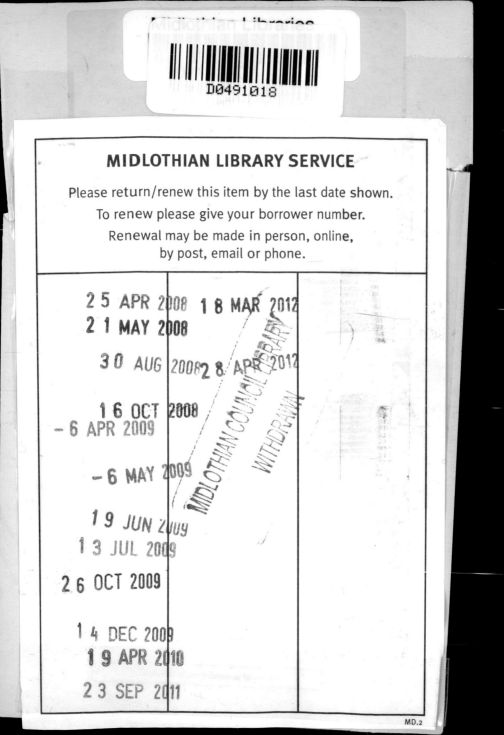

MIDLOTHIAN LIBRARY SERVICE

Please return/renew this item by the last date shown.

To renew please give your borrower number.

Renewal may be made in person, online,
by post, email or phone.

RAISING THE ROOF

Jane Wenham-Jones

BANTAM BOOKS

LONDON · NEW YORK · TORONTO · SYDNEY · AUCKLAND

RAISING THE ROOF
A BANTAM BOOK : 0553 81372 2

First publication in Great Britain

PRINTING HISTORY
Bantam Books edition published 2001

1 3 5 7 9 10 8 6 4 2

Set in 11/13pt Sabon by
Kestrel Data, Exeter, Devon.

Bantam Books are published by Transworld Publishers,
61–63 Uxbridge Road, London W5 5SA,
a division of The Random House Group Ltd,
in Australia by Random House Australia (Pty) Ltd,
20 Alfred Street, Milsons Point, Sydney, NSW 2061, Australia,
in New Zealand by Random House New Zealand Ltd,
18 Poland Road, Glenfield, Auckland 10, New Zealand
and in South Africa by Random House (Pty) Ltd,
Endulini, 5a Jubilee Road, Parktown 2193, South Africa.

Printed and bound in Great Britain by
Clays Ltd, St Ives plc.

For Felicity – my mother – with much love and deep appreciation

My thanks go to Shelagh Meyer and Lynne Patrick, who first told me I could do it, and my good friend Peter, who nagged me until I did. All from QWF and Midland Exposure for love and support when I needed it most and hangover cures even when I didn't. Rob Smith, Michael Winch, Peter Cocks and Eddie Robbins for supplying the technical bits. Jonathan Lloyd, for teaching me a thing or two. Gilly, for being a fan. My husband Tim, for not only bringing home the bacon but cooking it as well, and my son Tom for being the sort of kid to watch the same video fourteen times . . .

But most of all those brilliant people at Transworld for their taste and discernment. Especially lovely Sadie Mayne for great editing and the quite marvellous Francesca Liversidge – for making dreams come true.

Chapter One

Martin – Hope by the time you find this note, you'll have settled into your new life. We both know we're doing the right thing but I want you to understand that you will always be very special to me. Whatever I've said, I look upon our years together with love and appreciation. Hope you will never forget I am still – and always will be – your friend. Look after yourself. Love Cari xxxxx

Bastard! Bastard! Bastard! I watched Martin load the last cardboard box on to the back of the van and imagined what he'd look like if I shot him. I was just picturing him staggering backwards, blood spurting, when he smiled a last smarmy smile at the driver and turned a weary, sad one on me.

'Cari, I—' he began, as if he were in a made-for-television drama or capable of human emotion.

'Take care!' I interrupted brightly, although actually it would have suited me best if he'd been pulverized in a twenty-car pile-up on the M25. 'Speak to you soon.' And I kissed his cheek, noted with quiet glee the confusion in his eyes, turned and marched back up the steps to shut the shiny red door of the marital home behind me.

Pausing for a moment to see if I was going to fall into a crumpled heap, and finding that – strangely – I wasn't, I took up my position in the window to watch the van leave. As it pulled away, Martin gave a last, wounded, I-have-been-much-maligned look at the house and slid behind the wheel of his pretentiously numbered car. Then he drove away.

Martin gone.

I sat quite still on my window-seat – the scene of many a fine emotional crisis before this one – and waited to be desolate. Nothing happened at all.

Martin has left me.

I have been abandoned.

I live on my own.

I am an *ex*.

Nothing.

I tried an experimental gulp, just to see if any of the previously never-ending supply of tears – which had gushed all over the place at regular intervals yesterday – were on standby to burst out of my eyes but no. In fact, I found the smile I had created with which to bid him farewell felt quite comfortable on my face. And apart from a king-size hangover, which was sending inter-mittent signals to my shrivelled brain urging me to throw up, I felt very little pain at all.

How extraordinary.

Emotions are funny like that, though. Mine never do what I expect. I've always blamed it on the larger-than-average helping of loopy genes handed down to me (see later ramblings on mother and father) but in this case I think it was plain inexperience. I mean, all I knew about a Major Break-up of a Serious Long-term Relationship was that it gave me an instant ten points on the How-Stressed-Are-You? scale and all sorts of unwanted attention from my family. (Another ten points.)

Well, how would you know until you do it? And other people's examples can be dubious. My mother threw a lavish party with salmon twirls and champagne after she ran away from my father, whereas Auntie Maud, upon discovering Uncle Geoffrey packing his bags, slit her wrists in the bath.

A veritable queen of the mood swing at the best of times, I'd tried to take a middle road, dabbling in varying degrees of hysteria, gluttony and alcoholism between immense bouts of Positive Mental Attitude in which I planned my glittering new future, while always intending to keep this final day free to allow for hours of inconsolable sobbing as the need arose.

But now – how disconcerting life can be – the time had come (burst into refrain of Frank Sinatra's 'My Way') and here I was, irrevocably dry-eyed. In fact, if I analysed the odd mixture of tingling anticipation, sense of dramatic importance and sweet, poignant self-pity, I would have said it smacked of feeling strangely cheerful. Not, of course, that that was any long-term guarantee. A good rant always temporarily raises my spirits and there'd been plenty of weeping and wailing and throwing of cutlery the night before.

It was meant to be an adult parting of the ways, with wine-drinking, reminiscing of happier times, a last running-through of the details of our amicable parting. I'd slipped the note into his suitcase, prepared my good-wishes farewell speech for delivery on the doorstep. I had intended not to lose control until he'd gone. But my best-laid plans have never mixed well with alcohol, and by the time I'd drunk every drop of wine in the house and been reduced to climbing down the bottle of cherry brandy that a well-meaning aunt had given my mother two Christmases ago, I was screaming abuse about his new love (Sharon!!!!) and encouraging him to be extremely nasty back.

All the old grudges got an airing, of course. 'Nigel of all people! Cari, how could you?' (Bloody marvellous, isn't it? I have one drunken fumble I can't even remember. He disappears off to a conference, picks up someone's secretary, spends three nights banging away non-stop and decides he wants to *live with her*, and guess who gets criticized for being unfaithful?) But so did quite a few fresh and wounding ones (wouldn't stir my *fat* arse for him?) that he'd been silently harbouring against me but never thought to mention in the ten years we'd been together, all of which, it seemed, had been driving him towards the arms of another practically from the day he'd married me.

Eventually at four o'clock in the morning when he'd got down to the humiliating joke I'd made in front of his boss in 1993 and I'd deliberately trodden on his vintage Grateful Dead album, he threw a lamp against the wall and we both stood surveying the broken bits, panting at each other in exhaustion. Then, in one of the frightening U-turns that had once seemed exciting and now brought me to despair, he said, in a soft, reasonable voice, 'Don't be like this, Cari,' and I burst into tears, and somehow we clambered into bed together where I insisted he gave a final performance. Just to show I could.

After he'd fallen into dishevelled sleep, I lay on my back in the darkness until it thinned to grey half-light and listened to the mad squawking of the starlings outside and wondered whether I should have tried harder to keep him.

I think there was a point when I could have done if I'd really wanted to, but in the dithering, anxious, hurtful

12

weeks while I tried to decide whether to bring all my manipulative skills into play or accept that this was finally Fate taking a hand, Martin mooned about the place, apparently falling ever more deeply in love with this person he'd met only six weeks ago and seen four times since, and found himself a new job where she lived, in Brighton.

That is what saved me. That he would be a hundred miles away from Eastford. It was the crippling fear of being physically close but no longer in control, no longer a couple, that had kept us together this long. Imagine the exquisite pain of him roaming the pubs and wine bars, and parties of my friends, getting dinner invitations without me, being seen in cinema queues with the wrong blonde on his arm.

She'd already rung up three times with her phoney husky voice – not even having the decency to wait until he'd moved out of the marriage bed. After the first call, I made sure I answered the phone myself at all times, affecting a tone that would clearly warn Sharon that in due course she would discover what she had let herself in for and what I was very glad to be escaping. I called, 'Darling, it's for you,' just to confuse them both, and once added, 'It's your friend,' in the sort of sugary voice that suggested Martin and I shared it as a private joke.

Now, still on my window-seat, with Martin fifteen minutes closer to her, I hoped that he had neglected, in his sleepless state, to wash thoroughly and that he might arrive at Sharon's with a definite aura of shag about him so that their first day together was forever marred.

Really, for the world to be perfect – hah – ex-lovers should just vaporize. I had spent weeks willing him to die so that not only would I receive all the sympathy befitting a widow and none of the humiliating – if short-lived – pity directed towards a mere ex-wife, but so that nobody else could have him. Or, rather, so that he could have nobody else.

I did not want Martin (I did not! I did not!) so why did the thought of him driving towards Brighton, towards a flat with a blue door, to Sharon who'd told him he was the most exciting man she'd ever been to bed with (hah! again) and whose idea of a welcome was to come to the door wearing no knickers and carrying a carton of double cream (here I cursed my own addiction to demanding detail) make me feel quite sick in a way that had nothing to do with alcohol poisoning?

I remembered Louise sitting on my floor having drunk all the gin, sobbing into my cushions, bereft over Stuart. 'He's getting married, they're having a baby,' she had wailed. 'Why didn't he marry me?'

And I – who have never learned not to state the obvious – said, 'But you left him, you moved out and went to live with Robert,' unprepared for the howl of utter misery that would burst from my friend.

'I didn't know I wanted him then!'

Now, pushing down any notion that I might still hanker after even a hint of Martin, I considered what to do next. Since I had intended to spend the day locked in catatonic trauma and had wound up quite jolly about everything, I had a whole stretch of daylight hours to do with as I pleased. But I couldn't think of anything I wanted to do at all, so I began my first afternoon as a newly-amicably-separated single sitting on my window-seat, staring alternately out of the window and at the sink, reflecting how already the house felt quite different.

The window-seat thing was made out of old church pews and covered with a jumble of colours. Cushion covers from Mexico, a blue-patterned silk sari from India, an old tablecloth embroidered with flowers from one of my mother's rummages, a crumpled hand-stitched Victorian pillowslip from God knew where that was coming apart at the seams. Martin always said it looked a mess; I loved it. ('There you are, milord: our marital breakdown and grounds for divorce in ten words.')

Except you can never really boil it down to one thing, can you? It wasn't just about money, or him being unfaithful, or me being no great shakes in bed – a hitherto unknown fact that had emerged during our last screaming match and pretty damn rich considering! I nearly told him the truth then. 'Well, for your information . . .' I started to say, but I stopped. What would be the point now? At the end of the day, we'd just lost it – whatever 'it' is that makes the other person the one you want to collapse with on the sofa above all others.

I sat on my window-seat, with my arms around my knees, not ready yet to go and look at the gaps he'd left, and stared through the murky glass. (Martin sacked the window-cleaner in a fit of pique after he'd discovered him drinking coffee and explaining to me how God had come to him in a dream. I've been much more depressed since he left.)

In the early days of our marriage, I used to sit here waiting for Martin to come home, willing him to walk up the path, wondering why he was so late, afraid of who he might have taken to bed. Then, my heart used to give a little jerk when he came into view. Now, even as I heard his key in the lock, it sank. Lately I'd sat here hoping not to see him, unable to cope any longer with the weight of his disapproval, the palpable dis-appointment that hung in our home, wishing I could

15

summon the energy to get off the cushions and do something.

Eventually, on this historic day, I did get off them. I stood up, fetched the tin of chocolate fingers from the cupboard and the notepad from the drawer, and sat at the table.

And every time the cheeriness wavered, and the dull misery that started in the middle of my stomach began to spread outwards, I popped another biscuit into my mouth and studied the list of pros I'd felt-tipped three weeks before when trying to decide whether to allow Martin to move out.

This began with the minor details,

(1) Extra space in the airing cupboard

(2) More scope to eat junk food

and eventually on about number twenty-nine, got down to the bottom-line issues of being free to go and hunt down the sort of man I'd read about other women having but had never met myself (one with whom I might overcome My Problem?) and hinted tentatively at the possibility of being able to think now about having a baby, a prospect that Martin had found too repulsive to countenance and which, when I was first married at twenty-two, had seemed a perfectly reasonable view to share, but which now nagged at the corners of my mind, particularly when I found myself in a hormone-induced emotional state (mostly at the beginning, end and middle of each month).

I tore up the cons, averting my eyes from words like 'lonely' and 'frustrated' and 'spiders', and made myself a coffee and reminded myself of what my sister Juliette had told me about the best bits being in your thirties, and pushed to the back of my mind that she was a manic depressive and only twenty-eight. I scoured the fridge, found an out-of date strawberry

yoghurt to eat, and then walked straight to the bathroom, determinedly not thinking about how to move
the furniture to fill the spaces Martin had left. I ran a
bath and lay in it, listening to the relentless ringing of the
phone, which heralded the first round of friends and
relatives wanting to know if I'd fallen apart.

Chapter Two

Baths are a good way of putting off the inevitable. When I smoked, the day's natural punctuation points were created by lighting a fag. 'I'll just smoke this,' I used to say, 'and *then* I'll . . .' Baths are better than cigarettes. They take longer and have the added benefit of rendering you clean and fragrant (rather than wrinkled and tar-ridden). I seemed to be spending a lot of time in my bath. There is something about the suspension of your body in warm soapy water that allows you to suspend everything. Particularly the knotty and unpleasant problem of how I was going to earn a living.

Martin had been typically sneery. 'Now you'll *have* to get a job,' he said, practically crowing, when we were having one of our torturous conversations about the financial implications of our separation. Anyone would think I hadn't tried, was work-shy or incapable of getting employment, but I've had more jobs than Martin. I just have a slight problem in the holding-them-down area.

Of course, Martin and his mother had the Martin-Career-Plan worked out when he was about six. ('Go into computers, darling – that's where the money is.' Off he trotted . . .) But Louise, too, after much the same sort of performance at school as me – crap to middling – got a job the very moment she'd hung up her uniform and has since progressed from doing a bit of filing for ADF Chemicals – in the days when they occupied only one building on the industrial estate instead of sprawling over all of it – to the dizzy heights of having her own secretary, spending eight hours a day in important meetings and never going anywhere without her laptop.

Our friend Sonia does something weighty in insurance; Rowena was a deputy head about five minutes after she'd finished her teacher-training course. Even Juliette is heading towards a sizeable civil-service pension despite taking her full illness allowance, which seems to be about six months *per annum*, every year since she joined. Nigel – businessman *extraordinaire* – has a whacking great country pad in the most exclusive of the villages surrounding Eastford and gets called upon to after-dinner speak about being a self-made man.

And then there's me.

I started work on the industrial estate too, for a company that resolutely stayed the same size. Unlike Louise, I progressed from filing to more filing and then filing plus watering the pot-plants. Then I met Martin, who made it plain that he thought filing not much of a job for any girlfriend of his so I left and got another as office administrative assistant, a role that, though mostly photocopying, I thought I fulfilled with a certain aplomb until the firm suddenly closed down.

Since then there have been several appointments, largely utilizing my original filing and watering skills, and everyone has been perfectly friendly and pleasant but has never shown the slightest inclination to promote me or put me in charge of anything more challenging than the office aspidistra. Which rather leaves one wondering, What is wrong with me?

'Not sufficiently proactive' was the exact wording used by the personnel officer when she was explaining why I had been specially selected for voluntary redundancy the last time. What does that mean, for God's sake! How proactive can you get when running off five hundred copies of the annual report? 'It means you should be using your initiative,' Martin said loftily. (Like *he* did presumably, when the slimeball shot to the nearest condom machine the moment he saw Sharon's vacuous face across the table.)

Actually, just for once, he went through a phase then of telling me not to worry and to look around for a really good job with a proper salary that would fulfil my potential. And I thought he was being nice at last, until I discovered he just wanted me to be able to support myself so that he didn't need to feel guilty when he went off with the half-wit. Which he now had, leaving me unemployed. A fact that Louise, Juliette, my mother (twice), Sonia, Rowena and Nigel had all pointed out with varying degrees of subtlety – or not – each time they'd called to see how I was approaching my husband-less, jobless, potentially homeless state. (Answer: I am trying hard not to think about it and I am very clean.)

But I was also going to be in a severe state of financial decline if I didn't get something lined up soon. So even though Martin's parting assessment of my employability and general worthiness rating – 'right bloody parasite, useless at everything' – made the thought of a job interview even less appealing than it had ever been, I knew I soon had to get a grip.

I began in a small way by getting out of the bath and putting on lots of makeup, wishing that Sonia hadn't told me about eyelashes thinning after the age of thirty. Because now that I knew they did, I could see that mine were looking sparser by the minute. Whereas once lashings of black mascara gave one's eyes that thick-fringed exotic look, now, dead-for-several-days spider is more the overall effect. Still, on balance, there is no doubt I look one hell of a lot better with plenty of slap and shadow. Look Good and you'll feel Good! Or was it the other way round? Can't remember where that came from – either Sonia or Juliette in one of her up phases – but it makes sense.

I did some serious touch-up work with the concealer, plastered on the lipstick and leered at myself in the mirror, giving my biggest smile and practising the mantra once again.

I feel great!

I feel great, I feel great, I feel . . . (no – that is not my chin trembling) I feel . . . *great*!

Chapter Three

I felt rootless. I could not eat or cry. I sat, still, huddled, frozen, afraid to move. Afraid to take the next step or breath without him. When I did move the pain started . . .

Nigel hugged me, unable even at a time like this to resist having a minor grope while he did so and then, seeing that I was too distraught even to slap him, waiting sympathetically while I made the coffee. 'Martin's mad to leave you,' he said encouragingly, as I snivelled into the Nescafé jar and he tried surreptitiously to finger the front of my T-shirt. 'But I'm sure he'll come back,' he finished, as I leant my head against the cupboard and began to sob.

'I don't want him back,' I grizzled, because that is what everyone always says and I've never known what I *do* want.

'What you need', he said, laughing to cover all contingencies, 'is a damn good shag. It would brighten you up no end.'

I liked Nigel, whatever Martin said about him – though I had to admit Martin was generally right in what he did say. I also got immensely irritated by Nigel – particularly for his ability to make me feel that his ego should remain intact. I looked at him as I sniffed into several lengths of kitchen roll. 'You're probably right,' I said. 'How's Gloria?'

Nigel stared at me thunderstruck, clearly at a loss without my usual tirade of abuse. But recovery is his middle name so he was quick to answer while busily contemplating whether this meant I would finally capitulate and allow him to have me over the kitchen table. 'Gloria', he said happily, 'is wonderful.'

Gloria, I often thought, was amazingly wonderful to stay married to Nigel. He had made and lost at least three fortunes in his thirty-four years, written off four cars, been bankrupt twice, and had built up a powerful reputation for his honey-coated bullshit that found fame even in the building trade. Still, Gloria loved him. She was round and blonde and smiling, and would roll her eyes supportively over bank managers who made difficulties about overdrafts and investors who did not share Nigel's vision of the long-term. Only once had her composure cracked, when the bailiffs had started to tow away the trailer that not only carried her daughter's pony but the weeping six-year-old, who suddenly realized that she was going in the wrong direction for the Pony Club gymkhana. Even then Gloria showed remarkable restraint, containing herself until quite late in the evening when a minor disagreement over the remote control led her to batter Nigel so badly with a Le Creuset frying-pan that he needed five stitches in his left eyebrow.

Nigel put it around that she had severe pre-menstrual syndrome and that a specialist flown in from Jersey had put her on starflower oil. But I knew that the main reason why Gloria was serene again had been the tension-releasing pleasure of seeing him whimpering in a corner and her subsequent decision to take over the accounts and hack up Nigel's gold card. Since then, they'd been coining it in, for which Nigel naturally took the full credit. 'What are you going to do about money?' he asked now, jangling the keys to his new Porsche to underline his years of practice at facing such issues.

'I don't know,' I said bleakly, having studiously avoided ever facing them. 'Martin's paid off the mortgage – '

'Oh, well, then,' said Nigel. 'Easy, you just—'

' – on the understanding that I don't raise any money on the house, and it stays in our joint names. And sooner or later I've got to sell it and give him his whack or raise the money to buy him out and how the bloody hell am I going to do that without a job?' I finished, panic-struck, as the full enormity of it all hit me. 'At least his mother had the grace to die and leave him her money or I'd be out on my ear now,' I added, recalling with malicious pleasure the vision of the old bag croaking her last.

'How much did he get?' asked Nigel, whose eyes always gleamed at the thought of inheritances and whose life's regret was that he had no rich relatives.

'Enough for the mortgage and a bit more,' I said shortly, feeling faintly uncomfortable at discussing it with Nigel when I knew Martin would die rather than divulge the sum total of his penny-jar let alone his precious mother's legacy.

'Well, really, you know,' Nigel was casual, 'you're entitled to half of it.'

I shook my head. 'No, I'm not. It was her life's work to see I never got a penny. She only gave in and popped it once she was sure we were splitting up. She'd be turning in her grave and fighting her way out if she knew he'd paid this house off. He's been quite decent, really . . .' I trailed off, hating him.

'I've got a really good idea that would make some money for you,' said Nigel eagerly. 'I've been meaning to

24

put it to you for ages. Just because Martin's gone, it doesn't mean our business relationship has to end, or any other relationship come to that,' he added, predictably, sidling up to me as I spooned coffee into mugs and putting his arms round me.

We haven't ever had a business relationship, unless you can count Martin once investing five thousand pounds in Nigel's scheme to buy a bungalow, three lock-up garages and half a building plot, then sell them back to himself simultaneously in some clever legal manoeuvre with a dodgy solicitor he had known in the Scouts and which was supposed to make us fifteen thousand pounds in the space of an afternoon but somehow went wrong, so that we had to wait six months to recoup four thousand and thirty-five pounds of our original five. Martin, who prides himself on his business acumen and in-depth knowledge of world markets, had never recovered from this humiliating reflection on his hitherto sound judgement, while poor Nigel, once his dearest friend, best man and foremost drinking partner, had been rapidly downgraded to 'that wanker' or – ever since the incident when I got drunk last Christmas and ended up in the cupboard under the stairs from which Nigel had apparently emerged some time later – 'your boyfriend'.

Nigel was unfailingly hurt by this condemnation of his character and at great pains to point out that none of it had been his fault, which Gloria would vouch for. Now he was busily drawing room-plans on my blank shopping list. 'Tony the agent tipped me off,' he said, draining his coffee mug and winking at me encouragingly. 'It's not even on the market yet. Repossession – almost converted but the bloke ran out of money. No need to feel guilty, though,' he added hastily, knowing my long and loving relationship with that emotion. 'He was a nasty piece of work – used to knock his wife about.'

Here Nigel shook his head sadly at the surfeit of blokes in the world who weren't as nice as him.

'It'll be brilliant,' he said. 'It'll be easier if you get the loan but obviously I'll be right in there with you fifty-fifty. I reckon we can get it for fifty, spend fifteen or twenty on it – only needs a bit of cleaning up, couple of new showers and a few kitchen units. Three flats, four hundred a month each, that's twelve hundred a month less repayments – say, seven hundred. That's five hundred, or two hundred and fifty pounds a month each, profit for nothing. Now if we had twenty of those, you'd get plenty of lipsticks for that lot, wouldn't you?'

'Last year,' I said, 'I earned almost nothing. I don't have a job, I've no longer got a husband and Martin has taken away my Barclaycard. Who,' I asked, 'for God's sake, is going to lend me any money?'

'Everybody! With buy-to-let loans, they're throwing it at you up and down the high street. More expensive than a normal mortgage but all paid off in ten years. I've already spoken to a few people.' He produced a calculator and began jabbing at the buttons.

'I haven't got any income.'

'Leave that to me,' said Nigel airily. 'Don't worry about the details. Just get your short skirt out and put a bit of makeup on and I'll set up a few meetings. It'll be some money for you and a bit of a project for me that doesn't have to go through the books. We can pay you and Gloria four grand a year each without you paying tax and then, once we've done it up, we'll re-finance that to pay for the next one. It'll be great.'

'Nigel, what the fuck are you talking about, you cretin?'

'See? It's cheered you up already.'

Chapter Four

Juliette used to make me laugh. Her humour was the saving of her, for she lives on the brink of madness and we still hold on to her comedy like a rope. We hang on to either end, so that as she falls I can try to tug her back. Or, so that she can pull me with her.

Always stimulated by other people in crisis, Juliette kept pushing the kitchen roll hopefully across the table towards me, bobbing her head about to keep the sort of eye-contact recommended on her listening-skills day course, while she interrogated me about my feelings.

'I don't want to talk about it,' I snapped, continuing to unpack the shopping so that she had to wedge her head horizontally between the carrier-bags to try to hold my gaze. 'I am absolutely OK. I have nothing to get out of my system. And I'd be very grateful if you'd pass that on to our mother.'

Juliette smiled and sat up. 'Denial,' she said warmly. 'Divorce is a form of bereavement, you know, and the grief will be experienced in distinct stages.'

'I am not getting divorced,' I said, a small ripple of panic curdling the three Kit-Kats that were sitting in my stomach, 'and I'm fed-up with all your pseudo-psycho claptrap. You'd do better to stop reading all these books and take a good long look at yourself.' I could feel the familiar rage rising at the answering gleam in Juliette's eyes.

'Transference,' breathed my sister dreamily. 'I was like that when Sid left me. Do you remember how I screamed at the ticket collector at Victoria? I just screamed and screamed and burst into tears. It was because he reminded me of Dad,' she finished, beaming at me.

'You're always bursting into tears,' I said nastily, 'and for God's sake don't bring him into it.' I opened the fridge and surveyed the contents. 'Actually,' I said, 'I feel terrific. Every hour I discover further and more pleasing advantages in living alone.'

I held up a half-finished packet of bacon for her inspection. 'No Martin, no more gruesome bits of dead pig hanging about.'

'Have you become vegetarian?' she asked hopefully.

'Certainly not. And neither have you so don't start that again.'

'I only eat chicken and tuna.'

'You ate rabbit and goat when you lived with Sid.'

'Sid was trying to find his country roots. It was a way of reaching his mother.'

'Sid was a psychopath who would have eaten his mother!'

It got her off the track. She sat in chin-trembling silence for a moment, then gulped and pulled the kitchen roll towards her. 'Marlena says I allow you to undermine me because I'm still living out our childhood patterns,' she quivered. 'I was always in your shadow . . .'

Jesus! I'd heard this lot a thousand times before. I carried on emptying the fridge of various revolting substances and turned my attention to the new ones while she droned on in the background.

I was quite excited about this. Now that I had a fridge

all to myself it was my chance to put into practice the potentially enormous wealth-creating weight-loss breakthrough I had conceived years before and kept close to my chest ever since, terrified that someone else would pinch it and make their fortune before I'd got round to writing the book.

Namely: *The Shelf Diet*. This was such a deceptively simple but brilliant idea I was still shocked to think that I was the only person in the world to have thought of it.

It works as follows: you take one shelf of the fridge and put on it exactly one thousand calories' worth of food – no more, no less. Then you eat it. There are other rules, of course. Like you can't eat anything else that's *not* on the fridge shelf. The wonderful thing is that it's all planned beforehand. Temptation is removed, all the calculation is done before you start and you don't feel deprived because all that food is waiting for you. And it can be beautifully balanced so you can open the fridge door and say, 'Hey! What shall I have now? An apple or a Mars bar?' and know that you still have three boiled eggs, four bits of Ryvita and a tin of sardines in brine to choose from until bedtime. Except in my case I was going to prepare the whole week in advance – allowing myself the flexibility to pop a bottle of Frascati in the door – and fill the fridge with seven thousand calories' worth of food, on which I would live until next Tuesday. By then I would have shed pounds.

When I got round to writing the book, of course, I would supply a different shelf combination for every day and/or a full fridge option for every week. This should fill three hundred and sixty-five plus fifty-two pages very nicely, and might well lead to a supermarket franchise with shrink-wrapped plastic trays containing a day's choices all ready to carry home and place on a fridge shelf with no need to waste valuable time preparing it yourself. It would be an excellent method for those unfortunate enough to have gluttonous husbands and ghastly children filling the fridge with their own nasty food. The dieter could smugly eat from her own plastic tray and watch serenely while her children grew obese and spotty and her husband died of heart disease.

I wasn't quite sure how the videos would fit in, but if a multi-million-pound fortune had been made from a dozen books, six videos and a string of spin-offs from the basic premise of give-up-butter-and-you'll-get-thinner-legs then I was quite sure I could cobble something together.

Juliette had got to the point in our childhood where I had been sick over her German homework and nobody cared how *she* was feeling . . . and was evidently boring even herself because she suddenly snapped to attention and peered over my shoulder. 'Why are you putting Ryvita in the fridge?'

I had no intention of letting Juliette get an inkling of my invention. This was the woman who unburdened the full contents of her false-memory syndrome at the supermarket checkout. It would be all round town in no time. I muttered something authoritative about low temperatures and preservation of vitamins, which I knew would result in her loading every item of food she possessed into her own fridge the moment she got home, and tried to decide how many chocolate fingers at thirty-two calories each to allow for the week.

I was tempted by fourteen at two a day but this would have necessitated getting out the calculator – mental arithmetic not being a strong point – and Juliette's curiosity being further aroused, so I settled for ten, congratulating myself all the while on the sheer genius of a scheme where I could eat ten biscuits and still have 6,680 calories' worth of food to devour and would end up looking stunning. For there is no doubt about it, whatever all the fatties might say about being thin not making you happy: when you're thin you look fantastic, and that is bound to cheer anyone up, and when you're fat you just look fat. And that makes you miserable.

I looked fat. Martin had said so.

I had to get thin fast, not only because it is *de rigueur* when your marriage has fallen apart and waddling about does not elicit the same interest and concern as fainting from starvation but also so that I could look absolutely bloody terrific.

This was so that (a) I could soon be picked up by some gorgeous new man with lots of money and (b) when Martin next saw me he would be knocked out by how yummy and sexy I was, and pig-sick that I was now with someone else while he was stuck with blowsy old Sharon.

I couldn't fathom why this sought-after thinness hadn't started happening to me already since I hadn't eaten a meal for days. You would expect *some* gratifying removal of blubber after the hardship of surviving on red wine and peanuts for seventy-two hours. I remarked upon this to Juliette, who snootily informed me that there were fifteen hundred calories alone in the packet of nuts I'd eaten since she'd got there. I hate her sometimes.

'I'm getting my bulimia back,' I said, defensively, knowing it would make her jealous and that it was also a good cover story for all the food piled up on the table. She sighed while I considered the new packet of nuts, trying to decide whether to include that or three small tins of baked beans, four ounces of Cheddar, an avocado and six tomatoes. The truth is I'm something of a failed bulimic: I'm excellent at bingeing but rather lacking ability in the throwing-it-up-afterwards department. I compensate for this with my own carefully blended eating disorder called binge-and-starve, whereby you eat everything in sight for three days, feel incredibly fat, revolting and guilty then eat nothing for three days. This sometimes goes wrong too.

But now that I was fortunate enough to be living alone, all my weight problems would be over for ever. I decided to decant half of the packet of nuts to swap them over, if necessary, for the beans and surveyed the neatly packed fridge shelves with smug satisfaction. This could not fail.

I could see Juliette taking in the contents with interest so I shut the door smartly before she could cotton on to the fact that they were remarkably low-fat for a blossoming binger, and distracted her with tales of Nigel's concern. 'He's been so sweet,' I told her, 'so anxious about comforting me and helping me to make some money. Of course, I know really,' I said quickly, before she could, 'that he just wants to get my tits out.'

'Yes, well, Nigel', she said primly, 'is very insecure. And if I were you,' she added, all beady-eyed and emphatic suddenly, 'I wouldn't get involved in any of his schemes.'

I looked at her, wishing she'd go home so that I could start on the first shelf without being forced to share it and bugger up all my sums. I yawned so she'd think I was emotionally exhausted and best left to sleep all day, like she did when life got on top of her – which was frequently. 'I'm not going to,' I told her wearily. 'I'm not that stupid.'

The bank manager was one of the new breed who step forward briskly with a large smile saying, 'Hello, I'm Graham,' rather than skulking greyly behind their desks looking at you through those glinting little spectacles while you grovel for a car loan. Graham was ugly, though his wife and children looked quite normal as they grinned cheerily from their Perspex frame, perched among the coloured cubes of Post-it notes and garish pen-holders – evidently last Christmas's freebies from desperate customers whose overdrafts were due to expire on New Year's Eve. But he held the purse-strings, and he was a man, and as I've never really got the hang of talking to any who are over seven or under eighty without flirting, I gave him my firm don't-mess-with-me handshake and my best can't-you-just-imagine? smile and sat down, pleased, as I noticed a bit of interest send his mouth working.

I pulled out the folder and produced the two sheets of impressive figures that Nigel had made up. 'I'm looking at an investment property,' I began, in the smooth tones I had rehearsed earlier with Nigel.

'What exactly do you do?' he asked, in the irritating way people with company pensions tend to.

I smiled and began the fairy tale. 'My background is in sales and marketing,' I lied, 'but in recent years I have been engaged in running my husband's business with him.' I smiled warmly, reflecting that if Martin had had a business, I would have been the last person he'd let near it. 'You know, the accounts,' I simpered, 'customer liaison, that sort of thing. But,' I hurried on, as my stomach gave a sickening little flip at the thought of the liaisons Martin was probably engaged in at this very minute, 'the point is that this would be a stand-alone, self-financing project and would not need to depend on proof of earnings. Self-supporting, I mean,' I finished desperately, knowing the script had got jumbled and hoping I wasn't going to cry.

Graham looked at me curiously.

'And', I said, miraculously remembering it and getting back into my stride, 'the beauty is that if the housing market is buoyant then we'll make a capital gain on the increased value of the property after its renovation and if the market remains static then the rental market will remain strong and . . .' Here I faltered for a second as I saw Graham's mouth twitch again, more, I fancied, from having caught the whiff of bullshit than barely contained lust. '. . . and we'll get lots of tenants,' I finished brightly, cursing Nigel for not coming himself and delivering his own bloody speech.

'So, do you have any earnings?' Graham's hand picked up the silver pen with the orange and yellow cleaning-contractors' logo and hovered above his so-far bare A4 pad.

'Not exactly,' I began, switching rapidly to 'except for twenty thousand pounds a year.' Graham looked at me hard, evidently trying to decide whether I was trying to pull a fast one or was just stupid. 'It's quite a new job,' I babbled, 'well, not exactly new, more an old job I've just gone back to after my marriage broke up. I'm sorry to sound so vague,' I finished, on a sudden stroke of inspiration, which would have impressed even Nigel, 'I still can't quite get used to the idea . . .' I gave a small pathetic smile and let my chin quiver.

'Ah,' Graham said, visibly relaxing, evidently reassured by the concept of a woman being so bereft at losing her husband she couldn't remember whether she had a job or not.

'You could write to my employers,' I offered sadly, finding myself slipping into the role of helpless abandoned wife with worrying alacrity, 'for confirmation. I'm actually with a building firm, you see, and they'll do all the work on the project for me at cost, and I'll have all that expertise at hand to help me with the technicalities.'

Here I swallowed a bit and tried to look as if I was being brave while I tried to recall whether it was planning permission or building regulations that Nigel had said I must avoid talking about at any cost. 'Anyway,' I continued, in my brightest life-must-go-on tone, getting the hang of it now and beginning to believe my own fabrications, 'it means I know all about how the building world operates and the rudiments of basic conversions and now seems an excellent time – now there are no other demands being made upon my attention and I'm back in the workplace – to take up a fresh challenge in the form of this project.'

I paused for Graham to say something encouraging but he only grunted and began to study the sheets of paper I had pushed across the desk.

After absolutely ages, in which I stared around the office at an assortment of ghastly calendars and fiddled with my hair, he looked up and launched into a long, incomprehensible speech about rental yields and their percentage ratios to repayments, and how he was sure I understood the difference from the bank's point of view between open-market values and investment returns and something about seven times the gross rental income less ten per cent for maintenance and while my figures had an optimistic slant and his, of course, erred on the side of prudent caution we were not so far out as to be irreconcilable.

Not having an inkling of what he was talking about, I simply adopted what I imagined was an intelligent expression and smiled and nodded throughout, but it transpired that some answer was required for he waited expectantly when he finally stopped for breath. So I said, 'Quite. Yes. Absolutely,' which seemed to suffice.

Then he asked a few odd, unrelated questions about pensions and life assurance policies, to which I gave odd, unrelated answers, and finally got down to how much my own house was worth, which seemed to cheer him considerably. In fact, I saw a definite new respect creep into the manner in which he scribbled across his notepad from the moment he learnt I didn't have a mortgage. I implied that we'd paid it off through a series of shrewd and lucrative business ventures in which I'd played a prominent part and kept quiet about the fact that Martin's mother had kicked the bucket only days before Barclaycard had been going to take me to court.

Then he began a second and even longer lecture, with lots of accompanying hand movements and ruler-tapping, on the need for contingency planning, careful costings and how Valuation was All.

I guessed he had harboured a secret desire to be a teacher before his over-zealous mother had pressured him into becoming a bank manager. He probably dreamed of ending his working life as a great tutor in the hallowed halls of some far-off banking college where he could spend hours on end instructing a whole roomful of spotty trainees on how to bore people rigid.

'You must ask yourself,' he boomed suddenly, with an alarming transformation into Churchill-entreating-us-to-fight-them-on-the-beaches, 'what you will do if the tenants leave. What you will do if the flats are vandal-ized. What you will do if you cannot get insurance. If there is dry rot, woodworm, flood or fire . . . If', he lowered his voice to a menacing whisper that sent a shiver up my spine, 'it all goes horribly wrong.'

Tricky that. Slit my throat or pull off Nigel's bollocks?

'Whatever happens,' cut back to Churchill, 'you will have a commitment to this bank. Repayments must be honoured.'

'Oh, you don't have to worry about that!' I laughed heartily to dispel the uneasy thought that he might be being taken care of in the community and just pretending to be a bank manager as a change from basket-weaving up the road.

Then I selected a Margaret Thatcher intonation and gave him what I hoped would be a winning smile. 'Graham,' I said, 'I can assure you that there won't be any problem with repaying this loan.'

'How the bloody hell am I going to repay this loan?' I screeched at Nigel, later that afternoon.

'Stop worrying,' said Nigel jubilantly. 'We'll get him to roll on the interest until we get our first tenant. It'll be brilliant, you'll see. You have done well,' he went on admiringly, looking me in the eyes for once rather than down the cleavage. 'So he's going to give us two-thirds of the projected valuation when it's finished?'

'I don't know! He's going to give us whatever you asked for down on that bit of paper. Give *me*, I should say. I've got to repay this, Nigel!'

'Did you mention Wobbly Jackson valuing it?'

'Yes, he says it's fine. They're on the bank's list.'

'Excellent! Went to school with Wobbly. He was a boring bastard even then. I'll give him a call.'

'I haven't even seen the place yet.'

'I'll take you any time you want.' Nigel moved round to the back of my chair and nibbled at my ear. 'I'll do anything any time you want . . .'

'Sod off! I can't buy a house I haven't seen.'

'If Wobbly can do the valuation this week, the bank should get an offer out next week, so we can get old Greggie to start the searches now. Nothing to hold it up. It could be ours in two weeks' time.'

'Mine.'

'Cari!' Sorrowful look. 'We're in it together. I trust you or I'd ask for a partnership agreement in writing.

Don't worry, darling. I won't let you down. It's *our* debt. Yours and mine. And Gloria's.'

'Have you told her yet?'

'I've been so busy I've barely had time to ask how the kids are. Don't worry, Gloria will be fine. Gloria's as good as gold.'

'I think if you're involved in a business deal with another woman you should tell your wife. People might talk. I don't want her upset.'

'I will. They won't. She won't be.'

'You'd better tell her before the letter comes from the bank. They're going to write to you for confirmation of my salary.'

'Don't nag, Cari. It makes you look older.'

Bastard. He always knows where my jugular is. I smiled sweetly.

'Much better. You look all gorgeous again.'

'Do you think I look thinner?'

This is an example of how addled-through-trauma my brain was. Nigel takes questions like that as an open invitation to have a good feel all over while pondering his reply. 'Lovely and thin.' His voice was muffled against my neck.

'Get off!' I said, disengaging myself. 'And don't lie! Do I look as if I've lost weight?'

'Yes,' said Nigel firmly, clearly considering that this was his best option if he wanted me to trot along to the solicitor and sign away my life for a house I hadn't even clapped eyes on.

'Where?' I demanded, not letting him get away that easily.

'Your bum's smaller,' he said instantly, in the sincere tones that had sold half a million quid's worth of re-placement windows before he went spectacularly bankrupt in 1988. 'Not that it was big before,' he added

38

smoothly, remembering all the old patter. 'You've always had a wonderful body.'

I moved to the other side of the kitchen. I did feel thinner but I had vowed not to weigh myself until the end of the first week. The suspense was nearly killing me but I just kept thinking of the marvellous lift I'd get when I stepped on the scales in five days' time to find the best part of half a stone had melted away.

It was all going exceptionally well. So far I had resisted the Frascati altogether, which gave me a virtuous inner glow and a clear conscience about having a drink with Louise later. I had found that I was perfectly satisfied by the series of tempting little Ryvita-and-something snacks I'd been living on.

The trick was not to let yourself get hungry. I decided I would devote at least one chapter of the bestseller to this, entitled 'Hunger: the Dieter's Undoing', and expound on the importance of adhering to the principle of Little and Often.

Now that I was free of its tyranny I could see that a lot of fat was piled on through living under a husband-controlled regime where one was forced to eat three meals a day because that's what his mother always did, instead of the seven or eight delicate little nibbly ones, which one's internal body clock and I-feel-peckish mechanism in the brain knew was what Nature had intended. I could do a bit of research and put in a few scientific bits regarding the habits of sheep, who never stop eating and are altogether much more harmless and pleasant creatures than smelly, dependent dogs, for example, who have single huge meals that they gulp down in three seconds flat.

I was beginning to get hungry now and knew that it was time for the fridge to open and decision-time to begin. I didn't want Nigel to get wind of my money-spinning scheme any more than Juliette. Before I knew it he'd be appointing himself managing director of the plastic-tray-franchise side of things and planning when we would go public. Not to mention wanting to share the chocolate fingers in the meantime. He was definitely getting rounder – he might have benefited from a couple of weeks on the Shelf Diet himself. The drawback, though, while it was in its pre-patented phase, was that I had to keep throwing people out before I could eat. 'Right,' I said briskly. 'I've got Louise coming later, so I need to have a bath and things.'

Nigel looked at me in surprise. 'It's only five o'clock.'

'Since when has cleanliness depended on the hour of the day?' I retorted. 'Anyway, I've got phone calls to make and stuff. I've got to phone Martin back. He left a message on the answerphone.'

'Missing you, is he?'

'Don't know, don't care.' I wasn't about to tell Nigel that Martin was missing the money he'd lent me to tide me over and wanted to know when I was going to get that job. But thoughts of this unresolved issue brought on a fresh stomach-churning wave of panic and I clutched at Nigel's arm. 'What am I going to do about money? How am I going to pay for all this?'

Nigel clutched me back. 'Don't worry,' he said earnestly. 'I'll do some detailed figures over the weekend. We'll probably have enough from the loan if Wobbly comes up trumps but if not,' his voice was soothing, 'I'll put the rest down to some other jobs I've got on and we'll sort it out later when we've got some rent coming in. I'll look after you.'

For a moment I thought I might get carried away on a flood of sentimentality and throw myself sobbing into his arms, but I thought better of it and scowled at him instead. 'Why?' I asked as gruffly as I could manage.

'Because you're my friend,' with which – in one of the gestures that made him so forgivable and ensured that I would always love him even if he was a wanker – he kissed me gently on the cheek and picked up his phone, filofax and car-keys. 'I'll pick you up tomorrow at ten. We'll look at the house and I'll take you up to meet Greggie. Then we can start getting the boys in to give us some quotes.' He rubbed his hands together jubilantly. 'We're going to make some money here, Cari.'

He turned towards me the full force of the beaming smile that I can only imagine was what first swung it with Gloria, and I found myself grinning back, caught by his good mood. 'I hope you're right,' I said. 'Martin would go mad if he knew I was borrowing money.'

'You're making an investment,' said Nigel firmly.

I allowed myself a moment to luxuriate in the vision of myself with a string of houses to my name, looking immaculate and sophisticated (and thin), telling Martin, 'Darling, keep your little house!' And pressing a gloved finger on to the electric window button of my shiny new Seven Series and gliding off to my executive mansion in Waldorf Close, where Martin had always, always wanted to live, leaving him standing open-mouthed on the kerb.

'And it's nothing to do with him any more, is it?' asked Nigel cheerily.

My spirits plummeted. 'No,' I said grimly, as my stomach tightened. 'Nothing to do with him at all.'

Nothing.

'And that's what you're celebrating,' said Louise, firmly, wrestling with the champagne bottle. 'The fact that you're free. There!' She grinned triumphantly as the cork shot across the kitchen narrowly missing my right eye, and causing froth to spurt down the front of her jumper. 'Look at me,' she added, as we both scrabbled for glasses. 'Best thing I ever did, leaving Stuart. Never looked back.'

I held out my glass as she poured, seeing little point in reminding her about the sobbing-into-gin episode or that she was already having lots of second thoughts about the new love of her life, Robert, which were manifesting themselves in her regular shagging of the newsagent up the road, who was married with three children. 'I know,' I said. 'It's just that I feel – empty.'

I could also feel a whole lot of tears gathering themselves together and making a mad rush for my eyes, so I gulped the champagne and raised my glass to Louise, who was settling herself among the window-seat cushions and who suddenly looked as if, without much prompting, she might join me.

'I know too,' she said. 'It's shitty.'

We looked hopelessly at each other for a minute and then she grinned at me in the way she's been grinning since primary school and downed the contents of her glass. 'Best get pissed!'

Champagne is great stuff. There's nothing to compare with that light sensuous feeling of well-being that skips along your veins from the first mouthful. By my second glass I was thoroughly relaxed and beaming contentedly. By the third I was positively buoyant, planning my glittering career as a property developer and nodding indulgently as Louise ran through the impossibilities of balancing her cerebral affections for Robert with the animal lust she felt for the newsagent.

I think with hindsight our mistake was to open the Frascati from the fridge. I did have a moment of doubt, from the calorific point of view, but I figured that since today had already been a bit upset by the champagne I might as well put all the alcohol down to be deducted from the contingency allowance and replace the fridge bottle for the rest of the week tomorrow. In any case Louise was waving her empty glass at me imperiously, and, since she'd provided the fizzy stuff, it seemed the least I could do was to share my own supplies.

We were OK at first. In fact, we were laughing uproariously over something, which I now forget but which had been sparked off by a run-down of all our most disastrous sexual experiences – which were many – and had included a very funny description by Louise of Stuart with brewer's droop. But somehow we had had just one glass too many and toppled off that delicate knife-edge between laughter and tears because we suddenly stopped chortling and started staring at the carpet, and I found myself with a lump in my throat and a chocolate finger in my hand. By which time Louise was sniffing and talking about how little she'd ever demanded of any of them and how all she'd ever wanted was to be loved and valued, and how all they'd ever wanted was to get their leg over and then get down the pub.

I wasn't so gross as to point out that, under normal circumstances, this was spot on for her own agenda. Instead I went and sat on the floor beside her and patted her arm. But by then I was getting belligerent and composing an imaginary letter to Martin retracting all the nice things I'd ever said about him and outlining what a vile and odious creature he was. Materialistic, insensitive, completely engrossed in his own selfish pleasures . . . Round about the fifteenth paragraph where I was getting down to the nitty-gritty of his shocking taste in other women and his irritating habits with the plug-hole (Hairs! Yuck!), I was jolted back to reality by Louise wailing, 'And now Robert wants a bloody baby.'

We contemplated this in silence. I felt the anger dwindle and that sicky eat-something depression crawl up through my stomach.

'So do I,' I said sadly, standing up and getting the hidden half-packet of peanuts out of the cupboard, on the basis that since Louise was evidently in need of comfort food and would eat most of them it wouldn't affect the Shelf equation in any way.

'No, you don't,' she was slurring slightly. 'You just think you do because you've been drinking. You always want children when you're drunk. Think of Lukey!' she cried suddenly, sitting up and jabbing a finger at me.

'Pukey Lukey,' I said, and we both cheered up, snorted and giggled and generally fell about in a juvenile fashion, as I refilled our glasses with the rest of the Frascati and had a large mouthful of spirit-boosting peanuts. 'Only red left after this.'

'Horrible little sod!' said Louise gleefully. 'Remember the chocolate buttons?'

How could I forget? It is one of life's sadnesses that however much you love your friends there are no guarantees about their children. I only had to look at this particular brat to feel the stinging urge to give him a good slap. And the same was rapidly going for his mother Rowena too. Once a terrifying maths teacher who could silence the average eleven-year-old thug with a mere glance of her evil eyes, she had metamorphosed into a droopy pink-tracksuit-bottomed simpleton who could only talk about poo textures and who had, on the fateful day Louise recalled, sat with an indulgent smile on her face while 'Lukey' smeared chocolate across my cream sofa.

'I hate that child,' Martin had said with quiet venom. He hated him even more when he threw up over the Swiss cheese plant on his way out.

Ever since that day 'Lukey' had been a golden reminder of the need to be vigilant about contraception.

'Poor Rowena,' said Louise, adding, as she always did, 'she should never have married him.'

'None of us', I declared, searching for the corkscrew, 'should ever have married any of them.'

Louise – who never had – nodded fervently.

'At least,' I said, noticing that even to myself I was having difficulty getting the words out, 'Bernard's only boring. He's not a bloody grade A bastard like bloody bastard Martin.'

'He's a pillock,' said Louise, who had picked up the empty peanut packet and was now rooting about in my fridge. 'Why've you got tins in here?' she asked, emerging with a chocolate finger and my cheese ration for the next five days.

'Who is?'

'What?'

'A pillcock, pillock, bastard?'

'Bernard. Bearded boring bloody bastard Bernard.'

'Well, Rowena loves him,' I said vaguely, 'which is more than Martin ever did me.'

'He loved you in the beginning,' said Louise firmly. 'They always love us in the beginning.'

'I don't think he did, really,' I said sadly. 'He never looked after me – not in a nurturing, loving sort of way – or said nice things or made me feel needed. It was like he was OK with me being there but he'd have been just as OK if I'd gone. And as soon as someone else came along . . .' I gulped.

'But you still loved him,' said Louise, peering into her empty glass.

'Did I?' I asked tragically. 'I wanted him. I had to have him. Perhaps I just wanted him to want me. To show I could be wanted . . .' I was beginning to feel confused and still no nearer to getting the next bottle open. 'Find the corkscrew, Lou.'

45

She'd just finished ferreting among the cushions and was waving it triumphantly when the phone rang. We both looked at each other with a God-who-can-that-be? expression, an old habit from our guilty teens, which had been reincarnated in faithless adulthood.

With the sudden sixth sense that has saved me many a tedious conversation I leapt across the room and flicked on the answerphone.

'My mother!' I mouthed.

We sat and listened to her message: 'Oh, hello, darling, I'm phoning now because I'm out tomorrow, though I'll be back after four. I've got one or two things to say to you and I thought perhaps we could arrange a time later in the week to catch up. I've been thinking of you but I know you don't want to talk about it and you know how I am about respecting things like that. You might like to know – I thought you would be interested, though perhaps you're not, but just for information – there's a programme on at eleven o'clock on Channel Four about coping with loss or bereavement or something, but there might be some interesting bits and don't worry at all if you can't but if you did have a spare bit of tape you could record it and we could perhaps talk about it – only if you want to, you know how careful I am about boundaries. I do hope your father hasn't been interfering. I can just imagine how he'll want to get involved and you know what he is – if you give him an inch, darling, you won't be able to get rid of him . . .'

Here, thanks to my mother pausing weightily between sentences while she considered how to continue, the allotted three minutes of tape ran out and she was mercifully silenced by a shrill beep.

Louise threw herself back on the cushions and exhaled noisily. 'Bloody hell. I thought mine went on.'

'She's phoned every day this week,' I told her grimly. 'She'll be round here next, I know she will.'

We both yawned.

She arrived in the morning when I had the mother and father of a hangover and had only opened the door because I thought she was Nigel. She was smiling widely, finger still pressed to the bell, earrings dangling, ethnic scarf thrown fetchingly around her neck. Her arms were filled with gifts so that I couldn't tell her to sling her hook.

While I staggered back to the mirror to look at my smudgy eyes and blotchy skin, reflecting suicidally that one couldn't survive a night's drinking at thirty-two in the way one could at twenty, she began to unpack. 'Here you are darling, I just couldn't resist that scent,' she said, thrusting two bunches of freesias into my pasty white face.

I bet you bloody couldn't.

'And look, darling, Magnolia bath oil. I know how you love Magnolia. I said to that lovely supervisor in Marks & Spencer – you know, the one I went to pottery with – "It's for my daughter." '

Thank you.

'You look a bit tired.'

Once, I would have slapped on another coat of makeup, fluffed up my hair a bit and bounced out to greet another day. Now I looked about a hundred, and three tubes of Polyfilla wouldn't fix the great cracks in my face.

'How are you *feeling*?' Only my mother can make a seven-letter word stretch to five syllables.

Like shit.

When Nigel phoned for the second time to say he'd been delayed, I'd got rid of her but my nerves were still strung out with irritation. 'Well, get a bloody move on,' I said crossly, before banging the phone down.

My mother often does this to me. Other people think she's lovely. Rowena is particularly enamoured. 'Why do you get so angry?' she asked me once. 'What does she *do*?'

It's an excellent question and one to which I have never been able to provide an answer, despite hours spent with Juliette in quest of one. (Not that Juliette is the best candidate for the challenge, tending to get sidetracked on to what our mother *has done* in the past, namely not breastfeed for long enough, send her children to nursery school to be savaged, and marry our father, all of which have combined, it seems, to result in Juliette being more than averagely loopy even by our family's standards.)

When forced kicking and screaming into the present, Juliette will make long head-up-back-passage speeches about our mother not being appropriately parental and having problems about 'letting go', the importance of which my mother and Juliette spend long hours emphasizing without enlightening me as to what exactly one is supposed to be loosening one's grip on.

I think it is the way she breathes. Our mother has the equivalent of an entire musical range of breath at her disposal. There is the closed-eye thirty-second intake, in which her shoulders rise, her head is tipped back and to the right, her whole body sucks in oxygen as she prepares to make a momentous announcement. Then there is the elongated exhalation when her eyes are closed and her body slumps in defeat or disappointment before rising up again for confrontation (see above). Between these there is a whole spectrum of short breaths and long ones, sighs, gasps and moans that cover every emotion from rage (occasional) through long-suffering martyrdom (regular) to ecstasy (unheard of).

Today she had sighed in sympathy at my being abandoned, gushed breathily with enthusiasm over her gifts, and hissed with annoyance and hurt when I'd displayed my ingratitude by refusing to spill the beans about how I felt like topping myself. Why can't I tell her anything? Everyone else can: my mother has been a Samaritan; she's attended every listening-skills course known to woman; her friends would walk through the Siberian wastelands for the benefit of her echo-the-last-thing-they-said-and-thus-facilitate-further-outpourings technique. But it just doesn't do it for me. If I tell her I feel miserable all I am really saying is I want her to hand me a tissue. Instead it goes like this.

ME (*sniff, sniff, long face*): 'I'm upset.'

HER (*draws up chair, leans forward, positions eyes six inches from mine*): 'So you're feeling upset?'

ME: 'Yes, Martin has left me – the bastard.'

HER: 'So you feel he's a bastard?'

ME: 'Well, yes – he's a self-centred, self-seeking, smooth-tongued, wanker-worm.'

HER (*confrontational yet non-judgemental intonation and raised eyebrow to suggest meaningful and insightful moment has occurred*): 'Ah! Wanker-worm?'

I do not find this rabid interest in the inner workings of my emotional psyche a comfort. I wish she would be the sort of mother Louise has, who descends once a month, berates her about the state of the downstairs loo then spends three days scrubbing the kitchen and plumbing the murky depths of the laundry basket. She drives Louise mad, but what she does seems preferable to being forced to sit while my mother intones: 'Is there a particular association for you with masturbation and slimy creatures?' I'd rather she made me a cup of coffee and had a bit of a tidy-up.

Today, an hour of maternal love, and I was pacing the kitchen in fury, my insides twisting with guilt.

Nigel got the full benefit of my mood the moment I opened the truck door. 'If you can't even be on time,' I snapped, 'I'm not interested.'

'You'll have to find yourself a boyfriend,' said Nigel soothingly, while I fumed. 'Stop you being so frustrated.'

The house was in the grottiest street in town, tall and narrow with peeling paint, a kicked-in front door and broken windows. Ideas of becoming a property mogul with a designer wardrobe and a stream of brutish lovers faded. They evaporated completely when Nigel put the boot into the rest of the front door and we stepped on to a stretch of slimy green carpet. The smell of cat-piss was overpowering. As I turned to retch my way out into the fresh air, he pulled me in and shoved me towards the crumbling staircase. 'This is just superficial,' he said, with a smile to match. 'Jim'll sort out the cleaning – he's got no sense of smell.'

'Cleaning!' I squawked. 'The place needs demolishing!' I looked around and took in the broken windows, stained carpet, and the delicately spray-painted 'you're fucking dead' across what was left of the chimney breast.

'Wait till you see the top floors,' said Nigel. 'Much better,' he called, as he bounded up the rubbish-strewn stairs. 'They've started things up here, won't take long to finish.'

I scrabbled in my handbag for the bottle of lavender oil Sonia had recommended after our last confessional exchange about toilet trauma and went tentatively after him. By 'started', he meant gutted. The ceilings were down, radiators ripped from the wall. 'See?' he said triumphantly. 'All the pipework's in.'

Rubbing the oil lavishly around my nostrils I forced my head into the bathroom. The toilet was disgusting.

'We'll clean it,' said Nigel impatiently, affecting his disappointed-little-boy look at my lack of enthusiasm.

'We? *We?*' I squawked at him. 'I'm not putting my hands anywhere near other people's shit, thank you *very* much. I have enough problems dealing with my own.'

Nigel changed tack and smiled at me indulgently. 'Cari, really, I've seen lots of these houses. A couple of weeks and you won't recognize it.'

'I told the bank manager it just needed a bit of decorating,' I said furiously.

'It's really fine – just superficial,' he said, unperturbed, pulling at a piece of curling brown woodchip paper and watching clouds of plaster dust swirl towards us. 'You worry too much. It'll be brilliant. Look,' he waved his arm about expansively, 'we'll put a shower room over there, a kitchenette here – this will be the middle studio flat. Then upstairs—'

'What?' I interrupted. 'You expect people to live in this tiny space? It's not big enough to swing a cat.'

'It's how the other half live. You've been spoilt. You should see Johnny's flats – they're half this size and he has people queuing up for them.'

I stared at him in exasperation. 'This is just not going to work. The surveyor's going to take one look at this heap of shit and I'm going to be a laughing stock at the bank.' Already I was feeling protective of my new image as no-nonsense businesswoman.

Nigel gave a satisfied smile. 'Really?' he asked smugly. 'Do you think so?' I looked at him suspiciously. 'Funny that!' he said, thoroughly pleased with himself. 'I had a call from Wobbly this morning. I think he's going to see things our way.'

Nigel enjoys pretending he is part of a sinister Mafia underworld with the power to affect lives.

'Oh, yeah?' I said, unimpressed. 'He hasn't seen it yet.'

'He's seen the outside,' said Nigel, still in the same infuriating tone, 'and I've told him what to expect on the inside. It will be no problem.'

'We'll see,' I said, grimly, wondering if Nigel really had any influence over the unfortunate Wobbly.

'We will,' said Nigel. 'Now, we need to get the chaps in to have a look. You could help here.'

He gave the sort of encouraging smile you give a five-year-old who's going to help lay the table. 'I'll give you all the names and numbers and you can come and meet them here. Probably best to get Big Ben in first. Though we'll need Trevor too, by the look of this.' He pulled at a piece of bare wire hanging from the ceiling. 'We'll have to get the metering sorted out, plumbing shouldn't be a problem. Anyway, you can call up the agents – Tony's got the plans, so just show everyone those.'

'You call them! You said you'd organize all the work. You said I just had to talk to the bank manager and do the money. I don't know what to say.'

'OK, OK, I'll do it, but I'm just so busy – time's the problem with me. I thought you wanted to get involved. Take your mind off things a bit. And there's nothing to it.' He was already pressing numbers on his phone. 'Ben! How are you, mate? Good, good, no, I haven't forgotten, I've just been so busy, mate, haven't had a moment to get into the office all week. Yeah, I know, mate, I've got a pile of paperwork to get through. I'll sort it, mate. Now, I've got a new building needs converting. How are you fixed to come and have a look at it? Yeah, that's right, that's the one. Into three, yeah. Lovely stuff! Yeah, mate, I will. You too . . .

'See? Easy. Coming over Friday morning. You meet us here and I'll introduce you.'

I looked at him doubtfully but he was in full flow.

'They all know what they're doing. You just need to

52

check that they turn up when they say they will and make sure they've got enough money for materials and stuff. It's just a case of going to the bank. I'll be around too.' He patted his mobile. 'We'll get you one of these. Make life easier.'

'And a clipboard,' I put in, suddenly seeing myself as feminine and tough, delicate cheekbones beneath a safety helmet as I scaled the scaffolding to check up on the crew of only half-tamed navvies, board under one arm, phone clipped to belt as I leapt lightly across the tiles to gazes of admiration and lust . . .

'Clipboard, yeah, great,' said Nigel, clearly wondering why I couldn't just write everything on my hand or on the back of a crummy brown envelope as he did, but pleased to see some enthusiasm at last.

'Come on then!' I said cheerily, reflecting that here was yet another forbidden-by-Martin-delight that I could now experience. 'Let's go and get me a phone now!'

I was still fingering it lovingly and trying to decide between the five different ringing tones when the door-bell rang and a familiar head loomed up against the frosted glass. How can it be? Twice in one day!

'I was very worried about you this morning!'

No flowers and preamble this evening – straight in, wounded and fighting.

'I had a meeting to go to.'

'You barely spoke!' My mother breathed heavily and looked dramatically out of the window, fighting for self-control in the way she'd once seen Rose from *Upstairs Downstairs* do. 'I am very hurt.' Here she turned and glared into my eyes (same day course as Juliette) before lowering her lashes soulfully and exhaling loudly.

The wave of irritation that overtook me was so over-whelming I had to grab the side of the fridge to steady myself. While my nerve endings screeched, 'Leave me alone, for God's sake!' the small rational voice of experience reminded me how many heavy nights can ensue from a little biting back and how dreadful I would ultimately feel. She means well, it said. She is your mother, who loves you. Oh, yes. 'Sorry about that,' I said, teeth gritted, putting down my phone, other hand already reaching for the Frascati and nuts.

'I do *know*', she said, weightily, 'that this is a *very difficult time* for you. I am not *insensitive*.'

'Course you're not. Want some?'

'I did not come round here to intrude. That is how you made me *feel*.' (Four syllables and passionate raising of voice. She had obviously mistaken my crunching of peanuts for drawing of breath to contradict her.) 'Has your father been here?'

'No.'

'Has he phoned?'

'No.'

'He thinks of no one but himself.'

I could feel my insides curling themselves into a small tight ball. 'Do you want a glass of wine?' I asked pointedly, swallowing half of mine and topping it up again.

'Umm.' My mother took in a huge breath and let it out slowly. 'I don't think so, darling. I do feel like something but . . . Oh, all right, I'll just have a little one.'

One day my mother will answer a question with 'yes' or 'no'. The same day, no doubt, that a small rose-tinted porcine being floats through my window and bestows three wishes upon me. (*Make me rich, make me thin, send my mother to Australia* . . .) But at least she has a saving grace: she has very little capacity for alcohol. Within half a glass, she had forgotten her earlier displeasure and was drivelling on happily about how unhelpful and self-absorbed my father had been when Juliette had been forced to flee from Sid in the middle of the night (my mother and sister share a love of drama – on the night Juliette left, Sid was banged up in the local police station for doing something obscene in the middle of the new shopping centre that we never quite got to the bottom of, so she could easily have waited until morning) and how he was bound to be equally useless when he forced his way in here to demand all the intimate details about Martin.

'He won't do that,' I protested a couple of times, reflecting that the only person who ever barged in unannounced to interrogate me was right now knocking back my Frascati, but she didn't seem to hear.

In the end I gave up and sat programming in to my mobile as many telephone numbers as I could remember of the friends and establishments I might want to call now that I had it. Then I got out my address book to add in a few dozen more, seeing as it had a ninety-nine-number memory that might as well be filled.

This was quite time-consuming as I had to spell out their names for the phone-book search feature. And since Nigel had got the phone on the cheap because it came without a manual, there was half an hour of trial and error while I worked out how to bring up the letters in the first place.

By the time I'd finished, my mother was talking about something different, which seemed to involve her friend Molly and somebody not taking responsibility for the consequences of Transactional Analysis. (Not Taking Responsibility is a crime ranked alongside Not Letting Go and is another thing Juliette and my mother have long meaningful exchanges about while I yawn quietly in a corner.) She had got through most of the bottle of wine and had a slightly wild look in her eye. I was beginning to twitch because I hadn't had time to eat before she burst in on me, and I knew she'd devour everything in sight if I so much as opened the fridge. I also wanted a bath. Basically I wanted her gone but I knew that if this truth emerged too baldly we would go zooming back to square one and I would be forced to agree that although she had forced her way into my kitchen, drunk all my wine and ranted on about my sister's disastrous relationships for an hour it didn't mean she wasn't wholly sensitive to my current emotional state.

'Stuck!' she bellowed, banging her palm down on the table and making me jump. 'Stuck in adolescence! When I think of what he put us all through . . .'

Oh, God, not my father again.

'It's a good job he's not here now,' she continued, glaring at my slumped form. 'He'd say all the wrong things and upset you.'

Yes. Thank the Lord.

'Praise the Lord!' Neil and his inner glow climbed the ladder and started sloshing wet cloths about. 'Certainly are mucky, aren't they?' he yelled cheerfully, as I hovered at the bottom rung with his coffee.

'Are you coming down for this?' I called back hopefully. I couldn't wait to get him across the table talking about God's mysterious ways. It would be as soothing as the double-glazing man's lament and not nearly so demanding on the responses.

I've always been a sucker for being sold to. The top of my head tingles in the most sensual fashion when I am the subject of a salesman's undivided attention as he outlines his unique selling points and lingeringly reassures me about quality controls and guarantees of customer satisfaction. The advantage of being sold religion is that you don't get that sticky moment when they've exhausted all their patter and want you to buy something. With God you can just look moved and thoughtful and say, 'That's amazing. I've never thought about it like that before . . .' and they go away feeling gratified and loving towards you, instead of being all pissed off that they've wasted two hours for no commission.

I knew that once Neil had heard about Martin deserting me and my bitter cynicism towards men, family life and procreation he would be full of all sorts of delicious and fervent advice about turning to Our Father to which I could relax nicely for the next hour. And I needed to relax. My mother had stayed for three hours in the end, refusing to go home even when, in desperation, I started emptying all the cupboards and wardrobes. She sat on the end of my bed, flushed and indulgent, saying, 'That's right, darling, have a good clear-out, it's so *therapeutic*,' occasionally lurching to her feet to fondle some ancient summer dress that made me look like an over-stuffed bridesmaid, crying, 'Oh, isn't that *pretty*?' before sinking down again as I crammed the offending garment into a large black plastic sack.

By the time I'd bundled her into a taxi I was uplifted and energized by all the discarding of old crap, and strung-out, starving and twitchy from keeping a lid pressed down on all the rude things I'd wanted to say to her. Even the thimbleful of wine she'd left me and the rest of the chocolate fingers did nothing to calm my nerves. So, unable to sleep, I carried on sorting and throwing until I had six bulging bin-bags to show for my labours and could hardly keep my eyes open.

Knowing that since his rebirth he always rose at dawn to praise God, I'd phoned Neil at seven a.m., apologizing for and reversing my husband's peremptory dismissal of him and imploring him to come round and give me clean windows to go with my fresh start: the thin winter sunshine that had greeted me first thing had barely been able to filter through the mire.

'I'll get the top ones done first,' he had called, so that I had to carry his mug back inside and spend time moving things about the kitchen while I waited.

When eventually he appeared, I had worked myself into a lather of indignation over having a mad mother, a loopy sister and an eccentric father whom I barely saw, and was wondering what it would be like to have been brought up in a normal family where we all went on holiday to Spain or had a beach-hut instead of having mass nervous breakdowns.

I shared this dream with Neil as he stirred his now-tepid coffee and rather wished I hadn't as the conversation began to take an honour-your-father-and-mother turn which wasn't what I wanted at all.

'My mother was a wonderful woman,' he said dreamily. 'Eight of us in three rooms and we were a handful I can tell you. My brother Joe was in and out of Borstal more often than I was.'

It is apparently mandatory to have a wild criminal past if you want to be born-again so that disbelievers like me can marvel at the likes of little soft-faced Neil and reflect on how the presence of God had transformed him from a granny-bashing thug into a nature-loving cherub. 'Hmm,' I said, not wanting to discuss any sort of mother or brother but rather to talk about myself and be soothed by spiritual advice.

But it seemed that Neil was not such good value these days – probably because I didn't have the usual packet of Hobnobs to keep him rooted at the table. I vowed to buy some before his next visit, being careful, of course, to keep them away from the fridge. I tried stammering out a few self-pitying sentences about loneliness and isolation, but he just patted me on the shoulder, observed that God's love was all about us, and disappeared outside.

It was only later, after I'd spent half an hour staring sourly at his empty mug, that I realized he'd left without asking for any money. I looked up through sparkling glass and the sun came in a golden ray across the kitchen table and all at once I felt humbled and ashamed, uplifted and tingly. Perhaps Neil knew something after all. Either my alcohol-tolerance threshold was down to zero and I had another hangover or I had been touched by the hand of God. Whatever, there was fresh hope in my heart. I saw a new beginning.

Chapter Five

If ever a new beginning was needed it was here. On the second time round the house looked even worse. I stood in the stinking hallway, freezing, clutching my clipboard and mobile phone, and smiled brightly at the hairless gorilla before me. 'Big Ben' was absolutely bloody massive. He stood there in his dirty white T-shirt, apparently oblivious to the sub-zero temperature, and looked around him enquiringly. (Think King Kong before he smashes up the Statue of Liberty.)

'I can't think where Nigel's got to,' I trilled, thinking about what I was going to do to him when he finally arrived. He'd promised to meet us here at ten. It was now twenty past eleven and his mobile was still on divert.

'That's Nigel for you!' said Big Ben, with what I assumed was a smile but which had the eerie effect on my spine usually associated with the sort of late-night movie I only watched on someone else's lap. 'You're going to have to treat this lot,' he added conversationally, crossing the room and breaking off half of the window-sill in his huge hands. 'Rotten as a pear that is, darlin'. You're going to have to have all that out.'

'Yes, well, Nigel will be here soon,' I squeaked, as he moved towards what was left of the banisters.

'Cor, dear, love,' he said, kicking at the wooden panelling beneath the stairwell, with a great cement-spattered foot. 'And what have we got here?'

There was a splintering sound and Big Ben gave another flesh-crawling leer. 'Woodworm too! You'll have to go right through.'

'Nigel will know what we need,' I said nervously.

Big Ben folded his arms across his enormous chest and laughed openly, clearly not sharing this view of Nigel's capabilities. 'Well, if you say so. But Nigel's not really a builder, is he, darlin'? Don't get me wrong, lovely bloke, him and me go back a long way – smashing fella! But he's a bodger, love, slap-a-bit-of-paint-on-it'll-be-all-right, that's Nigel. That's why the old lady down at Bridge Street's suing him.'

Terrific. I smiled even more brightly and clutched my clipboard a little tighter. When I got hold of him! Though when that would be was another matter. I decided to take control before this animal destroyed the whole house before I'd even bought it. 'Right, then,' I said, trying to assume an efficient tone, and brandishing my pen over the virgin pad. 'What are we looking at, then?' (I had heard Martin speak like this to the weasel-like roofer who once came to clear our guttering.)

Big Ben looked at me curiously. 'You're going to be helping him, are you?' He bent his mouth into a crooked half-moon. 'Nigel's good at getting the pretty ones to run about.'

'I am not helping him,' I said coldly, making sure that right from the very beginning we both knew where we stood. 'I am in partnership with Nigel. This is my house and I'm going to be overseeing the conversion.'

Big Ben gave another House of Hammer Horror grin. 'Right! Who's doing the stud work?'

I beg your pardon.

It was quite obvious that what was needed – and what Nigel lacked – was ORGANIZATION.

I had a hardback book, my DAY BOOK – Nigel looked mystified – my clipboard with a DAILY LIST, things to do today, and a MASTER LIST of all the things that had to be done to get this house habitable. Clearly Nigel was a lot more slapdash than even I'd suspected but now that I had details of all the contacts and the plans it would be fine. I looked at my neat list of names and mobile phone numbers, some from Nigel, others kindly supplied by Ben, who had become quite human and friendly once Nigel turned up and he'd got his hands on the plans, and then I looked in the fridge.

Four slices of Ryvita, one tin of tuna, one egg, one banana, two bottles of Frascati (decided not to include alcohol in the calorie count – too confusing and, anyway, a thousand calories a day is so little that there's plenty of leeway for a couple of glasses of dry white in the evening without harming anything), no chocolate fingers. If I had the egg and one piece of Ryvita now for breakfast, the banana for lunch and the tin of tuna with two pieces of Ryvita for dinner tonight, that would leave . . . one slice of Ryvita and half a lettuce for the next two days.

Something had clearly gone wrong *again*. Namely Louise, my mother and Juliette all coming in and out willy-nilly and helping themselves. Right, well, I'd just have to eat it all up today and start a fresh week tomorrow.

I went upstairs to weigh myself, just to prove that it did work even if on this occasion – as well as the previous one – it had been buggered up. I got onto the scales, got off them again, got back on and started to stamp on them in fury.

Then I realized that I had my clothes on, had three

cups of coffee sloshing about inside me, hadn't had a pee since just after I got up and calmed down. What did I expect? What had Miss Simms taught us in the infants' class? *A pint of water weighs a pound and a quarter*. Well, there you are, then.

So I went downstairs, ate everything in the fridge and determined to start again at lunchtime. Then I phoned the electrician.

'Yeah?'

Trevor did not sound as thrilled to hear from me as Nigel had said he would. Far from being delighted at the prospect of a whole house to rewire and heat, he seemed more concerned that Nigel hadn't paid him for 'the last bleeding lot'.

Well, it would be me in charge of paying him this time, I explained proudly. He need have no worries on that score.

He was not mollified. 'You got three-phase in there, then?'

'Sorry?'

'Can't put storage heaters in without three-phase. Have the electricity board been in?'

'Er, no.'

'Well, you'd better get them in. It'll cost you, mind. Charge a bloody fortune, they do, these days. Then you wait around weeks for them to come back and connect the bleeding things. Not that they'll do anything without my certificate on the place . . .'

The plumber was much more accommodating if rather doddery-sounding. He gave the same response to every item on my list, 'I can sort that out for you, dear,' until I reached the horrors of the cranking, blocked-with-things-unspeakable toilet, when he varied it to, 'I'll bring my young fella round with me. We'll take a look and sort it out, dear.'

I wondered how young 'young' was. Any thoughts I'd entertained about having a passion with one of the string of musclebound macho outdoor types had been severely hammered by the experience of spending half a morning trailing round after Ben while he smashed the place up, and the undisguised hostility in the voice of Trevor, who I'd have the pleasure of meeting tomorrow. Thinking there might be safety in numbers, I arranged for the plumber-with-young-fella-in-tow to arrive at the same time.

I crossed off 'plumber' and 'electrician' from my Daily List, neatly wrote the appointments in my Day Book under 'Tomorrow' and felt very Businesswoman-of-the-Year-ish.

Emboldened by this new sense of purpose I decided to do now what I had been putting off for the best part of a fortnight and phone Martin. The telephonist who answered had the same breathy tones as Sharon – perhaps the Brighton air gave them all sinus trouble. 'May I ask who's calling?' she wheezed, in a sing-song advert-for-Philadelphia sort of way.

'His wife,' I snapped, knowing that Martin wouldn't have told anyone in his new life that he'd got one.

'Oh! Right!' said Breathy, who sounded a whole lot sharper all of a sudden.

Martin came on the line sounding irritable. 'Martin Carrington.'

I should have known it was doomed when I bloody married him and changed my name, shouldn't I? *Cari Carrington!* It even *sounds* ridiculous.

'It's me,' I said, adding helpfully as he spluttered in surprise, 'your wife, remember? You called me.'

I have found this before. They all ask, these girls. All demand to know who you are, why you're calling, what it's in connection with, and then they never pass an iota of the information to the person you want to speak to. I once went into a ten-minute description of how I'd come to drive into the back of some old dragon in a Metro during which the girl at the insurance brokers said, 'Right, yes, good, fine,' as if she were taking it all down only to be left listening to music for five minutes before being put through to someone else entirely who didn't even know who I was. Next time I phoned my husband, I decided, I'd tell Breathy to mind her own bloody business.

'I thought you'd phone me at home,' said Martin.

My stomach lurched and tightened. Home! Already he was so comfortably settled with Sharon that his abode of years was forgotten.

'I don't want to phone you *at home*', I intoned nastily, 'and hear that ridiculous woman's ridiculous lungs emptying themselves into the receiver. You phone me when it's more convenient!'

And I put down the phone and lunged at the tissue-box.

Seconds later the phone burst into life. Nigel was disgustingly cheerful and buoyant, and oblivious to the fact that I was in torment. His voice rang into my ear as I snivelled and shovelled another couple of spoonfuls of coffee into my mug and tipped the contents of the kettle over it, feeling caffeine as well as husband-depleted and pathetically sorry for myself to boot.

'We've bought the house!'

'What? Mr Gregory said it would take four weeks.' This was about the only thing the man had said clearly. 'Greggie' had been almost as incomprehensible as Graham from the bank, once he got going.

'To complete,' said Nigel slowly, so that all the children could understand. 'But you can exchange next week and Tony's let me have the keys back already so we can start work.'

Keys! The bloody front door was practically missing!

'Well, we haven't bought it yet, then, have we?' I snarled. 'And Mr Gregory said we shouldn't spend money on it until we've completed.'

Nigel was not to be deterred by mere legal advice. 'Greggie worries too much.'

By the time Martin had left his third message on the answerphone, sounding increasingly peeved as I wasn't there to leap to attention, and knowing me well enough to realize that I was sulking rather than out, I had got a grip on myself, was twitching with caffeine overkill and had begun the List of Objectives I intended to Sellotape somewhere prominent.

It read:

(1) Make some money
(2) Lose weight
(3) Find someone to have a grand passion with
(4) Become so rich and successful that Martin is consumed with jealousy and rage.

It went on to:

Ideas for Achieving This. Clearly the obvious one was to meet and fall in love with someone very rich who would give me lots of money and shag me silly so that I would lose weight, becoming so stunning that publishers would flock to buy my book and learn my secrets and I'd end up on *Parkinson* or *Oprah* or *Esther* or whoever was currently smiling from a squidgy leather sofa . . . But I'd long ago discovered that this type of man was in very short supply if not downright non-existent.

So instead the ideas were:

(1) Build huge property empire with Nigel – doubtful with Nigel's track record but perhaps more encouraging since he'd bought the Porsche and I was involved and had obvious flair for organization.

(2) Write wildly witty and it-really-does-work diet book *now* instead of just thinking about it for the next ten years. (Suppose it can't be that difficult – there was that poem about the water-rat I had published in the school magazine to great acclaim in the days before they started pressurizing me to leave.)

(3) Murder Martin so that all his life assurance policies come to me before he has a chance to imagine he might want to marry Sharon. (Fraught with problems: (a) my being squeamish, (b) I wouldn't cope with Holloway, (c) would have to glower at Sharon during funeral, (d) not sure he has any life policies.)

At this point I became both confused and despairing, and far too despondent to tackle setting up a new fridgeful of Shelves, so I turned to the one person who by sheer comparison is always guaranteed to make me feel on top of things and can perform a dramatic transformation into a supportive coper once I give in and whimper all over her. 'Juliette,' I said, when she eventually answered the phone. 'I need to come to lunch.'

I had to let her flat bell ring for almost as long as the phone until her voice, sounding remarkably bright and breezy, urged me to come in, which was difficult since she'd forgotten to press the entry button. By the time I'd climbed three flights of stairs I was feeling even grumpier than when I'd started and hoped she'd have plenty of gooey carbohydrates in the cupboard with which to cheer me.

No such luck. I found her in the kitchen presiding over a huge whirring stainless-steel thing and about sixty quid's worth of exotic-looking fruit and vegetables. She beamed at me. 'Juicing!' she shouted, waving a banana. 'Gets rid of your toxins!'

'How much did that cost?' I yelled back.

Juliette held up a tumbler of lurid purple liquid. 'Beetroot and tomato,' she declared importantly. 'Beetroot gets rid of pre-menstrual tension, tomato improves the symptoms of glandular fever, and now I'm doing apple and nectarine.'

As usual there was nowhere to sit. The only chair was groaning under a new heap of books – *Juice Your Way to a Whole New Life, The A to Z of Juicing Rescue Cures* – so I leant up against the doorpost and shrieked, 'Turn the bloody thing off!' until she did, and approached me with a serene smile.

'I can see you're very stressed,' she said soothingly. 'Come and sit down and I'll bring you some cucumber and kiwi fruit. No, hold on . . .' she picked up a green-stained leaflet '. . . celery. Very good for stress and anxiety. Lifts depression.' She picked up the tower of books and waved me to the chair.

'I hate celery,' I said miserably. 'You know I do.'

'You won't be able to taste it. I'll put peaches and raspberries in too.'

I still could. Celery's one of those tastes, all-pervading, creeps in underneath just when you think all the soft sweet fruits have spun their magic. A bit like Martin, who would sneak in to sour all my good new hopeful feelings. Just like he'd always bloody done.

I watched Juliette wrestle with a banana as I sipped at the thick pink goo. It seemed that God (here I thought wistfully of Neil, wondering whether, rather than drink it, it would be more conducive to lowering my stress levels to go home and smear the pulverized fruit over my windows so that I could call him out) had not designed the banana to be juiced. It seemed determined to turn into brown sludge and ooze into the peel and pips compartment rather than end up as golden yellow health-enhancing nectar in the tumbler Juliette was proffering.

Still, she seemed remarkably sanguine. She tossed the banana skins into the waste-bin and smiled philosophically. 'Oh, well, I've got all this other stuff.' She held up a plum. 'Want some more?'

I shook my head, and looked at her curiously. 'You seem very together.'

'Oh, I am. It's marvellous, this juicing. I'm relaxed, my skin's brighter . . .' Here she thrust the left side of her face towards me for inspection. 'I've more energy, I feel . . .' She picked up the leaflet again to find out what she did feel. '. . . this life-boost, a sense of regeneration . . .'

'And you're not worried about it exploding?'

Juliette giggled merrily. 'No! All my anxieties have disappeared. I can leave the house without rechecking all the locks. I even went to bed last night and left the television plugged in!'

We exchanged a glance of amazement. Juliette has been obsessive-compulsive since she was six years old when she would only sleep once she'd drunk her hot chocolate in exactly nine mouthfuls and all the teddies had performed their rituals. 'Oh, Cari, it's such a relief. I feel normal again.'

While I was digesting this stunning revelation, she scurried about the room gathering together newspaper and magazine cuttings, an assortment of leaflets and pages of her own curly handwriting. 'See? Do you want to borrow them? I cut these out from the Sundays; and this leaflet here I got from a juicing support group in Los Angeles. I spoke to this woman – Maria. She's had allergies for thirty years, so bad she couldn't leave the house, and now she has broccoli, orange, carrot and ginger three times a day and can eat eggs again . . .'

Something deep inside me gave a tiny puff of relief. 'Well, that's great,' I said, oddly reassured that nothing fundamental had changed. 'I'm really glad you're feeling better. I am too,' I added, having lost heart in the prospect of an emotional display. 'I've made all sorts of plans—'

'That's the thing,' interrupted Juliette excitedly. 'You feel the benefits from the very first glass. I think I'll go back to work soon.'

'And I'm going to write a book!'

Juliette looked at me blankly. Then she leapt up and began to tear her way through the tottering pile of newspapers that overflowed a huge cardboard box by the door. 'I just read it the other day,' she said breathlessly over her shoulder, as she flung papers all around her. Eventually she held one up triumphantly. 'Here! An article on writing your first novel. I don't know if there's a helpline number. Perhaps there's a society you could join?'

Chapter Six

If walking burns 240 calories per hour and it takes fifteen minutes to walk from my house to Turpin Road and I go there three times a week, that's three hundred and sixty additional calories I can eat without any effect on anything.

Or – pause while I searched for the calculator – eleven and a quarter gloriously chocolatey crispy Cadbury's Fingers to munch on in moments of particular need, without any worries about whether they were on the Shelf.

Thus I resolved to walk there and back, but the next morning I forgot and only remembered as I was squeezing into the last parking space in Turpin Road. However, I was too buoyant to care. Nigel was already at the house with a spotty youth who turned out to be Tony-the-agent, a shrivelled little toothless thing he introduced as Jim, and an old bloke of about a hundred who claimed to be the plumber. There was no sign of the 'young fella' or the charming Trevor.

I gave Nigel a dazzling smile, which startled him. 'I've just realized my car tax is about to run out,' I said breezily, 'which means the insurance must be up soon. All comes at once, doesn't it? Still, never mind . . .' I nodded cheerily at the plumber.

'Has Nigel shown you the problems?' I laughed. 'Well, the whole house is one big problem, really.'

Nigel smirked at the old boy, gave his salesman's guffaw in Tony's direction and grabbed my arm. 'What are you on?' he demanded, in an alarmed undertone as he steered me out through the space where the door should have been.

'Nothing.' I giggled. 'I'm just feeling happy, that's all.'

Nigel looked crestfallen. 'Who is it?' he asked. 'I knew it wouldn't take you long to start shagging again.'

'Nobody. The chance – as they say – would be a jolly fine thing.' I smiled again. (It was really quite easy now I'd got the hang of it.) 'I am just taking stock of my life, being positive, looking forward . . .' I wanted to say, 'And I've read a newspaper article that has changed my life,' but on the other hand I needed to save the surprise until I'd got an agent and a publishing contract, so I shut my mouth again and contented myself with grinning in the manner of someone who has simply stopped being an old misery and considers they have a future again.

'Brilliant,' said Nigel, clearly discomfited by this further change in my demeanour, but not one to let it put him off track. 'Come and talk to Tony, then, and we'll get Jimbo started on site-clearance, and show the old boy where the shower room's going. Come on!' he urged again, as I stood there replaying my brilliant first paragraph in my mind, picturing myself wafer-thin and glamorous, sipping champagne at the launch party . . .

As he was about to propel me inside, a white van drew up and parked on the pavement. A dark, glowering man got out, strode up to Nigel and scowled, ignored me, and pushed past us into the house. Before I could speak, Nigel had disappeared after him, pulling me with him.

'Another one of your bleeding messes, eh, Nigel?' The

new arrival looked around scathingly, thumbs hooked into the belt loops of his jeans, as if he was trying to look like the dark stranger in some crap western he'd seen as a boy.

Nigel turned to me, unruffled. 'Cari, this is Trevor.'

What a surprise.

Still dreaming of my forthcoming fame and fortune, it took me several minutes to realize that Nigel's introduction had been the precursor to him pissing off and leaving me to it. Before I knew where I was, he'd gone and I was surrounded by Jim, Tony, the plumber and the sinister-eyed Trevor, all of whom were looking at me expectantly. As I tried to remember where I had left my Day Book and assorted lists, Tony broke the silence. 'Well, I'll be off, then,' he muttered, shuffling his feet. Not knowing why he was there in the first place, I nodded.

And then my phone rang. The effect was electric. There was a mass scrabbling in pockets, a pulling at belts as all four men grasped their own mobiles.

I called, 'Excuse me a moment, won't you?' with desperate jollity, shot out of the door and dashed for my car.

It was Louise, wanting both to try out my phone and to report that she'd seen Juliette drifting around the fruit and veg section of Sainsbury's looking very odd, and perhaps I should check up on her because she might be going funny again.

Having reassured her that, yes, the phone had rung beautifully, even if it was the same model as owned by half a dozen revolting building types, and, no, Juliette was fine, I rang off, opened my car, gathered all my tools of efficiency together and marched back to the house to start again. Remembering the soothing effect that the sight of the plans had had on Big Ben, I decided to give them straight to Trevor while I phoned Nigel and asked him what the hell I was supposed to tell the rest of them.

But when I got back I found myself largely redundant. Tony had left, Jim was determinedly hacking plaster off the downstairs walls with an alarming-looking hammer thing several sizes bigger than he was and Trevor was rooting about in a cupboard, muttering.

I came up behind him, coughed a couple of times and called his name. When he emerged I held out the plans feebly and smiled ingratiatingly, but he ignored my out-stretched hand and looked at me with distaste. 'He's shown me,' he said, with a curt nod towards Jim, and went back into the cupboard.

I found the plumber upstairs, ensconced in the putrid bathroom, measuring things with a long metal tape. I tried to give the plans to him instead. 'It's all right, dear, I'll sort it out for you. Jim's explained what we want.'

It seemed that Jim, for all that I hadn't heard him utter a sound, was a veritable fount of knowledge and in full control. Which was just as well, really, for Nigel, of course, was on divert.

Having called cheery goodbyes and been ignored by everyone except the plumber, I got back into my car, noted down a few details of time and positions in my Day Book and drove home to reread Juliette's newspaper and the words of encouragement from my new role-model.

Jessica Jackson was my age, even if she looked a sickening twenty-five, with no sign of any wrinkles and with those cheekbones that only people in photographs have. Still, no doubt the touch-up people would be able to do much the same for me in due course. She had just taken the publishing world by storm in getting a huge six-figure sum (here I'd paused to work out how much this might be – why couldn't they just say, 'More than a hundred thousand pounds'? It's like those irritating American novels where they keep giving everyone's weight in pounds, necessitating a wasted ten minutes every three chapters while I take the house apart searching for my calculator so that I can divide by fourteen and work out how grossly obese or malnourished they are in real terms) for her first novel, which she wrote in eight weeks on some remote Windward Island where she'd been sent by her rich father to recover from the trauma of her fiancé running off with an overweight occupational therapist who was fifteen years older than him and considerably more ancient than heartbroken Jessica. The similarities were so uncanny it felt like a sign. Right down to the stammery alliteration of our first and second names. True, my father had had to be blackmailed before he'd pay for our school uniform, let alone a two-month holiday, and Martin had disappeared with someone pointedly younger than me and I had lots of wrinkles, but it was close enough to send a shiver of anticipatory excitement skipping up my spine. Jessica had never written a thing before and had all sorts of uplifting advice about just letting it all pour out and there being a bestselling novel in all of us just waiting to be set free. She said she couldn't understand all this fuss about it being impossible to get published these days because she'd had six publishers and three agents fighting over her and one had said her writing was the 'brightest, freshest, most exquisite prose' he'd ever read. (There was a photo of him looking as if he'd had too much lunch.)

Anyway Jessica, with her if-I-can-do-it-anyone-can logic, had given me just the boost I needed. And underneath her bit were a lot of helpful hints from various nobs in publishing saying what it takes to have her sort of success, and it all seemed perfectly straightforward.

All agreed on the importance of the first paragraph leaping off the page and grabbing the unsuspecting reader by the throat. After that you just had to keep them turning the pages for a hundred thousand words or so and you were home and dry.

I'd worked it out on the calculator. A few introductory chapters explaining the philosophy behind the creation of the Shelf Diet (say, ten thousand words), fifty-two different combinations for each week of the year with seasonal notes and witty words of encouragement (say, 1,635 words each) and a five-thousand word conclusion, outlining how revolutionized the reader's life would be. I thought of having a section of glowing testimonials from people who'd tried it and been amazed but, of course, this would necessitate having to reveal how it worked and they might give away the secret. Then I toyed with making up the testimonials but this might not go down well with the publishing giant's legal department so I decided to leave those till the second print-run. And there you would have it. A hundred thousand words of groundbreaking weight-loss truth that would be grasped eagerly by millions of women all over the country – the world, indeed, must make sure the agent is up on translation rights, Jessica said – and turn me into a household name.

I had spent the whole evening working on my first paragraph, producing seventeen different versions until I hit my dream formula. Now I determined to write on, completing my target of 1,785 words per day to complete the book in eight weeks *á la* Jessica. I hadn't got a clue where you dug up an agent for when this marvellous work – amusingly titled *Left on the Shelf* – was completed but I guessed I could sort that one fairly easily when the time came.

Meantime, I had to stay very strictly on the Shelf

myself so I stopped off at the supermarket to stock up on components including lots of fizzy water which, apparently, Jessica drank by the gallon to keep her mind clear. ' "I don't drink alcohol," says Jackson' (of course I didn't have to follow her literally) ' "but I ought to have shares in Perrier. I cannot begin to work without a glass beside me." ' Know the feeling, Jessica.

As I was loading my trolley full of virtuous things (the new plan was to have nothing in the house that anyone else would want to eat, no peanuts, no – *deep breath. I can do it! I can do it!* – chocolate fingers), Henry strolled by, looking rotund and important in his badged grey suit. 'Hello, my love, how are you doing?' Henry has spoken as if he was forty-five since we were in the third year at secondary school. He left the minute he could, desperate to start stacking shelves in the same supermarket where his mum was on the checkout and his dad wheeled boxes of cat-food about, and had now risen to the dizzy heights of manager, with a permanent beam at his good fortune on his podgy face. Broadrange Food Stores Ltd was his life.

'I'm fine, thank you,' – little point in saying, 'I'm broke, fat and my husband's left me' – 'and you?'

'Never been better.'

'Oh, good.'

'What are you doing with yourself, these days?'

It's always the same. The times in my life when I've been employed no one has asked me what I do, not once. I used to have to pin people against the wall at parties and demand that they listen to my job description while I still had one. The minute I'd left, been fired, or the company had gone bust, wham! Every bugger from the milkman onwards wanted a graphic breakdown of my career. 'Oh, this and that – you know . . .' I changed the subject rapidly. 'Henry do you have a diet-foods section in this store?' (You have to talk about the 'store' these days. Call it a 'shop' and Henry gets close to tears.) He looked at my hips. 'What do you need diet foods for?' he asked gallantly, before leading me two aisles down and pointing into a frozen-food cabinet. 'Our own brand in there,' he said proudly, indicating a couple of square yards of brightly coloured cardboard packages. 'Forty-two varieties.'

Walk into your local supermarket and see what they have to offer in the way of calorie-calculated foods. A few shreds of chicken in orange sauce squashed into a tiny plastic sachet? Four teaspoons of rice? And you're paying three pounds forty-nine for the privilege? Ask yourself: Can't I do better than this?

'Thank you, Henry,' I said, as I realized he was still standing there expectantly. 'I've certainly got plenty to choose from here.' I pretended to be absorbed in this limitless choice until he'd wandered off.

On the Shelf Diet you have the whole store to choose from. Relax, take your time. Pick up anything you fancy, safe in the knowledge that it can be integrated into a full-week option and eaten without guilt . . .

I made a mental note to get hold of Juliette and borrow a couple of her you're-only-fat-because-you're-full-of-suppressed-rage-and-not-because-you-eat-too-much books and crib a bit of psychobabble about why traditional diets fail. Then I headed for the checkout. I couldn't wait to get home and get started.

In the event I got home to an incomprehensible letter from Graham-from-the-bank and a great sheaf of papers from Mr Gregory the solicitor, and was forced to phone Nigel for a translation, then spend the rest of the day fretting and pacing up and down.

Graham, it seemed, had flatly refused to co-operate with the smarmy letter Nigel had sent him, signed by me, which basically asked him if we could put off making repayments till we had tenants and instead was insisting that we started paying back hundreds of pounds a mere month after we'd bought the house.

Mr Gregory was asking me to call in and sign things because the vendors were pressing for immediate exchange and completion within a week since they'd dropped the price a few more grand (a masterstroke by Nigel, courtesy of Wobbly, which he'd omitted to share with me at the time but which he now used to deflect me from the panic of buying a ramshackle heap of shit I couldn't afford), and pointing out complicated things about boundaries and planning permission for a shop on the broken old stretch of car park at the back.

It sounded to me as if he was implying that this could be all sorts of trouble and warning me against buying the house but Nigel said that solicitors, and 'Greggie' in particular, always talked in tones of gloom and doom but it was still an absolute bargain, would make us a fortune and if Greggie really thought it was a bad move he'd come right out and say so because he was the best in the business.

On the Graham front, Nigel was equally confident. What he'd taken with one hand, he'd given back with the other, Nigel assured me. Since the house was now cheaper there'd be more money for conversion and plenty to take out from the loan account with which to make repayments until we were coining it in.

And even though it didn't seem to be quite right to borrow money from the bank just so I could use it to pay it back again, and I could just imagine what Martin would have to say on the subject, Nigel is nothing if not persuasive, and I soon found myself caving in and agreeing to sign myself into dungeons of debt at the next possible opportunity.

Chapter Seven

'Well, you'll just bloody well have to.' I waved Louise towards the kettle, glanced in the mirror to discover with despair how revolting I looked first thing in the morning, and squawked over the top of Nigel's placatory noises. 'I can't understand a single word of it, and they want diagrams, and Trevor absolutely refuses to help . . . You'd better!' I banged the phone down and waved the electricity board's three pages of gobbledegook at Louise. 'I can't cope with my days starting this early. What are you doing here? It's eight fifteen!'

Louise smiled the superior smile of one who is suited and made-up with every hair in place, in stark comparison with a dishevelled, sleepy-eyed lie-in-bed slob and handed me a cup of coffee. 'I was early and I haven't spoken to you for ages so I thought I'd pop in and see how you were. Rowena's coming down in a couple of weeks and wants us all to go out.'

'Who's all of us? I can't spend an evening with Bernard and Lukey.'

'The girls, she said. I thought you could get hold of Sonia.'

Rowena and Sonia. Should be scintillating! Rowena, the Bore of Potters Bar, reliving her birth experience for the forty-third time, and Sonia drawing attention to my blossoming crow's feet.

'You could ask Juliette, too, if you like. Cheer her up a bit.'

Juliette? With those two?

'She doesn't need cheering up – she's really good at the moment.'

'Not in Sainsbury's yesterday she wasn't.'

I decided Louise must have misinterpreted Juliette's new sublime I-am-full-of-vitamins-and-new-found-joy look – understandably, given that Juliette is better known for being off work with manic depression – because my sister still sounded on top of the world when I phoned her on another book-borrowing exercise. Or maybe it was what my mother and Juliette would call either transference or projection – I never remember which is which – that funny little number where in fact it was Louise who was miserable and she just *thought* that Juliette looked equally suicidal.

I knew Louise was miserable. I've known her long enough to know that she doesn't arrive practically at dawn, looking stunning, just to herald the arrival of a long-lost schoolfriend. When Louise appears with half the Lancôme counter spread all over her face, she's feeling dreadful.

But her work beckoned, and all I'd managed to get out of her was that Neville the newsagent was prepared to sell all his shops and run away with her if only she'd leave Robert, but she loved Robert even if he didn't thrust her up against the wardrobe door with quite the passion and aplomb of Mr Newsprint. And Robert still wanted to get her pregnant and was getting shirty because she kept avoiding the issue by having two-week-long periods. All of which I'd heard before and which got us no further forward.

Except that it set me thinking. I wanted her sort of passion more than anything. But it never lasts, and before you know it you're embroiled with them in a sticky intertwined sort of way that hurts like fuck when you try to pull yourselves apart. Which is why Louise would hurt whoever she chose to tear herself away from.

Martin and I had had passion long ago. Or I'd had it anyway. Now I couldn't even remember what it felt like. And, once, Juliette and Sid could barely let go of each other. In the beginning Juliette got separation anxiety if he went to have a bath (infrequent as that was) but still ended up revolted by him – finally falling in line with how the rest of us had felt for years. Even my mother, in a rare moment of truth after three Cinzanos, had confided that when she was eighteen the sight of my father made her knees tremble. She'd quickly added the rider that, these days, he made her want to vomit – as if I might not have noticed.

I looked at Juliette as she packed a carrier-bag with two dozen books I might find useful if I was worried about weight gain, and considered once more spilling out my emotional *Angst* all over her kitchen and letting her do some List Therapy on me. This was something she particularly enjoyed. Last time, she'd elicited from me twenty-seven issues to worry about and then we'd gone through them carefully, analysing each one and deciding whether (a) it was really worth worrying about; (b) if it was, whether there was anything I could actually do to alter the situation; and (c) if there was, what it should be and when I should do it.

Then we crossed out all the As, things like the woman in the pub over the road thinking that Martin was lovely and I was an old dragon who made his life a misery, and all the Bs – my mother being barmy and the fact that I still got spots – and whittled the whole thing down to nine Cs from which we made a neat Action List:

(1) Buy some anti-wrinkle cream
(2) Chop up my credit card
(3) Make a dental appointment, though Juliette consulted her *Dictionary of the Unconscious* and her personal dream-notebook and concluded that having nightmares about your teeth falling out was more a sign of my inability to grow up – thanks, Sigmund – than underlying gum-disease.

It was undoubtedly beneficial, even if only because after three hours of minutely examining each aspect of every conceivable anxiety we were too exhausted to do anything except go home to bed and certainly far too knackered to worry about anything. But remembering it now and Juliette's several volumes of dream-notebook, fully indexed with dates, I began to wonder if in all this writing down of things there wasn't something genetic afoot.

True, it was a matter of degree. Juliette had a whole shelf of compulsive-obsessive notebooks and so far I only had a Day Book, but I'd already found myself writing down odd thoughts instead of sticking firmly to how many thousands of pounds Trevor was demanding with menaces and whether Nigel had forgotten to order the plasterboard again. If it meant I might be on my way to the Juliette state, in which she recorded everything from how often she ate sprouts right through to their lavatorial end-result, it was faintly worrying. On the other hand, my mother was famous for her lists of things-to-talk-about-when-I-see-you-darling and subsections of things-I-forgot-last-time and, to my knowledge, it had never developed further than that. And my father, during one of his depressions, had once written a rather torturous *History of the Town*, which nobody wanted to read, and he still passed for normal. So, there was the cheering thought that writing might be in my blood even if mine was the commercial money-making sort as opposed to the downright doo-lally variety.

I suddenly realized I'd been staring into space during these reveries and had been taking no notice of Juliette, who had probably been talking to me. However, a quick look at my sister confirmed that she, too, was staring into space with a peculiar expression on her face. 'Do you remember', she said meaningfully, 'when we went to look for my roots?'

'Do you mean when we went in search of the inner-city rat-infested tenement building our father was supposed to have struggled for survival in that turned out to be a semi in Beckenham?'

Juliette looked irritated. 'Do you remember that none of my photos came out?' she asked deliberately.

'Yes. You'd left the lens cap on.'

'No, I hadn't! They said in the shop the film wasn't in right but I've been wondering . . .'

'What?'

'Well, don't you think it's significant that I went to journey back to find out where I'd come from and all I got was a blank film?'

'Not if you'd left the lens cap on.'

Juliette considered me for a moment then obviously decided (rightly) that her sort of logic was beyond me. 'I'll talk to Marlena about it,' she said dismissively.

'Ah, yes, how is your dear therapist?' I'd never met the woman but I hated her on principle ever since she'd pronounced me an insatiable attention-seeker who had squashed my sister's personality underfoot in order to be controlling.

'She's fine.' Juliette brightened. 'We're talking about Dad at the moment.'

Lovely.

'And I've been having terrible panic-attacks!' She beamed again. 'At first I thought there was something wrong with my chest. You know, a healing crisis revealing hidden blockages from all the juicing I've been doing. But Marlena says it's just anxiety . . .'

All back to normal, then.

I escaped after a glass of revolting carrot and potato (very good for stomach ulcers!) with another three armfuls of books, including one ominously entitled *Bond or Bind – A Study of Sibling Rivalry*, which was, no doubt, a comprehensive breakdown of all my shortcomings, and a free magazine for budding writers Juliette had sent off for via a coupon in one of the papers. There was always the drawback in confiding any new interest or hobby to Juliette that I would be inundated with paperwork on the subject for ever more (she still cut out articles on stamp-collecting for me, even though my mother gave my stamp albums to a jumble sale when I was thirteen) but in this case I was touched and pleased.

I got into my car, clutching the magazine to my chest, longing to get home and read the 'How to Find that Publisher' article tantalizingly billed on the front cover. However, remembering the sobering bank statement that had arrived in the same post as the electricity bumph I thought I'd just pop into the house on the way to reassure myself that we really were making the huge strides Nigel had outlined so glowingly this morning.

Why do I ever believe a word Nigel says? True, the house didn't smell any more. And now that it had been bashed about, it seemed really quite spacious. But every floorboard in the place was up, there were pipes everywhere, half-finished dividing walls all over the place, and Jim, Big Ben, Trevor, the plumber and the young fella –

who looked extremely young – were all sitting down having a fag and a cup of tea.

The plumber held out a chipped, brown-stained cup with its handle missing. 'Want one, dear?'

I politely declined. 'Has Nigel been in?' I asked.

They all shook their heads and Big Ben laughed as if I'd made a particularly funny joke.

Trevor produced a sheaf of papers and addressed my left eyebrow with distaste. 'I'm done here for the moment. Send that lot off with the forms they've sent you and let me know when they're coming. I'll have to be here. Can't trust their blokes to do anything on their bleeding own. And here's my bill. Tell Nigel I want paying this side of Christmas.'

'I'll see to that,' I said smoothly, taking all the crumpled sheets and wondering what the rest of it had meant.

'These fire-door stops,' said Ben. 'They're supposed to be one inch.'

'Right, great, one inch it is, then.'

'Nigel's ordered half-inch.'

'Oh.'

'And really you should have tumescent strip round these doors – I know old Nigel likes to cut corners but if you have a fire in here, darlin', it's your neck on the line.' He gave an evil grin and fingered a piece of wood.

'Right, well, I'll talk to Nigel about it.'

'And is he putting the alarm system in or not? There's no point us finishing off these new walls if Trevor's got another cable run to do.'

Trevor glared at me. I looked at Ben. 'I haven't heard about that. I'll ask him.'

Ben stood up and walked away from the others, indicating to me that I should follow him. His eyes fixed on mine. 'You should put it in, really, darlin'. It's on the plans. Heat and smoke detectors. And those upstairs aren't regulation fire doors. I told Nigel—'

'Yes, yes, I'll speak to him straight away.'

Ben considered me for a moment, and I squirmed under his gaze. Then he wiped his hands on his jeans and laughed ominously. 'Well, you'll have to hurry up. We need to get the rest of this up and finish treating upstairs if you've got a tenant moving in at the end of the month.'

What?

'Stop panicking, Cari! I was going to tell you. I've just been so busy.' Nigel stepped back against the kitchen cupboard as I continued screeching.

'And look at this,' I shrieked, thrusting the latest missive from Graham into his face, 'and this,' a bill for thirteen hundred pounds from the electricity board, 'and this,' my own demented-looking column of figures that showed something had gone seriously wrong.

Nigel sighed. 'Just calm down, stop worrying and let me have a look.'

I sat down at the table, fuming, while he read.

Something had gone haywire with the calculations. We'd worked it all out in a neat list – well, I'd done it neatly: Nigel had scrawled it all over the back of his cheque book – with the jobs to be done on the left-hand side and the estimated cost on the right with the actual cost in brackets after it where we'd already paid.

And, yes, Big Ben had ended up charging us seven hundred and fifty pounds more than he'd thought because of all the extra wormy bits he'd found and the dry rot in the cellar. On the other hand, the plumber had come up trumps: he had managed, with Jim and some evil-smelling acid stuff that Big Ben said they used to dissolve bodies in where he grew up, to restore the existing bathroom without replacing anything. And Nigel had got all the stuff for the new shower-room at a fraction of the real price in a closing-down sale.

So all in all we had saved thousands. But according to the figures we still needed to spend sixteen thousand and there was only £7,856 in the loan account. Even allowing for the fact that I'd had to live off it a bit and Graham had just taken a horrendous arrangement fee for doing bugger all, it was still clear that something had gone very wrong indeed.

Nigel put down the Master List and was as soothing as only Nigel can be in the face of disaster. 'Building's like that,' he said helpfully. 'It always costs more than you think.' He put up a hand to stem a fresh torrent of abuse. 'But there's really no need to worry. We'll have to pay the electricity lot or they won't connect us, and of course we'll pay the lads. First rule of building: always keep the trades happy. But the suppliers can wait. And', he paused to preen a little, 'this tenant I've found is going to be brilliant.'

'Tenant! The place isn't habitable and we can't afford to get it so. Paying the blokes is going to clean us out. What about decorating? What about this alarm thing? Ben says we've got to have it.'

I was still ranting. Nigel was still looking maddeningly pleased with himself. 'Ben sees problems everywhere. Always has. And the tenant's going to do the decoration himself. He's a nice chap. Very reliable. Doesn't mind if the flat's not finished. He said as he's got no deposit or references he'll take it as it is.'

'Why hasn't he got any references?' I asked suspiciously, remembering Graham's dire warnings about wayward tenants.

Nigel filled the kettle. 'Oh, some trouble with his wife or something,' he said airily. 'He's had a difficult time lately. Nothing to worry about.' He smiled encouragingly. 'So just you chivvy Ben and Trevor along.'

'Chivvy Trevor? He hates me, and I don't know what he's talking about!' I pulled all the mystery bits of paper out of my Day Book and shoved them at him.

Nigel glanced at them briefly. 'Oh, that's all standard stuff. Write me the cheque and I'll send it off, and that will be all the electricity and heating sorted.' He'd adopted his bedtime-story-for-simple-infants voice. 'Now, you just hurry the plumber along and tell Ben to stop winding you up about fire regulations, and I'll tell Gary he can move in in a couple of weeks, and then we'll have some rent coming in.'

'But Graham wants to inspect it now.'

'Tell Jim to tart up the outside a bit. Graham will drive past, see how smart it's looking and turn his attention to the customers he really has to watch. By the time he does visit it will all be done.' He grinned triumphantly. 'And you're looking yummy. Have you lost more weight?'

I should have done. A quick look at the interior of the fridge while I got the milk out for Nigel's coffee revealed shelves still stuffed to bursting with fruit and vegetables and goat's milk yoghurt – the latter recommended in combination with bananas for instant pound-shedding in the only one of Juliette's books that was remotely readable – so I couldn't have been eating much.

Of course, there had been the night when Louise had rowed with Robert and turned up with fish and chips, and the day when I was overcome with sugar-depletion and had to burst through Henry's doors at a minute to six for an emergency box of chocolate fingers. But apart from that I had stuck to the Shelf with almost religious fervour. Which reminded me that enough time had passed for me to be able to contact Neil again.

My writing was also progressing. It had turned out

that my daily target had been a little ambitious, what with having to hare backwards and forwards to Juliette's on research missions and being tied up with my property-development career, but I had lots of it sorted out in my head and had made lots of useful notes in my Day Book for tempting autumnal options when I'd got that far. (Must find out how many calories in an average-sized toffee-apple).

However, the secret of success (I was informed by a Juliette-leaflet found lurking inside the yoghurt book) was to prioritize. So, no more writing for the moment. I was going to direct all my energies towards getting that house sufficiently complete to install rent-paying Gary.

Who, as Nigel had assured me, was going to save the day.

Chapter Eight

I was beginning to enjoy myself. When you've been married for ten years to someone whose general view of you is that you are hopeless at everything, it's very easy to end up believing it. But here I was, Day Book in hand, mobile attached to jeans pocket, being a proper foreperson with an air of authority, which would surely have impressed even Martin. I felt stimulated, useful and successful. I could now talk about second fixings, rendering, repointing, tanking and stud work with the best of them.

The walls were plastered and the new windows in. Trevor had spent a day scowling at two cheery blokes from the electricity board and the hall was a mass of shiny new meters. Gary's flat was approaching habitable. Jim had finished tiling the kitchen and I was finally sharing the vision Nigel had had all along. When it was cleared of all the bits of wood and plasterboard, when it was painted and clean, it would be very nice – and I had organized it!

Of course, the secret was in having used the right people. Jim and Ben were pretty good at getting on with things – in fact, Ben was a mass of information and I had picked up valuable knowledge that would come in handy when we did the next one. Indeed, Nick – the young fella

– was already clearly recognizing my areas of expertise: when the ground-floor loo had flooded for the fourth time, he went into a huddle with the plumber and then came to *me* to consult as to the best solution in a manner that was particularly gratifying. 'We think a section of the soil pipe has collapsed,' he said.

'Dear me! Really?' I said, in tones befitting the gravity of the situation.

'But we can re-route the duct.'

'Oh. Good.'

'We'll cut out the old section and sleeve into the second soil pipe to the old outside toilet.'

'Right.'

'Cheaper than digging up the whole backyard.'

'Oh, yes! Indeed!'

'So, that all right with you?'

'Yes, that sounds fine,' I said grandly, seeing that he was waiting expectantly for my approval. 'Do go ahead. Thank you, Nick.'

'We'll sort it out for you, dear,' said the plumber, who had wandered up during this exchange.

I nodded, feeling a satisfying tingle of power as they disappeared to do my bidding, and made an immediate note in my Day Book to the effect that I had now solved the plumbing problems and we were well on the way to completion of the first flat. At this rate, I would probably even be able to get a job as buildings manager for some big local firm with a fat salary that, coupled with my rental income, would resolve my financial instability altogether.

I would definitely employ the plumber again. And Nick, who was really, I decided, not only an excellent judge of character but rather sweet in a fresh-faced innocent sort of way. Rather too innocent for his own good, it turned out, since while I was outside supervising

93

Jim's painting of the railings, he chose to confide his marital problems to Big Ben and Trevor – who'd rolled up again, after all.

'You want to sort her out mate,' Ben was saying, when I came back in to find them on tea-break. 'These girlies,' here he winked lecherously at me, 'if you give them an inch . . .'

There followed various ribald comments and a selection of downright pornographic jokes until I said, 'Do you mind?' in my best I-am-your-boss-and-paying-your wages way, at which they all guffawed.

'I wouldn't bleeding well put up with it,' said Trevor. 'Ask her who's paying for the roof over her head and putting the food on the table!' I think Trevor must have based his whole life on a film.

Nick looked downcast as he fiddled with a bit of wastepipe. 'It's not as easy as that,' he said diffidently. 'It's just not worth the aggro sometimes – it upsets the kid.'

Big Ben shook his head sadly. Jim sucked his gums. Trevor glowered at me, as if, by merely being a woman, I was mostly to blame.

Only the plumber rose to the occasion. 'Never mind, lad,' he said. 'You'll sort it out sometime.'

The afternoon passed in a string of skirmishes between the roofers and Big Ben over what came first, the new roof joists or his anti rot/worm kill-everything spray and whether the scaffolding was sufficiently robust to take six blokes carrying three tonnes of roof tiles.

My aura of authoritative foreperson did not have quite the same effect on Ben. 'There's a safety issue here,' he said, twelve times. 'If one of us breaks our neck and you haven't got insurance for it, darlin', you'll be for it.'

Eventually I sneaked into the backyard and phoned Nigel, who laughed. He turned up and offered Ben fifty quid more to shut up and work over the weekend without moaning. Ben clapped him on the back and took Nigel off into a corner where I imagined he was regaling him with the lurid details of what he'd do to Nick's wife if he was married to her and she wouldn't shut up, while I stood there seething and trying to look prim.

Later, I began to feel responsible, thinking that, as a caring employer, I should do my bit. 'Actually,' I said kindly to Nick, just as we were all going home, 'you might find that if you do stand up to her and demand to be treated better she'll back off. My husband used to dominate me – well, bully me, really – till I grew up and learnt to fight back. Then, because I stood up to him, he stopped.'

We looked at each other with the sort of new warmth that sprung from sharing confidences. I didn't add, 'He also left me,' because I didn't see any point in upsetting the poor boy further. I just smiled and patted his arm in an I-understand-you-can-always-talk-to-me gesture of support and left him to it. Which was a mistake: the others took him to the pub and got him absolutely slaughtered, filling him up with an unrealistic fire that he couldn't hope to sustain.

The next morning he turned up three hours late with a black eye and a broken nose. While I was gasping with horror and Big Ben was grinning, the plumber said, 'Hey, lad, what happened to you?'

It was to me he answered. Wryly, and with a self-conscious dab at his swollen blue-black flesh, he said, 'I stood up to her.'

Chapter Nine

Martin didn't want to sleep with me on his last night. He said he felt guilty about Sharon and the thought of those words still makes the inside of my stomach curdle.

Guilty about Sharon? I am his wife, whom he promised to love and honour until he pegged it. There is no loyalty these days. Nigel laughed when I said that to him. 'You're as bad,' he said. 'You've been eyeing up other men for ages. You know you have.'

It's true. I had counselling once. Juliette made me go. She wanted me to talk about my anger at her being born but instead we spent all our time examining the fragility of my self-esteem. Amazing. Twenty-five pounds an hour to be told you have a self-confidence problem when friends will confirm for free that you have an ego the size of a house. An ego that needs the daily top-up of some bloke leering at me with his tongue hanging out.

They don't whistle from building sites any more. I've gone downhill since they stopped. Ageing is now a grim reality that hits me each morning as I stare at my withering skin. 'Come off it – you're gorgeous. Great tits.' That's what Nigel said. I need Nigel more than he knows.

Isn't time weird? Sometimes the clock charges round, sometimes it ticks slowly through each second of every minute. One day I was at school, ashamed of my vest and flat chest in the wake of all those sprouting breasts. The next, I am staring hopelessly into the mirror as my tits begin their inevitable journey towards my knees . . .

Nigel had buggered off again. I stood there on the pavement, trying to think nice thoughts in the spring sunshine while two thugs tried to take down the scaffolding, Big Ben blocked their way and Jim rolled his eyes at me while he swung a large metal bucket of black tar backwards and forwards.

'I'm just following instructions, mate,' said Thug One. 'We've been told to get this down this morning.'

Big Ben looked at me. I shrugged. This was Nigel's box of tricks.

'They haven't sealed round the dormer window,' said Ben. 'You'll have to get the roofer back or you'll have rain in there and it'll all go rotten again.'

I tried Nigel. We managed three sentences between us before the phone line crackled and died. 'He says it's nothing to worry about,' I offered, 'and he's in a bad signal area. And I don't know who the roofer is,' I added, before Ben could speak.

Big Ben looked at me with a don't-say-I-didn't-warn-you expression and nodded towards Jim. 'It'll only take half an hour for him to seal it. If the roof leaks later you'll have to put all this scaffolding up again.'

Remembering the cost of the scaffolding, which Nigel had assured me was 'dead cheap', I wavered. 'Well, maybe . . .'

Ben nodded, satisfied. 'Come back this afternoon!' he bellowed at the thugs.

Thug Two glowered back. 'That's another day's hire charge, then,' he said nastily.

Oh, God, not more money. Suddenly, remembering Nigel's amused words of advice about not falling for Ben's scare tactics, I fixed Ben with a rapidly constructed I-wasn't-born-yesterday look and spoke firmly. 'I'm not convinced this is entirely necessary. I've learnt enough about you lot to know you never have a good word to say about each other's workmanship. And we haven't got money to burn, you know.'

Ben looked back at me, an unfamiliar gleam in his brown eyes. 'That's not true,' he said, looking me up and down. 'Anyway, there's one way to sort it. You come up and I'll show you.'

I felt some interest stir between the thugs. They shuffled a bit closer. Jim grinned.

'What? Up on the roof?' My voice squeaked a little.

Ben grinned. 'Yep. Then you'll see the problem for yourself.'

I looked up at the rickety arrangement of ladders and scaffolding that had been declared a death-trap only days before and gulped.

'You go first and I'll come behind you. Then if you fall, I'll catch you.' Ben gave a shark-like grin and jerked his head at Jim. 'Get up there, Pops.'

Jim went up the ladder like a monkey. I stared after him as he leapt lightly from plank to plank until he was grinning down at us from on high. The thugs sniggered. My stomach gave a couple of twists.

And then Trevor rolled up in his van. He swaggered across the pavement and gave a general sneer. 'What's this? Bleeding mothers' meeting?'

That did it. 'Come on, then!' I said briskly, and put my foot on the first rung. The expression on Trevor's face continued to be worth it for about the next ten rungs until I began to feel a tingling in my knees and made the mistake of looking down.

'Go on!' said Ben, behind me, as I clutched and swayed.

I went on.

Half-way we reached a little platform and I stopped and grasped the metal pole, my knees now jangling unbearably. 'I don't think I can do this,' I gasped, looking downwards for a sickening moment then gazing upwards at the equally horrific gap between me and the top where Jim was jigging about, waving his bucket.

'Yes, you can.' Ben's voice was deep and strong behind me.

I thought of Trevor and the thugs and started climbing again. By now the ladder had given way to another vertical set of bars and my arms as well as my legs were quavering alarmingly. *Keep going, don't look down*, I repeated to myself hysterically, until at last I was level with Jim. I stepped on to the wooden planks, clutching the pole for all I was worth and hoping I wasn't going to ruin my super-cool image by throwing up.

Behind me I could hear Ben breathing. He came to stand beside me. 'Over there.' At the word of command, Jim scampered off again. Ben stepped over a huge gap in the scaffolding and proceeded to walk along a tiny ledge to the front of the roof.

I froze in horror. 'Ben, I can't!' My voice was distinctly trembly now. In fact, it sounded as if I might be dangerously close to bursting into tears.

He turned and walked back towards me. As he did so, a huge gust of wind whooshed around us and I felt the whole structure sway. My legs buckled and I clutched at the metal poles, whimpering. Ben stopped opposite me, straddled one great leg across the gaping hole and held out his hands.

I took them.

I think that at that moment I would have married him.

He was big and solid, warm and reassuring. He held me as I crossed the abyss then kept his arm round me as I tiptoed along the ledge, his great bulk shielding me from the terrifying drop. Then he propped me up against a fresh set of poles on what seemed like a vast expanse of platform in comparison to the wood shavings I'd been teetering on earlier and patted my shoulder. 'All right now?'

I nodded, trying to arrange my face into a nonchalant smile while keeping my mouth firmly shut to hide that I was hyperventilating. After a couple of snorts, I had regained my composure enough to peer over the poles at the dormer window, although I was still too glazed with terror to focus. 'Oh, yes, I see. Well, we'd better do it, then,' I said, in the most businesslike voice I could muster, while trying not to look at Jim who was skipping among the chimney-pots in a way that made my stomach go into spasm.

'Look at that view,' said Ben.

His voice sounded different and I lifted my eyes, which had been locked on the roof tiles, a fraction, and swivelled them. A sea of roofs and chimney-pots and tower blocks stretched into the distance. Far away on the horizon the sea was a silvery ribbon. 'Lovely,' I croaked.

I looked at Ben. He was gazing out to the horizon, with an almost dreamy expression on his face. He turned towards me with a half-smile that was uncharacteristically human and started to speak but then, despite my best intentions, my eyes slid downwards.

The thugs and Trevor were dwarfs on the pavement. My legs felt as though they might collapse as the great drop between me and them seemed to suck me towards it. I shuddered.

'Come on,' he said.

Going down was even worse than coming up, except

this time I abandoned all pretence of being brave and grasped both Ben's hands in mine the moment he started to move. He grunted once we'd bridged the return gap.

'I'll go down first this time,' he said, 'then I'll still catch you.'

Once I'd completed my journey to the ground and was propped up against the railings, he gave a sort of smile. 'You did well there,' he said gruffly. 'Your knees still yet?'

Then he turned to the thugs, who were staring at me with what I like to think was open-mouthed admiration but was probably just disappointment that I hadn't landed in a squashy heap at their feet and said, 'You'll have to come back after lunch when Jim's finished. That's what she's decided.' He winked at me, and my legs and stomach did something that wasn't altogether to do with my fear of heights, as he finished casually, 'And she's the boss . . .'

Behind me Trevor choked.

Chapter Ten

The guy on the radio was singing his heart out, telling me how it must be Love. 'This strange new feeling I have for you . . .' I crooned along softly.

Louise was sitting on the floor, with a corkscrew, telling me I must be mad. She sighed, loudly. 'You're kidding!' she said, opening the second bottle of Chianti, which was the only thing she would drink since she had read a scientific study proving it did not give you anything like the hangover ordinary red wine did, and reaching for my glass. 'You're never having fantasies about one of those bloody builders. You said they were all oiks.'

'I know,' I said absently, turning up the stereo a little louder. 'What can I do about my heart . . . The way I feel about you . . .'

Of course it was pathetic. Of course it was the wine. And the candles I'd lit, and too much listening to Radio Two on my own. Lack of food from the empty Shelf. After-shock from almost plunging to my death. I just kept seeing his hands and his eyes. The feel of his soft shirt against my face as he held me safe . . .

'For God's sake!' said Louise, looking as if she might vomit. 'It's a good job we're going out next week. I think it's making you peculiar staying in here every night.'

'I just want, you know, to be protected and looked after. I've always wanted it. It's that basic need to crumple and be held up again. To surrender oneself and fall into safe arms . . .'

'Cari, have another drink.'

'Not with Ben! Cari, be very careful. He's got a terrible reputation. He shags anything!' Nigel looked uncharacteristically agitated when I told him that Ben and I had reached a new understanding.

'What do you mean "not with Ben"? I'm not going to do anything with anyone. I'm just saying I like him better now, that's all. He respects me.'

'You want to get his kit off. I've seen that look on your face before. You know he's married with two kids?'

I looked at him.

'I don't! I've never been unfaithful to Gloria, you know I haven't. It's just you I find irresistible.'

He put an experimental hand up the back of my shirt to see if my hormones were in sufficient uproar for me to allow him to ravish me and sighed as I moved crossly away. 'Just be very careful that's all. I worry about you.'

Neil approached the whole matter from an entirely different angle. 'There's lust,' he said, carefully considering the packet of Hobnobs, 'and then there's love.' He took a biscuit and dipped it thoughtfully into his coffee.

I slumped in relief over my own mug. After a tempestuous and largely sleepless night, during which I'd tossed and turned and dozed off occasionally to awake hot and ashamed from a jumble of pornographic dreams about Ben, one of my old maths' teachers and, inexplicably, Trevor, this was just what I wanted. Half an hour of soothing oratory on the temptation of the devil and the carnal pleasures of the flesh, uplifting words about God testing me, saving me from myself, seeking out in me the hidden reserves that would one day bring me to fulfilment. I didn't mention the dreams to Neil, of course. I didn't want to frighten him. I concentrated on the power of the life-changing moment. The touch of Ben's fingers on mine. 'It was all so symbolic,' I told Neil. 'He held my hand for a brief moment. He closed a gap. He shielded a gaping hole and helped me pass.'

Neil nodded. I'd hoped this would be his cue to retell the delicious story of how his heart filled when they pushed his head beneath the baptismal waters, but he was far more concerned with the sanctity of marriage this morning. 'Before God came into my life,' he said slowly, 'I was driven by lust.'

I looked at him with interest, trying hard to imagine him in the throes of passion.

'But now I know what true love is. It's commitment. It's knowing you're there for better or worse and drawing comfort from that.' He peeled back the wrapper on the biscuit packet and picked out another one. 'Linda knows I can still be tempted. But now I turn to God and ask for his strength. Love', he said, looking hard at me, 'is more important than passion.'

'Is it?' I said, suddenly realizing I was munching a Hobnob myself. 'I loved Martin and look where that got me. Depressed. Yesterday I felt high. Sort of raw and exhilarated . . . the way I want to feel. Like life is powerful and exciting . . .'

'That's how I felt', said Neil, 'when Jesus entered my heart.'

I didn't dare go to the house. I was only in fantasy-crush mode so far. If I saw Ben again too soon and he so much as asked me how I was, I'd swoon into full-blown obsession.

It's happened before. There, I've been. Too much to drink at a party. Sitting behind the sofa, sobbing, as you do, and along some bloke has come and given me a tissue. And that's been it! Half a minute of undivided attention and concern and I'm composing Martin-I'm-sorry-I'm-in-love-with-another speeches and writing excruciating poetry.

Luckily for all concerned, when drunk I've had a husband in tow, and the sober light of day has usually brought home the grim reality of what is bound to be their smelly feet and unalluring underpants so I've been saved the guilt-ridden consequences of a dismal coupling even before the bubble has well and truly burst.

But I didn't feel so safe these days. I couldn't cope with all that heart-thumping and disillusionment again so I didn't go out.

I stayed on my window-seat, curled up with mugs of coffee and chocolate fingers (this was an emergency and Henry had looked so pleased to see me last time I'd dashed in to buy a packet) and did sobering calculations of how little money we had left, and made sensible grown-up notes in my Day Book on how best to approach Graham for a small overdraft, and wrote down several thoughts about the compartmentalization of foodstuffs and how thinness was all a matter of attitude.

And gradually the afternoon passed until I realized it was getting dark and I was almost falling asleep and there, filling three pages, was an amazing convoluted doodle that was flowers and leaves and girls' faces and hundreds of little boxes. And right in the centre was a spiral twisting inwards, inwards, inwards, with a little picture in the very middle – of someone. Martin? Ben? I don't know. Just someone.

Chapter Eleven

'Surprise!' Rowena twirled in front of us, holding out the billowing green top – presumably for our gasps of admiration.

Louise stared.

'Very nice!' I said quickly, reflecting that, if anything, her taste in clothes had got worse.

'I'm pregnant, silly!' Rowena laughed. 'Look! I'm showing already!'

'Oh!' Didn't her stomach always look like that? 'Congratulations! Wonderful!'

Imagine. Two Lukeys.

Louise still said nothing.

'You all right, Lou?' I gave her a manic wake-up-you're-supposed-to-be-enthusing smile and trilled, 'Isn't that lovely news?'

Louise smiled back wanly. 'Yes, that's lovely, Rowena,' she said limply. 'I expect Bernard's thrilled.'

'Oh, he is!' Rowena beamed. 'But we were both surprised at how quickly I fell. I mean, goodness, we've barely had the energy since Lukey was born. I think we only did it once that month and bingo . . .'

I looked sideways at Louise as Rowena rattled on. She'd been quiet since she'd arrived and was now staring at Rowena, looking positively anguished. I nudged her arm. 'Are you OK?'

She shook me off. 'Excuse me a minute, Rowena,' she said, as she scuttled off in the direction of my bathroom.

Fortunately Sonia chose that moment to ring my doorbell, giving me the chance to cry out, 'Would you mind, Rowena?' and charge after Louise before Rowena had a chance to do so herself.

I found her sitting on the edge of the bath clutching her stomach and staring desperately at the ceiling. 'What's the matter?' I asked, in the time-honoured fashion, though the answer had already come to me with a sickening certainty. When she didn't answer I went straight on to, 'Are you sure? Have you taken a test?' wondering how early I could decently demand to be godmother.

She looked at me blankly. 'What?'

'Are you pregnant?'

Her answer was drowned in a whoop of delight from the doorway, which was crammed full of Rowena and Sonia peering in to see what was going on.

'You're not! How marvellous. I thought you were looking pale. Oh, it's so exciting. Fancy us both carrying at the same time! What does Robert say?'

Rowena shoved past me and crouched at Louise's feet, taking hold of both her hands as if preparing to deliver the baby herself there and then.

Louise glared at me and spoke quietly to Rowena. 'I am not pregnant. I'm just not feeling too well.'

She smiled warmly at Sonia. 'I'll be fine once I've had a drink.' And, with an unconvincing cheery chuckle at them and another glower in my direction, she flounced out of the room.

Rowena's face fell.

We drove to the wine-bar in Rowena's car ('Well, I can't drink, of course, so I might as well . . .') She and Sonia kept up a thrilling exchange on stretch-marks in the front and Louise stared out of the window in the back. I nudged her a couple more times and mouthed questions but she just frowned and turned away.

'What *is* the matter, then?' I hissed, when we'd sat through Rowena's attempts to park ('It's my hormones. Bernard always says I'm a liability when I'm pregnant . . .') and we were safely on the pavement and the car finally wasn't. 'What've I done?'

'Nothing! I'll tell you later,' she hissed back, adding, 'Sorry, I meant that the other way round.' And leaving me to tie myself in knots trying to work out which was the answer to which question, she strode ahead to open the wine-bar door.

I sensed the way the evening was going to go as soon as we all sat down.

Rowena, who had given us all a brisk lecture on foetal alcohol syndrome, was sipping sanctimoniously at an orange juice. Sonia, who has the most sickeningly perfect skin you have ever seen but who is even more neurotic about wrinkles than I am, was sipping fretfully at a mineral water and Louise was toying with half a centi-metre of Chianti she had poured out from the bottle we were supposed to be sharing. I had already gulped down one glass and was busily setting about my second.

'There was this dermatologist on the radio,' Sonia was telling me. 'He said you might as well put Vaseline on your face. Ageing is about cigarettes and sunlight and alcohol. Well, you know I never go out without factor thirty . . .'

Rowena, secure in the bloom of procreation, was more interested in sharing her birthing plan. 'We thought we might go for a water birth this time,' she said happily.

'Bernard doesn't think he can cope with seeing me in all that pain again. I mean, last time, I had thirty-seven stitches. Bernard said when the head came out it was like the sound of ripping canvas.'

'For God's sake, Rowena,' I said crossly, looking at Louise who had gone green, 'you'll put us all off for life.'

Rowena gave a tinkling laugh and I thought sadly of her pre-Bernard days when she'd once got so drunk she'd danced on this very table. 'Oh, don't be silly,' she said. 'It's the best thing I ever did, having Lukey – you soon forget all the agony, you do, really. Mind you,' she continued, oblivious to our glazed expressions, 'I'm not looking forward to all those broken nights . . .'

I poured a third helping of Chianti. Louise swirled her few droplets round in the bottom of the glass. I held up the bottle encouragingly, mystified when she shook her head. Rowena was still going: 'Lukey's still such a dreadful sleeper. He has all these little habits you know, he's such a funny boy. Dippy Duck has to be in just the right place and if his cloth isn't tucked under his chin then he just gets beside himself. The health visitor says it's because he's so intelligent but Bernard and I feel that if a child can't feel secure in his own bedroom . . . and, of course, he's got Bernard's bladder . . .'

I wanted to get back to Sonia and this week's useful tips for hanging on to our collagen, but Rowena was unstoppable and Sonia and Louise were either gripped or asleep with their eyes open. I drank on.

After the next glass I felt more mellow. I was managing to keep up an interested smile while indulging in a pleasant little fantasy about Ben catching me as I stumbled and fell from something – I couldn't quite decide what this might be but nothing *too* high – and being so overcome with concern and relief that I hadn't fallen to my death that he had to make wild, passionate love to me right there and then up against the wall . . .

Then I realized that they'd all stopped talking and were staring at me and that the bottle was almost empty. 'Shall we get another?' I said casually to Louise, as if she had contributed to drinking the first one. She ignored me.

'What were you thinking about?' asked Sonia. 'You had a really funny look on your face.'

I ignored her. And then the door opened.

I have never been so pleased to see my sister. I sprang to my feet, grabbed an empty glass from the next table, poured the last millilitres of wine into it and thrust it into her hands. 'Here you are. You like red. I'll just get another bottle.'

Juliette thrust the glass back at me and beamed round at the assembled company. 'I'm not drinking,' she declared proudly. 'I'm on anti-depressants.'

I left them to it. I got another bottle of wine, and refilled Louise's glass, so that no one could say I'd drunk it all myself. I pretended I hadn't heard Rowena ask Louise whether she thought, now I'd lost my husband, I might be turning into an alcoholic, and Sonia's sorrowful contributions about the drying effects of drink and its accelerating effect on fine lines. Then I sat on a stool at the bar and chatted to Ellie, who was serving and could always be relied on to be enjoyably indiscreet about who'd been getting drunk with whom lately, and pointedly took no notice of the table behind me, where the other four – even Louise – were all chatting and laughing merrily now they'd got rid of me.

I was just thinking that, in my friendless state, I might as well call a cab and stagger home when in came Henry, looking even rounder than usual in a tight pink shirt, accompanied by a tall, skinny bloke I'd seen on the butcher's counter in Broadrange. He came up to the bar, looking touchingly pleased at the sight of me. 'Cari! Let me buy you a drink.'

I started to explain that I already had a bottle on the go, then saw how much was left and changed tack: 'A glass of Chianti would be lovely.' Even to my ears it came out a bit slurred, though Henry – bless him – didn't appear to notice.

'I'll have a glass of water as well, please,' I said to Ellie, remembering Sonia and wrinkles, and thinking briefly of tomorrow morning. This time my words sounded quite clear so I tried a few more. 'Come and sit here, Henry,' I said boldly. 'Tell me what you've been up to.'

The skinny bloke sidled off. Henry looked amazed and delighted, and settled his fat buttocks on a bar stool with astonishing alacrity. 'Well,' he said, 'I've had rather a good week, actually . . .'

He was really quite sweet, I decided, as I listened to his earnest explanation of the philosophy behind the new incentives for managers of Broadrange Food Stores Ltd, the wonders of the profit-sharing scheme and how he'd met his targets. How marvellous to be so sure of what brought you fulfilment.

'And next year,' he was saying, 'the managership of the new superstore will be up for grabs. If I could get that, I'd really be on my way. A couple of years' success there, then maybe area manager before I'm forty. Do you know? One of the chaps on the board started like me. When I got this manager's job, they said to me, "Henry, the only thing to hold you back is you." ' He stopped and sighed. 'That was the best day of my life.'

'Where is the new superstore?' I asked, thinking I should contribute a few intelligent questions rather than just slumping into my glass.

'That bit of old ground behind Turpin Road.'

'Really?' At last. I've been waiting for this moment all my life. I am somebody. I have business interests. 'I've got an investment property down there.'

Henry looked as impressed as impressed could be. I preened and then he ruined it. 'Your husband's in property, then, is he?'

No! My husband is shagging a brainless blonde in deepest Brighton. Deep breath. Serene smile. Matter-of-fact voice. Try not to slur. 'I'm not with Martin any more. We're separated.' There! That wasn't too painful. 'This is something I've started myself. Makes a lot of economic sense.'

Except half-way through the last sentence something went wrong because my eyes were burning and my lip was quivering and Henry was saying, 'Oh, my love, I am sorry,' and producing a huge handkerchief and attempting to mop at my chin.

God, how embarrassing. Yes. Thank you, Henry. I will have another drink.

'Didn't you know about the new store, then?' he asked later, when I'd swallowed some more restorative alcohol, he'd patted me on the arm a few times, and decided it was safe to put away his hanky.

'Yes, of course, it came up in the searches. I'd just forgotten. My solicitor deals with all that. I don't question it. He's the best in the business . . .' I did vaguely remember 'Greggie' saying something about permission for a supermarket out at the back and Nigel saying how sought-after that would make our flats with tenants being able to nip over the back fence as easy as winking the moment they ran out of beans.

Henry peered at me as if he didn't quite understand. He probably wasn't very worldly in the ways of solicitors. 'It's going to be marvellous,' he said, obviously trying to cheer me up. 'We actually call it an ultra-store. There's going to be a coffee-bar, crèche, soft-furnishings section, a petrol station . . .'

Didn't Ben say he might have some work pulling down those old factory buildings behind the car park? That must be to make way for the dream store. I could drop by, just to see how he's getting on . . .

'. . . and so the new chairman wants us all to mingle. He's trying to foster warmth and comradeship at all levels from the cleaners to the members of the board . . .'

My eyes were getting heavy. I needed to go home.

'It used just to be the Christmas do but now there are these special regional get-togethers planned. They're usually pretty good, lots of good food, the wine flowing.'

There was a sudden silence and I looked at Henry fearing I had missed a question. But he was fiddling with a beer mat.

'The thing is', he said, still not looking at me, 'that they all take wives or girlfriends, and it's a bit awkward—' He broke off and turned his glass round and round in his meaty fingers.

I made a supreme effort to sit up and concentrate on his dilemma. 'You mean, not having anyone,' I offered helpfully.

'That's right. It's all right for all the young lads but all the other managers, well, they're married with kids and things. And the invitation says "and partner".' He stopped, looking even more uncomfortable. Then he gave an embarrassed laugh and studied the beer mat again. 'Don't suppose you'd like a night out, Cari?'

I was filled with warmth and affection, pity and admiration for this dear, shy, decent man. 'What? Come to the do with you?'

'It was just a thought,' he said miserably.

'Of course I will. I'd love to.'

Henry's face broke into a huge grin. 'Shall I get you another drink?' he asked eagerly.

Things were swimming slightly and my stomach felt uneasy. I gripped the edge of the bar. 'No, you'd better not.'

Going home was a bit of a blur. I remember Louise propping me up against the front door and taking my key from me, and seeing Rowena drive off into the night. I can recall her in the kitchen, saying, 'For God's sake, have another glass of water, you're going to feel terrible,' and my laughing and trying to say that that was a bit like shutting the stable door after the horse had bolted but finding myself incapable of getting my tongue around any of those words and Louise saying crossly, 'What are you talking about? Go to bed.'

After that, nothing. Until I woke up to find that I had gone to bed, was still there, had a pounding head and a raging thirst and Louise was lying beside me, on top of the duvet with her clothes on, staring at the ceiling. I sat up, groaning, reached for my water and tried to work out what the clock said. The room was greyish, but after a few moments I got my eyes to adjust and focus on the bedside table and found out it was ten past five. 'What are you doing here?' I asked Louise. 'God, I feel like shit.'

'I can't go home. And you were so drunk I thought you might die of alcohol poisoning during the night. What was wrong with you?'

'What was wrong with *you*?'

She sat up and looked at me. Her eyes were two smudged panda circles. She ran her hand upwards over her forehead and through her hair in an old, familiar gesture of despair. 'I am pregnant.'

Oh, God. 'Have you done a test?'

'Shut up about tests, Cari. I'm pregnant. I'm a week late. My breasts hurt. I feel sick. I'm pregnant. I spoke to Rowena about it.'

'What? You told her?'

'No, of course not. I just got her talking about what it feels like.'

'Look, you don't know for sure until you do a test,' I said stubbornly. 'It can feel the same as just being late and your hormones being up the chute. Don't you remember when I thought I was? The very next day I came on, after I'd wasted seven pounds ninety-nine. We'll get one when the shops open.'

Louise got up and began walking about. 'I just know I am,' she said furiously. 'And I don't know what the hell I'm going to do.'

I watched her pacing. Rowena with a baby inside her meant nothing to me, but the thought of a tiny little being curled deep inside Louise was the most peculiar thing: I felt this great gap between us. Suddenly she was somewhere I'd never been. Part of me wanted her back, for me, empty-wombed. Another part already wanted to hold that baby. 'Robert will want you to keep it.'

She stopped and looked at me miserably. 'It can't *be* Robert's! I haven't slept with Robert!' she said. She began pacing up and down the room again.

Oh, no. Not Neville the newsagent. Not him with his three kids already. 'What? The other one! Haven't you been using anything? Oh, God, Louise, why not?'

Louise flung herself back down on the bed and burst into tears.

I wriggled across and put my arm around her, trying to make out the words that were being sobbed into the pillow. 'The bastard told me he'd had a vasectomy.'

*   *   *

115

I took two painkillers and went back upstairs with the coffee I'd made. I found Louise under the duvet, her hair spread across the pillow, her eyes closed. I put the mug beside her and climbed into bed. It was light now, and the birds were screaming the place down. I felt exhausted. I took a mouthful of coffee and snuggled down.

'Your coffee's there,' I said.

She murmured sleepily.

'It'll all be all right, I know it will,' I told her, sitting up again, feeling all emotional. 'I'll be here for you. You're the best friend I've ever had. I do love you, Lou.'

She rolled away from me. 'You smell like a brewery,' she said. And went to sleep.

I was woken by the phone ringing.

Juliette sounded flustered. 'I was worried about you. I thought something had happened.'

'It has. You've woken me up when I wanted to be asleep.'

'Are you depressed? Is that why you're in bed?'

'No! I'm in bed because I have a God-awful hangover and I want to die. Now, can I go back to sleep and phone you later?' I put the phone down and buried my head back in the pillow. Then I remembered Louise.

The other side of the bed was empty. It gave me a peculiar jolt to see the indentation on the pillow, the crumple of duvet where someone else had been. It was the first time the bed had looked truly slept in since Martin had left.

I got out of bed, put on my dressing-gown, swearing to myself I was never going to get drunk again. So much for Chianti and its non-hangover-giving properties. I went downstairs and in and out of the bathroom, establishing

116

both that Louise had gone and that I looked terrifyingly ancient and ugly.

I went into the kitchen, put the kettle on, then had to collapse on to the window-seat, shuddering with nausea. It was several minutes before I noticed the note on the table: 'Gone to face the music. PS. Love you too.'

Chapter Twelve

'Your sister was saying some funny things last night,' said Sonia, who had rung to enquire after my hangover. 'And Rowena thinks Louise is definitely getting broody. How are things with Robert? She wasn't very forthcoming.'

It was a question I badly wanted answering myself. I'd phoned her number at least a dozen times only to be greeted by the answering-machine. I had to keep telling myself it was only dehydration and the fertile workings of my hormone-ravaged pre-menstrual mind that was causing me to picture her having gone home to Robert and confessed all and ended up in a pulp on the floor. Not that Robert – a rather quiet, contained sort of person – was given to displays of unimaginable violence, but that was no guarantee as a hundred newspaper articles out-lining the budgie-loving habits of the average psychopath would testify.

I got shot of Sonia as soon as I could, wanting to keep the phone line free for emergency calls from Louise, but it seemed that everyone wanted to talk to me this fine Sunday afternoon. Rowena was next. She was also intent on getting the low-down on Louise's home life and keen to debate the likelihood of Louise getting her ovaries into action. She also wanted to get

Juliette back to work. I had no interest in discussing either.

'You know these government departments,' I said, deliberately sounding as bored as possible, which wasn't difficult, 'you can have months off sick before anyone starts jumping up and down.'

'Well, if she's that stressed,' said Rowena fervently, 'perhaps she should consider medical severance . . .'

'Hmm,' I said, emptying my purse and examining a piece of paper scribbled over with what looked like it might once have been my writing but was now indecipherable, 'she's much better these days.'

'I didn't think so,' said Rowena bossily. 'I thought . . .'

But I switched off from what she thought because I'd realized that half of the paper contained Henry's phone number and I was reeling with horror at the memory that I'd pledged to spend a whole evening with him at some ghastly dinner-and-dance and the other half was the name of some wondercream that Sonia said all the glossies had trialled and then sworn that it *really did work* and that I must go out and spend all the rest of my credit limit on it, and I couldn't for the life of me read it.

By the time I was concentrating again, Rowena was explaining that Bernard and Lukey were on their way down by train to drive back with her, because Bernard was worried about her negotiating the motorway back to Potter's Bar with her hormones unbalanced and there'd probably be time for them to pop in and see me before they left . . .

I spluttered out a jumble of excuses involving Nigel and tenants and problems that needed sorting – remembering, just in time, not to use the one about my mother since Rowena adored her and would certainly turn up regardless – and tried not to feel guilty about the huffy tones emanating from the other end of the line.

I was still feeling ill. Boring husbands and revolting children were the last thing I needed.

My lies have always had a way of coming back to haunt me. If ever I've phoned in sick to work and claimed to have been throwing up all night then before I know it I'm in the bathroom with my head rammed down the loo. Pretend I'm stuck with having my mother over for dinner and guess who turns up on the doorstep looking hungry. Juliette would say it's hysterical suggesta-phobia. Neil would no doubt cite divine retribution. Nigel just laughed and said, 'Hurry up and get dressed. Gary's moved in and we need to get the paperwork sorted.'

'Why can't you all leave me alone?' I grumbled, having got comfortably immersed in the cushions with my fifteenth black coffee and my writing magazine, discovering how to approach literary agents who would get you two-book deals and six-figure sums. From what I could gather there was no need to write the book at all. A synopsis and three chapters seemed to be all that was required and I was quite confident I could knock that out over the weekend. It was only a matter of joining up all the little bits I'd jotted down already.

Nigel jangled his keys. 'Come on,' he said, 'you want the rent, don't you?'

'Why can't you go and do it?'

'Because you're the landlady and you're going to have to sign the forms.'

'What forms?'

'And you can meet him and see what a nice bloke he is, and we can have a talk about what there is left to do.'

'The whole of upstairs, that's what, one and a half flats, and we've got no money left. What forms?'

'There's not that much left to do. It's only finishing and decoration now.'

'Top one looks like a bloody bombsite. Nigel, if you don't tell me what forms, I'm going back to bed.'

'Housing benefit. Makes it all easier, anyway. They'll pay the money direct to us.'

Terrific. Gary not only has no deposit and no references, he's got no rent either.

But when I stood on the pavement I was filled with pride. The freshly painted railings gleamed blackly, the glossy white door shone brightly. Nigel had been right: a lick of paint made all the difference.

I pushed open the door and stepped into the emulsion-filled hall. Yes, magnolia and white were very effective, after all. I hadn't even noticed the cornice work in the beginning – now picked out in Dulux's most brilliant gloss – up against the high ceiling. Wonderful.

Nigel had been right all along. This was going to be a success. I breathed a sigh of relief as I pushed open the inner door to the first flat. There wasn't quite the same effect in here. It was still unpainted and most of the floor was filled with black bags of clothes and card-board boxes of compact discs but you could still see the potential, and Gary didn't seem bad at all. He bounded forward, spiky hair bobbing, various rings glinting from various places, stuck out his hand, grinned cheerily and said, 'Thank-you-I-do-appreciate-this,' about six times and waved a pot plant about and explained how he was going to make it all homely. 'I thought,' he said, producing an enormous can of emulsion, 'I'd do the walls pale green, and those twirly bits in this.' He held up a tin of dark olive.

'Whatever you like, mate,' said Nigel jovially.

'Carpet same colour as the walls,' went on Gary. 'And it's OK if I knock up a few shelves, is it?'

I nodded.

'I'm one of those people, see,' he said happily. 'I like things nice.'

I smiled at him, thinking it was lucky he couldn't see the general unfinished mayhem on the floor above.

'Just got a bit of paperwork here,' said Nigel.

Gary signed his name obligingly on both the bottom of a thick white tenancy agreement that Tony the agent had provided and the crumpled brown booklet thing Nigel produced from his Filofax, and promised to trot down to the job centre forthwith to get an apparently crucial blue form duly stamped. 'I'll get down there tomorrow,' he said, shaking hands. 'You'll have to come and have a look when it's all finished,' he offered. 'I do appreciate this,' he said again.

'There!' said Nigel, as we drove away. 'Didn't I tell you?'

'How do you know about all these claim forms and things?'

'I asked Johnny. He's got twenty-seven of these. It's a piece of cake. Money for old rope. You'll see.' He delved into the overflowing glove compartment. 'Here, you sign this and we can send it off first thing tomorrow.'

I looked at the neatly typed letter confirming the rent on Flat One, 106 Turpin Road, and was punched with an unexpected vision of Ben's big hands breaking down the banisters. 'This is going to be all right, isn't it?' I said.

'Of course it is. Cari, trust me.'

'How's Gloria?'

'Wonderful. Well, a bit pissed off I wasn't there for lunch but she knows we've got to get this up and running. Why do you ask?'

Ben's hands were now doing all sorts of other things. 'I need a pep talk on the sanctity of marriage.'

'Cari, if you just want sex you can shag me. For God's sake, don't start falling in love.'

'Nigel, what are you talking about?'

'Cari, I know you better than you remember. What did you tell me when we were in that cupboard last Christmas?'

God only knows. What cupboard?

Chapter Thirteen

I let my friends imagine that Martin was desperate to marry me. They think he wanted it to pin me down and keep me faithful. They do not know how I was the one who begged and cajoled and threatened until he had no option but to scurry to his mother and break the good news.

I wanted him so much then. Needed him to be mine. Funny how I should stop loving first. How soon none of it was enough and I was lying with closed eyes and tight-shut limbs. How even before he consoled himself with the soft, easy flesh of Sharon, I had dreamt of myself prowling, perfumed and perfectly poised for what I wanted, on the look-out for fresh blood . . .

What a shit day.

Monday, for a start. And one that brought bucket-loads of rude awakenings after a delicious, snuggly, cushion-filled Sunday evening where I'd become so deeply relaxed and involved in my blossoming literary career that I'd put aside missing friends and unpaid bills, avoided getting sidetracked by hopeless unobtainable sexual fantasies – or nasty jealous stomach churnings about Martin and that woman – and had experienced a phenomenon I had been striving to experience all my life. *I had forgotten to eat!*

Yes, it was true. Apart from some hangover-suppressing toast and the previously mentioned three gallons of coffee, I suddenly realized around midnight that I had been so absorbed in my writing that not a morsel of anything had passed my lips for hours and that I was feeling much better.

I went to bed quickly before the fridge door beckoned.

This morning I felt that flat-stomached virtuous glow from not eating, the wash of sweet relief that my hangover had gone, and a whoosh of excitement that I had a whole bundle of pages all neatly written out, which I had only to get typed before taking the first steps to stardom. In short, I felt great. Until I picked up the post.

(1) A letter from Graham, talking about limits being exceeded and draw-downs reached, insufficient funds noted and site visits proposed, from which – even without Nigel's translation skills – I was able to infer that we were overdrawn, all the loan money had gone, and he wanted to come and see what we had spent it on. (Oh, God.)

(2) A red statement from the building-supplies lot saying we owed seventeen hundred pounds and they wanted it *now*.

(3) A thick white letter with bold black print from the electrical-bits company, saying we owed £2,252, and if we didn't cough up within seven days flat they'd take steps to recover it.

(4) A note from Henry, saying he was thrilled I was coming with him to the regional do and he'd pick me up three weeks on Friday at four thirty. (Half past four?)

(5) A recycled brown A4 envelope from Juliette stuffed full of newspaper and magazine cuttings, which started with 'Could You Be Psychic? Hearing the Voices

Within' and went on to the pros and cons of colonic irrigation, an in-depth description of a new fat-burning food-combining eating plan, which guaranteed to shift seven pounds in seven days, and a copy of a magazine entitled *Alternative – The Health Magazine for the Busy Life You Lead* on which she had stuck a pink Post-it note and written 'see page 22', adding three exclamation marks.

I turned quickly to the latter, fanning the vain hope that it might feature an appeal from a top publisher for anyone with a breakthrough diet plan to contact him immediately and receive half a million quid but it was simply an advertisement for an *Unlock-Your-Potential-and-Be-a-Whole-New-Person* day school at which I was promised revolutionary new insights and fresh channels of positive thought that would make every dream I'd ever had come true. This day of delight was taking place in Eastford adult education centre no less and I presumed from Juliette's frantic circling of the advertisement that she thought I would benefit. A whole day with a whole roomful of Juliette-types? You have got to be joking.

And then, just as I was moving towards the phone to dial Nigel and scream, 'For Christ's sake what are we going to *do*?' the bloody thing rang and it was traitorous, drop-me-in-the-shit Martin.

He was phoning from work, speaking smoothly in his we-both-know-I-have-always-been-the-voice-of-sweet-reason-while-you-have-been-a-screeching-fishwife tone, and trying to ask me nicely, 'So don't start yelling at me, Cari. Just keep calm,' what progress I had made towards either getting a job so that I could buy him out, or putting the house on the market so that he could have his share of the proceeds. And he didn't want to pressure me (not much!) but he wanted the money he'd lent me sometime.

'Well,' I began, in equally smooth tones, just to show him that I only screamed like a banshee when he was ruining my life by living with me, 'I'm working on the job thing, got quite a few things in the pipeline, you know, and I'm trying to decide what to do about the house,' though even as I said it I knew I did not want to leave this house, which really felt like mine now that I'd shifted things about and thrown out lots of old crap, and not as if it had ever even remotely belonged to Martin, 'it's all going to take a bit of time.' But as I said that I was filled with despair because I could see all the letters lying on the table and I didn't know how I was going to get myself out of this, unless Nigel could pull something amazing out of the bag. I changed tack brightly and said, 'How are you, anyway?' hating myself for the way I felt when he told me how wonderful everything was and trying to think of a plausible answer to his next question.

'What sort of jobs are you going for?' he said, repeating it. And when I still didn't answer, he went on, rather more sharply, 'How long is this all going to take? I can't wait for ever, Cari. I've got to get my finances sorted.'

'I suppose you want to buy somewhere with Sharon.'

He didn't answer and I imagined digging my nails into his self-satisfied cheek.

I wondered whether to appeal to his better nature – he must have had one once – and ask him to give me three months to get things sorted, but then he spoke again, reverting to his Mr-Supersmooth-Salesman-you'd-never-guess-I-was-just-about-to-stab-you-in-the-back voice: 'We don't want to have to get solicitors involved, do we?'

And I thought, What's the point of trying to be all grown-up and reasonable and speaking to Martin as if he was a friend when I'd survived perfectly well without him for weeks now and I hadn't got any money to give him back and I didn't want to sell my house and I could just imagine the bitter recriminations that would come blasting down the phone if he got even a hint that I was on the verge of financial ruin and Nigel was right on that verge with me? So I took the only approach I could think of to deal with him in the short term.

'Fuck off,' I said, and put the phone down.

I answered the phone when it rang again because I hoped it might be Louise, who I still hadn't heard from and who might still be lying in a heap somewhere, or Nigel, who might have some wheeling-dealing idea to get us out of this mess, or even Big Ben, who might have decided to leave his wife and children and spend the next three weeks shagging me.

Or, best of all, in a world where dreams really did come true, it might be Sharon, to tell me that Martin had just dropped dead of a rare disease and had forgotten to change his will so I was his sole beneficiary and not only got the house but all those shares his over-indulgent mother had salted away for him over the years.

In the event, it was my own over-indulgent mother, though having been struck with guilt about wishing paternal abandonment on Ben's perfectly innocent children, yet not at all repentant about wishing away Martin's life, it took me a couple of seconds to realize it and by then she was in full flow. 'Because we don't seem to have caught up for ages, darling,' she was saying, 'and I've got a couple of things I want to say to you.'

'What are they?' I asked suspiciously.

'Oh, nice things,' she said quickly, though there was a pause for the sort of deep breathing that meant something else was coming too. 'And I'm rather concerned about Juliette.'

'What's wrong with her now? She was fine the other day.'

'I'll tell you when I see you. So, are you coming to me or am I coming to you?'

Difficult one. If she came here she'd settle in, and I might not get rid of her for hours and then I'd have to feed her and that would mess up the Shelf quantities *again*. If I went there, she'd make me eat lots of cake.

'I'll come to you.'

'Lovely. I'll see you this evening.'

Tonight? I'd missed that bit.

'I can't really come this evening . . .'

'You just said you would. I'll make us both something to eat. Because I told you – I thought you weren't listening – the rest of the week is busy. I've got Molly on Tuesday and my art group on Thursday, and did I tell you about Paula and Yasmin taking me to the operetta on Friday?'

'I'll see you tonight.'

'You'll be glad you did. I've got such a surprise for you.'

Can't wait.

'The main thing', said Nigel, 'is not to panic. We'll write back to Graham and put him off for a few days – he always writes letters like that when the cash-flow gets sticky, he doesn't mean them. By the time he comes round Gary will have done his place up and we'll get Jim to have a tidy round upstairs and start slapping a bit of paint on. Then you tell Graham you've already got all the gear and paid the blokes and it's almost finished. He won't know the difference. And by then Gary's rent will have come through and he won't care anyway.' He smiled. 'Now, make me a very quick coffee. I was supposed to be at the accountant's half an hour ago.'

'And what about these?' I squeaked, pointing to the other letters.

'I'll sort something out.'

'But Gary's rent won't be enough for the loan repayment.'

'I'll find another tenant for upstairs.'

'But it's not finished.'

'Trust me.'

Of course Nigel was right. This was a temporary hiccup. There would come a time in my affluent future when I would look back to this moment and chortle heartily at my lack of faith.

In the meantime, as Nigel said, there weren't debtors' prisons any more. There was nothing Graham could actually *do*. And he'd laugh on the other side of his face in ten years' time when the house was unencumbered and we were raking in thousands of pounds each month in rent and had a string of other properties into the bargain.

Putting aside this latter unlikely vision, I decided the best way to stop my stomach knotting was to shift mental responsibility for the problems of the house on to Nigel, avoid facing the issue of my dwindling building-society account by spending no money whatsoever, and put far from my mind the prospect of the credit-card statements that would arrive in the next few days.

Instead I turned my energies to tracking down Louise and ascertaining whether there were now two of her. I phoned her at work to be told she was off sick, phoned her at home to be greeted by the machine again, considered trying to phone Robert at work to shriek, 'What's happened? What have you done to her?' and finally decided to drive across town and glower into Neville the newsagent's window to leave him in no doubt as to what a conniving, deceitful bastard he was.

Then I was gripped by panic and drove round to her house instead. She opened the door almost before I'd taken my finger off the bell. She was dressed in a pair of old tracksuit bottoms and a huge baggy T-shirt, with her hair all over her white face looking, it has to be said, truly dreadful.

'My God, what's happened?' I said, following her along the hall.

'I saw you pull up,' she said weakly, and tottered off into her sitting room where she sank on to her sofa. I gathered from the blankets, magazines, and little piles of crumpled tissues that she'd been there for some time.

'What's happened?' Why does no one ever answer my questions these days?

'I keep being sick,' she said, looking as if she might be about to throw up right now just to prove it. 'I've been doing it ever since I left you.' She clasped her stomach. 'Oh, why did I stop taking the pill?'

'Because the doctor told you to,' I reminded her helpfully. 'It was making you fat and spotty.'

She glared at me. 'What did you come round for?' she asked sourly.

I looked at her, hurt. 'Don't be horrible. I've been really worried about you. You didn't phone me back. I thought Robert had gone berserk or something.'

'I haven't told him anything yet. And *he* says he *has* had a vasectomy, and how could I think he was lying to me, and then he got all funny with me about me being pregnant by Robert and I said, 'What the fuck do you do with your bloody wife every night then? Play dominoes?' I haven't spoken to him since. Bastard,' she finished, with feeling.

'He is a bastard,' I agreed, 'always bloody has been. But you said you hadn't slept with Robert for weeks.'

'I haven't!' Her voice rose. 'So I must be much more

pregnant than I thought. It must be months.' She looked at me in anguish.

'Have you done a test?'

'Cari!' She leapt to her feet in fury and lifted her T-shirt. 'Look at me!' she snarled. 'Do I need to piss on a stick? I look like an elephant!'

I considered her protruding stomach. She did look pregnant but no more pregnant than I'd looked after a heavy weekend on the chocolate fingers. 'Well, perhaps you'd better go and see the doctor and find out just how far gone you are,' I said cautiously.

Louise sat down again and burst into tears.

I decided to walk to my mother's, both for appreciation-of-the-changing-seasons reasons – at last it was warm enough to wander about outside in only a few clothes without hunching against the elements – and non-drink-driving ones. And because, if wearing-shorts time was rapidly approaching, I needed to shift some cellulite. Also Martin and Louise had upset me and I needed to shake that off, together with all the other residual feelings from my horrible day.

So there I was, meandering along Broad Street, looking idly in restaurant windows and despairingly in shop ones, when a laughing group emerged from the new brasserie. I focused on the women first because they were all so beautifully dressed and made-up, enveloped in a soft cloud of perfume that wafted up the pavement several yards before they did.

But then I saw *him* and my stomach jolted.

As our eyes met, I tried to conceal my surprise. I thought of Martin, running a hand over the hips of his designer jeans, making disparaging comments. 'Manual workers are like that,' he'd sneer. 'When they wear overalls all day they can't wait to go out on a Friday night all dressed up in their cheap suits . . .' But there was nothing cheap about Ben's suit. He looked delectable.

When I realized he was going to stop and talk to me, my heart began to thump.

'How's the house?' He even sounded smoother.

'Oh, fine, yes, we've got the tenant in there now . . .' I just sounded squeaky.

Ben nodded. 'Off somewhere nice?'

'Just going to visit my mother.' I looked down, conscious of my old jeans and sloppy T-shirt, unruly hair and lack of makeup. I wondered which of those immaculately groomed women walking away along the pavement was his wife.

When I looked up again, he was watching me closely, as if I was about to make some important pronouncement, so I smirked in the way I do when I don't know what to say, and twittered, 'Good meal?'

He glanced over his shoulder at the restaurant. 'Oh! We just had something quick. We're off to the opera.' *Opera in Eastford?* 'Didn't you know? There's a really good touring company at the Playhouse. They're doing *La Bohème*.'

'Right!' I said, startled. *My mother, yes. But Ben?* 'Well, hope you enjoy it . . .' My voice trailed away.

He began to move off.

'Have a good evening.'

'And you.'

Blimey. I took a surreptitious look over my shoulder as he caught up with the rest of the group and fell into step between another bloke and a glossy redhead. What had Louise called him? My heart was still beating faster than it should have been. My *bit of rough*? Well, not tonight he wasn't . . .

*   *   *

My mother was panting with excitement. I sat down obediently on her sofa among the handprinted-in-the-Third-World cushions and various throws in fetching ethnic prints and waited while she settled herself in a similarly attired chair opposite me and gave a wide smile. 'I've got a present for you,' she said. 'I can't wait to see your face.'

Oh, God, save me from another handthrown joss-stick holder in the shape of an elephant's foot.

'Look at this first.'

It was a photocopy of the same page 22 that Juliette had flagged for me earlier. 'Discover your hidden assets, unlock your talent . . .' Spend an excruciating day on money you can't afford.

'I've booked you in!'

What?

'They had one place left! It's a present, darling. A chance to enjoy yourself. Juliette says you've been very stressed and, of course, I know it must have been dreadful. I haven't invaded your space because you know I'm very careful about things like that. I know what it's like. I remember how I felt when I finally broke free from your father. But it will help you with strategies to recharge your batteries. And get yourself focused.'

'Look, it's really nice of you but I don't think—'

'You need a day out. We all do sometimes.'

'I've got all this stuff with Nigel going on.'

'I've paid for it now. And how's your novel?' she said, while my mind was still reeling. She exhaled loudly and fixed me with a wounded look. 'You haven't told *me* about this. What's it about?'

'It's not a novel and I haven't told anyone,' I said feebly. Thank you, Juliette, O Queen of the Confidences.

'You've always been so creative. I'll never forget what

Miss Marshall said about that lovely poem about the otter.'

'It was a water-rat.'

'We all express ourselves in writing. There's me doing my words-and-images collection with the group and you writing a novel. Of course, Juliette would have been able to write too, if your father hadn't stifled her.'

'She never stops writing. What about all those notebooks? And it's not a novel, anyway. It's a sort of diet book.'

'Diet book?' My mother looked around for her tin of Kit-Kats. 'You don't need to diet. I hope you're not working out your anger by punishing your body.'

We had pasta with courgettes and a peculiarly shaped garlic and parsley loaf. ('Have you been in that little baker's by the dry-cleaner's? Super bread and such a lovely woman. You'd really like her, I know you would.') And salad and a bottle of red wine which I drank most of.

My mother told me all about Molly's cousin's nervous breakdown, and why she thought Juliette had never been the same since Sid, and how it was my father's fault that she was attracted to men who abused her. (Which was a bit rich, since Juliette had once confessed that one of the reasons Sid had thrown so many temper tantrums was that she was squeamish about tying him up and knocking six bells out of him with a bamboo cane.)

Still, it was probably best not to let my mother get her teeth into that scenario so I nodded and grunted and behaved as my mother and Juliette love best by offering a couple of anecdotes of my own about what a dreadful snob Martin was and how he'd deprived me of the right to childbirth because he'd never worked out his twisted complexes about his dreadful mother, while my mother showered me with the adoring looks I always get when I have come back into the fold.

'Isn't this lovely?' she said. 'We haven't had a proper chat like this for ever such a long time,' and I was overcome with shame.

'Yes, it is. Look, Mum, I really appreciate you giving me this day thing but it's not a good time right now and I'm really busy. Why don't we get the money back and I'll do something a bit later in the year when I'm more settled?'

'I thought you'd like it. Molly and I are going.' Wonderful. 'I tried to get Juliette to come too but she won't. I'm a bit worried about her spending so much time on her own. I thought for your birthday I could buy you both a weekend away doing something.'

Oh, God, can't we just have bubble-bath or something?

I eventually left at midnight having had to wait three-quarters of an hour for a mini-cab, so that I wouldn't get attacked by the hordes of muggers and rapists my mother envisaged on every street corner, during which I was treated to a further diatribe on my father's failings as a parent which, my mother was convinced, had now transformed Juliette into a committed agoraphobic as well as a neurotic and confirmed victim.

'I will, I will,' I said, for the eighth time, after she'd extracted a promise that I would not only visit my sister but insist she came out for a walk with me and watch her face carefully when she refused. Really, I thought, the best thing my mother could do for Juliette would be to park *herself* round there for half a day. A few hours holed up in her flat with our mother and she'd soon see the appeal of open spaces.

She was still talking as I got into the cab. In fact, she had her head stuck so far through the window that she was nearly garrotted as he drove off.

'Goes on a bit, doesn't she?' said the driver cheerfully, as we went round the corner. 'Mine's the same. Specially since my old man died. They get lonely, don't they?'

No, in my family they don't. It's not allowed.

Chapter Fourteen

Henry was engrossed with a customer, a small determined woman who seemed to be complaining about damp grapes and unhelpful attitudes in Fruit and Veg. 'At Broadrange,' I heard him say, 'we pride ourselves on customer service. I shall select your grapes personally, madam, and have a word with the young man concerned.'

I had come solely to quiz Henry on the details of the forthcoming night from hell, but since I had to wait while he pacified what was clearly a professional complainer, I did a little wandering up the biscuit aisle while trying to picture what I had left in the fridge. Quite a lot, if I remembered rightly. It was all going remarkably well. I was definitely eating less and had lost four whole pounds, which nobody had noticed.

I was hovering by the chocolate biscuits when Henry bustled up to me. 'Sorry about that.' He stuck his fat fingers beneath his lapels and rocked back on his heels, looking at me anxiously. 'You are still coming, aren't you?'

'Yes, of course I am.' How could I not? Even I'm not that rotten. 'I'm just a bit concerned about what to wear.'

'Well, the directors' wives wear long black things,' he

said vaguely. 'Velvet, I think . . .' He scratched a plump cheek, as if trying to remember. 'But some of the girls wear pink.'

This was not exactly helpful.

'But it doesn't have to be long? A sort of cocktail dress would do?'

Henry looked perplexed. 'I don't really know about ladies' clothing,' he said unhappily. 'We wear dinner jackets.'

'OK, I think I know what you mean. I'll find something.' God knows what. I gave every remotely suitable garment to charity the night I was trying to get rid of my mother.

'I could get Maureen to come and help you,' he added suddenly. He brightened at this idea and rushed off to find her. Disheartened, I picked up a packet of chocolate mint creams.

Maureen turned out to be a stout woman with a mouth that turned down at the corners. She looked me over with distaste while Henry beamed. 'Cari, this is our assistant manager, Maureen.'

At that moment an even larger figure appeared at Henry's side. 'Mr Chapman, if I could have a minute.' She was about twenty and probably a similar number in stones. Her navy cardigan was stretched to bursting point across her great white-bloused bosom, her matching skirt tight above her hugely fat knees. She was gazing at Henry adoringly.

'Oh, Rosie.' Henry touched her arm. 'Cari, this is our office manager, Rosie. I don't know what I'd do without her.'

Rosie's round face glowed.

'If you'll just excuse us,' said Henry.

They disappeared, Henry looking positively slim beside Rosie's bulk. What did they do in this place? I wondered, hurriedly shoving the packet of biscuits I was holding back on to the shelf. Eat everything that was past its sell-by date?

Left alone with me, Maureen looked pointedly at the mint creams, which were now on top of the shortbread triangles, then back to me. 'Mr Chapman tells me you want a word . . .'

By the time he'd come back all I'd got out of her was a lot of disapproving sniffs and the information that a lot of 'the young ones' wore things that were 'unsuitable' and which showed too much of 'everything they've got'. She clearly couldn't decide whether I was some old floozy likely to turn up in similar attire or whether I was Henry's nice new girlfriend, who wanted heartfelt advice on the right sort of floral frock. To cover all eventualities she alternately glared at me menacingly and bestowed on me motherly smiles until Henry returned with the invitation (white card, gold wiggly edges, curly black writing) and held it under my nose. Then she smiled ingratiatingly at him and left.

'Where is this?' I asked, reading the address of the Majestic Hotel.

'Sussex. Just along the coast from Brighton.'

Brighton!

'It's a brand new hotel. Lots of leisure activities. You can have a jacuzzi before breakfast.'

Breakfast?

'Oh, no, Cari, don't worry,' he said, seeing the look of horror and alarm that must have crossed my face. 'I mean, we all stay the night but of course we won't . . . you know.'

'You mean, I'll have my own room,' I said kindly, relief making me feel sorry for him in his discomfort.

'Well, no – well, yes, sort of. They'll book us into one room but you can have it and I'll go and share with

Barry. You know Barry,' he rushed on, still pink. 'He was with me the other night.'

The skinny butcher.

'Well, that's fine, then. Brighton, eh? I wondered why you were picking me up so early.'

Henry passed a hand across his forehead, grinned gratefully at me and resumed his usual tones: 'Got to allow plenty of time for the journey.'

Chapter Fifteen

What a shit month. Apart from the light relief of indulging in all sorts of delightful daydreams about crossing the marble foyer of the new luxury Majestic Hotel, looking stunning on the arm of some rich supermarket baron who'd never married and had spent the evening lusting after me, and bumping into Martin with Sharon, who was looking rather tired and ordinary, things had gone from bad to worse all round.

The last week had begun with the following Action List on a clean blank page of my Day Book, which was filling rapidly as I toyed with endless calculations and ideas to dig myself out of the deep dark hole of financial ruin.

(1) Find out what to do with my opening chapters in the hope that someone would pay me a hefty advance that I could chuck at the above. (I had been dreaming about this for days.)

(2) Go to the house and relieve Gary of the elusive blue form that was apparently the only thing standing between us and a fat rent cheque (which I'd been trying to do for two weeks).

(3) Cancel the unlock-your-potential day of delight and get my mother's money back (which I'd been putting off for three weeks in the hope that I'd break a leg or my

mother would have a change of heart and cancel it herself).

(4) Find something to wear for Henry's blasted do. (Which I'd been dreading for three and a half weeks.)

(5) Make Nigel do something – i.e., get Graham off my back and deal with the increasingly stern letters from the building-supplies mob, who were threatening legal action. (This could take a lifetime.)

(6) Make it up with Louise.

Now it was Monday again and the list remained.

Nigel had been strangely elusive. His mobile was constantly on divert and he'd stopped returning my calls. The only time I caught him he was in a terrible hurry, just about to go into a meeting and would say only that he had it all in hand, I wasn't to worry or panic and he'd sort everything out in a few days. All I had to do was get Gary's confirmation of income from him, which was the blue form and which he should have received by now from the benefits lot, and post it off to the council.

This was easier said than done. I'd been to the house a dozen times and Gary was never in, nor had he responded to my bits of paper pushed through the door asking him to call me on my mobile. I'd peered through the windows the first couple of times and been reassured to see the start of a painted wall and a step-ladder in the middle of the room, which at least meant we'd soon have one civilized flat to show Graham, who was now insistent about visiting and was not going to be fobbed off for ever with tales of wet paint everywhere, but since then curtains had gone up and they always seemed to be drawn.

On the hefty-advance front, I'd read my writing magazine from cover to cover and had gleaned only that I needed something called *The Writer's Handbook*, which the bookshop didn't have and which would take a week to come in.

Leaving aside the telephone call that should take care of Mother's grim idea of a present, this left items four and six – Louise and the dress – and the obvious solution was to combine them. Louise and Robert went to a lot of dos. She had a whole wardrobe of black cocktail numbers, long floral summer ball get-ups, and pink pastel matching-hat-and-shoes ensembles that she tripped around weddings in. She would know exactly what I should wear, would be reassuringly bossy about choice of handbag and would probably kit me out from head to foot. But for some reason I could not get my head round, Louise had spent the past three weeks trying to avoid me and was spending her life slumped on the sofa while an alien fatherless child swelled relentlessly within her.

The last time I'd phoned she'd been bad-tempered, snapping at me when I asked a few simple questions, like what was she going to do and had she been to the doctor's, and finally accusing me of not understanding anything at all. Since then I'd left her to it, even though that, too, had left an empty bit in the pit of my stomach.

So I didn't do anything. I sat on my window-seat with my head in my hands and reflected on the hopelessness of life and how much I wanted someone to cuddle me, tell me they'd look after me, look at my list, zip through all the problems and then – probably – take me to bed.

I picked up my Day Book and looked at the list again. *I want a hug*, I wrote deliberately across the bottom of the page, then cringed.

Get a bloody grip, I thought. The uneasy memory of Mad Auntie Maud writing in lipstick all across the bedroom wall came to my mind. Oh, God, I'd forgotten all that.

Item seven. Visit Juliette.

But in the meantime, I thought, jumping up before any more barmy old relatives could shove their way into my head, I will start at the very beginning again. And with snatches of Julie Andrews singing Do-Re-Mi going round my probably also-barmy mind, I set off for the house, phoning Nigel on the way.

The bastard was still switched off. There was still no answer from Gary. I stood outside, wondering what to do. The bored girl at the housing-benefit office had been clear on the phone: no blue form from Gary, no rent for us. He hadn't answered their letters and he hadn't been in when their man called round. If they didn't get proof that he lived there, they weren't paying out any money. And, in fact, if they didn't get all the information they wanted by next Friday the claim would be cancelled anyway and we'd have to start all over again.

I shuddered at the thought. If I didn't get some money paid into that bank account soon, Graham would start on the 'further steps' he'd hinted at.

I had spent far too many grim hours with Louise ever to entertain any real fantasies about a married man but once again I felt my heart thud even as my brain was still processing the information that Ben had appeared round the corner of the house and was sauntering along the pavement towards me.

'How you doing, darlin'?' The old builder tones were back.

'OK.' Fairly desperate, actually – in all senses of the word. 'What are you doing here?'

He had on a tight blue T-shirt, very short sleeves, great muscular arms like tree trunks . . .

'Got one of the contracts over the back. The new superstore.'

'Oh. Have they started?'

'Phase One's going to be finished in three months, if

they ever stop arguing about where to put the car-wash. Right bunch, those architects.'

I looked at his paint-splattered shorts and wondered if the other evening had all been a dream.

'And how was the opera?'

'Excellent. Breathtaking Mimi. And a Rudolpho as good as Carreras. Wonderful deathbed scene. Do you like Puccini?'

I looked at his enormous legs, feeling that he was teasing me but not understanding why. 'Er, yes. Oh, right, well, I'm here just checking over the house, you know, seeing how we're getting on.'

Ben grinned as if he knew I was gibbering inside. 'I've got a few lads working with me so we can still help you. Let me know when you're ready to finish it off.'

He looked into my eyes and I saw a certain gleam. I looked back and returned it. I just couldn't help it. Old habits die hard. Then I sighed. 'We've got to get some money in first.'

Ben grinned again. 'From him?' He jerked his head towards the downstairs windows, curtained in a variety of shades and firmly drawn. 'Is he all right?' he asked.

'Yes, he's fine. He's making it very nice in there. Why?'

'Have you seen his eyes? Trust old Nigel to find one of them.'

'One of what?'

'He's a druggie, isn't he?'

Is he?

'If I were you, I'd get in there and take a look.'

Oh, my God.

'I haven't got the key with me.'

'Excuse me!'

A suited, middle-aged bloke, complete with briefcase, went past me up to the front door and rapped smartly.

'He isn't in,' I called helpfully.

He turned and came back down the step. 'Do you live here?' he enquired.

I smiled the smile of the property-owning classes and fixed him with a cool businesswoman's look. 'I own the house. I don't actually live in it.' Then, inspired, I asked, 'Are you from the council?'

'I am.'

'Oh, good. Well, I'm sorry he isn't at home, but I can definitely confirm that Gary does live here. He moved in over three weeks ago, and I'm glad you've come because we haven't had any rent yet.'

The suit bent down and opened his briefcase. He had dandruff on his shoulders. He stood up again, holding a pad and pen. He looked at me. 'And you are?'

'The landlady.' I gave him my best flirtatious don't-you-wish-I-were-your-landlady beam and tossed my hair about a bit. The sooner he scuttled back to the office and reported that Gary was firmly in residence, the sooner I'd get some desperately needed dosh.

He stared back stonily. 'Your name.'

'Oh! Umm – Cari. Cari Carrington.'

I sniggered. Beside me, Ben gave a deep chuckle.

Mr Dandruff looked distinctly unamused. 'And Mr . . .' he stopped to pull a cardboard folder from his briefcase, giving me another close-up of his flaky scalp complete with thinning, gleaming pink patch '. . . Mr Saddleworth is your tenant.'

'Absolutely!' I tried another dazzling smile, even though the sight of his head had made me feel quite nauseous.

'Do you have any other tenants in there?'

'No, not yet. The rest of it's not finished.' Ben's fingers closed around my elbow and I jumped. I looked round at him in surprise but he was gazing down the road apparently taking no notice of what was being said.

Suppressing the minor shudder of excitement that went through me at the illicit intimacy of this little gesture, I turned back to Dandruff Head and tried to bring matters to a close. 'When do you think we might get some rent for our tenant?' I asked, in my nicest tones.

'Miss Carrington,' he emphasized the single title, confident in his assessment that no man would have been fool enough to promise his life to me, 'I can tell you that you should not have *any* tenants in occupation. We have no record of an application for building regulations on this property, and without our inspection and final certificate on the building, it is not considered fit to be used as rented accommodation. And I shall say so in my report.'

I stared at him aghast.

'You'll be hearing from my department.'

Just as I was starting to splutter, Ben stepped forward, clamping a heavy hand to my shoulder. 'It's all been done to regs,' he said, in a deep voice, moving fractionally towards Flaky, and fixing him with the look I remembered from our first meeting. 'A bit of a mix-up with the paperwork, I expect. You know what some of these builders are and the builder's the agent on her behalf.' And while I was trying to fathom what he was talking about, he reeled off Nigel's name, address and mobile number and relieved Flaky of the paper he was still holding. 'I'll pass it on,' he finished, turning me round and starting to walk me back along the road. ''Bye now,' he called over his shoulder.

We turned down the little road by the side of the house, and Ben stopped. 'You'll have to be a bit careful with him. He can make you do all sorts. I mean, some of it's all right. I made sure there were double skins on all the ceilings and the walls were insulated, whatever Nigel said, but you need all your fire precautions in place.

That means heat and smoke detectors, proper doors, mode of escape in communal areas, fire extinguishers and blankets . . .' On an overdraft? '. . . I've told him time and time again but old Nigel will insist on doing everything on the cheap. I'll give him a ring and put him in the picture for you.'

'We shouldn't have given him Nigel's details. Will he get into trouble?' Even to myself I sounded pathetic.

Ben gave a big, booming laugh. 'Nigel! Old Shiny Suit?'

I looked at him, not understanding.

'Shit never sticks to him.'

The little road had led to a couple of old factories and a few square acres of pot-holed car park. Now it had been transformed into a huge building site filled with diggers and cement-mixers and blokes wandering about stripped to the waist. 'That's my crew.' Ben waved to a bloke in a plastic helmet, who was perched on top of a huge steel structure beneath an enormous Broadrange sign. Another great burly thing in a boiler-suit swaggered past and nodded at us.

'All right, guv!' Someone whistled. A few more heads appeared over the concrete slabs.

Ben bellowed up at them, 'All right, you lot, get back to work, show's over.' He grinned at me.

'I didn't know you . . .' I gestured around me.

'Didn't know I was a real builder. I do a bit for old Nigel because someone's got to do things properly for him and, anyway, I like the bloke. Went to school with him. He was a terrible liability even then.'

I looked at Ben suspiciously. 'School? Nigel went to Kingsmead House.'

'So did I.'

'I thought you said you were brought up in grinding poverty.'

'I got a scholarship.'

I was still trying to fathom which bits of Ben were real. Years of Nigel had given me a reasonable nose for bullshit but Ben didn't seem to be talking your run-of-the-mill bollocks. Mind you, he *was* still talking about Nigel. 'Terrible taste in tenants. You mark my words, darlin'. You get in there and see what that druggie's up to.' He winked at me. 'And if he gives you any bother, you know where I am.'

Typical. A lifetime's fantasy teetering on the brink of fruition. An enormous bloke prepared to charge to my side and protect my honour. A huge macho pile of muscle, who suddenly wasn't evil or oiky at all but strong, powerful and benign. My own personal giant with whom I could be frail and precious and helpless . . . My knees were quivering at the very thought.

And he was bloody well married.

Chapter Sixteen

Tuesday of the week from hell. The woman on the phone would not budge: no refunds on any cancellations made within fourteen days of day schools. It was stated quite clearly on the booking form. I tried everything, explaining about batty mothers and double-bookings and friends in crisis but she was adamant. 'It's all been a terrible mix-up,' I whined. 'I'll still be in Brighton on Saturday.'

'It begins at ten,' she said coldly, and rang off.

Why does my mother do this to me?

I tried to approach the problem from another angle: perhaps I could use it to wriggle out of Henry's clutches.

I phoned Broadrange and explained the impossibility of staying the night in Brighton when my mother had booked me a surprise present back here that began at dawn. Henry began to beg. 'Please come, Cari. I'm so looking forward to taking you. It's really important to me. I'll do something for you – anything. And we can get up really early and I'll drive you home in plenty of time.'

What was that book Juliette gave me for Christmas? *Never Say Yes When Your Heart Says No*.

Wish I'd read it now.

*   *   *

Wednesday. There was still no answer at the flat and Nigel hadn't arrived to go in and find out what was going on.

I was toying with the idea of wandering round to the back and engaging Ben to accompany me when my mobile rang. Nigel announced he'd be with me in ten minutes, so I sat on the step in the sun and reflected that I had two days in which to find an outfit for Friday night and that I still hadn't got round to seeing Juliette, about whom my mother had left a third answerphone message last night when I was hiding in the bath: 'Do go and see her before you go, darling. I expect you're up to your eyes in packing, aren't you? But if you can make time I'd like to know what you think. I still don't think she's getting out enough. I invited her to Molly's rummage evening but she didn't seem very keen. Anyway, darling, I'll let you get on. Are you excited about Saturday?'

Ecstatic, Mother. Especially as it will be a whole day with you when what I really need is for it to be packed with *men*. Tall, sensitive, intellectual ones, who would cleanse my soul of all these impure thoughts about macho-muscled builders. Who would whisk me away from all my financial problems. The biggest of which was just drawing up in his truck.

Nigel bounded out. 'Sorry! Sorry! Got held up. But I'm putting a great deal together. If it all comes off I'll have enough money to finish this place off for us.' He grinned at me. 'You're not still worrying, are you?'

'Did you sort out the council bloke?'

'Yep. He's fine. I told him it was already converted and we've just been tarting it up a bit. He's going to come and have a look sometime but it's nothing to worry about.'

'But it only got planning just before we bought it. They'll know it wasn't already converted.'

'A bit *had* been done! Anyway, planning's different from building regs. Different departments. You know councils – one hand doesn't know what the other's doing.'

'He said we couldn't have tenants in there.'

'Oh, they say things like that but they won't do anything. They can't go round evicting people. Anyway, he was fine on the phone. Obviously just doesn't like women.' Nigel beamed. 'You do panic, don't you?'

I gritted my teeth, exasperated. 'I'm just not used to all this dodgy stuff. And if we don't get some rent in soon I don't know what we're going to do. Graham's started phoning up now. Luckily he's got the answerphone so far.'

'All right, all right,' said Nigel. 'Let's go and sort Gary and the rent out. Have you got the keys? Well, open the door, then.'

'I'm not going in first. He might be dead on the floor.'

'Come here!' Nigel turned the key in the lock and stepped into the gloom of the hall. He knocked on the inner door to Gary's flat. 'Gary! You there, mate? It's Nigel.'

He knocked again. 'He's not in. Come on, let's have a look.' I hung back while he fiddled with the second key and pushed open the door.

'Are you here, Gary?' I could hear Nigel walking through the rooms and I moved cautiously into the doorway. There was the same patch of painted wall I'd seen three weeks before with the step-ladder in the same position. A tin stood on the floor with its lid off, a brush standing stiffly in the centre of the hardened paint.

Strewn all around it was a variety of gruesome-looking underwear and an interesting array of foil takeaway containers with furry remnants. The room had a thick, warm, unwashed atmosphere. I retched and backed out hurriedly.

From the bedroom, I heard Nigel say, 'Come on, mate, wake up! We need to talk to you.' And then, more loudly, 'Cari! Come in here.'

I tiptoed in with my nose buried in the crook of my arm and went through to the room beyond. Nigel was pulling back one of the curtains. The sun flooded across Gary's bedroom and I instinctively stepped back. Yuck. Unshaven, skeletal, half-dressed drug addicts sprawled across beds in their socks and boxer shorts had not been in the deal when Nigel assured me of a fast fortune. I felt in my handbag for my lavender oil. 'Just tell him we need that form,' I hissed. No oil. I must have left it behind when forced to venture into the loo behind the bus-station.

Gary shifted and groaned.

'Go on!' I prodded Nigel, while I looked around at the debris. The flat was in a worse state than when Gary had moved in. I peered at the heap of newspapers in the corner, the overflowing ashtrays and beer cans littered across the floorboards and held my nose before I could retch again.

Nigel was crouched down trying to make out what Gary was saying. He looked as though he hadn't eaten for weeks. 'Doing my head in,' he muttered, his eyes opening and rolling. 'Fucking all of them are.' He fell back into a stupor.

Nigel shook him. 'Come on, Gary. We need to get your rent sorted out, mate, or you'll have to move out.'

I felt myself sway. 'Open the bloody window, Nigel,' I gasped. 'Or I'm going to pass out.'

Nigel went to it, wrestled with the catch and slammed his shoulder against the frame. It creaked and opened suddenly, sending him toppling forward.

'Shit!' Gary sat up, looking around wildly. 'What's going on?'

Nigel walked back and stood over him. 'Have you got your proof of income from the benefits office yet?'

Gary stared back at him, his head on one side. Then his eyes narrowed. 'You're one of them, aren't you?' He fingered the ring in his left nostril. 'I'm saying nothing.' He lay down and pulled the grimy-looking duvet on top of him. 'This is doing my fucking head in,' he muttered, and appeared to fall asleep.

I looked at Nigel, who shrugged. I turned to go outside, beckoning him to follow me with a furious jerk of my head. Back in the mercifully fresh air, I exploded: 'Well, that's bloody terrific. Well done! You said he was all right. You said he'd do the place up. Look at him! He's a fucking filthy nutcase and we're stuck with him in there with no rent and the bank manager about to barge in any day. I must have been mad to listen to a word you said.'

An old lady came past, staring at me, obviously wondering what he'd done to make me start shrieking like a demented seagull, but I was well past caring.

'*You*', I was breathless with rage, determined to stick the knife right into his jugular and turn it, 'are what Martin always said you were – a complete and utter wanker.'

I stopped, my chest heaving. Nigel's shoulders drooped. He looked hurt. From behind me came a deep voice. 'Don't beat about the bush, darlin', just come right out and tell him how you feel.' I swung round. Ben stood there grinning. 'Need a hand, mate?' he asked Nigel.

Bloody men.

Nigel spoke sadly to me. 'I'll just go in and have a look round for that form. He might have got it all ready.'

'Of course he hasn't,' I said nastily.

'Look, Cari, I'll sort it.'

'Bollocks!' I said, and stomped back to my car.

Juliette next. Oh, what a day of joy this was. I rang her bell about five times then drove off. So much for my mother and rampant agoraphobia. Pity those two hadn't been around this morning with a real-life crackpot to test their counselling skills on. I'd like to see my mother doing her deep breathing on Gary.

I phoned Louise on my mobile which, amazingly, was still connected, even though it was paid for on my credit card, which must have exceeded its limit by now. Answering-machine. I called her at work. They said she was with someone. I felt ridiculously put-down and excluded. Still, at least she was off that bloody sofa.

I drove around a bit and thought of phoning Sonia to see if I could go round this evening and poke through her dresses, then decided the only thing I wanted to do this evening was go to bed, so I went home. When I got in I ran a hot deep bath, wondering whether it wouldn't just be easier to follow dear old Mad Maud down the primrose path and top myself while I was about it.

I was wandering naked about the kitchen, looking down at the bits of me that still wobbled despite endless weeks of undernourishment when the doorbell rang. I looked wildly around for something to put on. Oh, God! Suppose I waddle down the hall to the bathroom for my robe and whoever it is looks through the letter box and sees my huge bottom? 'Who is it?' I bellowed, screwing my head round the door and wondering if I could make a bikini out of two tea-towels.

'Nigel.'

'Hang on.' I scuttled upstairs for a tracksuit, put it on and grudgingly let him in. 'What do you want?' I asked sourly.

'You're so unfair to me.' He paused to look suitably

wounded. 'I came round to tell you I've sorted it all out.'

'How?'

'Gary's going, and I've told Jim to get in there and finish the decorating. I'll pay him,' he added quickly, as my mouth opened.

'Oh.' I closed it again. Then I remembered. 'We still haven't paid Trevor.'

'I'll pay him too.'

'What about Graham?'

'Don't worry about him. The thing is', explained Nigel, 'you just have to keep these accounts active. All the time money goes in and money comes out they don't mind. Just keep it moving.'

'How the hell can I when I haven't got a bean?'

'You can't hit a moving target,' continued Nigel smoothly.

'We haven't got any bloody money to keep moving with!' I said furiously.

Nigel gave a small, pleased smile. 'I've got together a couple of grand.'

'Where is it?'

'I'll pay it in for you in the next couple of days. Just waiting for a cheque to clear. That'll keep Graham off your back. And I told you I've got a great deal about to come off. Then I'll have loads of money again and I can finish upstairs. We'll soon get new tenants and it will all be fine.' He smiled widely.

I made him a coffee while he explained how Gary was going to be removed and we would soon be back on track to make a fortune. 'You just have to trust me,' he said, for the fourth time, as he tried to put his arm around me.

'Did Ben go to your school?'

'Er, yes.'

'Why didn't you tell me before?'

'Never thought about it.' He looked shiftily at his mug.

'Well, he's a funny old mixture, then, isn't he?' I persisted. 'Apparently a right oik but went to a posh school and visits the opera in his spare time.'

Nigel frowned. 'Cari, don't be taken in by Ben.'

He refused to elaborate and I changed the subject, not wishing to be reminded either of Ben's marital status or of my hopeless addiction to the wrong sorts. 'So you will make sure you pay the money in, won't you?' I said instead.

'Yes, Cari, I will. Please don't worry,' Nigel said earnestly, giving me his warmest you-can-rely-on-me smile and I felt the knot in my stomach almost undo. 'Just you go away and have a lovely time with Henry and forget everything,' he finished brightly, quite his old smoothie self. 'If you're lucky you might get shagged.'

Huh!

Thursday. One day left to get something to wear. Mother on the answerphone, reminding me to call my sister. Ten minutes wasted while I jump around the room, John Cleese-like, screaming, 'Yes! Yes! Yes! I'm going to. I'm going to *do it now*!'

Juliette's phone: ring, ring, ring-bloody-ring. She's got a bloody answerphone. Why won't she use it? Then I could leave a message and clear my conscience in one sentence. Answer: because she has to unplug everything every bloody night in case the bloody things explode and strike her dead in her bed. She should be so bloody lucky.

I spent an hour sitting at the kitchen table with my chin in my hands, staring at the list with 'Dress. Louise. Juliette' written on it and thinking how grim my life was.

Then I made a cup of coffee and went and sat on the window-seat, staring out into bright June sunshine, thinking bitter thoughts about the group of giggling sixteen-year-olds who went by in crop-tops showing lots of smooth, flat, brown stomach, and tiny shorts revealing a similar amount of smooth, slim, brown thigh. I mean, what was the bloody point of thinking about slinky black numbers if I was still going to look white, lardy, wrinkled and so generally loathsome that the only man who'd ever loved me had to flee to Brighton?

In the middle of these cheering reveries the phone rang. My sister was in buoyant mood. 'I one-four-seven-oned you,' she told me brightly. 'I was still in bed.'

'I came round yesterday afternoon.'

'I expect I was in bed then too. I'd been up all night making amazing discoveries. I've put it all down on a chart. Would you like to see it?'

'Have you got any slinky black dresses?'

It was a stupid question. Juliette's thin clothes have always been far too thin for me, her fat ones far too fat.

Later, I looked at her as she reduced broccoli, onion and potato to a pulp amid the roar of machinery. She was definitely getting very thin indeed. Must be all that juicing, I thought enviously. I wondered if I could dig out an old gross picture of her with several chins and persuade her to be a before-and-after for the Shelf Diet once it was safely patented. Put her on it for a week and I could probably covince her that it had brought about a three-stone loss anyway.

'Our mother thinks you're agoraphobic,' I told her, once the noise had subsided and she was stirring thick green gunk with a wooden spoon.

'Ah, well,' she said. 'I've done a lot of thinking about our mother too. Look, isn't this fantastic, the way the potato separates straight into juice and starch? Look!' She held out a second bowl of white sludge. 'Our mother', she said deliberately, 'is locked into her past. Have you ever wondered why she cannot let go of our father?'

'She divorced him!'

'But she holds on to her anger. She's afraid to forgive him because then she'd have to let go of her rage and what . . .' Juliette paused for dramatic effect then went on in a hush-the-murderer-will-now-be-revealed tone '. . . would she replace it with?'

'Another art class?'

Juliette looked at me sorrowfully. 'I told Marlena how resistant you are, and she says you're probably in denial because of the abuses of our childhood.'

'What abuses? Having barmy parents doesn't count as abuse.'

'Look at this.' My sister abandoned her culinary efforts and dragged a huge roll of white card from the corner. 'Move those books off the table and just see.'

It was a mass of thick black pen, interconnecting circles and arrows and scribbled notes with occasional Sellotaped newspaper cuttings and family photos. 'It's a family tree of emotional trauma,' said Juliette excitedly. 'Now look, here's our father. See how he connects to his mother who used to lock herself in the broom cupboard and her cousin who had the nightmares. Then there's our mother with a line to Maud. In the bath, remember? And look here – Peggy. Our father says she looked after him when he was a baby. Our mother says she was clinically depressed. There's a picture of me when I was six. And what's my middle name?'

'Margaret.'

'Exactly!' Juliette was triumphant.

She wouldn't drink any of the wine I'd brought

160

because she was still on tablets and 'Marlena says I must learn not to hide behind mind-altering substances,' but she tucked into the tasteless grey-green glue with gusto. I nibbled at the gluten-free crispbread and worked my way steadily down the bottle.

'Do you remember', she said suddenly, 'when I told our father about Sid being arrested for indecency?'

I laughed. 'And he said, "Try not to think about it, dear," and our mother hit him with a washing-up bowl.'

'She was like that with the policeman. She kept saying, "I am her mother. Her father's going to be very frightened by all of this but I am here." '

Suddenly we were helpless with laughter.

'While I was packing the night I left Sid she waited in the garden with a shovel. I don't know what she thought she was going to do. Sid was in a police cell!' Juliette spluttered and choked on her soup.

'She'd have hit him with it,' I said confidently, the wine making me feel warm towards and proud of my mother. 'It's funny how she always gives us this stuff about her being the downtrodden one and our father the ogre. She's much fiercer than he is.' I giggled. 'Do you remember that Christmas just before she moved out? He disappeared and hid as usual because the neighbours were coming round, and she hauled him out of the cupboard in front of them all shouting, "Take responsibility, Rodney!" '

Juliette pushed away her bowl and clasped her stomach, tears running down her face. 'He was just so frightened of everything,' she managed eventually. 'Remember when number thirty-six was broken into and he wired up our garage and we had to go out in shifts so the house was never empty in case . . .' She doubled over, gripping her middle as if she were in pain.

'Our mother,' I squeaked three times, unable to get

any further without becoming hysterical, 'he made our mother . . .'

Juliette screamed in mirth. 'Yes! Yes! Made her go into the house in a dress and hat and come out in a scarf and trousers so that watching burglars . . .'

My stomach muscles were hurting. '. . . would think there was still someone at home,' I finished, 'and – and—' It was useless. I collapsed in gales of laughter.

Juliette ploughed on stoically. 'And we had to call out, "Bye-bye, Auntie!" when we all went down the path.' She snorted.

'It's a wonder we're as sane as we are,' I said, wiping my eyes.

'And it's his fault', added Juliette happily, 'that I worry about things exploding. If he hadn't insisted on turning the electricity off at the mains every time he changed a light-bulb . . .'

'And the water off in the road,' I put in, 'if we went away.'

'That's why we were attracted to Sid and Martin,' said Juliette importantly. 'We needed someone to take charge.'

'Got more than we bargained for there!' I chortled, reflecting that I hadn't laughed like that in ages and that I'd forgotten how good it felt. 'Martin's a complete control freak and Sid was totally bloody mad!'

Juliette looked pleased. 'Yes, he was,' she agreed, 'wasn't he?'

I hugged her when I left. 'Let's do this again soon,' I said. 'I'll cook pasta or something and tell you all about Henry's do.'

She smiled, looking like the sister I used to giggle under the bedclothes with. Then she hugged me back. 'That would be lovely.'

162

Chapter Seventeen

Friday. Seven hours to find something to wear tonight.

An eight a.m. poke through my wardrobe had revealed not only that I had nothing remotely suitable for Henry's do but that I had given away all the clothes I most loved to the woman in the Save-Everything-Unfortunate-Shop (who'd simply said, 'Thank you, dear,' and hadn't even bothered to get down on her knees and make a fervent speech of gratitude) and I hadn't got any credit left with which to buy new ones.

Now I had to track down a dress pretty damn quick and decide from my meagre supply of horrid garments what to wear for this cohort-with-peculiar-people-and-find-yourself day, knowing there would be all sorts of earache from my mother if I didn't look as though I'd made an effort.

I phoned Louise at work and threw myself on her mercy. For a change she sounded remarkably sanguine and friendly and promised to meet me at her house at lunchtime and give me the full run of her cupboards. 'Of course you can,' she said warmly, as if she hadn't been completely vile for the last three and a half weeks. 'I'll make us a sandwich and we can have a natter as well.'

I decided not to spoil this new age of golden peace

by mentioning pregnancy tests. No doubt I'd find out later. Instead I rang off, dragged a variety of dust-laden luggage receptacles from beneath the spare bed and opened all the drawers in a fruitless search for sexy knickers and tights without holes.

Louise was definitely bigger. Even her face had filled out and had an unfamiliar roundness to it. 'Don't know how much is the baby and how much is all the biscuits I've been eating,' she said cheerfully, pulling a packet of digestives from her kitchen cupboard. 'Still, at least I'm not feeling sick any more.'

'What have you told Robert?' I asked cautiously.

'Nothing yet.'

'But you're going to.'

'Yes, of course I am.' She was getting impatient again. 'I've just got to get used to the idea first.'

'Have you spoken to the other one?'

'No.' She bit savagely into a biscuit and pulled a loaf from the bread bin.

'So you still haven't been to the doctor's.' I don't know what it is with me, I just have to keep asking.

'No, I haven't.'

'Well, you'd better go soon. I mean, you need to know when it's due.' I had a sudden image of a small wrinkled mini-Louise warm and snuggly in one of those little towelling Baby-gros, tiny fingers curled round one of mine. Mind you, I got all gooey over Lukey when I visited Rowena in hospital. Little did I know he'd be a fat drooling blob in a matter of weeks. I looked at Louise with a mixture of frustration, envy and disappointment. 'Anyway, you should have a check-up.'

'Look, shut up. You don't know what it's like.'

No. And at this rate I never would.

Louise sat on the end of her bed eating her sandwich while I trailed up and down with her clothes on. 'That'll get them all going,' she chortled, as I squeezed into a black lacy-fronted affair. 'You look like Barbara Windsor.'

I looked in the mirror and tugged it off again. I actually looked like a bloke in drag being a milkmaid in a panto. 'I'm not that much bigger than you,' I said crossly, looking at her chest.

'Not now,' she said, thrusting her breasts towards me. 'They've got enormous. But I never had as much as you before.'

'What about this?' I said sulkily, standing in front of the mirror in a salmon-pink silk shift thing that looked terribly expensive and elegant on the hanger but didn't create quite the same impression stretched across my stomach.

'Not quite your colour,' Louise said tactfully.

She was not at all diplomatic about the next one. 'No, no, take it off,' she shrieked, rolling across the bed in mirth and knocking her plate on to the floor. 'It always looked terrible on me but it looks absolutely horrendous on you.'

I pulled the shiny, beaded bodice back over my head and threw it on to the floor. 'Well, what did you buy it for, then?'

'I don't know.' She was still giggling, her good spirits evidently fully restored.

'Well, apart from amusing you,' I said irritably, 'this is getting me nowhere.'

'Hold on.' She got up and started ferreting about in the back of the cupboard. 'I know what will do perfectly. Here.' She handed me a long, flowing black thing swathed in dry-cleaner's plastic. 'It was always a bit big for me,' she added helpfully.

It was a suit with soft wide trousers that looked like a

165

skirt till you moved, and a long buttoned jacket. All in floaty, drapy black stuff with classy-looking buttons.

'Wonderful!' she proclaimed, as I twirled. I examined myself in the mirror. It looked great.

'Look,' she said, grasping my hair and twisting it up into a knot, 'and these,' she added, reaching for a pair of earrings on the dressing-table with her other hand and holding a large gold twirly one against the side of my face. 'You'll look terrific.'

I looked and nodded. Already I had an air of sophistication about me. It was amazing.

'I've got some shoes,' she said, letting go of my hair and rooting about in the bottom of another cupboard, 'and somewhere – ah!' She held up a small black bag triumphantly. 'This! You'll knock Henry dead.'

I smiled at her. I'd hoped for someone a bit more promising than Henry.

When I went she threw her arms around me. 'Have a lovely time. Perhaps you'll pick up someone rich and famous.'

'It's a supermarket do.'

'Well, you never know.'

'Thanks for all this, Lou.'

'Sorry I've been an old bag.'

'That's all right.'

Chapter Eighteen

There must be an art to travelling light. I once went on an executive suck-up-to-the-punters-so-they'll-buy-something weekend with Martin's company, struggling under the weight of three suitcases containing clothes and footwear for every eventuality, while the wife of the top-dog-grovel-most-to-bloke tripped into the hotel carrying one slim zip-up bag and still appeared immaculately turned-out in a different crisp outfit each evening with colour co-ordinated shoes and matching handbag. How?

I'd read an article only the week before about taking two T-shirts, three sarongs and a swimsuit with you on holiday and creating six different looks to last you the fortnight, but I was still surveying my bulging overnight suitcase and running through its contents fretting about what I could have forgotten when Henry rang my doorbell. 'All ready?' He grinned at me and bobbed up and down on his heels, looking rounder than ever in a green checked shirt and flapping cream trousers. 'I'm going to change when we get there,' he said unnecessarily.

'So am I,' I said, nodding at the suit on the back of the door to reassure him that I wasn't intending to sit down to dinner in my frayed shorts and washed-out pink T-shirt.

'Right, then,' said Henry heartily, manfully swinging my suitcase about. 'Let's go.'

The roads were full of Friday-afternoon home-goers. We sat in a queue at the traffic lights and Henry lowered all the windows, wiping a handkerchief across his glistening pink brow. 'It'll cool down once we get out of the town,' he said.

I got my sunglasses out of my handbag, trying to remember whether I'd packed my back-up pair and if I'd thrown in the emergency evening bag to decant everything into if the strap on the first broke.

The lights changed and we crawled forward.

I'd got a pair of jeans and a sweatshirt to wear in case it was cold when we came home at daybreak, and a spare pair of shorts and a T-shirt if it wasn't. And a flower-sprigged dress if I relented and arrived at the day thing dressed as Dutiful Daughter, and a pair of dungarees with holes in the knees if I didn't. And a caftan-type-robe affair in case there was a stay-up-till-the-early-hours-sitting-on-somebody's-floor-discussing-the-futility-of-life situation.

The cars all started to speed up and Henry put his foot down happily. 'We'll be on the motorway in ten minutes.'

And I'd got a spare pair of shoes and all my make-up and the new perfume given to me by Louise, who claimed that whenever she wore it she had to beat off men with sticks (knowing my luck it would make them beat a hasty retreat to the other side of the room). And, of course, I'd got all my stuff for the do tonight. I'd packed Louise's handbag and shoes and earrings first in case I forgot them and – oh, God!

Henry overtook the car in front. 'I reckon we'll do it in a couple of hours even at this time of day.'

'Umm, Henry, it might take just a little bit longer than that.'

'Why, my love?'

'My suit's still hanging on the back of the door.'

He was very good about it, really. By the time we reached the third set of traffic lights for the second time, he was humming again. Martin would have seethed silently all the way to Brighton.

Henry simply got straight into the fast lane of the M20 and bulldozed everyone out of the way. 'Soon make up the time,' he said, as we joined the masses on the M25. 'No harm done.'

Martin would have stored it up to trot out in the next row under the subheading Why You Are Stupid.

Although I guess I must have been to marry him.

We got there without further mishap, save the inevitable slow-downs and leftovers of other people's pile-ups.

Henry carved people up with aplomb and grinned merrily all over his chubby face when a couple of skin-head youths held their horn down and could clearly be seen making masturbatory gestures in our direction with expletives to match.

My stomach gave a peculiar little flip once we were on the M23 and Brighton started appearing on the road signs. I wondered for a wild moment about asking Henry to take me to see the house before we left in the morning. The house that contained the flat that my husband was probably walking into, home from work, at this very minute. Or perhaps she met him on Fridays. Perhaps they went out for a few drinks then something to eat the way we used to. In the beginning.

I found myself staring out of the window as Brighton came closer. Imagined seeing them arm-in-arm crossing the road. Laughing together. 'Do we go through Brighton?' I asked Henry casually.

'No. Ring road round it. We're going down the coast towards Shoreham. Hotel's about half-way along.'

'Oh, good.'

Not that I'd mind seeing them. It would just be better if I was already rich and famous. And not with Henry.

'Brighton's not what it used to be,' Henry said. 'Full of drug addicts, so I'm told.'

So is Turpin Road, mate. You should worry.

The hotel was a big, modern, lots-of-enormous-glass-windows-and-huge-green-plants place with a tinkling fountain in the foyer. Henry beamed at me as we checked in. 'What do you think of this, then?'

Very nice.

The room had peach-and-blue-flecked wallpaper, peach-and-blue-flecked matching quilt covers on the twin beds and a watercolour print of peach-and-blue flowers. Henry held open the door in the corner to reveal the pale-blue-tiled bathroom with peach accessories. 'Look!' he said proudly.

Lovely.

I put my case on the bed and raised my eyebrows enquiringly at him. 'I'll, um, get myself sorted out, then, shall I?'

'Oh, right, yes. I'll, er, go and find Barry.' He picked up his bag and stumbled off.

'Shall I meet you in the bar?' I called after him.

He turned in the doorway. 'Oh, no!' he said, looking shocked. 'I'll come and knock on your door. We'll go down together. Seven twenty-five?'

'Sure.'

I lay in the bath, letting the hot deep water swirl about my neck. Twenty-five minutes left to make myself look a million dollars. I could do it. I wanted it all to go right tonight, my makeup to slide on smoothly, my blotches not to show, my fat bits not to wobble. I wanted to turn heads and feel beautiful.

I rinsed off the grit from the exfoliating face rub, sat up and reached for a towel. I wound my wet hair into a turban then packed all my lines with the Sonia wonder-cream. I still couldn't decide whether it really worked or not. My face did seem smoother a lot of the time, but who knows? Maybe anything would have worked. When you've spent a frightening amount of money on a very small pot, you feel duty bound to actually scrub your face and layer the stuff thickly all over it each night instead of just falling drunkenly into bed with your make-up still on.

I allowed myself a further three minutes in the water, letting the steam rise to open the pores and the cream to soak into them while I was in a relaxed state, as Sonia had instructed, then got out and started to dry myself, deciding to make up my face first, then dry my hair so that I didn't end up with mascara in the wispy bits, then put my clothes on so I didn't end up with hairs all over my shoulders – must consult Sonia and Juliette about hair loss, definitely getting worse. Sonia would know about cripplingly expensive shampoos, Juliette about vitamin and mineral mixtures.

I collected my makeup bag and stared into the mirror in amazement. It had worked! I was visibly younger, smoother and firmer. The lines around my eyes had evened out. All this in three minutes of steam-and-cream! Why hadn't I listened to Sonia before?

Trembling with excitement, I got out my foundation and started to smooth it in. The effect was miraculous. My face took on a soft, even glow. My cheekbones leapt forward. I couldn't wait to finish. At record speed I got all my eye stuff on and carefully outlined my lips, filling them in with a deep, luscious shade of plum.

Then I stood back in wonder at the sight of me and my face. It was the painted mask of a twenty-year-old.

I went into the bedroom, tracked down the hairdryer, threw off the towel and bent forward to dry my hair into a wild fluffy cloud that I could put up, leaving lots of fetching tendrils cascading around my suddenly beautiful features.

When it was almost dry I stood up, ran my fingers through the tangles and moved back to the mirror to start arranging it. I stopped in horror. I was back to normal – in fact, worse than normal! My face was all red from hanging upside down, and my eye makeup had already smudged. Worse, all my wrinkles were back, and my saggy cheeks, and that crease above my nose where I frowned. What had happened?

Stomach churning I peered at myself more closely. God, I looked about fifty. Was it the hair? Was I one of these people who actually looked younger without any? I pulled it up off my face and imagined it with the towel around it. As I tugged upwards the answer came to me with sickening clarity.

The towel had given me a facelift.

My God, I'm so ancient and ugly that already I need surgery! I wound the towel round my head again, pulling it savagely tight. All at once I lost ten years. Presto! I was young again. I took off the towel and stared the sad truth in the face. I pushed my thumbs across my cheekbones towards my ears and my index fingers up above my eyes towards my hairline. Yes, it all smoothed out. I looked once more as I had long ago. I would remember this day for ever. The day I faced my lost youth. Friday the fifth of June. Facelift Day.

I turned and flung myself across the bed.

Henry knocked on the door.

'Are you ready, Cari?'

No, Henry, I am not ready. I am old and decrepit and feel like slitting my throat. I am in the depths of despair and cannot come downstairs and mingle with twenty-two-year-old beauties when I have a face that has been so ravaged by time that it hangs in folds. Fuck off, Henry, and leave me to die.

'Just give me five minutes.'

'Wow!' Henry, a vision in black and white, stared at me. 'Cari, you look fantastic!'

'Really?'

'I can't wait till the others see you.'

We walked down the hotel corridor.

'Your hair looks lovely,' he said fervently.

'Thank you.'

In the end I'd just twisted it up and stuck a couple of combs in it. It would probably be all around my shoulders in no time.

'And what you've got on.'

If only the lights would be kind. I'd slapped on enough foundation to plaster my derelict flats and put three more layers of colour on my eyes and lips. As long as the illuminations remained low I could probably get away with it. A hint of neon and I'd be revealed as Bette Davis's Baby Jane. I vowed not to go anywhere near the ladies' until I was desperate.

'Oh, it's trousers,' said Henry doubtfully, as I stepped into the lift. 'Well, never mind,' he said bravely, as I got out of it again, 'you look very nice.'

He offered me his arm as we entered the Maple Room and, still glazed with the shock of discovering that I was even more undesirable than I'd thought, I took it.

The room was quite full already. Clumps of penguins stood about interspersed with women in alarmingly bright dresses. We took glasses of purple fizzing liquid from a small girl in a frilly apron.

'Kir Royale,' said Henry proudly. 'Our own brand, ready mixed.'

It was vile.

Henry looked around, then took my arm again and headed purposefully towards a group of noisy twenty-somethings who were all laughing uproariously. 'Come and meet everyone,' he said. 'Sandra, Kevin, this is Cari.'

A smooth-faced blonde in shiny green satin, with a chest looking like mine had in the milkmaid dress, turned round and giggled. 'Hello, Mr Chapman.'

The one called Kevin leered at her. 'You can call him Henry tonight,' he said. 'New chairman says we're all one big happy family.'

There was further raucous laughter all round. Two more wrinkle-free nymphets in glittery dresses smiled politely at me in the way you do at someone old enough to be your mother. A few weedy-looking youths chortled.

Henry cleared his throat. 'Well, we'll see you later.'

'Hope those two aren't going to drink too much and make fools of themselves,' he said pompously.

I took another Kir Royale from a passing tray. Then I followed Henry as he crossed the room, weaving in and out of the groups until he reached a small gnome-like man standing with a large woman in floor-length yellow.

'My area manager,' Henry said importantly, as I obediently shook the gnome's hand, 'and Dorothy.'

Dorothy offered damp, limp fingers and went back to fanning herself with what looked like a copy of the fire regulations.

A waitress came by with a tray of little circles of brown bread with a salmon snipping on top. I grabbed one, bunged it into my mouth and took another to toy

174

with. When I was in mid-chew, the gnome spoke. 'So you're the new girlfriend, are you?'

I swallowed and waited for Henry to intervene with something explanatory but he merely grinned inanely, which seemed to confirm things for the gnome who cut straight to, 'What do you do?'

Here we go again. What shall I start with? My varying attempts at becoming bankrupt or my sterling efforts in the biscuit-eating department? 'I'm writing a book,' I said, before I could stop myself. Henry looked startled. I found I'd put the second salmon-round into my mouth after all.

Dorothy sprang to life. 'Is it a romance?' she asked hopefully. 'I read lots of them.'

Married to him, who wouldn't? I shook my head and swallowed hastily.

The gnome wrinkled his forehead and scrutinized me. 'Have you got a publisher?' he asked, in the manner of a man used to getting straight to the bottom line.

'Not yet.' I smiled sweetly. 'It's still in the early stages.' I glanced sideways at Henry, wondering whether he had any intention of rescuing me. He was still sporting a fixed grin. I narrowed my eyes at him, meaningfully.

'I like the historical ones best,' volunteered Dorothy, fanning her meaty face with new gusto. 'Such lovely clothes.'

'Seen the seating plan yet?' asked the gnome jovially.

Henry sprang to attention. 'No,' he said, looking around.

'Over in the corner.'

'Shall we go and look?' I asked Henry quickly.

'Oh. Yes. Of course.'

'Lovely to meet you,' I trilled, moving off quickly and praying that they wouldn't appear right next to us on said plan.

'Are you really writing a book?' asked Henry, as we made our way through the groups once more.

'Absolutely.'

'What's it about?'

I looked pointedly at his straining jacket, fed up with him already. 'It's a diet plan.'

Barry was one of those blokes for whom a dinner jacket worked wonders. I didn't recognize him as the meat-cleaving in-store beanpole until he'd got through several sentences. He'd waylaid us on the way to the seating plan, nudging Henry in the ribs and giving him a run-down on who looked a-bit-of-all-right. Then he winked at me with a sort of and-so-do-you-look, which cheered me – until I realized who he was.

'They've mixed us all up,' he said to Henry. 'Only one I know on my table is Greg from Stores. They could have put me next to Sandra – or her,' he added, winking at the waitress who was circulating the salmon again.

I looked round for the one with the drinks tray, but she had gone. Instead I spotted Rosie, standing alone in a turquoise blue tent. I nudged Henry and we went over to her. Her face lit up at the sight of him, then fell in disappointment when she saw me. 'You look nice,' I said awkwardly, wondering how I could make it plain that I was only doing Henry a favour and that he was still a free man.

'So do you,' she said gloomily.

Before I could say any more, there was the sudden high-pitched whine of feedback and the crackling of a microphone, and the noise began to die down. A short, round, bald man had climbed on to a small platform at one end of the room and was addressing the assembled gathering. I missed his first few words because Henry was shushing the Sandra and Kevin group, who had drifted up behind us and were carrying on telling jokes regardless. By the time they had shut up, the small man had become quite impassioned. 'And all of us together as we strive onwards in our quest for the highest standards, the finest quality, the greatest . . .'

Beside me, Henry was standing to attention, his head held high, fat chin wobbling reverently. Over his shoulder I saw Kevin murmur something in Sandra's ear. She grinned and repeated it to one of the nymphets who giggled. Henry's neck grew crimson, and he swung round and glared at them.

'And, above all, customer service!' The bald man was reaching a crescendo. 'At Broadrange Food Stores, customer service is all. Never forget, ladies and gentlemen, friends and colleagues, without our customers we would not be here!'

This nugget of wisdom brought forth a storm of applause, mostly – it seemed to me – provided by Henry, who was clapping wildly and becoming very red in the face.

Baldie beamed. 'Please take your places for dinner.'

Henry's joy knew no bounds. 'We've got one of the directors on our table,' he told me excitedly, when he'd returned from the crush around the seating plan, 'and he's sitting next to you.' I could see that he was itching to remind me to hold my knife and fork properly and not to tell any filthy stories but good manners restrained him. Instead he contented himself with giving me a rundown of the man's career history and character profile as we moved through the double doors into the dining room. 'Name's Mr Winterbar. He'll probably tell you to call him Bill. Lovely wife – Cynthia. Always remembers everyone's names. He's a bit of a maverick. Worked his way up from the bakery department where he started when he was sixteen – he was the one who wanted me to be manager. He recognized we were two of a kind.' He was still hissing in my ear as I sat down. 'Tells a lot of jokes. They're not very funny but if you can try to laugh . . .'

Thank you, Henry. I'll try.

Bill was rather charming, in an oldish, crumpled way. 'Ever been to one of these before?' he asked me.

I shook my head.

'Lot of nonsense,' he said conspiratorially, 'but the wine should be good. I had a word with Geraldine over there. Told her we wanted the proper stuff this time.' He nodded at the next table, where a small droopy-looking woman in sequined pink was hugging her chest. 'Organizes things every year, bless her. Cynthia always writes her a nice letter afterwards.'

His wife – an immaculate bleached fifty-year-old who looked stunning in black velvet and exquisite white-gold jewellery – leant across the table. 'Is Bill being boring already? I love your suit, dear. Very tasteful. You look perfectly delightful.'

Cynthia, I love you.

Next to her, Henry forgot his earlier reservations and swelled with reflected glory. Cynthia continued, 'I keep saying to Bill I'm going to start wearing trousers to these things myself. They have such lovely evening ones, these days, don't they? And long skirts are such a fuss. I wanted to buy some before we went on our cruise but he got all grumpy about it as usual.' She smiled across at her husband who was busily trying to attract the attention of a waiter. 'He wouldn't buy a new suit from one year to the next if I didn't make him.' She laughed as if I might share a personal experience of the difficulties of getting a man into a clothes shop. 'Dreadful, aren't they?'

The waiter appeared and Bill took his arm. 'Can we have some wine on this table? Now!' He turned back to me. 'Her clothes fill every room in the house.'

'Wish mine did.'

Gratifyingly, this amused him and he guffawed and filled my glass with white burgundy.

Heartened by the way he knocked back his own, I drank half of mine straight away and began to feel better.

Cynthia had turned to Henry. 'Now tell me all about that mother of yours, dear. Didn't you say at Christmas that she'd lost her cat?'

The prawns came and I ate them while the man on my other side, who was called Gordon and was a manager in Bromley, gave me an in-depth description of his daughter's wedding and the difficulties of fitting a marquee into the garden of your average semi. His wife, seated opposite him, had a face like a hatchet and glared at me unrelentingly throughout the tale. Bill filled my glass at regular intervals.

'Are you enjoying yourself?' Henry leant across as they were bringing the chicken *à la mode* complete with stunted carrots.

'Very much.'

Thank God for Bill. He'd just signalled to the waiter to bring another bottle.

By the time the strawberry gateau was on the table, I was feeling quite mellow. Cynthia had worked her way round the entire group asking after their various ailments and custody battles while Henry looked on adoringly. Bill and I had finished the latest bottle of red and were discussing the supermarkets of the future.

'You see,' Bill was saying, 'we may call ourselves Broadrange Food Stores but in fact fifty per cent of what

179

we sell is not food. There's videos and CDs, clothing, beauty products—'

'Not in Henry's branch there isn't,' I interrupted. 'We haven't got any of that stuff. It's all rotten old tins of custard and frozen peas.'

Bill laughed.

Henry spluttered through a mouthful of cream. 'They'll have all that in the new one,' he said. 'You know, we're building the ultra-store on the old factory site in Eastford, Mr Winterbar.'

Bill looked at the label on the wine bottle. 'We're having a lot of problems with that one,' he said. 'Right cock-up with the plans.'

Henry blinked nervously.

'Our local one's frightful too,' Cynthia put in kindly. 'I wouldn't shop there at all if we didn't have a discount card. I prefer Tesco's, to be honest. Much better range.'

Bill frowned. 'Cynth,' he said reprovingly, 'you shouldn't say things like that, my sweet.'

Cynthia laughed indulgently. 'Don't be so silly,' she said, quite unrepentant.

Henry looked as if he might dissolve into tears, but we were saved the discomfort of such a sight by the reappearance of Baldie at the far end of the room with his microphone. First he thanked us all fervently for being there, then started waving rolls of parchment about and announcing various awards. Silver carriage clock for Gladys – forty years at Broadrange Stores. Clap, clap, clap. Little gold cup for the Bournemouth Branch – greatest increase in turnover due to imaginative displays. Clap, clap. Bunch of flowers for Droopy Chest for organizing such a splendid evening. Clap.

Henry, fully restored, sat bolt upright, smacking his hands together enthusiastically as various pink-faced individuals trailed across the dance-floor to receive their accolades.

As Baldie reached the end of his list, Henry leant forward. 'It could be us next,' he said, in a low voice across the table.

Us?

'And finally,' Baldie waited for the last lot of applause and some not-quite-fitting shrieks of ribald laughter to die down, 'we have the prize for best overall performance on the incentive targets for the last three months.' He paused to create maximum suspense. Henry's eyes bulged with expectation. 'The Eastford Branch in Kent! Would the manager, Henry Chapman, like to come up and collect the award on behalf of all his staff?'

Henry blushed scarlet, leapt up and began to squeeze his fat frame through the spaces between the chairs to a sea of clapping hands.

As he waddled up to get his cup, I spotted Maureen – of the sartorial advice – encased in high-fronted purple, smiling round proudly. Sandra and Kevin's table let out a roar of 'Yeah!' with a few whoops for good measure and, for some inexplicable reason, a muted cry of 'Get 'em off.'

When he came back we all toasted him with the brandy Bill had thoughtfully demanded to go with the coffee, and listened to Bill's long, complicated joke about a man who took his crocodile to the doctor's, which I now forget but which produced gales of laughter from everyone, with the exception of Cynthia, who said, 'Oh, no, Bill, not that one again.'

Then they were clearing the tables and a band appeared at one end of the room, surrounded with flashing disco-lights, and struck up a hearty rendition of 'Light My Fire'. Kevin, Sandra and all the Sandra look-alikes started jigging about the dance-floor.

Henry came and stood beside me. 'Usually all the directors slide off at this point,' he said. 'Fancy a dance?'

'Maybe a bit later,' I said, thinking that some things were probably beyond the call of duty and that Henry blobbing his way through 'Hi-Ho Silver Lining' could well be one of them. 'Look, there's Rosie all on her own. Why don't you ask her?'

I went to the bar to get a damage-limitation glass of water while I was still vaguely sensible, and found Bill, far from disappearing off home, drinking a large gin. He lifted his glass towards me. 'Can I get you one?'

'I only came for a glass of water,' I said cheerfully, climbing on to the stool beside him.

'You want to watch that stuff.' I laughed as he ordered two doubles and found myself wondering idly what he'd be like in bed. It's always a sure sign that I've had too much to drink when I start fantasizing about balding fifty-year-olds. I remembered Martin dragging me furiously out of a party when he'd found me snuggled up on the sofa with somebody's uncle singing, 'I'm just a girl who can't say no . . .'

'What's funny?' asked Bill.

'I was just thinking about my husband. Ex-husband,' I added, thinking how remarkably pain-free the words were. Wonderful stuff, alcohol. 'He didn't like me getting drunk. Said I always made a fool of myself.'

'Oh, Cynth says that about me. And she's probably right.'

We sat in companionable silence and contemplated our tonic bottles. Out of the corner of my eye, I saw Henry coming towards us then sidling away.

'Thing is,' I said, 'I like getting drunk. It just makes everything seem so much better, even when it's not.'

Bill nodded. He seemed to be getting maudlin. 'I wanted to be in Marketing,' he said morosely, 'but

182

they're all young whippersnappers straight out of university. All the bits of paper, not an idea in their heads. In my day we worked our way up. Learnt about what sells by selling it, not reading about it in some fancy textbook.' He gazed sadly into his gin.

'Henry's worked his way up,' I said comfortingly, taking the lemon out of my empty glass and sucking it.

'I'll get you another,' said Bill. 'See, the thing is now,' he went on, 'they're all working on the convenience factor. Meal solutions, they call it, Chinese meal for two all packed up in a carrier-bag, bottle of wine included. Just pick it up and walk away.' He waved my glass at the girl behind the bar. 'I had the idea years ago and nobody listened. "Take the worry out of it," I said, "work it all out for them, put the right combinations together." Nobody listened. You're Logistics they said, not Marketing.'

The girl put another gin in front of me and plonked down a bottle of tonic.

'All in?' asked Bill, picking it up.

But I was hardly listening, my brain was churning so fast. 'Look,' I said, suddenly seeing how the whole evening had been a wonderful twist of fate and how my chance of fame and fortune was staring me in the face, 'I've got a bloody brilliant marketing idea, which would go like hot cakes in your supermarkets and sell my books at the same time. We could work together.' Taking a swig of gin and throwing earlier caution about patents to the alcohol-driven winds, I told him all about the Shelf Diet. 'Do you see?' I finished excitedly. 'It's just like you said. All the individual decisions gone, all the worry lifted, all the calculations made for you, all there on a plastic tray.'

Bill nodded thoughtfully. 'It's a very good idea,' he said. 'In fact,' he grinned at me, looking suddenly like a kid, 'you're quite right. It's bloody brilliant. I'll speak to old Keith about it.'

'Who's Keith?'

'Trading director. Good fellow. Not here tonight. He drew the short straw. Had to go to the one in Middlesbrough.' He felt in his pockets. 'I should have a card here somewhere. Or maybe it's in Cynthia's bag. And we need some paper to write your phone number down on. There'll be a few quid in it for you if they take it on.'

'Well, I don't want it on the shelves till the book's out,' I said, getting carried away with the idea of my name emblazoned on a million cardboard packets.

'Who's the publisher?' said Bill.

'I haven't got one yet.'

Maureen went past on the other side of the room and waved. I tried to wave back and nearly fell off my stool.

'Careful,' said Bill, putting out a hand to steady me while still searching in the folds of his suit. 'We'll have to get paper from the girl behind the bar,' he said eventually.

Cynthia appeared at his side. 'What are you looking for, Bill? Here.' She produced a pristine white pad and small silver pen from her minute evening bag and handed them over. 'And if it's anything important, for heaven's sake give it to me,' she told me. 'He'll lose it before bedtime. Ah, Barbara dear,' she moved smoothly forward to kiss a woman in orange on both cheeks, 'how lovely to see you again. How's Derek's chest?'

She added to Bill, in an undertone, 'Do take your hand off Cari's knee.'

Bill looked down in surprise. 'Sorry about that,' he said.

I giggled. 'Not at all.'

Henry was still hovering nearby, watching us anxiously.

'I think,' I said to Bill, aware that my mouth was moving more slowly than it had been, 'Henry may be worrying that I'm saying all the wrong things.'

'Well, if you are,' said Bill, 'I won't remember them in the morning. Another gin?'

I held out my glass.

By the time Henry came to accompany me upstairs, I was almost falling asleep. In my bag I had two folded pieces of paper: one with Bill's direct-line phone number on it and another with the details of someone called Charlie-boy with whom Bill played golf and who was in publishing. If only Bill could still remember who I was in the morning, my glittering career might be under way.

'You were getting on very well with Mr Winterbar,' said Henry enviously, as he propelled me out of the lift. I staggered along the corridor until I reached room 234. 'What were you talking about?'

'Henry, I've got to go to bed.' I was trying to get the key out of my handbag where it had got caught up in a tangle of mirrors and lipsticks. Henry took it from me and fished it out while I watched, stupefied. 'I'll tell you tomorrow. I'm really tired.'

As if to prove the point, I walked into the doorpost. Henry grabbed me and steered me through the opening. 'Will you be all right now?'

'Yes, of course. Just sleepy, you know.'

'Yes, I know. Good night, Cari.'

'Night, Henry.'

Somehow I got my clothes off and cleaned my teeth. At least, I remember grinning at myself in the mirror and seeing the toothbrush sticking out of my mouth and watching my face crinkle into hundreds of wrinkles and still grinning and thinking, So what, I'm going to be famous instead of Oh, God, I'm going to kill myself, so I must have been pissed but lucid enough to remember bits of it.

But then nothing, until I was in bed and there was this tapping noise and I got out of bed and staggered back to the bathroom and found the towelling robe the hotel had thoughtfully provided for such eventualities and dragged the door open and there was Henry. 'Cari, I'm really sorry about this. It's a bit awkward.'

'No, I've had a great evening. I'm just going to sleep.'

'No, Cari, listen. It's Barry. He's taken that waitress back to his room.'

What?

'I've got nowhere to sleep, Cari.'

Oh, save me.

I must have passed out the moment I dropped back into bed. When I woke it was to a strange rumbling sound that reverberated alarmingly round my head.

I sat up, heart pounding, and fumbled about in the darkness for the bedside light. I switched it on, saw Henry's pyjama-striped mound in the next bed. His mouth was open and out of it came a stream of bubbling, snorting snores. I groaned. God, I felt dreadful.

Then more things came crowding into my head and I groaned again. I'd given Bill a big hug before I'd said good night, right in front of Cynthia and Henry. And I'd had some sort of further exchange with that area manager dwarf and his gruesome wife, but I could only remember Henry gripping my arm and leading me away.

What must they all think of me? When was I going to grow out of drunken debauchery?

Another great explosion issued forth from Henry's bed and I turned to see his rubbery lips vibrating as he gave a further grunt and shifted his great bulk in the bed.

Cringing at all the flesh-crawling horrors of being an

out-of-control sex-starved alcoholic, I shrieked, so loudly that I even took myself by surprise, '*Henry!*'

He opened his eyes and thrashed about. 'What? What?'

'Bloody well shut up!'

The next time I woke it was light. The sun was beaming into the room in a harsh shaft through the two-inch gap in the curtains. The crumpled bed next to me was empty and Henry was nowhere to be seen.

I sat up, my head drumming, looked for the robe I'd flung to the end of the bed, went into the bathroom in search of water and accidentally glanced into the mirror.

It was a horrendous sight.

Imagine being famous, poking your head out of doors for the milk, finding tabloid reporters in your front garden and being photographed just like this, then discovering yourself spread all over the front pages, knowing that blokes up and down the country were pausing in munching their Shredded Wheat to say, 'Here! Look at that old dog,' while their wives and girlfriends looked anxiously into their mirrors for reassurance, patting their hair and fingering the sides of their eyes, muttering, 'She's only thirty-two . . .'

I sat on the loo and concentrated hard on not throwing up. Then I drank two glasses of water and carried a third back to bed, got under the covers and tried to pass out again.

There was a knock on the door.

'Cari, do you want some breakfast?'

I think not.

I'd have stayed there all day if Henry hadn't stood over me, pleading, 'Cari, it's eleven o'clock – I've made you coffee.'

I can't move.

'What about your mother's thing?'

You must be joking.

'It's past midday. We have to vacate the room.'

Sod off.

'Cari! Please!'

Eventually he got me into the car.

It was like an oven. I felt as sick as a dog.

The painkillers I'd managed to secure from Barry's waitress hadn't worked. I looked and felt worse than the worst I'd ever looked or felt. Henry would not stop talking.

'I knew we were in with a chance,' he said, for the third time, 'but when he actually called out my name, well . . . And she's very nice. Carol, her name is. Barry seems very keen. First time for him, I think, since Julie . . . Isn't Cynthia wonderful? Such a hostess. And Mr Winterbar may be a bit eccentric but he's very well thought of on the board . . . He didn't say anything about the new manager for the ultra-store, did he? Well, I suppose he wouldn't.'

Congratulations. How nice. Yes, she is. I'm sure he is. No, he didn't. Henry, stop the car. I'm going to vomit.

Henry stopped at a garage and bought me a bottle of water, a tub of paracetamol, some wet-wipes, a copy of *Woman's Weekly* and a packet of cheese and onion crisps. 'Good for hangovers. It's the fat content,' he said cheerily, as I collapsed beneath another wave of nausea.

He drove on. I slid down in my seat and wallowed in self-revulsion. Guilt and hangovers have always gone together. I was still cringing at the thought of how drunk I'd been. Good job dear old Cynthia was there, that's all I could say. Otherwise I might have made an embarrassing attempt at seducing Bill. I shuddered at the memory of Barry's leery grin this morning. 'Sleep well, did you?'

188

he'd said, winking as I staggered across the foyer on our way out.

'Not really,' I'd said pointedly. 'Henry was snoring too loudly from the *other bed*.'

Henry had laughed self-consciously, and I had glared at the revolting Barry, who looked as gruesome as ever now that he was back in his ordinary clothes. Surely, even on four gallons of gin, no one could think I'd do anything worth winking about with Henry. Could they? This was crunch time. Really, honestly, I was never going to drink like that again.

Henry had started chuntering on again as I closed my eyes. I remember putting my arms around the bottle of water and then I fell asleep. When I woke up, feeling stiff, thirsty and muzzy-headed, Henry had parked outside my house. 'Can you manage?' he asked, as he hauled my case out of the boot.

No, Henry, obviously I cannot . . .

Chapter Nineteen

Whoever was on the doorstep seemed fairly determined. They'd rung the bell three times and, from my vantage point on the kitchen floor where I was lying with my neck craned round the bottom of the door trying to make out the shape through the glass, they were showing no sign of moving off.

I'd been hiding all week, refusing to answer the phone or the door, knowing that my mother would not be fobbed off with the croaky descriptions of food-poisoning I'd left on her machine as an excuse for not turning up on Saturday to Unlock Myself, and it was only a matter of time before she arrived on the doorstep with an armful of herbal remedies.

I couldn't face her.

Or Henry, who might be back to check on my welfare and blather on about his moment of glory.

I wriggled backwards into the kitchen.

But, then, if it was Louise, here to tell me she'd had her first scan, it was twins and she'd brought me a bottle of champagne to celebrate my double godmotherhood . . .

I had another look.

Or Nigel with a cheque? Even Nigel without a cheque. He had to get me out of this mess. I needed Nigel more than anyone.

I stood up.

Except the man from the Premium Bonds. I did have one, a two-pound one, bought for me by a drunken uncle a hundred years ago when I was christened and two pounds meant something.

The doorbell rang again.

I walked up the hall.

A small group was gathered on my doorstep: two short-haired men in suits, a curly-haired leather-jacketed bloke and a girl in skinny black clothes and bright purple lipstick. She was pointing a camera straight at me.

The first suit stepped forward smartly. He nodded his neatly combed head, flicked a speck of something from his clean grey lapels and smiled engagingly. Then he informed me I had fourteen days in which to pay £2,743 to the electrical-bits company or he would be forced to return and seize goods and chattels to that value.

My heart thumped. The camera whirred. Leather-jacket thrust a tape-recorder beneath my nose as I spluttered. 'What's going on?' I asked, glaring at the camera as it clicked again, no doubt capturing my mad-aunt-Maud look in all its glory.

'That's enough, Carla,' said Leather-jacket.

Carla pouted and wandered off down the steps.

'It's all right,' he said to me. 'We probably won't use it.'

'Who are you?' I asked, but Suit One was still talking about recovery and possession, and just as I was reflecting that he'd be hard pushed to find goods to any amount in my Martin-stripped house, he wound up by announcing that his clients were aware that I was the registered keeper of a blue Ford Fiesta, which would be considered when the time came to put possession orders into practice. I could feel myself swaying. I grabbed the doorpost, gibbered something about my business partner being away now but coming back to sort everything out very soon, and tried to shut the door, vaguely aware that half of the doorstep contingent were trying to come through it.

This wasn't really happening, was it? Must be stress overload. Mixed messages to the brain causing delusions of persecution. Surely I was still upstairs in bed. I leant my hot forehead against the cold glass and closed my eyes.

When I opened them and turned round, Leather-jacket was standing patiently in front of me while, through the doorway, I could see Carla Purple Lips sitting on the corner of my kitchen table. One high-heeled black boot rested on the floor while the other swung restlessly back and forth.

'Are you OK?'

He had a deep, gravelly voice – probably the result of hours spent in front of the mirror perfecting it – lots of dark hair, a suntan, and crinkly smiling eyes. The sort of man who made one wish that one was not in an old towelling robe of Martin's, hair unwashed, wearing no makeup and looking as though one should have been the subject of a mercy killing several days earlier.

I stared at him, unable even to summon the where-withal to ask what the hell he was doing there. I nodded dumbly.

He moved forward. 'Guy Matthews.'

Obediently I held out my hand.

'And this is Carla.'

She had one of those smiles that switches on for a split second then freezes off again.

'What do you want?' I asked weakly.

Guy was a smooth talker with the mixture of charm and concern that gets me every time. Instead of throwing him straight out I allowed myself to be taken gently by the elbow and settled on the window-seat.

'I write for *Macho* magazine. You may have heard of it.'

I shook my head.

On the table, Carla sighed and shifted her weight to the other leg.

'It's a new, ground-breaking upmarket men's glossy – a sort of male *Cosmopolitan* – addressing the needs of today's modern man. Know the sort of thing I mean?'

Become Prime Minister, cook the perfect mushroom Stroganoff and still have a hard-on all night long? 'I think so,' I said.

He smiled, flashing lots of white teeth. 'We're doing a feature on the sexual magnetism of men in authority. Carla and I have spent time with the police, today we're with Debt Recovery, tomorrow we're with the Medway Fire Brigade and—'

'We're stuck in this hole,' put in Carla sulkily.

'And I wondered . . .'

'Yes?'

'If you'd be prepared to talk about how you felt when that bailiff wedged his foot in your door and—'

'He didn't!'

'When you realized he had the power to affect your life. Could swing in here and grasp your dearest possessions while you stood helplessly by.'

'They're going to take my car!'

'Were you turned on?'

What?

Carla made tea with very bad grace while Guy enlightened me. 'Lots of women become aroused by men in positions of power. Do you, for example, find men in uniform attractive? Are you drawn towards men who have helped or rescued you in some way?'

Ben, oh, Ben.

'Have you any special feelings towards your doctor or bank manager?'

Graham?

'These are the sort of questions I'd interview you on. We don't have to use your real name.'

'Do I get a fat fee?' At the thought of the bank my stomach had contracted into a tight hard ball of anxiety.

'I'll buy you dinner.'

'I'm on a diet.'

All the time I was getting ready I was asking myself why. As I smothered my face in a thick layer of makeup, I told myself it was just vanity, so that he'd see I wasn't as repulsive as he'd first thought.

As I plastered my lips with the lipstick I'd got free when I'd spent an amount equalling most people's mortgage payment on firming cream – the salesgirl had assured me it was in this summer's thrilling new shade but it made me look like one of those ancient old crones who paint in lips that disappeared years ago – I decided I needed a night out to escape the horrors of my situation and was also being helpful to a fellow writer.

But as I checked myself in the mirror – definitely an improvement though it was a shame I couldn't wear a towel round my head for the rest of my life – and sprayed myself liberally with Louise's perfume, I knew that the reason I was off to meet Guy had nothing to do with altruism. It was the unexpected jolt of yes-I-would that had gone jerking through me the minute we touched hands. Even through my post-traumatic stress I had seen his potential. Not as tall or big as he could be but lovely eyelashes . . . And apart from a moment of feverish fantasy on the roof, I hadn't been anywhere near a bloke since the night before Martin moved out . . .

'Face it!' I said, looking into my thickly mascaraed eyes and pursing my painted-in lips. *You want to shag him.*

Chapter Twenty

I slept with Martin the first night I met him. When he loved me he admired me for it. 'You don't play games,' he said. 'Don't think you have to say no when you want to say yes.'

Later, of course, he called me a tart. Men are like that. Want you to be all blokey and shag them as soon as look at them. Then when you do, leave with a vague sense of disquiet, knowing you're not quite the girl their mum would have chosen.

'I am not the sort of girl men want to marry,' I warned Martin long ago. It was his cue to fall upon one knee and plead. A cue he missed.

Truth will always out . . .

When I walked into the hotel they were already at the bar. Guy smiled warmly, took my arm and pressed a large gin into my hands as if he'd known me for years. Carla yawned and slid off her stool, smoothing down three inches of leather mini-skirt and shrugging into her jacket. 'See you later,' she said, not looking at me.

We watched her toss back her hair and stride away.

'She's not going because of me?'

'No, no, dinner's not Carla's scene. She's after more exciting night-life.'

'She'll be lucky in Eastford.'

Guy grinned at me and I got that jolt all over again. 'Carla's bored,' he said. 'She wants to get back to London.'

'When are you going?'

'Tomorrow evening.'

Perfect.

Another gin?

Yes, please.

Shall we have one more here?

Why not?

A last one before we eat?

Absolutely.

We walked down the road to the Italian.

Well, he walked. I tottered in that let's-pretend-my-heels-are-a-bit-treacherous-and-the-four-gins-on-an-empty-stomach-are-quite-coincidental sort of way.

He held the door open. I tried hard not to fall through it.

The place was empty, apart from a long table of giggling girls. The waiter led us to a table in the corner and lit a candle.

Guy touched my shoulder as we sat down, and smiled meltingly at me over the top of the wine list. I felt that forgotten thrill of being out with a new man. The plump expectancy of it all. The delicious possibilities . . .

I studied him as I ate my pasta. He was attractive. I needed a fling. Someone new to erase the memories of Martin's reluctant body and Ben's unattainable one. He'd be gone tomorrow before I could get too attached. The Barolo was going down nicely, and now that I was safely seated I felt mellow and relaxed.

'So, what sort of men are you drawn to?' he asked, munching a lamb chop with obvious relish.

'Those with a gold card,' I quipped.

He grinned and made some reply, which was lost in another gale of laughter from the back. 'Hen night,' he said, without looking round.

Guy had a flat in Notting Hill and had worked for *Macho* for six months. He didn't press me further for my views on desirability but regaled me with the feature he had done last week, which involved three days at a nudists' retreat so progressive they had an arrangement with the local cinema for special naked viewings of the latest films – I simply wouldn't believe the sort of things that went on in the front row, never mind the back, he told me.

I found myself telling him all about Nigel, the house and my financial predicament. Aware of the wine now coursing its warm way around my veins, hot on the heels of the gin, I did stop to wonder vaguely whether it was wise to spill the beans about my failed marriage, breaking of local authority regulations and possible impending bankruptcy to a reporter I'd barely met, but in my normal few-drinks-inside-me-and-I'll-worry-about-that-in-the-morning fashion, I ploughed on regardless.

I'd just started to give him the rundown on the Shelf Diet – between mouthfuls of tiramisu – when the door of the restaurant opened and the girls at the long table broke into a chorus of fresh shrieks and giggles. I turned to see an oil-slicked pile of muscle prancing up and down in a minuscule leopardskin thong-thing. He stopped at the head of the table where a dumpy brunette – presumably the bride-to-be – was presiding over the proceedings in a tight shiny top and flashing hairslides.

'Good God!' I said, as he produced a silk scarf and began to wind it round her head.

The rest of the girls were now beside themselves.

'Go on Trace! Get in there!'

Trace screamed unconvincingly, as Leopard-knickers

thrust various bits of himself towards her blindfolded face.

'We can go back to the hotel for coffee if you've had enough of it here,' said Guy, craning to see over my shoulder.

I licked a little cream from the corner of my mouth. 'Good idea.'

'I thought you were quite enjoying it, really,' he said, as the waiter placed a cafetière in front of us.

I looked at him and he looked back at me. I was still clinging to the last vestiges of sobriety so I knew exactly what sort of look we were giving each other but I was sufficiently plastered to have no sense of shame about it. 'I hate that sort of thing,' I said. *But the sooner I get you stripped down to a loincloth the better.*

'I started a book myself once,' he told me. 'I had this idea for an erotic novel, but not the normal old stuff. This was a murder mystery as well. You see, most erotic literature is purchased by women – aged thirty-five to forty, professional types, upper income bracket. Surprising, yeah?'

I watched his hands while he spoke. They had dark hairs on the back. They moved all the time. The occasional shiver of excitement went up my spine.

'Well, of course men would like to read that sort of thing but they want a different sort of plot. Not a romance where she spends the whole book finding Mr Right, but a proper story, a thriller with lots of action. Now my idea . . .' His face was animated, alive. God, at last, a man with passion. '. . . and the female detective basically screws her way round all the suspects until she discovers who did it. Then you can include some variety – a bit of bondage, three in a bed, lesbian scene, you know – got to please everybody.'

My heart was beating faster than usual, so I took the coffee pot and poured myself some. Then Carla appeared from nowhere and stood by our table, pouting. 'This place is dead. I'm going to bed,' she said. 'There's my Pete out on the town at home, drinking himself senseless, and I'm stuck here with a load of geriatrics.'

'Thank you very much,' I said. 'Would you like some coffee?'

Carla smirked. 'I didn't mean you.'

She went. Guy smiled at me. I smiled back. Again we knew the sort of smiles they were. But we were both acting as if we were going dutifully to different beds. Funny how we all play the same game.

'Shall I call you a taxi?'

'Yeah, in a bit.'

'More coffee, Cari?'

'Yes, please, Guy.'

And then, Guy . . . And then . . .

We both gave up the niceties at about the same time. He leant across the table and took my hand just as I was positioning my foot to slide accidentally up his ankle.

We had our first kiss in the corridor outside, were tugging at each other's clothes by the time we reached Guy's hotel room.

Blame it on the red wine and my desperation to escape the grim mundanity of my debt-ridden life, the pleasing symbolism of metaphorically saying, '*Screw you*' to the bailiffs, the heady surge of hormones that charge around my body at certain times of the month. Whatever it was, it came upon me as a savage need.

The moment he'd closed the door behind us, I ravished him.

Later, we lay in an exhausted heap and he stroked my hair. 'There was no need to pretend,' he said.

What?

'You don't have to do that with me.'

'What are you talking about?'

'You know. All that gasping and groaning. It may be OK in scenes in films set in American diners but we all know real women don't come like that.'

Don't they?

'Just tell me what you want. We can take as long as you like.'

Oh, shit.

Isn't it funny how you end up telling the strangest people the oddest things? I never expected to make the confession in a hotel room to someone I'd barely met. Well, it's embarrassing, isn't it? Embarrassing and unbelievable. Particularly years after *Cosmopolitan* has taught every other woman in the country to Be Responsible for Your Own and have multiple ones while waiting for the bus.

In fact, I never thought I'd want to share with anyone this other area of fantastic non-achievement, hoping that one day it would happen all on its own – you know, just as I happened to be sitting idly on the washing-machine or sliding down the banister or, if Victoria Wood is to be believed, filling up with petrol. Though, blimey, how big are these women's tanks? Naturally, after seeing Victoria on TV, the next time I had cause to go to the garage – about half an hour later – I had a bit of a fiddle with the hose and even I could appreciate the potential of its pulsating vibrations, but how long would it take? How much petrol would you have to buy? I'd have to hang about the forecourt all night offering to man the pumps for all-comers, surely, to have the faintest chance of becoming one myself. In the meantime, it was back to fruitless hours of grinding away and many more magazine articles trying to discover what was wrong with me.

The latter were of no help as the world – apart from me, of course, Mrs Unemployable *and* Sexually Duff – has moved on from the days when various girlfriends with a few drinks inside them would admit that the earth had not actually stirred for them yet. Now it is assumed you just knock one off whenever you feel the urge, and the main thrust of the message for the modern woman – How to Have Yours First Every Time! Twenty-five Positions for Mega Multiples! Manage Your Own G-Spot Till Your Eyelids Tingle! – was concerned only with increasing quality and quantity.

Nowhere did I find any advice for someone such as myself, who had never had an orgasm at all.

I muttered it into the pillow.

Guy sat bolt upright and hauled me up with him. 'Never?' He was incredulous.

'That's right.'

'But you said you'd been married for ten years.'

'What's that got to do with it?'

'Everything! What was he doing?'

'He didn't know.'

'You mean he fell for all that wailing and panting and thought you had?'

'Fuck off.'

This was utterly humiliating. I pulled myself free and scrabbled about looking for my clothes, all my earlier elation draining away.

'Hey, where are you going? Don't go. We can sort this. You've obviously never had the right man.'

I'd found my shirt but my knickers had disappeared. 'Look, I've got to get home.'

He grabbed hold of me again. 'You're going nowhere. You're not leaving this room till you've had an orgasm. Wow. Thirty-two years without one! It's going to blow your mind.'

We were awake for the next four hours.
It did.

When I woke, the room was filled with sunshine. Guy was standing at the end of the bed, pulling on clothes. 'Breakfast finished hours ago. I'm going to see if I can rustle up some room service.'

I looked at him and it all came back to me. Oh, marvel of all marvels. Bloody hell and other such words-fail-me type sentiments.

I stretched in the bed, wriggled my fingers and toes, ran my hands through my hair; all sorts of warm pleasurable tingles in all sorts of places at the very thought of the night before.

He came round to the side of the bed and took my face in his hands. 'God, you were fantastic.'

I pulled back the duvet and tugged him towards me. God, so were you.

Afterwards, he brought us tuna sandwiches, peanuts and champagne. I felt absolutely bloody wonderful. I couldn't stop grinning at him. The champagne made me giggly and high.

I filled my mouth with it, cheeks bulging out, then drizzled the foaming golden liquid between his open lips. I felt beautiful, sensual and happy. I lay back across his chest, my cheek turned against the smooth skin of his shoulder. He wound his arm around me and popped a peanut into my mouth.

'Hey!' I said, sitting up. 'What happened to the firemen?'

'I sent Carla. Another sandwich?'

'No! I'm writing a diet plan. I've got to look thin.'

'You look great. You've got an unbelievable body.'

'It feels unbelievable.'

'You want to write in some stuff about good sex burning up four hundred calories an hour.'

'How many does bad sex use? It's a diet book, not a bonking manual.'

'Shall we go for another one?'

'Now you're talking.'

Chapter Twenty-one

And people say it was 'only sex'. Only?

What else could lift your senses, fill your body with vigour, relax it so deeply, make your mind soar, brighten a whole day?

I have been re-created. This is my first day of newness. I feel that deep circling of pleasure again and again. Bursting flowers of violet intensity . . .

We'd been awake since six.

'I wish I could have sex as a woman,' said Guy. 'Just for a day – or a night – to see what it feels like.'

'It feels wonderful.' I felt drunk on it. 'I've never wanted to be a man,' I told him. 'Except occasionally when I've been dying for a pee out of doors.'

Guy laughed.

I ran a hand over his hard stomach. 'And all those horrible baggy, wrinkly bits,' I went on, not meaning a word of it. 'The male form isn't beautiful, is it? Not like the female. I'd rather look at a naked woman if we're talking aesthetics.'

He pulled me on top of him. 'So would I. Even if we're not.'

'The thing is,' I said, when I was sitting up again, flushed and glowing, watching him empty sachets of coffee into the cups, 'I literally didn't know what I was missing. I mean, I've always quite enjoyed it, even if the earth didn't move. I just felt I must be a bit odd.'

'It's not that unusual. They reckon up to twenty-five per cent of women say they've never had an orgasm and a much higher number than that don't have one through penetration alone. But what's interesting is that—'

'How do you know so much about it?'

'We had a survey in the magazine. And the thing that makes the difference is doing Kegels. Now what you should do—'

'Kegels?'

'Exercises on the vaginal muscles. Now, try squeezing.'

'No. Yuck. Stop it.'

'It's not yuck.'

'It is. My friend Rowena was obsessed with them after she'd had her baby. It's all that stopping in midstream stuff. It makes me squeamish.'

'Don't be silly. It's just a muscle like any other. If you increase the blood supply to the muscle and the blood-flow to the pelvis . . .'

'Stop it, I feel faint.'

'. . . you'll intensify the levels of arousal and therefore . . .'

'I don't want to hear.'

'. . . have bigger orgasms!' Guy finished triumphantly. 'They work wonders. You try them and see. And it stops you being incontinent when you're old and grey.'

'Thank you very much.'

Guy insisted I practise a minute of Kegels, which I did with gritted teeth. He nodded, satisfied, when I'd finished. 'I've got to go and do those interviews today.'

I got out of bed and looked around for my trousers. 'My God, look at me!' I peered into the mirror in disbelief. I looked like a different woman – sort of wild and flushed yet calm, wide-eyed and serene.

My skin had the glowing, rested look I'd spent about five hundred pounds so far this year on trying to achieve and that had now happened effortlessly – even though I'd spent thirty-six hours away from my moisturizer – with a mere half-dozen shags.

'Ah,' said my new walking-sexual-encyclopedia, 'regular sex raises oestrogen levels and the increased hormone improves skin condition. You'll be giving out lots of pheromones as well – the chemical substance that attracts a mate. The more sex you have the more you make.'

So that was Louise's secret. Nothing to do with perfume at all.

Guy threw his tape-recorder on to the back seat of his car and kissed me lingeringly. 'I've got other stuff I can do around here. If you like, I could pop down again next weekend and stay a few days. You can show me the sights of Eastford.' He tightened his arms around me. 'Or the sights of your bedroom anyway . . . Is that all right?'

I was mellow, fulfilled and sanguine. 'Very all right,' I told him.

I've been waiting to feel this way all my life. Is it love? Or just lust?

Who cares?

I walked home hugging myself with joy. I had a bloke, I was orgasmic. Everything was going right again.

Orgasms were like alcohol, I decided: capable of making the world a different place. It was just a matter of where you were looking from.

I'd *thought* I was on the edge of financial ruin, my life in shreds, but really, just by a bit of positive application, I could see that I was teetering on the brink of a multimillion-pound supermarket deal and an incredible writing career.

Think Bill. Think diet-food empire. Think Jessica Jackson and six-figure-sum blockbusters.

My steps seemed lighter, my head clearer. Happiness bubbled beneath my every surface.

I was going to make a whole new Action List the moment I got in.

Number one: Write the letter to Bill's Charlie-boy publisher.

I crossed the road, almost skipping, my mind already composing the life-changing missive: *Dear Charlie . . .* Too familiar? *Dear Charles Merriman, Your friend Bill suggested . . .* How many Bills are there in the world? *Your friend Bill Winterbar that you play golf with . . .* No, no, he knows who Bill Winterbar is. Forget the golf. *Dear Mr Merriman, I recently had the pleasure of meeting* no point in mentioning the gin *a friend* golfing colleague? *of yours, Bill Winterbar, who kindly suggested . . .* I dug in my handbag and found my phone. Not very good at letters. Phone Louise first. Much better idea.

She was on the line immediately, complaining that she'd been calling my mobile and it was always switched off and that she'd wanted to tell me how she'd changed completely, was ecstatic about the baby, how Robert was also delirious with happiness and how she'd got a doctor's appointment for Wednesday week and she wanted me to come with her and share in the excitement.

At this point I became ecstatic myself and told her about Guy, my two days in bed and my new status as Complete Woman.

She made a series of flabbergasted noises, not – I like to think – because she was amazed I'd been able to pull a bloke but because, of course, throughout the last sixteen years of our friendship, I'd omitted to tell her that I was non-orgasmic. I told her this was because I'd convinced myself it was completely unimportant and not that I felt inferior as she, Louise, had been having multiple ones since she was about eleven.

'That is marvellous,' she kept saying. 'I can't wait to meet him. Oh, and Cari, you're going to be godmother. Do you think I'm having a boy?'

I bounded up my steps.

Even the sound of my mother on the answerphone – clearly having no truck with my food-poisoning story – didn't dampen my spirits: 'I want to speak to you, Cari!'

(*'Why weren't you at the day school, Cari? You were supposed to be discovering hidden talents.'*

'I have been, Mother, I have been . . .')

However, the smile on my face started to dim when I heard the next three – two from the bank demanding I contact them and a slightly shrill one from the building-supplies company wanting their bill paid – and it was wiped away completely when I picked up the post.

Forget post-shag-euphoria versus being-pissed comparisons. Had I been drunk, I might have tossed it all on to the table and said, 'Bollocks', at least until the hangover kicked in. Being sober, all my new-found joy dwindled away to a cold clammy puddle of dread.

There was a bank statement. (Thank you very much, Nigel. What happened to the two grand?)

There was a letter from a Mr Farquar at the council about building regulations, enclosing pages of alarming-looking legal blurb about contravening various acts and demanding I contact his office.

There was a letter from a company called Grantham & Sons, the bailiffs acting on behalf of the Electrical Bits lot, who were confirming that I had ten days or else. (They'd said fourteen on the doorstep!)

There was a nasty letter from Graham at the bank, saying I must get in touch immediately as he had been unable to reach me by phone.

And I found a note from Ben, written on the back of an envelope, saying he'd called round to let me know that he'd noticed 'the druggie' had broken a couple of windows.

I phoned all Nigel's numbers and listened to a series of answerphones and on-divert messages. Where the hell was he? What about the money and the eviction?

I stood and clutched my stomach. Panic scuttled up and down my arms. God, oh, God, what was I going to do?

I got into the car, which I might as well drive into the ground before it was snatched from me in a week's time, and went round to Turpin Road. On the way I did lots of deep breathing, still nurturing the vague hope that if Gary hadn't been thrown out he had got over his drug addiction, repaired the windows, finished decorating and got together six weeks' rent.

The house looked dreadful, almost as bad as it had before we'd bought it. The two front windows were, indeed, smashed, while overflowing bags of rotting rubbish were piled up against the railings and an old mattress now filled the well beneath the steps. The new front door already had several dents and the glass had been replaced with hardboard.

I took a deep breath and went up to it. Somebody had stuck up a piece of card, saying, 'Bell not working.'

Beneath it someone else had added, 'Arsehole.'

I stood on the top step, leant over the railings, put my hand gingerly through the hole in the jagged glass to try to pull the curtain out of the way so that I could see inside. As I grasped it a voice behind me said, 'Can I help you?'

I turned to see an old woman, arms folded, at the bottom of the steps, wearing an overall and a ferocious expression. 'Oh, yes, it's OK. It's my house.'

She surveyed me with suspicion. 'Oh, is it? Well, what are you going to do about this rubbish, then? And the noise. And the foul language. People coming and going all night long! We've had the council round, you know. And the police. It's not good enough.'

'I'm sorry,' I said faintly. 'We've had a bit of trouble with the tenants.'

'So I see! Where'd you find 'em in the first place? This used to be a nice street. Times were when you could leave your doors unlocked and money on the table. Not any more. You lot come along with your money-making schemes, fill the place up with riff-raff and won't take responsibility. All you care about is lining your pockets.'

If only!

'No, it's not like that.'

'Oh? What is it like, then? You tell me, young lady. Because all I see is you taking the rent and me afraid to let my grandchildren play on the pavement. There's hypodermics in them rubbish sacks. I've been on to Environmental Health and they're going to be after you!'

Oh, Christ. Not another council department to add to the growing list of official bodies after my blood.

'I'm sorry,' I said again. 'Look, I assure you . . .' I stopped. What could I assure her? 'I'll go and talk to him,' I said.

'Him?' She snorted. 'There's at least a dozen of 'em in there now.'

The one who opened the door had a shaved head and a tattoo on his forehead. He poked his pale clammy face through the six-inch gap and looked at me blankly. 'Yeah?'

I swallowed. 'Is Gary in?'

211

'Nah.'

He started to close the door, but I jumped forward – immediately longing to jump back again as I got the full close-up of the sweat glistening on his pimply upper lip. 'I'm the landlady,' I said bravely, trying desperately to introduce a note of authority into the proceedings. 'I need to talk to Gary.'

He stared at me for a moment. 'Right,' he said, uncomprehendingly.

Behind him a voice shouted, 'Who is it?' and a second head lurched over the first one's shoulder. This one was even more unsavoury than the first.

I looked into the two bleary eyes that peered out of the veiny red face and wondered if I really wanted to insist on gaining entry. 'I need to talk to Gary,' I said again.

'Ah'm,' Veiny seemed to be making a huge effort to move his mouth into the right shape, 'Ah'm his shtep-father.' He staggered against the doorpost, evidently in a state of collapse after this exertion.

Sweaty-face – clearly relinquishing responsibility for the interview – let go of the door and disappeared. While the drunk was recovering himself the door was left open and I was able to stare at the sight beyond. A mound of dingy blankets indicated that someone or something was asleep in the hall. A mangy-looking Alsatian lay slobbering over the inert form. Another figure lay slumped across the stairs, staring at the ceiling, can of lager in one hand, suspiciously fat roll-up in the other. A couple of kicked-in televisions sat at his feet. The electricity meters dangled on the end of thick black cables that led to a large hole in the wall. Abruptly the ceiling began to vibrate with the heavy thump of mindless music overhead. Oh, God, they'd got in up there too.

I took a sharp step backwards.

'I need you out!' I cried shrilly, while the drunk peered at me. 'Tell Gary you've all got to go!'

He staggered forward and waved an arm towards me as I recoiled further. 'Lishen to me,' he slurred.

I listened.

'Ah'm his shtepfather,' he said. And fell over.

As I stumbled down the steps the old lady reappeared. 'Well?' she demanded.

'I'll deal with it!' I rushed away from her.

In desperation I went round the back to where the new superstore had risen to remarkable heights in the week or two since I'd last seen it. There were still men and diggers about but no Ben.

Eventually I spotted someone who looked a bit like one of the leering-over-the-top lot I'd seen last time. I asked him if Ben was around. 'No,' he said, and walked off.

I tried another. 'I was wondering if Ben was here.'

This one had wet, rubbery lips and most of his buttocks on display. 'Not at the moment, love. Anything I can do?' His lower lip flopped open helpfully.

'No, thanks. Um, if you see him, can you say, Cari says . . .' I stopped. What could I say? 'Please come and rescue me. Please single-handedly remove a dozen assorted drunks, drug addicts, smelly dogs and make my house fit for human habitation. Find a way I can quell an irate bank manager and half the local council. Get me out of this unspeakable shit'?

'Could you just tell him I came?' I finished feebly.

He grinned at me lecherously. 'Sure can, darlin'. Bet he'll be very glad to hear it.'

I left him chortling at the brilliance of his own wit and repartee, and went home morosely. How the hell was I ever going to get out of this one?

Chaper Twenty-two

Denial Action Plan
Make neat pile of post in middle of kitchen table.
Leave answer-machine switched on at all times.
Spend as much time as possible in bed.
When not in bed have a bath.
When all else fails, get drunk.

Ring, ring. Ring, ring.
Cari, it's Louise. Pick the phone up. I know you're there!
No, I'm not. I'm far too miserable and bad-tempered to be around the unborn child.
Ring, ring. Ring, ring.
Miss Carrington, it's Graham from . . .
I haven't got any bloody money to give you!
Ring, ring. Ring, ring.
Cari! Why aren't you returning my calls?
Because you'll bleat on about your bloody day school.
Ring, ring. Ring, ring.
Cari, it's Martin. I need to talk to you.
Sod off!
Ring, ring. Ring, ring.
Hello, this is the credit-control department of . . .
Join the bloody queue.

Ring, ring. Ring, ring.

Cari! I need to speak to you urgently . . .

Don't you always, Mother?

. . . phone me back at once!

Don't you understand?? I am not speaking to *anyone*!

Ring, ring. Ring, ring.

Cari! It's Ben. Did you want me? I'm on my mobile 0468 . . .

Agggh!

Leap out of bath, run dripping to phone.

'I'm here! Don't hang up!'

But he already has.

Chapter Twenty-three

Don't be taken in by Ben.

No. But it's all right to be taken in by you, isn't it? I thought bitterly, as I put down the phone on Nigel's answering service once again. Had he died and no one thought to tell me? Where was Gloria? What about the kids?

If he was living it up in Marbella on ill-gotten gains while I was left here to face the music and Graham, I'd bloody well kill him.

I was still quivering from my interview with Trevor, who'd appeared without warning on my doorstep, shiny black boot shoved forward, thumbs in loops of jeans, face like thunder.

'Trevor!' My voice was squeaky with surprise.

Trevor did not waste time on pleasantries. 'What about my bleeding invoice?'

'Nigel—'

'Thought you said it would be you who was paying.'

'Yes, but Nigel—'

'I'm not a bleeding charity.'

Neither it seems is your average high-street bank. I put my card into the machine – a triumph of desperation over reality, I can see with hindsight – and it was promptly gulped away into the bank's innards. *Please refer to your branch*. I frantically pressed all the different buttons, in the hope that it might change its mind, while the queue behind me shuffled and sighed or craned their necks to see why I'd been so evidently and humiliatingly denied cash.

I sighed loudly and impatiently, as if it was a technical error and one to which someone such as myself was certainly not accustomed, swept away and pushed through the swing doors into the bank so that the assembled company would realize I had nothing to be ashamed of and was going straight to the top to sort it out. (The plan, of course, had been to meander about a bit at the back, examining the paying-in slips and leaflets on setting up your own business then scuttle out again red-faced, once the people outside had disappeared.) But the bank was empty. With half of its customer base outside on the pavement smirking at my misfortune there was not a single person in the place.

As I marched in, not one but two smiling cashiers looked up eagerly and smiled the welcoming smile of the bored witless longing for a bit of human interaction, one even going so far as to trill: 'Good-morning-how-can-I-help-you?' Bloody typical. If you wanted service she'd be too busy telling the other one what her boyfriend had thought of *Coronation Street* last night.

I ground to a rapid halt, wondering how I could best slink out again without it looking like a bad case of cold feet to all those voyeurs outside.

And then I remembered the deposit account.

It was in joint names. Martin had opened it to pay in some proceeds from his ever-loving mother's never-ending supply of there-you-are-my-darling-boy shares so that he could claim my capital-gains tax allowance as

217

well as his own, or some other smarmy dodge from which I had never reaped any benefit.

The keener of the two cashiers was still beaming at me so I approached her, thinking how bloody marvellous it would be if Martin, in his Sharon-besotted blindness, had forgotten its existence and had left thousands in there about which he'd never told me, and how at least I had a *bona fide* excuse for being in the place that didn't involve admitting to a massive and unauthorized over-draft.

'Good morning!' I beamed back, 'I was wondering if you could tell me the balance of my deposit account.'

Keenie's smile didn't falter. It remained in place even though I didn't have the account number and she had to do a lot of tapping at her screen. Even when she had to disappear off to one of the desks at the back and have a long involved conversation with a white-shirted sideburns who in turn tapped into his own computer.

She smiled at she handed me the slip of paper that told me I was the joint owner of £4.72. And she still smiled when she added that, since I happened to be in the branch and he happened to be free, then the manager would just like a quick word.

For a wild moment I thought about fainting and having to be carted away in an ambulance but in the end I walked meekly into Graham's office and sat down, clutching my handbag tightly on my lap so he wouldn't see how much my hands were shaking.

There was no smile today. Even his family seemed to stare accusingly from the middle of his desk as he con-sulted various bits of paper and listed my misdemeanours in the shape of missing loan repayments and unanswered telephone calls. 'Yes, I'm sorry,' I said feebly. 'I've had a few problems.'

'You can't just ignore them,' said Graham severely. 'The bank needs to be kept informed.'

I tried to listen but I found myself glazed with terror, fixated by the bubble of saliva that kept forming at the corner of his mouth then popping.

'Already exceeded the bank's criteria . . .' Pop. 'Twenty-five pounds charge for each unpaid item . . .' Pop. 'Would expect by now to see income generated . . .' Pop.

My stomach had twisted into a hard, tight knot, it was stiflingly hot in the small room and I needed to go to the loo.

'The council payments are taking a long time to come through,' I blurted suddenly, feeling that awful achy-tingling in my throat and nose and knowing I might soon cry.

Graham appeared to swell. His shoulders rose and fell as both hands came up, as if in prayer. He balanced his chin on the point of his joined fingertips, breathed out heavily and fixed me with small stony eyes. 'There is an arrangement between us, Miss Carrington,' he said, with slow menace, 'according to the facility letter you have signed . . .'

I could feel myself getting hotter and redder.

'. . . yet after only two months you were in default . . .'

My mind was going round and round in circles. Should I just confess all and throw myself on his mercy or buy some time by promising him Nigel's famed two grand and hope I could get hold of the little bastard double quick? Would it help if I said I'd put the house straight back on the market? What the bloody hell would he say if he could see Gary?

Meanwhile Graham had fallen back on his Churchill impression and was half-way across the desk.

'This bank has a *duty*!' his voice reverberated around the room and I felt myself shrink back.

'A *duty* not only to *ourselves* . . .' his hands were now open wide entreating the country to sit up and take notice '. . . not only to our shareholders, our depositors, our customers small and large . . .' he was now staring fanatically at a point somewhere above my left eyebrow '. . . but to *you*, Miss Carrington,' he bellowed, making me jump.

His glinting eyes fixed on mine and he dropped abruptly to the terrifyingly silky tones of the serial killer. 'We need to make sure you are running your business appropriately, Miss Carrington. Perhaps you'd like to let me have your cheque book, Miss Carrington.'

My heart was now thudding alarmingly.

'Because, Miss Carrington,' he finished pleasantly, 'I could legally and legitimately call in your loan this very afternoon.'

I kept swallowing and breathing deeply but it was no good, tears were now trickling out all over the place. I fumbled about in my bag for tissues.

Graham got brisk and started firing questions at me I didn't understand about my 'own resources' and my house and, for some inexplicable reason, Martin's earnings.

I gulped and rubbed my eyes and reminded him that Martin was long gone which made me cry all over again, which embarrassed him because he pulled a huge black diary towards him and brought the meeting to a close. 'I'm out of the office for a few days,' he said, as though it might be a matter of regret to me, 'so the earliest I could get there now is Friday week. Ten a.m.!' he barked, slamming the book shut. 'I'll meet you at the property.' He stood up. 'The works are fully completed now.' He made it a statement, his

tones implying all sorts of dire consequences if con-
tradicted.

'Just a bit of decorating left . . .' I said faintly.

He held open the door. 'I imagine it will be finished by
Friday.'

I fled.

Chapter Twenty-four

I now thought about money all the time. My mind was a running column of figures, a seething mass of calculations of how much I needed to put things right.

My father – in one of his vague attempts at being parental – had a long, philosophical lecture on the subject of finance, which he delivered periodically throughout my youth. 'However much money one has, dear,' it ran, 'one always needs more.' And 'A thousand pounds may seem a lot of money now,' (this was at a time when I had about 49p in my money-box and a thousand pounds seemed an unspeakable fortune) 'but there will come a time, dear, when you'll find a thousand pounds, ten thousand pounds, even a hundred thousand pounds doesn't go very far . . .'

I never understood the purpose of the lecture or the point he was trying to make but ever since, at any given stage in my life, there has always been a particular sum that I don't have and I long for, knowing that if only it would turn up, magically and unexpectedly, my life would be complete. Once it *was* only about a thousand pounds, enough to pay off Barclaycard before Martin found out how much of a bill I'd run up. (Martin's purpose was always very clear: amass as much money as possible and prevent me spending it.)

Then it grew to about ten. Enough to feel I had 'independent means' so that Martin would stop being horrible about my employment record and I could buy a pot of moisturizer without there being a public inquiry. But by the time of our separation it had escalated to well over fifty grand, for me to buy out Martin's share of the house and purchase several jars of moisturizer and pay the bills till I got a job. Now, well, it was an awful lot more than that . . . I had become used to the hard knot of anxiety that lived in the pit of my stomach but it was getting worse.

Money was the first thing I thought of every morning, the last thing before I fell fitfully to sleep. And when I woke in the night, as I did frequently, hot and sweating from a panic-filled dream, the enormity of my debts pressed in on me and I found myself gasping for breath. For the first time, I understood what Juliette must go through with her panic attacks: how anxiety and fear could pervade everything, how the simple daily acts of getting up and living through a day could over-whelm . . .

There will come a time, I told myself repeatedly, when I will look back at this and if I don't laugh then at least I will shrug. It was what I used to tell myself, years ago, when I was still terrified that Martin would discard me. What hurts now won't always hurt. This is only one small point in the whole of your opportunity-filled life. Things will get better. Oh, I knew all the philosophies. But still my stomach churned.

Friday. I had a week to sort something out. I sat on the step, waiting for Guy. It was one of those soft evenings when the light's fading but the air is still warm. I wanted to feel excited but last week seemed a lifetime ago. I swirled the last mouthful of wine around in my glass and tried to recall that perfect joy I'd felt, lying in the tangled bed, drinking champagne. But already I had lost faith in us. My mind was full of overdraft and unpaid bills. Nothing was going to transport me to those heights again. I picked a weed that had sprouted up through a crack in the concrete and began to pluck at its leaves. I heard the car draw up and the door slam. I kept my head down as long as I could.

But it wasn't Guy's feet that came up my path. My heart jolted as I looked up at the great figure looming above me. 'Got your message, darlin'. Got a problem?'

Ben listened in silence to my tale of woe.

'Well, sweetheart,' he said eventually, 'I've been in this situation myself. Have you spoken to a solicitor?'

'No.'

'How many of them in there?'

'Too many for you to chuck out.'

He laughed.

'Well the legal situation is, you *can* get them out.'

I felt a small slump of relief. 'Thank God for that.'

'You'll need to issue a section twenty-one notice to quit. Normally that would give them two months' notice.'

'*Two months?* I've got to get them out quicker than that!' I clutched at my knees in fresh panic. 'I've got the bank manager coming.'

'But in this case, with rent arrears and nuisance being caused, you can get it down to two weeks.'

'OK.' I breathed deeply. 'I suppose I could try and put him off a week. So, I can get them out in a fortnight, but what about the rent owing?'

'That's if they leave. Which they won't.'

My heart plummeted again. 'What then?'

'If they don't vacate voluntarily, you'll need to make

an application to the court for possession and at the same time you can file an application for monies—'

'Court?' I squeaked. 'How long does that take?'

'If they don't turn up for the hearing it can be awarded against them in their absence but these things can drag on.'

'How long?'

'Could be months.'

Oh, my God, oh, my God. 'By then they'll have smashed the place to smithereens. And who's going to pay the court costs and what about the council? The bank won't wait for ever. Graham's already said—' I bit my lip, willing myself not to cry again.

Ben's eyes gleamed. His voice was deep and sinister, menace overlaid with treacle. It sent mysterious shivers down my spine. He spoke slowly. 'There is another way . . .'

He'd just settled himself on the step with me and I was just gazing at him in adoration when the gate creaked open for the second time. Guy looked smaller than I remembered him.

I stood up abruptly. Beside me, Ben got to his feet.

'Ben, this is Guy . . .' I felt myself hesitate for a fraction then blush furiously '. . . a friend of mine.'

Guy swung his weekend bag from arm to arm and stuck out a hand. Ben shook it and turned to me. 'Well, I'll be off, then,' he said heavily.

'Yes, OK. Umm, thank you. Thank you very much,' I twittered, alarmed by how embarrassed I felt that Guy had arrived, and how disappointed that the moment had been broken.

I watched Ben's back go down the path. *He's married. You couldn't have him anyway.*

'Bet you keep the bananas out of reach when he comes round,' said Guy cheerily.

'What?'

'Striking resemblance to his ancestors.'

I felt myself bristle. 'He's been very helpful to me.'

This one's for you. He's single.

I held open the door as Guy carried his bag into my house.

Suddenly, strangely – in fact, bloody ridiculous, considering the abandon with which I had tugged off his clothes the previous week – I felt awkward. *Please don't let it be one of those awful ones when I no longer fancy him and have to spend the weekend cringing.*

My fears were realized the moment he tried to kiss me. I pecked him hurriedly on the cheek, wriggled away and went to the fridge. 'We could sit outside,' I said, grabbing the bottle. 'It's a bit of a jungle out there, I'm not into gardening.'

But Guy had settled himself on the window-seat. He stretched out a hand. 'Come and kiss me.'

I fussed with the glasses. 'Frascati OK?'

'Come here.'

It began to feel better once he had his arms around me. I ground my face into his shoulder. 'I'm sorry. I'm just really stressed out.'

Guy rubbed my shoulders while I gave him the edited highlights of my debt development. Then he began to kiss my neck and things felt better still. 'I've been looking forward to this for days . . .' he murmured.

'Mmmmnn.' At last I could feel the old stirrings of last week's wild, reckless frenzy of desire. I'd always known that window-seat had potential.

I opened the fridge again. 'Look, it doesn't matter. I don't care.'

'I know. I just want you to have a good time.'

'I did. Just leave it.'

'Sure. We've got all weekend.'

I stared out at the darkening sky.

'Stress can have an adverse effect on one's ability to climax.' Guy adopted a reassuring tone as I filled both our glasses. 'As can alcohol.'

Later, looking pointedly at my crotch, he asked, 'Have you been doing them?'

'What?'

'Your exercises.'

'No, I haven't. I don't like them.'

'You'll never manage three times in a row!'

'What are you? A bloody sex therapist?'

He put his arms round me. 'I just want to make you feel nice.'

I wrapped my arms round him, overcome with guilt and gratitude. 'I know.'

The phone had rung twice while we were at it. When Guy had gone to have a shower, I scowled at the answer-machine and pressed the replay button.

The first message was from my mother, sounding more than usually peeved. Was she ever going to forget about her blasted day school?

Guy appeared in the doorway, a tiny towel wrapped around his waist. He raised his eyebrows at me in invitation. I ignored him and listened to the next. Also my mother. This time she simply said, 'For heaven's sake, Cari! Where are you? I've been phoning you all day.'

I looked at Guy who had removed the towel and was lounging naked in the doorway. 'She only wants to have a go at me,' I said crossly.

'Ready for another try?'

I shook my head.

*   *   *

227

We lay in my bed. Guy was asleep. I stared at the ceiling.

I went over and over it all obsessively. If I could find somebody to lend me a couple of thousand to keep Graham at bay and a bit more to pay next month's loan and Ben's plan worked and I could quickly get some new tenants and Jim would decorate and wait a bit to be paid . . .

I turned over restlessly. Oh, God, and Trevor! I squirmed as I remembered his expression. Guy shifted a bit closer to me and I rolled away from him. It felt strange to have another body there. I was sweating. I needed to stretch out into the coolest reaches of the bed. I threw back the duvet. Suddenly I wanted it to be morning with us up and clothed.

Above all, I wanted Nigel.

'Do you know where Nigel is?' I had asked Ben.

'You know Nigel,' Ben had said. 'He'll turn up.'

But he hadn't looked at me while he was saying it and, once again, I had the feeling there was something hidden between the two of them, some exclusive blokey secrecy from which I was excluded. Nigel would have some slick dodge we could employ to keep the bailiffs from the door. Nigel would tell me not to worry.

Martin would just be furious. But even he would know what to do. At the thought of Martin, I felt flushed with a hot guilt at my stupidity. Martin, for all his faults, would never have let this happen.

The phone jangled in my ear, sounding monstrous in the quiet room. I jolted in shock, squinted at the clock-face and picked it up.

'Oh, Cari, you're home.'

'I'm in bed!'

'I need to—'

'Look! I was ill, all right?'

There was a pause. Just for once I couldn't hear my mother breathing at all.

'Are you still there?' I snapped.

'Oh, Cari,' my mother sounded uncharacteristically hesitant, 'it's Juliette. We've got to get her to hospital.'

Chapter Twenty-five

I have been reminded of my first death. Grandmother herself, with her fat, smothering arms, was no loss but the sight of my father's tears touched me with shock and exhilaration. My sister cried but I was thrilled by it all.

For a hideous moment Juliette's madness was like that. I felt that frisson as I heard my mother's voice telling me what Juliette had done, that trembling anticipation of facing an emergency. I could tell she felt it too.

She was calm as we made Juliette get into the car, but as we drove through the night, her eyes fixed on the black road ahead, I knew she was invigorated . . .

Juliette's flat was in chaos. All the books were off the shelves, piled in tottering towers around the room. Her cardboard chart was Sellotaped to the mirror. Juliette herself was on the phone when we entered the room. She stopped and clutched the receiver to her chest and eyed us suspiciously. 'Where have you been?' she said to our mother.

'I was letting Cari in. She's going to drive us.'

'I've got to make phone calls.' Juliette's eyes were darting, anxious. 'I've got to let everyone know.'

'It's OK, we'll do that.' My mother's voice was soft

and melodic, a forgotten echo of childhood, of warm laps and bedtime stories.

I was afraid. I went to my sister. 'What's the matter?' I felt a deep sense of unreality. I heard my own voice, trying to be cheery, normal. She looked at me. She was afraid too. Her hair needed washing. Her skin had an unhealthy sheen. But it was her eyes that frightened me most. I wanted to run.

'There are things happening here,' she told me. 'It all makes sense now.'

My mother took the receiver from her hands and put it back in its resting place. 'We're going in Cari's car now,' she said. 'Dr Kendrick's arranged everything.'

Juliette stared into the distance. 'But who am I going as?' she asked.

Before I reached the edge of town she was asleep in the back like a child. My mother, in the front next to me, took off her bangles and turned them round and round in her hands. 'It took me a day or two to realize,' she said. 'I thought she was just, you know, having insights. I thought she'd be all right. I thought she was just—' She broke off and looked ahead at the dark road. 'I called the doctor,' she said, 'but it wasn't until he came that I really knew. Of course, I should have done. After all I went through with your father . . .'

It was very dark. I turned my headlights on to full beam, and followed the bright strip of white line that ribboned away down the centre of the curving shiny road, thanking God for putting me on an alcohol go-slow tonight so that I could still drive. I thought of Guy at home in my bed. I felt curiously detached from reality. There was just us three in the car, moving along, swallowed up by the black night. 'She was OK when I saw her,' I said. 'She was the best she's been for ages.'

'She called herself an ambulance,' said my mother. 'She told them the world was going to explode.'

The hospital was due to be closed, but one ward was still open, a set of small square lights below the turrets, in the blank walls of dark Victorian brick. 'The new unit's not opening till next month,' my mother told me, as we turned the corner of the creepy winding drive and pulled into the deserted car park. 'In the meantime, there's nowhere else for her to go.'

As I switched the engine off Juliette woke up. 'Turn the sound down,' she said. 'Turn the cameras the other way.'

I opened the car door and my mother and I looked at each other as the light came on. I saw the pain in her eyes. 'They'll know what to do,' she said.

We spoke to someone at Reception then walked up a bleak stone staircase. Juliette went ahead with my mother.

'Who have I come as?' she asked again.

'You have come as yourself,' said our mother.

For a hysterical moment I wanted to laugh. 'Fat chance of that in our family,' I might have shrieked. But I walked silently behind them, carrying a plastic bag full of Juliette's clothes.

At the top of the stairs a door was opened by a male nurse.

My mother took Juliette's arm and propelled her towards him. 'I am her mother,' she said.

A second of hushed silence, the drumbeat of expectant music as the mystery figure reveals herself.

'Right,' the nurse said, clearly wearied by another late-night lunatic, with accompanying relatives to pacify. 'Come into the office.'

It was a tiny grey room with a cluttered desk and plastic holders full of curling leaflets on understanding your medication and helplines to call if the mental strain of being nuts was all too much for you.

Juliette sat on a plastic chair. She still did not know who she was.

The doctor came in, wanting 'background'.

My mother is good on background. She launched into a long, energetic speech outlining my father's short-comings and genetic weaknesses while Juliette sat motionless. The doctor looked at me doubtfully, perhaps wondering if there had been some mistake over who to admit. I smiled at her.

Juliette refused to count backwards from twenty or to supply the date or time. 'They're listening to me,' she whispered, when the doctor left us.

Another nurse brought us thick pale tea that none of us touched. I stood in the doorway and looked out at the day room. The television was blaring and nobody was watching it. People wandered about. A woman, hunched in an armchair, sobbed unnoticed.

'We'll take her to bed now,' said the first nurse return-ing. 'Phone in the morning.'

My mother kissed Juliette. I put my hands on her arms and said goodbye. But she did not move. She just looked at me with empty eyes and would not speak.

My mother talked all the way home. I drove through rain and darkness and her voice hammered on. I don't know what she said. I felt high, charged with energy and disbelief. I kept seeing Juliette's face when I'd entered her kitchen, hearing her high wails of fear as she clutched at me before we left her flat.

'We had to do it,' said my mother as we turned into her road. 'She hasn't eaten for three days.'

I switched off the engine.

* * *

233

'She phoned your father, you know.' My mother handed me yet another cup of coffee. 'Of course, he'll be *terrified* by the whole thing. I shall warn the hospital about him. I've already told Dr Kendrick. I said, "Of course, Juliette's father has a long history of mental illness himself." '

'That's a bit of an exaggeration,' I said uncomfortably.

'It is *not*,' returned my mother hotly. 'Dr O'Connor said to me when your father had chopped up the piano, "Your husband is ill." And, of course, I was too weak and pathetic to stand up to him then. It makes me wild when I think about it.'

'Don't go into all that again. He hasn't been diagnosed as anything. He hasn't been hospitalized.'

'Only because it was Boxing Day,' said my mother firmly. 'You know very well what he's like. Why are you defending him?'

'I'm not. The whole bloody family's barmy. We all know that. But there's no point in ranting on about it.'

'I do not rant.'

It was almost light when I got home. I felt that strange shivery high from lack of sleep and a trembling sickness from too much caffeine. I wanted to sleep for a week but I was collecting my mother again at eleven.

Guy was sprawled out in the bed. He woke as I was getting undressed. 'Mmm, I've missed you. Come and get under the duvet.'

'I feel all dirty and sticky.'

'Lovely! Nothing like an earthy woman.'

'I'm going to have a bath.'

The bathroom felt different. There was a black hair on the soap, more hair around the plug-hole. My towel was a damp, scrunched heap on the wicker basket. I ran a deep, hot bath, pouring in the remains of my relaxing bath-foam.

Before I got in, I locked the door.

The water was so hot it turned my legs lobster red, but I was frozen with fear about Juliette. I kept thinking of her lying alone in that horrible place, kept seeing the dead look in her eyes. I wrapped myself in my big towelling dressing-gown and went back up to the bedroom.

'Can you give me a cuddle?' I asked, as I climbed beneath the covers.

'I'll give you more than that.'

'A cuddle's all I want.'

And as he was giving it to me, I realized that what I really wanted was the bed all to myself.

Juliette was sitting on the edge of the bed. When she saw us her mouth opened square like a child's. There was a soundless moment while her face distorted and then she began to cry, sobbing my name over and over again.

I was grateful for the noise. I had been afraid she would be quite silent and just stare with those frightening eyes. I knelt before her, holding her cold hands. 'Don't cry,' I said. Then I gave her a tissue. Her nose was running, a glistening trail that ended in her open mouth. She began to weep more quietly, rocking back and forth, occasionally stopping to gulp in air. After a while she stopped altogether and sat contemplating me, sniffing.

Her skin was grey. But it was her hair that shocked me. Stale oil to its very ends. My mother would always remember her blank, dead face but I was riveted by the horror of that hair.

'Your hair needs washing,' I said. When she first left Sid she was always bathing and showering and shampooing. Any time you went round there she had a towel on her head. I looked at my mother. 'She must wash her hair.'

My mother was busily putting things into Juliette's locker. 'I'll talk to the nurse,' she said absently.

Juliette spoke: 'I've seen the doctor.'

My mother straightened immediately and came to sit on the bed with her. 'What did he say?' she asked eagerly.

'She,' said Juliette slowly. 'She said I've got to try to eat.'

'Good,' said my mother encouragingly. 'What else?'

'She's going to phone Daddy for me.'

'Oh!'

Juliette gave a sort of smile. 'I've got new tablets,' she said dreamily. 'She says I have an affective disorder.'

I don't know what I felt when I looked at her then. Some huge sense of loss and displacement, guilt at my rising sense of horror and recoil. This person sitting in front of me was not my sister Juliette. It was not her but I could see the place where she used to be.

Her eyes widened again and filled with tears. 'I'm afraid,' she said breathlessly. Her tongue dabbed anxiously at her dry, cracked lips.

'I think,' the words came in short bursts, 'when you get in the car,' her voice was high and trembling, 'it will explode and you'll die.'

'Don't be ridiculous,' I snapped, alarmed. 'Nothing whatsoever will happen to me.'

She was crying again. The sound of her despair twisted inside me and jarred at my fingertips. I felt so helpless. I leant out and took her hand. Her fingers were cold. 'I'm sorry,' I said. 'I didn't know.'

Was that true? I did know, really. But it was an old knowledge – one we've always lived with. Juliette is not

236

your average run-of-the mill sister. She has funny ideas, weeps and wails, gets in states. That's how she is and sometimes it's worse and sometimes it's better and the main thing is that it doesn't seem odd any more. My mother told me she was worried. But I didn't see it. Was I too selfish to look properly, or when I went to look, was it not there? 'We're all so used to how she is. It's not easy to tell.' Last night my mother had tried to let me off the hook. But all the same I should have seen.

'Don't cry,' I said again now. But as she cried on, I began to find the sound peculiarly soothing. I closed my eyes, exhaustion pressing in on me.

My mother touched my shoulder. 'I'm going to find the doctor,' she mouthed, in a stage whisper, and left us together.

When Juliette stopped crying she looked more like herself again. I rubbed my eyes and found myself wondering whether anyone would be able to tell which of us was the visitor if we both had clean hair. I was still holding her hand. It lay unresponsive against my palm. I could feel all her bones. I wanted to say something that would bring her back but I didn't know what or how. Part of me wanted to hug my sister. The rest of me, shamefully, didn't want to go anywhere near that hair.

I tried to concentrate on the road. I felt sick with tiredness and Juliette's warnings about crashes were still ringing in my ears.

My mother was talking very fast. 'She said it's a severe depressive state, a psychotic depressive state. Affective disorder. I shall have to look it up. But she says Juliette will get better once the drugs start to work. And she's going to set up a meeting with the social worker about support networks at home. Gabrielle Markham's the one with psychiatric responsibilities. I'm sure Molly knows her. I shall phone Molly as soon as I get in. She phoned me herself this morning. Of course she's very concerned . . . And I can just imagine what's going to happen when your bloody father turns up. I don't think that's going to be a very healthy combination at all. He's bound to make her worse.'

'How', I asked, stopping at a red light, my insides contorting with fury, 'could she be any worse?'

When I got in Guy was sitting reading the paper. He jumped up and put his arms around me. 'Some bloke came looking for you. I told him you were all mine.'

'What did he look like?'

'Um – don't know really. Dark hair.'

Nigel?

'Suit.'

Not Nigel. 'Was he fat?'

'No.'

Not Henry. 'What did he want?'

'He left you a letter.'

Oh, shit.

Juliette had temporarily pushed the house to the back of my mind but now, staring at this latest communiqué from the council detailing their intent to make me practically rebuild the place, it all came flooding back.

I ignored all Guy's recommendations about the best ways in which to relieve stress and went for another attempt at my own sure-fire method – screaming abuse at Nigel.

His mobile was switched off – surprise. His answer-machine at home was switched on.

I started out calmly enough, listing the problems with the bank, the squatters and the bailiffs. My voice began to vibrate a bit when I moved on to the things Nigel had failed to do: pay the bills, pay into the bank, get some bloody rent in or the bloody tenant out. And it was definitely juddering when I relayed the most recent problems with the environmental health department. But when I got down to the nitty-gritty in that I was desperate, didn't know what on earth to do and my sister had gone round the bend, I found myself screaming hysterically. I collapsed into a sobbing heap even before I put the phone down.

Guy picked me up and hugged me. 'This isn't a very good time for you, is it?' he said. 'What can I do to make you feel better?'

Afterwards I fell asleep. When I woke up, it was seven o'clock in the evening and Guy was putting a coffee on the bedside table. He got back into bed and put his arms around me. I felt suddenly hot and stifled and sat up, reaching for the mug.

'I can't spend my life in bed,' I said. 'I've got to sort things out. Though God knows how,' I added, as it all came back to me on a wave of despair.

'I thought it would lift you up a bit,' said Guy, stroking my back. 'Get your endorphins going. I had an aunt like your sister,' he went on, nuzzling at my neck. 'She was in and out of hospital all the time. They gave her electric-shock treatment dozens of times but it only lasted a few months then she'd be raving again.'

'God, how awful.'

'She was single too.'

'What are you saying?'

'Well, nothing, really. It's just that I've noticed that a lot of these batty women have one thing in common.'

'Which is?' Dislike can turn up quite quickly and grip with cold fingers around one's heart.

239

'Well, no bloke. You'll find that's half the problem. They're just not getting screwed.'

I shifted away from him. His hairy arms had lost their appeal. 'When are you going back to London?'

Louise was both fascinated and appalled.

'It's terrible,' she said several times.

'I know,' I said. 'Actually, I can hardly bear to talk about it.'

I had now told Juliette's story a dozen times. As the word got round, the well-meaning had been phoning up for details, making my nerve ends jangle and my skin cringe as I had to go through it all yet again. Each time my guilt deepened. It seemed so painfully obvious now how ill she'd been and how I'd let her down.

I had longed to speak to Louise, but had deliberately avoided phoning her before her doctor's appointment, not wishing to distress her with sagas of woe at a time when she was bursting with happiness.

But in the vitamins section of Broadrange she'd seen Sonia, who'd heard about it from Rowena, whom my mother had taken it upon herself to phone and update with all the gory details. Apparently Henry had waddled past during this news bulletin and had declared that he would be round to offer comfort post-haste. Which was just about all I needed.

'Tell me about Guy, then. I can't believe you've chucked him out before I've even had a chance to take a look.'

'I couldn't handle it. My sister's had a major break-down, I've got bailiffs after me, Nigel's disappeared and left me in the shit, the bank's screaming for my blood and all he could say was: "Did you know that sixty-five per cent of all men come within two minutes of penetration whereas women take an average of twenty minutes," ' I sighed. 'I mean, it's all very well but there are other issues in life apart from achieving ever-greater sexual heights.'

'Hmm . . .' said Louise doubtfully, then added, more briskly, 'Well, he obviously wasn't the one for you long-term.'

'What about yours?' I asked.

'Oh, him!' she said, derisively. 'Just a cheating bastard. Thank God this baby's Robert's, that's all I can say.'

I said nothing.

Louise was looking at the table where I'd made a desultory start on the post. She poked a finger towards the red electricity bill. 'Cari, do you want to borrow some money?'

I hurriedly covered up my credit-card statement. How many thousands have you got? 'No, no, it's all going to get sorted soon.' Come on, Ben, don't let me down. I told her about his plan to rid me of unwelcome tenants.

'There's a letting agent in the high street,' she said. 'You could get some decent tenants with proper references.'

Who'd want a proper flat that was habitable. 'Yeah. Sure.'

'I can lend you some money, if you want.'

'I know. Thank you. I'll be OK.' *I hope.*

I shoved all the new post into a pile and hid it under my Day Book while she went to the loo. There was no point in opening it and depressing myself further. Part of me wanted to break down and confess all to Louise, share with her the full horror of my situation and beg for help. The rest felt a sense of responsibility towards my future godchild and a duty not to overburden his mother and – if I was honest – a sense of shame that it was always me who was inept with money, in debt and generally inadequate, while Louise had had the good job, flash cars and a personal pension since the day she left school.

Later I would drive, while I still could, out to Nigel's

and see what had happened to the bastard. In the meantime, I was going to focus my attention on the one and only happy event in the vicinity. 'Do you want a coffee before we go, Lou?' I called down the hall towards the bathroom.

But she appeared in the doorway looking ashen. 'We've got to go now, Cari. I'm bleeding.'

'Look, try and keep calm,' I told her, as I waited impatiently for the lights to change. 'Do you remember, this happened to Rowena and she was fine? She just had to rest for a few days and it was all OK again.'

Louise shook her head. 'I'm going to lose it, I know I am. It's my punishment for what I've done to Robert.'

'No, it isn't. It's going to be fine.'

We had the same conversation all the way to the surgery. Once through the door I gabbled at the receptionist, who disappeared into a room at the back then returned and hustled Louise off.

I felt sick. First Juliette, now Louise. I had a sudden horrible moment of panic that my mother was slumped, grey-faced and breathless, at the foot of her stairs with nobody any the wiser. Hot on the heels of this came the realization that this was precisely the sort of scenario Juliette would imagine and with which she would torture herself, which frightened me even more. 'Stop it!' I muttered to myself, ignoring the curious looks of the runny-nosed brat on the next chair.

I picked up a magazine and flicked through it. It contained articles on how to look younger, how to feel fitter, how to lose weight and how to waft around with a younger man in tow. All recommended not drinking. It used to be smoking. When I smoked, every page I turned screamed about what it would do to my wrinkles, teeth, hair, unborn baby – imagining that the cigarettes didn't kill me stone dead before I got a chance to get my leg over – heart rate and lung capacity. As soon as I gave up, everyone forgot all about smoking and started shrieking on about the dangers of alcohol, which now apparently gives you every fatal disease known to man and makes you look about a hundred while you're dying from them. No doubt if I become teetotal they'll discover that it was fresh fruit and vegetables all along that did the damage. Especially if you combined them with chocolate fingers.

I looked up. DRINK PROBLEM? screamed the poster opposite.

I looked down again, stared sourly at a photo of three women who claimed to be fifty-nine, sixty-one and seventy but who all looked a jolly sight younger than I did – a phenomenon they put down to drinking a gallon of water a day and having their eyelashes tinted. I threw down the magazine in disgust. Then I picked up *Good Housekeeping*, and stared at 'Twenty Ways with Courgettes' for about half an hour. Afterwards I couldn't have told you one of them. I kept wondering what they were doing to Louise, whether she'd emerge beaming, saying the baby was fine and it was just one of those things, or whether she would be stretchered out, blanket-covered, white-faced, to be taken to hospital to lie on some narrow bed in a corner somewhere while we waited. I couldn't bear it for her. I was sitting clenching my fists, desperately willing the tiny being inside her to hang on, my head filled with gory pictures of blood and kidney dishes and half-formed foetuses in technicolour. Rowena had a book, each page a huge colour photograph of the baby in the womb a little bigger, developing fingers and toes . . .

I jumped up and went to ask the receptionist what was happening just as Louise came down the corridor towards me. She'd been crying but, as I rushed towards her, she just shook her head and walked on towards the door. I caught up with her as she stepped outside.

'I've got to get out of here.'

'What's happened?'

'I'm not pregnant.'

I stared at her stupidly. 'You mean you've lost it?'

'No! I'm not pregnant. I never was.' Tears ran down her face again.

'What, not at all?'

'No!' It came out as a howl of anguish. 'What am I going to say to Robert?'

'Where is Robert?' I asked, when we were back in my kitchen and I'd given her a cup of tea, containing a generous pouring of brandy I'd found in a sticky old bottle at the back of the cupboard filled with cake tins I never used.

'He's at home,' she said, sniffing and gulping the tea. 'He's working there this week. He wanted to come with me but I said I'd go with you and then go back and tell him all about it. Cari, why am I in such a state? Why am I always crying these days?'

I picked up the brandy and poured the last millilitre into my own mug. 'It's all the shock of being pregnant and not pregnant. What did the doctor say?'

'He said it was probably a hormone imbalance, causing missed ovulation. He felt inside me and said I definitely wasn't pregnant and I said, "I'm bleeding," and he said, "Yes, you're having a period." ' She exploded into a series of snorting noises that were half sobs and half laughter. 'I feel so stupid. He must have thought I was completely mad.'

'But what about your stomach and getting big boobs and stuff?'

'I don't know. He just went on about too much

progesterone and these things happen, and there was no reason to suppose I wouldn't get pregnant next time with no problem.'

'Well, there you are, then,' I said comfortingly, although I felt ridiculously disappointed too. 'Now you know that you want a baby you can try for a proper one.'

Louise stared at me, her bottom lip stuck out like it had when she was seven. 'I don't want a proper one,' she said crossly. 'I want the one I thought I had.'

I drove her home. She kissed me and walked up the path. The front door opened and Robert appeared in the doorway. I saw him hold his arms out and Louise walk into them. In my last glimpse of them, he was hugging her tight and stroking her hair.

Nigel's truck was in the drive but his car was gone and so was Gloria's. I parked in the lane, climbed over the gate and crunched across the gravel to peer through the garage window. Empty.

I went and knocked at the door but it was obvious that the place was deserted except for Sam, their ageing, smelly Labrador, who came waddling round the corner and sniffed, in his usual disgusting fashion, at my crotch. 'You revolting animal!' I shoved him away and wandered around to the back of the house. A fat brown pony was standing under a tree in the paddock. A child's bicycle lay discarded beside the barbecue. Several empty beer cans littered the picnic table.

I peered in through the french windows. This was not the plumped-cushions-fresh-flowers sitting-room that Gloria usually kept. More beer cans on the table next to the sofa. Newspapers on the floor. But no sign of life. I wondered where they all were. Neither of the animals looked starving but the place had a neglected, abandoned air about it that I'd never known before.

I went back to my car and rooted about for something to write on. Ironically it was Trevor's final invoice. Locating a biro from the bottom of my handbag I scrawled, 'Urgent! Nigel, please phone. Am in deep shit', and pushed it through the letter box.

As I walked back down the drive, an old man in blue overalls came towards me carrying a bucket. We stopped and looked at each other. 'They've gone away,' he said flatly.

'Where? How long for?'

He shook his head. 'All they says to me is feed the animals and cut the hedges.'

'Who said? Nigel?'

The old man shook his head again. 'Only saw her.' He began to move on. 'Took all the kiddies' toys with her,' he said, over his shoulder. 'Didn't look to me like she was coming back.'

When I got in I went straight to bed. I hadn't yet changed the sheets, and there was still a whiff of Guy's aftershave on the pillows. Part of me felt a pang. The rest knew I would cringe from his hairy, sweaty masculinity.

It was still light. I could hear cars going by, shouts of laughter as feet tramped past my gate. I curled up into a ball, my arms wrapped around myself. Why would Nigel go away without telling me? Nothing felt safe.

I longed for sleep but I lay awake for a long time. As darkness came my head filled. Graham's stony disapproval, Trevor's disdain, Juliette, unreachable, crying alone in her hospital bed . . .

I wanted to turn the light on, but I couldn't move. I lay stiff and still, watching car headlights cross the ceiling. With each passing hour, fresh fears came rolling in.

Chapter Twenty-six

Neil stirred his coffee. 'God would help you, you know,' he said. 'If you opened up your heart, you could overcome anything. "Perfect love casteth out fear." John, chapter four, verse eighteen.'

I wiped a hand over my tearstained face. 'I'm sorry I haven't got any biscuits,' I said.

'I don't want any,' said Neil, looking hard at me. 'What else is wrong?'

'Everything,' I said miserably. 'Everything is a complete mess.'

'Go and have a bath,' said Neil. 'It will make you feel better.'

'I thought I'd found love the other day,' I told him. 'Well, better than love. I thought I'd found passion. But it was only sex.'

Neil cleared his throat and went to the sink to fill his bucket. 'You're tired,' he said. 'When you've had your bath get yourself back to bed.'

'What is passion, Neil?'

'Forget all that,' he said. 'The fruit of the spirit is love, joy, peace, long-suffering, gentleness, goodness, faith . . .'

'Right.' I wasn't sure I was quite so comfortable with this Bible-spouting Neil.

There was an odd light in his eyes as he continued, '. . . meekness, temperance.' Was it my imagination or was he looking pointedly at the empty Frascati bottle on the draining-board? 'Galatians, chapter five, verse twenty-two.'

'I don't think it's too much to ask,' I went on doggedly, determined to have my say. 'I need someone in my life to share things with but I want them to move me, to excite me . . .' Carry me away from here, pay off my debts . . .

'What you need', he lifted his bucket of soapy water and prepared to go outside, 'is a friend.'

Well, I know God moves in mysterious ways but did he have to bring Henry to me at that particular moment?

No sooner had Neil spoken those words than who should waddle up the steps and press a podgy finger to the bell? Neil opened the door. 'There,' he said, pleased, as I groaned. 'You've got a visitor.'

'Oh dear,' said Henry, taking in my dishevelled appearance and blotchy face. 'What's happened to you, my love?'

'I came', he said later, when I'd offered a rather pathetic-sounding and somewhat-edited catalogue of woes, 'to say how sorry I am about your sister. Thought I'd just pop in on my way to work, see if there's anything I can do.' His plump cheeks wobbled with concern.

'Thanks, Henry. She's better than she was.'

'Are you all right?'

'Just tired, that's all.'

We sat in silence.

'Um, look, would you like to go for a drink or something? Cheer you up a bit, you know.'

He fiddled with his jacket and I examined my shirt

button as I formulated my stressed-out, overburdened, thank-you-very-much-but-I've-no-time-for-anything-like-that excuses, but I was saved a reply by the postman marching up the steps outside and slotting a wodge of sinister-sounding envelopes through the letter box. They fell on the floor. Thwack. We both looked round.

'You stay there,' said Henry kindly, rising from the table and heading towards today's bundles of delight, while I clutched at my stomach and tried to quell the feelings of dread that were already churning about inside it.

'Oh, I'll look at them later,' I said, in what was supposed to be a casual tone, but which definitely had a tell-tale squeak to it, but Henry seemed reluctant to put the envelopes down. He was staring at the top one with wide-eyed disbelief.

'You've got a letter from Head Office here!' he said excitedly.

'Head Office?'

'Yes, look!' He held out an envelope that bore the Broadrange logo.

'What . . . ?' he started to ask, then, blushing, changed it to: 'Oh, sorry, I didn't mean to pry . . .'

'It's all right. It's from Bill, I expect,' I said, feeling immediately cheerier.

Henry stared at me, wonder-struck. 'Mr Winterbar?'

'Yep. He was going to find out about an idea for me.' I took the letter from Henry's reverent hands, excitement bubbling up in me now too. 'Wasn't that good of him to remember after all those gins?' I said.

Henry nodded mutely.

I looked at the envelope. This could be it. The turning point. The first real step on the road to me getting out of this mess.

Bill might be about to tell me that he'd spoken to the

rest of the board and they were about to launch the On the Shelf range of products forthwith and make me a mint. Once Charlie-boy heard about it, he'd snap up my book and I'd be made.

Maybe, *maybe*, Bill had already told Charlie-boy when they played golf on Sunday. Perhaps at this very minute Charlie-boy was writing to me too. Maybe there was already a letter waiting in that pile, begging me to send in my manuscript.

With trembling fingers, I tore open the envelope. Henry watched me, eyes bulging.

It was typed on Broadrange headed paper, addressed to Ms C. Carrington. '*Dear Cari, I've now had an opportunity to speak to our Trading Director . . .*' The letter was remote and polite. Its tone bore no resemblance to the Bill I'd sat on a bar stool with. '*. . . feels that . . . while a good idea in principle . . . something which will evolve naturally with prepared meal-solutions already featuring nutritional information including calorie counts . . . problems regarding exclusivity . . . not an idea that could remain unique to Broadrange . . . ease with which rival stores could adopt similar product . . . sorry to disappoint you in this instance . . . welcome any future innovations . . . thank you for your interest in Broadrange . . .*'

'What does he say?' Henry could not contain himself any longer.

I put the letter down, before it got blurry. 'He says, "Sod off, Cari, your idea's crap." '

Henry looked horrified. 'He doesn't!'

I handed it to him.

He read it and looked back at me misty-eyed. 'What about the handwritten bit at the bottom?'

'I didn't see that.' I took the letter back. Beneath his signature Bill had scrawled, '*Great to meet you. Don't forget to send your book to Charlie. I've told him it's coming.'*

'Well,' said Henry, 'you obviously made an impression.'

'Yeah.'

Who had I been kidding? Of course no self-respecting supermarket would want any idea of mine. Any more than Charlie-boy would want my pitiful attempts at a book. I put my head in my hands.

'Who's Charlie?' asked Henry.

'Some publisher in London.'

'And are you going to send your book to him?'

'No point. That's crap too.'

'Well, Mr Winterbar obviously thinks there's a point or he wouldn't have mentioned it. Or given you a personal introduction . . .'

'It doesn't work like that,' I said, thinking that the golfing crony of someone you once got drunk with was not the most promising of contacts.

'Well, if Mr Winterbar says—'

'Yes, thank you, Henry. I know you mean well but you don't understand. Look I'm having a bit of a bad day . . .' For God's sake, *leave*, Henry. Go to work. Go anywhere. Just bugger off.

'Yes, I know. I'm sorry. But perhaps if you send your book off it will cheer you up. Give you a focus, something to look forward to.'

'Yeah, another letter saying it's crap.'

'That's not the attitude. Look, where is it? I'll post it for you now on my way in. It'll be on his desk on Monday.'

'It's not even typed.'

'I'll get Rosie to see to it.'

'I haven't finished the letter.'

'I'll sit here while you do.'

251

'Why are you being so nice to me?'

Henry blushed again. 'That's what friends are for.'

He made us both a coffee while I fetched the notepad, found the letter, and copied out the address Bill had given me. 'There,' I said, 'he'll throw it in the bin but who cares?'

'Come on,' said Henry, 'look on the bright side. Now, where's the actual book?'

'It's not a book yet,' I said. 'It's just the beginning.'

'Well, where is it?'

'Under there somewhere.' I indicated the mass of papers, bills and tottering pile of unopened letters covering the table. We both started to move bits of paper about. All we found were red bills and frightening-looking official brown envelopes.

Neil came back in and put his mug on the side.

'This is my punishment,' I wailed. 'Everything is crumbling around me because I'm such a dreadful person.'

'No, no,' said Henry soothingly, still digging among the court orders. 'It will all be all right.'

' "The souls of the righteous are in the hand of God," ' said Neil, and started to rinse out his cloths, ' "for though they be punished in the sight of men, yet is their hope full of immortality." Wisdom of Solomon,' he told Henry.

'Very nice,' Henry replied.

The front door was still ajar. I'd just located the manuscript stuck between the pages of my Day Book when, over Henry's shoulder, I saw a figure stop on the pavement outside and turn towards the house. Then as they mounted the first step I realized who it was. 'Tell her I'm in bed,' I squeaked, thrusting the book into his hands and rushing upstairs. 'Let yourselves out,' I called.

I ripped off my clothes, dived beneath the duvet and

closed my eyes. I heard Neil's voice going on at length. Then Henry calling, 'I'm off, Cari. I'll get this typed up and see you later.' The front door closed and then I heard lots more of Neil, with her voice interjecting from time to time.

The bed was warming up, I felt sleepy and heavy. Hopefully she'd go and I could just have a bit of a sleep, then get up, get washed and start trying to decide what to do. Must find Nigel . . .

I heard the front door close and then silence. Good – they'd both gone. I let myself drift.

'Cari!' My mother was in the doorway. 'What are you doing in bed at this time of the morning? You've got to get up.'

My eyes opened wide at the injustice of this remark. 'I couldn't sleep. I've been awake all night!'

My mother glared at me. 'I've just cleaned your sink. It was disgusting.'

When I'd dragged myself back downstairs in my dressing-gown, she said sternly, 'I came round to tell you that we need to go and sort out Juliette's flat, but perhaps we'd better start on this place first.' She looked round the kitchen and then at me. 'Look at the state of you! For heaven's sake, go and have a bath or something, and what on earth's going on in that window-cleaner's head? All those quotations. What do they say about *him*? That's what I'd like to know. We had all that with your father. Hadn't been inside a church for years and suddenly it was "What God has joined together let no man put asunder." The hypocrisy of it!' My mother gave a savage snort and banged down the Ajax cream.

I sat down at the table. 'What are you talking about?' I asked weakly.

It turned out that my father had arrived at Juliette's

bedside bearing fruit and flowers and a rather sickly get-well card, had been rapturously greeted by my sister, and had then gone on to explain to the nurses that the reason Juliette had gone doo-lally again was that she had never got over my mother leaving him twelve years previously. Whereupon my mother had gone one step further. She had hauled the doctor away from another bed and insisted that both she and a visiting consultant listen to a full run-down of all my father's acts of mental cruelty over the years and how she'd been a nervous wreck for months (just imagine!) after she'd finally gathered the courage to leave and taken her poor defenceless children with her. (I had been twenty at the time and had left home two years earlier.) At this juncture, Juliette had had the screaming ab-dabs and both of my parents had been thrown out of the hospital.

My mother was now frothing at the mouth, determined to get Juliette out of there and under her own caring wing, and had apparently spent the previous afternoon and evening phoning everyone from Social Services to our local MP demanding that my father be banned from interfering with her. Quite why she felt so vitriolic towards Neil – apart from the obvious fact of him having a penis – wasn't clear, but she was in no mood to be questioned or trifled with.

The up-side of this outpouring of fury was that she was cleaning at the same time as yelling at me. As she detailed my father's emotional and intellectual incompetence she was scrubbing away at the taps like a woman possessed. She went on in high rage down the work-surfaces, barking, 'Move that lot!' as she grabbed a fresh J-cloth and headed, still enraged, for the table. I gathered up all the post in my arms, stood aside as she steamed across it, snarling, 'He's got a bloody nerve,'

254

and jumped away as she started jabbing at the backs of the chairs, crying, 'Stuck at the anal level.'

It was when she started knocking the stuffing out of the cushions on the window-seat that I decided to call a halt. 'Stop!' I yelled. 'This isn't going to help anybody.'

She glared at me, her chest heaving. 'We've got till the weekend to get her flat ready. Meeting with the social worker eleven on Monday. Bring her home in the afternoon.'

'OK. I've got to visit house, find Nigel, placate bank, do post,' I said, finding I was gasping and talking in shorthand myself.

My mother sniffed. 'Well, you'd better get dressed, then.'

I was just putting the plug into the bath when the doorbell rang. I stiffened then shot back down the hall, sliding sideways into the kitchen where my mother was repacking her handbag. A quick glimpse *en route* of shape-through-glass suggested someone tall but not hefty.

'Get rid of him!' I gasped.

My mother looked up. 'Get rid of who?'

'At the door. Say I'm out. Or dead.'

My mother closed her eyes and exhaled. 'Are you asking me to tell lies for you?'

The doorbell rang again.

'Please! Please just say I'm not here.'

My mother glared meaningfully at me and sighed some more. 'I'm not happy about this.'

I sank on to the floor by the window-seat and pulled my robe more tightly about me. 'I'll tell her when I see her,' I heard my mother proclaim, and then the front door closed.

I raised my head and snatched a quick look at the back of Trevor descending my steps.

She was now standing over me breathing heavily. 'He says you owe him money. Cari!'

I turned back to look at her. She had her hands on her hips and her I-will-keep-on-until-I-get-an-answer expression fixed firmly on her face.

'Cari! I'm talking to you. *What's going on?*'

I told her as little as possible, blaming Trevor's appearance largely on Nigel and a misunderstanding. She gave me the full range of her most telling breathing noises, a short lecture on not being a rescuer and Nigel being responsible for himself, and then she dropped it.

She left when I'd promised faithfully to meet her at the flat at ten the next morning and had sworn to God I would not let my father 'get away with anything'. Since I imagined that he was, at this minute, lying in a darkened room in the recovery position, this last vow seemed largely unnecessary but I couldn't cope with setting her off again.

Finally alone, I stood in the middle of my strangely scrubbed-looking kitchen, gazing at the heap of envelopes piled accusingly in the centre of the now dust-free table. I resisted the urge to crawl back into bed and continued with Option Two of the Cari Carrington School of Avoiding Facing Things. When the bath was neck-high with bubbles I climbed in, closed my eyes, and heard myself go, 'Aaaa,' aloud, as if I were in some put-your-feet-up-and-have-an-unspeakable-hot-milky-drink commercial.

I lay and stared at the taps, cursing myself for not redirecting my mother towards the limescale problem rather than stopping her cleaning altogether, and closed my eyes against the grim reality that was my financial position.

They all appeared accusingly in the dimness. Graham, Mr Dandruff from the council, Trevor, bailiffs, Ben . . .

The water was getting tepid, my eyelids were heavy. Really, I should face things, get a grip, get organized . . . but I was tired. Tomorrow I would do all sorts of things.

But today I simply had to go to sleep.

Chapter Twenty-seven

Juliette's flat looked even madder empty than it had with her in it. 'God, where do we start?' I said, looking at the piles of books, magazines, clothes, charts, notebooks, cups and glasses that covered every surface.

'You just get on with it,' said my new, brisk mother, dressed for the occasion in a blue-and-white striped shirt – sleeves rolled purposefully up – and a pair of baggy white trousers. 'Come on.' She shoved a roll of black bin-liners into my hands and pushed me towards the kitchen. 'Throw everything away. We'll go shopping for more later.'

I looked at her as she strode around the living room, gathering up magazines, and suddenly had the strangest feeling. It was like the sort of homesickness I'd suffered as a child if I slept in any bed other than mine. All these years I'd wished my mother would stop asking me how I felt every five minutes and just help out with the ironing, but now, suddenly, I missed it. I didn't like all this tidying. I wanted her back in flowing cheesecloth and tinkling beads, showing endless fascination for the inner workings of my psyche.

'This is all dreadful,' I said, experimentally.

She did not look up. 'Get a move on.'

I opened the fridge and stepped back. A pool of brown liquid had gathered at the bottom. As I looked, there was the plop, plop of further brown drips joining it. The shelves were packed full. Every available inch was taken up with apples and bananas, apricots, plums and lettuces in varying stages of decay. I pulled a – thankfully still sealed – Cellophane bag towards me. The label said, 'Ready-washed spinach.' The contents had turned to brown sludge. Thank the Lord my sister was a quasi-vegetarian when she went round the bend and not still in her cold-mackerel-and-pasta phase. Luckily for a chronic retcher like myself, rotten fruit and vegetables have a sweet, composty, farmyardy smell, which is just about bearable, and I was able to get the contents of the fridge into one of the black bags without throwing up.

I searched in her cupboards for cleaning stuff and found dozens of unopened bottles of bleach, disinfectant and spray-on kill-everything liquid. I squirted the one that claimed to zap salmonella *and* listeria *and* e. coli all round the inside of the fridge and mopped away until it glowed with hygiene. Then I washed my hands and went in search of my mother.

She was flushed and breathing heavily, her arms full of clothes. She had transformed the living room: the books were back on the shelves, magazines in neat piles on the coffee table, the sofa clear, its cushions nicely plumped. When she saw me she put the clothes down on the floor. 'Look at this.' She handed me an A4 pad, picked up the bundle again and left the room.

The writing was so scrawled that it was almost unrecognizable as Juliette's but I could make out most of the words: '*Cari came round this evening . . . They've put a bug in here somewhere . . . I could hear them playing back our conversation. Peggy, Margaret, Mother, Maud. Mad Auntie Maud. I may as well be dead. I may as well be dead. I may as well be'* . . .

My mother had come back into the room.

'I thought she was really good that night,' I said to her, finding I was trembling. 'We were laughing.'

'She could always dissemble when she wanted to.' There was an odd, broken tone to her voice.

I was gripped by fear. 'I didn't know,' I said, guilt sitting sickly in my stomach. 'I had no idea.'

My mother did not answer. When I looked up I saw she was in tears. 'Don't,' I said, shaken. I put my arms round her, feeling how strange and awkward it was, but she hugged me back, tightly, fiercely, and I felt her warmth.

'I love you both so much,' she said, in a funny, muffled voice.

'And I love you,' I said, wanting to cry too.

She let me go and blew her nose. 'Come on. Let's go shopping. I've a feeling your bloody father will be round here next.'

But the only other person I saw was Henry.

He turned up minutes after I'd got home. I wasn't going to open the door but no one else makes that shape through the glass so I let him in, relieved it wasn't the even-heavier mob come to strip the house.

'Did it!' He beamed, bouncing up and down on the doorstep. 'It took Rosie quite a long time. She had a bit of trouble with your writing but she said it's ever so good and it's all been sent off.'

'Thanks.'

'First step to fame, eh?'

'Yeah. Sure.'

'Fancy going for that drink yet?'
'Still not quite myself, Henry.'
'Oh, right. I understand.'
' 'Bye, Henry.'
Thank you.

Chapter Twenty-eight

Another soft summer's evening. I was half-way down the bottle of Frascati before I realized the irony of my taste in music. The CD player was somehow set on repeat and I couldn't drag myself off the window-seat to alter it. So I sat and listened to all those beautiful voices from seventy-five years of the BBC, over and over again, singing to me about what a perfect day they'd had.

As the alcohol numbed me I felt my senses rise and the music seep into my pores. I felt touched by an exquisite sense of loneliness. I had no one to be glad I'd spent the day with. Louise was with Robert, my mother had gone to Molly's, even Juliette was lost to me, turning to the voice inside her head for company.

I wanted someone, anyone, to come and pick me up. But Guy would just want to shag me, Nigel would let me down, Martin would be all the things that Martin had always been, and Ben . . . I didn't really know Ben. Hah! That was probably the appeal.

I laughed and poured myself another glass of wine. A small, uneasy part of me wondered if my genetic heritage wasn't finally coming home to roost. Maybe they'd find me in days to come wandering around the house muttering . . .

I wanted to forget *my*self.

I looked at the pile of envelopes on the table, the flashing of the answerphone I still hadn't replayed. I thought about the debts and the council and Gary the druggie and not having a job and having to pay off Martin and having let my sister down and been rotten to my mother . . . The song was coming to an end. All the voices mingled. Do you reap what you sow?

I poured another drink.

I was lurching a bit as I got ready for bed. Twice I dropped the toothpaste. Drinking on an empty stomach – that was the problem. I put a hand on it: not only was it empty, except for the Frascati, it was flatter too. I looked at the scales. Must weigh myself in the morning – see if all that bonking had paid off.

As I was scrubbing my teeth the phone rang. I paused, mouth full of froth, and listened to the answerphone cut in. Then I spat it all out and ran for the phone. 'I'm here! I'm here!' I said, startled to hear his voice. Ben was the last person I'd expected. I listened as he repeated what he'd said. 'Tonight?' I asked stupidly. 'What's tonight?'

With hindsight it wasn't one of my best ideas, but I wanted to see those miserable bastards who had caused me all this trouble get their comeuppance. I wanted to be in on the action. I felt reckless and brave.

I was hoping that Ben himself might decide to come along and watch.

I was pissed.

So there I was, at two in the morning, on the other side of Turpin Road, crouched down behind the wall, feeling like George from the Famous Five. True, she'd have had a torch and Timmy the dog, and all I had was my mobile phone and what was left of the bottle of Frascati decanted into an empty brandy miniature, but I felt like an intrepid investigator, about to witness the darkest secrets of criminal underlife.

There wasn't a soul about. I'd seen one old drunk weaving his way along on my walk down here – I'd been weaving a bit myself – and now I'd been here for what felt like hours and all I'd seen was one bloke (not Ben, sadly): he'd gone up to 106 and rapped on the door. An upstairs window had opened, a head had come out and shouted something. A moment later the front door opened and the bloke disappeared inside. He still hadn't come out. The lights were on upstairs and I could hear the distant cha-thump-cha of the obligatory head-banging music, but, apart from that, nothing to report.

I was beginning to yawn and shift my cold, stiff limbs about, wondering whether perhaps Ben's 'mate' had got it wrong and I'd done too much reading as a child, when I saw another bloke sauntering along the pavement.

And then, my heart pounding with the thrill of it (Guy would have been pleased!) I saw all the others, black shapes creeping along the railings several houses back.

Bloke One was now going up the steps and banging on the door. Again the window opened overhead. This time some longer exchange went on, but I couldn't make out the words. Then the front door opened and it seemed that the bloke was going to get in, but the door started to shut again. There was a bit of a scuffle, the door slammed and then all hell broke loose!

The shapes all came running up the road towards the house – I could see their dark padded jackets as they darted beneath the street-light. Two of them leapt up the steps and charged at the front door with a metal pole. There was a splintering, crashing sound as the door caved in and they all pounded inside.

I stood up in alarm, staring at my front door hanging

264

drunkenly off its hinges. Even from across the road, I could hear the bangs and thumps and shouts coming from within. Up the road, a dog barked. Then a white police van careered round the corner and screeched to a halt. Simultaneously, upstairs, there was an explosion of breaking glass as the big front window shattered. Something flew out and crashed to the pavement.

My excitement gave way to horror. The place was going to be completely smashed up! Oh, my God, what would Graham and the council say?

Out of the van came two more padded jackets. They ran up the steps and through the open doorway, the first one aiming a hefty kick at the sagging front door for good measure as he went. Before I knew what I was doing I had dropped my bottle and was running across the street shrieking, 'Stop that! Don't break it any more!'

They'd disappeared by the time I entered the wreckage of the hallway. The bare lightbulb was swinging crazily like something from the worst sort of late-night film. I stood there, knee-deep in fag ends and empty lager cans. The door to Gary's flat was closed and silent but more kicking-in-of-wood sounds emanated from above.

'Stop!' I screeched again, as a shaven-headed violent-criminal type came tearing down the stairs towards me, with a padded jacket in hot pursuit.

'Fucking move!' the VC snarled, shoving me aside. I flew back, hit the wall and slid down it. The padded jacket stampeded over me as he rushed after his prey.

Overhead, a stream of obscenities punctuated with crashes and thumps suggested that the occupants were objecting to being arrested. There was more smashing glass and a couple of body-sized thuds. I scrambled to my feet, head ringing, and headed for the foot of the stairs.

I had to leap back and cower against Gary's door as a

thundering of feet heralded the approach of half a dozen assorted bodies being frogmarched down the stairs and out through the front door.

Behind them, swaying and staggering into the wall, almost pulling his escort with him, came the delightful spectacle I recognized as Gary's stepfather. He crashed into the banister above me and for a horrible moment I thought he was going to vomit all over me, but he strained away from the padded hand that gripped his arm and a pair of red, bleary eyes met mine. 'Ah shtop-fuckish wassah zeesh,' he slurred, slumping to his knees. He was unceremoniously hauled to his feet.

'That's the lot. Bring her!'

I looked round to see who they were talking about. As I did so, the door behind me swung open and I almost fell backwards. I grabbed the doorframe and twisted round to find myself looking up into the face of my tenant – dear pay-your-rent Gary. He stuck his head out into the hall, eyes staring wildly, hair on end, so emaciated that his forehead and cheekbones stuck out like ledges. 'Got it coming,' he said, to nobody in particular. Then, as a padded jacket suddenly lunged at him from nowhere, he grasped my arms and, with surprising strength, yanked me into the fetid interior of his flat and shut the door after us.

Jesus Christ!

'Let me out!' I cried shrilly into the darkness, my fingertips jarring painfully as adrenalin raced around my body. Gary had let me go, and I could feel him shuffling about near me. For a split second not only my life flashed before my eyes but that ghastly scene in *Silence of the Lambs* where she's stumbling about in the dark, knowing that somewhere nearby is that bloke who wants to make a dress out of her skin.

Just as I was contemplating a really good scream, a

light came on. Gary was standing over a home-made lamp constructed from a 100-watt lightbulb stuck in the neck of a bottle. It threw out one harsh yellow circle of illumination. Its great thick cable trailed away into the darkness and piles of putrid best-not-to-look-too-close.

I fixed my attention on the figure in front of me. 'Gary! I want to go out!'

But Gary was busy. Working at great speed, he was slotting thick planks of wood into great metal bracket-things either side of the door. 'Fucking conspiracy,' he muttered, as he heaved another massive beam into place.

Outside, someone had already started to hammer at the door. 'Open up!'

Gary was across the room now, manhandling a decrepit sofa towards the door. As he came back into the glare of the bulb I could see the sweat beaded all over his unhealthy white face. 'Please let me go,' I begged.

He stopped, facing me, but his glazed eyes fixed on a point somewhere above my left eyebrow. 'It's them,' he said. 'If we don't stay here, they'll get us.'

'They' were now beating at the door in earnest.

Gary shoved the sofa into its final position and began to drag a table across the room while I stood wringing my hands, concentrating hard on not breathing too deeply or letting my eyes stray into the corners.

The pounding on the door intensified. '*Police! Open this door now!*'

Gary stopped and looked across at me. 'Are you one of them?'

'*No!*' I squeaked. 'No, no, no! I'm . . .' I made my best effort at a sickly, ingratiating smile '. . . I'm one of you.'

Gary nodded. He didn't seem about to kill me after all. He sat down on a huge pile of clothes and lit a cigarette, indicating with a jerk of his head that I should sit down too. I looked around. The floor was a definite health risk and there was nothing else that wasn't being used as a barricade.

Not wanting to upset him, I squatted on my heels and leant against the wall. 'We could climb out of the window,' I ventured.

Gary shook his head. 'They're fucking everywhere,' he said. 'They watch me all the time.'

I thought about speaking to him like actresses do in films when held hostage by psychopaths, in casual I'm-not-scared tones to befriend him, or soft, wide-eyed social-worker ones, designed to reduce him to tearful reminiscence of the indignities of his childhood – but he wouldn't have heard me above the noise.

They seemed to be attacking the door with some sort of battering ram now. There was a series of loud, splintering noises but Gary's planks held firm. They were clearly going to get in and rescue me fairly soon, though, so I breathed deeply (not too deeply: oh, how I longed for my lavender oil) and volunteered a smile in Gary's direction. He looked at me suspiciously and drew deeply on his fag. It was hard to reconcile this slit-eyed wraith with the cheery spiky-haired chap I'd first met.

There was a moment's quiet outside – presumably while they considered what fresh tactics they could employ to smash my house down – but as I tried to settle myself more comfortably, my seventh sense, which is highly tuned for this very purpose, sent all the hairs on my arms to an upright position, and my back hurt with the spasm that ran down it.

I turned my head. There it was, only inches away.

A fucking great spider.

I screamed and leapt to my feet, running across the room with such force and speed that I went full tilt into Gary, and ended up a tangled heap with him on top of his festering clothes. He gave a sort of howl and tried desperately to pull his arms and legs out from under me.

Across the room I stared back at the huge body and eight great legs, and screamed some more. In fact, by now I couldn't stop. The full horror of the thick, unwashed fug of the room closed in on me and, as I struggled to my feet, I screamed the bloody place down. Gary had freed himself now and was gasping, panting and crawling about the room like a wounded animal.

Outside, it sounded as if the whole of the Eastford police force were kicking the door in.

I screamed on.

Suddenly, one of the beams crashed down, a padded jacket had a leg through the gap and was clambering over the sofa. Then the room was full of them and Gary was handcuffed while I stood there sobbing.

'Get the girlfriend.' One took hold of my arm. The rest of the planks were wrenched from the door. As the doorway reappeared the man holding me pushed me towards it.

'I'm not,' I gulped, 'he pulled me in here.'

He ignored me.

'What they all on?' I heard one say behind me.

'Box of syringes here, Gov.'

I kept trying to explain myself all the time I was being marched into the hall.

'What are you doing?' I could hear my voice, unnaturally high and wobbly as we all went down the steps. 'I don't live here,' I pleaded, as we reached the pavement. 'I was just watching.'

Lights had gone on next door and further up the street. The van doors were open, the jacket put one hand on my head and started to push me into the back.

'No! *No!*' I screamed, going rigid, wondering hysterically if this time I'd really overdone the Frascati and was hallucinating. This surely could not be happening to me. 'I'm not one of them. It's my house!'

I heard one of the jackets laugh, and the one holding me said, 'Yes, love. You can tell us all that down at the station.'

I found myself sitting on a narrow seat opposite a girl with dirty blond hair, vicious black eyeliner and her front teeth missing. She fixed me with a poisonous look.

'All right!' The jacket sitting next to her banged on the partition separating us from the driver.

We drove off. My heart was pounding and I was afraid I might be sick. I put my hot head in my hands in utter disbelief. I had been attacked, held prisoner, terrified beyond all belief and now I was being arrested!

I nearly slid off my seat as we went sharply round a bend. In the corner of the van, Stepfather threw up.

'Cup of tea.'

'I hate tea,' I said petulantly.

'Coffee?'

I nodded.

'Get her a coffee.'

'Black,' I said.

I glared at the two figures sitting opposite me. So far the sergeant had been quite friendly and avuncular, the policewoman stony-faced.

'Can I talk now?' I said. 'I am not a drug-dealer or a tenant. I am the owner of the house.'

The sergeant smiled. 'I see, madam. Very good. You'll be pleased to know we've got a representative from the electricity board here with us tonight. Small matter of the metering being tampered with. I expect they'd like to interview you next.'

He disappeared – presumably to establish whether my name was on the deeds of Turpin Road or whether I was suffering from the sort of delusions you pump into your arm through a needle. I seemed to have been here hours but there was no natural light in the room and they'd taken my watch. 'Can I have my phone back?'

The policewoman looked at me disapprovingly. 'You can't use it in here.'

'There's a number in it I need. I want that phone call he offered me.'

I'd shaken my head the first time. Who was I going to phone?

Your husband? Martin? Abandoned me.

A friend? Louise? Traumatized.

A relative? Juliette? Hospitalized.

Your solicitor? Greggie? Can't understand a word he says.

What was the bloody point? Might as well save the phone call for a taxi home when this lot finally let me go.

But the hours were dragging on and it occurred to me that there was one person who could very quickly verify my story. And if it got him in the shit with his wife for being called at dawn, then tough. Who'd got me into this bloody mess in the first place?

They left me sitting in a cell-like room with a bench thing down one side. Outside the desk sergeant was trying to persuade a drunk to empty his pockets. What was that song? 'If My Friends Could See Me Now' . . .

When we got outside it was well and truly morning, bright light, birds singing, sun shining down on my filthy clothes and hair.

You'd think I'd be grateful, wouldn't you? Appreciative of him rushing away from his breakfast to get me out.

The moment I hit the air I was consumed with fury. 'Do you know what you've done? The house is wrecked!'

Ben looked at me impassively as I stood there panting with indignation. 'You wanted them out.'

'Yes! I wanted them out. And you said that if they were dealing and you tipped off your mate Tommy in the Old Bill, they'd move them on! You didn't say they'd smash the bloody place up while they were at it.'

'Well, at least they've gone. We can board it up to stop anyone getting back in and then—'

'I've got to sell it. Get some money back. Who'll want it in that state? I've got the bank manager coming tomorrow. What the bloody hell am I going to tell him?'

'We can—'

'*We*? *We*?' I was squawking now, waving my arms about like a demented scarecrow. 'You're all the same, you lot. You're as bad as bloody Nigel.'

Ben's brow darkened. He pressed his lips together and said nothing. For a moment I wondered if I'd gone too far but then rage overtook me again. 'This is a right fucking cock-up!'

'I'll drive you home.'

'I'll walk!'

I stormed off along the road. Jesus Christ! How did this *happen*? One minute I've got a comfortable non-life with a crap husband, no job and a few minor credit-card problems but nothing *serious*, the next I'm up to my ears in debt, with half the local authority on to me, the electricity board breathing down my neck, a bashed-up house I owe thousands on and any number of people longing to take me to court.

I stomped on. My eyes felt tight and shiny from lack of sleep. Soon I would have to make some decisions, but right now all I wanted to do was get into the bath and then go to bed and die. A white van pulled up beside me and a door opened. 'Get in, Cari.'

'Sod off.'

'Look, I'll help you sort it out.'

There was a split second when I might have fallen on him, weeping with gratitude but it was only fleeting.

Even so the words that were out of my mouth before I could stop them surprised even me with the depth of their bitterness. 'Go back to your bloody wife.'

I woke with swollen eyes and a thudding head. I'd spent the best part of twenty-four hours alternately crying and sleeping, trying to block out reality. Now it was Friday morning. Twenty past seven. Two hours and forty minutes before I was due to meet Graham.

Tears were already oozing down my face again. I just wanted to put my head back under the covers and sleep. But I knew I had to get up and get dressed and go and face the wreckage. I had to say, 'Sorry, Graham. I fucked up. I'll sell it and pay you back.' But I wouldn't be able to sell it all smashed up.

I wondered whether to turn up at all, whether it might not be simpler just to lock the windows and doors and stay in bed until someone came to arrest me or they sold everything over my head and kicked me out on to the pavement with a cardboard box.

Or perhaps I should go. Just breeze along and clap my hand to my mouth in horror at the sight of the trashed house and pretend to be as shocked as Graham would be. For a brief, gleefully relieved moment, I thought of a massive insurance claim and then I remembered we only had the basic buildings cover. Nigel had said the accidental-damage option was far too expensive. Not that this damage could be called accidental.

I dithered until twenty to ten. I wandered about and threw a bit of water at my body and got half dressed, then sat down on the bed again. I still hadn't decided to go when I was walking down the path. My legs just

273

seemed to take me. Before I knew it, I was driving reluctantly to Turpin Road to view the embodiment of my financial ruin.

At ten past ten I pulled up outside, steeling myself for the sight of the windowless, doorless shell that had been meant to make me a fortune. I spotted Graham immediately, briefcase in hand, engaged in earnest conversation with the old woman from next door. She was wagging her head and waving her arms about while Graham leant attentively towards her. No doubt she was filling him in with all the gory details of two nights ago. For a moment I closed my eyes in horror and nearly drove off again. Then I opened them and saw my house.

It was a 106 Turpin Road I wasn't expecting, in which every window-frame was sporting a complete pane of glass, the rubbish had been cleared and a new front door was miraculously in place.

I blinked.

Graham was now looking up and down the road. I got slowly out of the car. Had I dreamt it all? Had Nigel mysteriously returned to pull us back from the brink of disaster?

I crossed the road to where Graham was pointedly looking at his watch. 'Sorry I'm late,' I said vaguely, still looking in disbelief at the transformation.

Graham looked at me coldly. 'Shall we go in?'

'In?'

'Yes, Miss Carrington. In. I have come to view the property as we arranged.'

I looked at the new door. 'I haven't got the keys.'

Graham's face seemed to turn to stone, his eyes were little narrow flints, his nostrils flared.

'The door's been changed,' I explained, and a curl of hysterical laughter bubbled in my mouth. Come to think of it, it hadn't occurred to me to bring the keys to the old kicked-in door either.

But Graham was not amused. Graham was angry. 'Very well, Miss Carrington,' he said, appearing to do some strange little dance where he lifted himself up on his heels and swung his briefcase about. 'Then you leave me no alternative but to start on the proceedings I warned you about. Good morning!'

I looked after him stupidly as he clicked his way smartly down the pavement. 'No, it really has—' I started to call after him, all hints of laughter now dead and buried.

The old woman, who had backed off when I'd arrived, shot out of next-door again, flapping her apron. 'A right carry-on!' she snapped.

I looked at her dumbly.

'Well, perhaps that'll teach you,' she went on fiercely, 'now you've had to spend some of that rent on new windows.'

'I haven't had any rent,' I said. 'Not a penny. In fact, the house will be repossessed very soon. It's all been . . .' I could feel my chin beginning to wobble '. . . a bit of a nightmare . . .'

Come on, God, if you don't stop me bursting into tears every five minutes, I'm going to die of dehydration.

Her name was Elsie. I didn't have the heart to tell her I didn't drink tea so I sat in her kitchen and stirred the orange liquid round and round, hoping she'd get distracted long enough for me to pour it into a potted plant, of which there were many.

'Don't take on, love,' she said again. 'When you get as old as me you'll know you never trust the men with anything important. You don't let them get involved with the money. They don't know how to deal with it, love. They're all big babies at heart. And he is big, your fellow, isn't he? Was that this partner of yours putting on the front door?'

'I don't know. What did he look like?'

'Great huge chap. Short hair. Turned up in a van.'

I went guiltily round to the Superstore site. Ben wasn't there.

I phoned his mobile. It was switched off.

Ben was probably as pissed off with me as everyone else.

I got back in my car and went home.

And who was just coming down my steps?

I was past caring or hiding. I stopped in front of him and just said, 'I'm very sorry . . .' but he interrupted with one of his usual scowls.

'I've written it out like he wanted. Put it through your door.'

'What? Who wanted?'

But he was already stalking away.

'Trevor! Wait! Have you seen Nigel?'

He turned out of my gate and strode off down the road. As I fumbled with my key, I heard the slam of a van door.

On the mat was a windowed envelope with what looked like another sort of invoice thing inside. I didn't even bother to open it. There was no way I could pay it till Nigel showed up.

Where are you, you bastard?

As it happened, the answer to that burning question had been available to me for some time. When I got home, the answerphone was still flashing away and I finally decided to listen to it before exhaustion overcame me.

Nigel sounded tired and woebegone. He apologized for not calling me back sooner. He was very sorry for what I

276

was going through but he was having a few problems of his own and wouldn't be able to see me until he'd sorted them out. He gave what I think is known as a hollow laugh then explained that Gloria had left him and he was under investigation by the VAT office.

Chapter Twenty-nine

It is raining. I sit by the window. There is something pleasingly relentless about heavy rain. I like the smudging greyness of it. The feeling of being cocooned inside until it stops, the hammering of the water on the wet pavements. I don't know what to do. Perhaps if I sit here long enough, it will be done for me . . .

Someone was bashing determinedly at the door again. I was skulking equally determinedly on the floor of the kitchen. My car was hiding in a side-street some distance away. I clutched the keys and took deep breaths.

I'd finally been doing the post. So far I'd opened three envelopes.

Number one was from the bank, who had now drafted in a Mr Cox to write to me in no uncertain, legal-sounding and incomprehensible terms warning me of the dire consequences soon to befall me.

The second was Trevor's, which wasn't a final demand at all but a receipt showing he'd been paid in full. So Nigel had produced some pennies after all. Slightly cheered by this upturn in events I ripped optimistically at the third, which was a thick white envelope with a London postmark. For a wild, hopeful moment I thought it might be from the publisher – impressed rotten with

278

the Rosie-typed manuscript and solving all my problems with one swoop of his pen.

But no. It was from some solicitor. I saw the words 'Re: 106 Turpin Road' and shoved it back in the envelope. Graham and Mr Cox had obviously started on those famed 'proceedings' before I'd even read the letter warning me about them. Shit.

That was enough opening of correspondence.

Why didn't I just kill myself? Because it was easier and less messy to pass out.

I went upstairs and lay down on the bed. When I woke up I really would deal with everything. Slit open the rest of the post and decide whether to do the same to my throat. Phone the bank, explain everything and throw myself on Graham's mercy. Probably call an estate agent and find out how much this place was worth.

'You're only a house,' I told the bedroom ceiling. 'I can soon get a smaller one with what I've got left when I've paid off Martin and paid off the overdraft . . . Or a flat anyway . . . Or a rabbit hutch.' Better try and get a job too. Oh, God, better go to sleep . . .

I woke up small in a world of giants. I was the tiniest being emerged fresh and spindly from a golden egg. I clambered among monstrous cups and oceans of saucers. And then he picked me up. Held me warm and safe in the palm of his hand, choosing not to crush me.

'Get into my pocket,' he said, voice deep and warm, booming, echoing like a long fall from a dangerous cliff. He lowered me down into a deep warm cave of blue cotton. It was full of fluff, one blue-stained Polo mint in crumpled foil, a coin, a hairband. No, no, that's my pocket. It's my pocket! *Let me out!*

I sat up screaming. It was ten to seven. It took me a few minutes to work out whether that was a.m. or p.m.

After a bit of bleary-eyed examination of the light out-side the bedroom window I decided it was evening and I'd been asleep all afternoon.

I got my crumpled self downstairs and made a cup of coffee.

I looked at the envelope-laden table. 'Right!' I said out loud. 'Time to get this lot sorted.'

I looked around for my Day Book, in which I could make a morale-boosting Action List. I couldn't see it anywhere. Perhaps just a quick bath first. Just to wake me up a bit . . .

I lay in the water, reflecting that I seemed to be spending ever-increasing amounts of my life in the horizontal position. Dreams are funny things, I thought. In the past I'd made them up for Juliette, just for the pleasure of hearing her analyse them.

But truth is always stranger than fiction. Dreaming I'm trapped in my own pocket, huh?

I didn't need Juliette for this one. The details may have been a scramble of fear, stress and alcohol abuse but I recognized the warmth of that great hand. *It had been a dream about Ben.*

Chapter Thirty

I have lost my sister. She has been stripped open so all I can see is the scrawny clutching misery of her insides. The outer layers have already dropped away like rotten fruit peel. And I cannot see how we will ever be able to put them back . . .

Gabrielle had a huge beaked nose and narrow lips. She perched on the edge of her chair waiting to swoop like a vulture on our emotional scraps. She leaned forward and brought her eyeballs up close to my face. 'I can hear that you are very angry, Cari. That is a quite normal response when someone we love is ill. There is that resentment that they are not well, that they are not here for us.'

I glared at her. My mother was nodding away like one of those dogs people used to have in their back windows when they got bored with furry dice. 'Can we just get on with it?' I asked coldly, thoroughly fed up with them both.

We were supposed to be discussing Juliette's 'support network' before we picked her up and took her home. So far we'd had forty minutes of Gabrielle leering at us and making all sorts of assumptions about our 'feelings'. My mother, of course, was in her element. She'd delivered a fifteen-minute speech on 'Why Juliette's Father Is

Damaged', a ten-minute presentation on 'Why Juliette Is Damaged', which was largely the same, and then she and Gabrielle had got very animated about 'Talking to the Empty Chair'. This involved my mother holding forth at length about manipulation, addressing her comments towards a battered and stained teak-armed orange-velour-covered item of furniture in the corner of the room and which, I gathered, we were supposed to imagine had various people sitting in it. Gabrielle wagged her head up and down encouragingly throughout this display, clearly adoring my mother and loathing me, as I sighed and muttered loudly about the time it was taking.

Now she fixed me with a pitying look and said, in irritatingly slow and soothing tones, 'Well, since Juliette has been stabilized, our aim is to give support to ensure she is prevented from having another episode.' At which point my mother leapt in with some total irrelevancy about the son of a member of her pottery class who was schizophrenic and went twice a week to make hand-printed lampshades, and I switched off altogether and looked out of the window.

By the time we were rising to leave, all I knew was that someone called Marion was going to visit Juliette on Tuesdays and Fridays to 'befriend and support', and I had been offered the opportunity to sit in a circle every second Wednesday with Gabrielle and other unfortunate relatives of the insane 'exploring my anger'.

'No, thank you,' I said, through gritted teeth, picturing my hands around her scraggy throat.

'She's very skilled,' said my mother brightly as we crossed the car park, 'I think she's got the measure of your father.'

'You made him sound like a raving lunatic,' I said crossly.

My mother beamed.

Juliette looked pale but her hair was clean and she smiled at me. 'Can't wait to get out of here,' she said. While my mother was engaged in dialogue with the nursing staff, she rolled her eyes and added, 'I've got lots to tell you.'

I was glad to get out of there myself. There was something profoundly disturbing about wandering among such mental torment. These were not jolly lunatics oblivious to their saner surroundings, grinning village idiots or even dangerous axe-swinging psychopaths. They all looked so sad, so lost, so frightened. I did not want Juliette in that place. I did not want any of us there.

Back in Juliette's flat, my mother made her tea. Juliette was still smiling. 'It was really weird, Cari. I thought I was part of a film. I thought they were making a documentary about me. When you left last time, I was convinced they'd put a microphone in your handbag.' She laughed. 'I can't believe it, really.'

My mother fussed about with the tea-cups. 'Well, you're better now. That's the main thing.' She mouthed something to me that I couldn't understand, then went on to Juliette, 'Gabrielle's going to phone you later. See how you're doing.'

Juliette took her hand. 'I'm still frightened,' she said.

My mother put her arms around her. 'I'm going to stay with you. I'll be here.' When she came to see me out, she said, 'She's still not right.'

'She never has been, really, has she?'

'I'll look after her.'

'I know.'

When I got home, I sat by the window. I wished it would rain again. I wanted to be lost in the greyness.

Chapter Thirty-one

While I've never been a particular one for clouds having silver linings, it does seem that it is a rare crisis that doesn't have some little hidden pocket of benefit. I mean, there I was, no apparent glimmer of hope of beginning the long slow clamber from the wreckage, only seven pounds in the building society, five pounds and eighteen pence in my purse and the phone about to be cut off, when it occurred to me that I hadn't eaten a chocolate finger in weeks. I was supposed to be taking Decisive Action, phoning Graham and generally Getting On With It, but with my usual flair for procrastination, I delayed crisis management to go into the bathroom and weigh myself.

Praise the heavens, I'd lost half a stone!

Joyfully, I pulled off all my clothes and weighed myself again. In fact, I had lost eight and a half pounds. Without even trying! I turned sideways and examined myself in the mirror. I was thinner than I'd been for ages. I stood on tiptoe and held my arms above my head. I was positively skinny. I put my hands on my hips and thrust my breasts at the glass. Yes! Yes! Yes! Somebody, come here right now and capture this with a soft-focus lens. Immortalize me on film before the inevitable happens and I pig out and revert to being a fat blob.

I sent up a short prayer. Look, God, I know I've already asked you to consider sending me some mystery millions with which to pay off my debts and to make Ben forgive me and bring Nigel back before the house is repossessed and to try to make my sister as close to normal again as is possible, given that she is my sister, but do you think I could make just one more titchy-witchy request? Can I always look like this?

As I paused reverently for my message to reach home, hunger stabbed at my stomach. A savage, light-headed, trembly hunger that said, If I don't have four packets of biscuits right now, I am going to drop in a dead faint to the floor. Guess that's a 'No' then.

Without bothering to re-dress, I rushed to the kitchen and threw open all the cupboards.

Naturally they were bare. I hadn't been to the super-market for weeks and didn't feel inclined to go now. Instead I went round the corner to the baker's for a large, squidgy egg-mayonnaise roll and into the news-agent's for a packet of crisps and a Kit-Kat and while I was there I bought a newspaper.

And I really wished I hadn't. Because apart from cleaning me out, I was already feeling nauseous from ramming all my purchases down my throat in about three minutes flat, and when I'd finished reading it I felt really sick.

Ridiculous to be so upset over someone you don't even know. OK to cry over sisters and mothers and ex-husbands, but a first-time novelist you've seen in the paper once? It was just a little tiny heading on an inside page but it leapt up at me and made my heart thump. Jessica Jackson – my inspiration – was in a clinic recover-ing from a suicide attempt.

I felt shocked to my core.

No doubt my mother and Juliette (in the old days) and

Gabrielle (every day) would be falling over themselves with excitement at my sobbing.

What is it in her you see in yourself?

When you identify with the despair of her wish to kill herself which particular aspect of yourself do you think you wish to destroy?

Oh, transference! Oh, transference!

Louise would simply yawn and say, 'Come off it, Cari, people try to top themselves all the time. It's got nothing to do with you.'

Still, I couldn't escape the emotional symbolism. My chosen role-model, the paragon of literary endeavour to which I had hoisted my star, had felt her life to be so worthless she'd taken an overdose. It just about said it all.

Jessica's father had said the newspapers should leave Jessica alone; it was a family matter. Jessica had reportedly declared that money and fame weren't everything.

Indeed not, Jessica, but for some of us they'd be a bloody good start. While I was drinking my coffee, still steeped in Jessica-grief and inertia, my mother phoned to say that my father had been making a nuisance of himself, as expected, but had finally agreed to go home to whichever unfortunate woman he was living with these days, but was intending to visit me on the way. Although, knowing him, my mother added, he probably wouldn't, reliability never having been a strong point with him, but she was letting me know anyway because he might well phone. And I wasn't to believe anything he might say about her having been unpleasant to him because she had been the voice of calm and reason. He was the one who'd bleated on about himself, as usual, and so upset Juliette that she'd been quite rude – to my mother, of all people – but of course my mother wasn't taking that on board, darling, because Juliette is unwell and your bloody father has that effect on everyone.

During this, I said, 'Um,' a couple of times and 'Aha' once or twice, but even that seemed an enormous exertion and when I'd put the phone down I felt so exhausted I tottered upstairs and once more lay on the bed.

When the phone rang a few minutes later, I lay and looked at it until the answerphone cut in downstairs. I didn't mind seeing my father *per se*. It was the thought of having to listen to his own rambling account of this latest family interaction that put me off. And the knowledge that even if I interrupted him and said, 'I'm almost bankrupt and about to be thrown into debtors' prison and nobody in the world cares,' he'd only look vaguely about him and say, 'That's nice, dear,' before launching back into his favourite subject of I-don't-know-why-your-mum-is-so-hostile-to-me, which had been his one and only enduring topic of conversation for the last twelve years and on which he could have written a thesis. That was what filled me with the need to be unconscious.

But it sounded like Louise's voice floating faintly up the stairs. I'd phone her back in a minute. Then get up and sort things out. Never mind Jessica. It could all be done. Cut your losses, that's what you had to do in these situations. Sell the house, get a job . . . Start again . . .

In the meantime, somehow, I went to sleep.

I woke with a start and went rigid, feeling my fingertips jangle. What the fuck was that?

I sat up, fear gripping me. I heard it again. Somebody was downstairs.

I looked at the phone, wondering whether to dial 999 or just throw myself out of the window and land in the road outside to scream for help. But I found myself croaking, 'Who is it?' while trying frantically to remember what I'd been doing just before I'd ended up on this bed and whether I could have left the front door open, or which window the burglar might have smashed to force his way in. All the time the bizarre thought went through my head that while others might criticize Enid Blyton for giving children housekeepers and making policemen appear stupid, what always got me was the way that eight-year-olds would leap out of bed at any hour of the night, prepared to tackle strange noises. I was thirty-two, it was broad daylight, and I was cowering under the bedclothes. 'Who is it?' I screeched again.

'Is that you, Cari?'

I was shot through with relief, rapidly replaced with fury. I hurled myself down the stairs and into the kitchen. 'How dare you come in like that, you shit? You terrified me.'

'Sorry, I thought you were out.' Same old smooth tones, same ready excuses.

'What are you doing here?'

'I need to talk to you about things.'

Great. One bent business partner, lots of debts and bailiffs, a local council on the warpath, and now (peculiar tunes are running round my head – I am clearly on the way to full-blown lunacy) a partridge in a pear tree?

No.

Bloody bastard Martin.

'Sharon kicked you out, has she?'

'No.' The smooth tones had disappeared. His eyes were little shiny beads of malice. 'Have you read this?' He thrust a piece of paper towards me and I saw, with disbelief, that it was the last we're-getting-tough letter from Mr Cox of the bank.

Rage made my voice quaver. 'How dare you read my post! Bloody hell, Martin, you've only been in here five seconds. And you've got a bloody cheek using your key anyway. You should damn well—'

'They sent me a copy.'

'What?'

'I have been sent a copy of this letter because I am still a joint owner of this house, and the bank, as you know, is shortly going to be taking steps to repossess it.'

I stared at him, trying to comprehend what the hell was going on. 'Not *this* house,' I said stupidly.

'Yes!' he exploded. 'This house! I don't know what you've done, you stupid bitch, but it seems you owe them money, and, as mortgagees, they're coming after this property to pay it off.'

'You said we didn't have a mortgage.'

He slammed his hand down on the table. 'I left a hundred quid on it so that they looked after the deeds. Wouldn't have been able to trust you with them, would we?' he added nastily. 'Look!' He was really yelling now, waving the letter in my face. 'They're applying for a charging order.'

I stared at him in incomprehension. 'What's that?'

'What do you bloody think it is, you silly cow? The right to have a charge over this house. So they can make you liquidize it to pay off your debts. So they can repossess it if they want to. What have you done? How much are we talking about?'

I sat down at the table. I was shaking. 'Just stop shouting and I'll tell you.'

Martin paced up and down the kitchen while I related the tale, his mouth in that old, tight downward line I'd forgotten. I tried to keep my voice calm but my stomach was in those sick knots it got into whenever we rowed and I could already feel myself shrinking from his rage and disapproval.

'God, you're thick,' he said, when I'd finished. 'Haven't you learnt anything about Nigel? No wonder the bank are coming after this house. That other one is probably worth less than you paid for it, if he got a bent valuation. Not that you'd be able to sell it anyway if the council's after you. You're going to find yourself in court, Cari, as well as bankrupt.'

I stared at him miserably.

'And what's this bloody lot?' He picked up a handful of letters from the table and threw them down again. 'You haven't even opened half of them. And what's this, for God's sake?'

He pulled a sheet of thick white paper from one of the envelopes and started to read it. 'You never did have a bloody clue, did you?'

Suddenly, with a great hot flash that almost made me fall off my chair, my dejection was overtaken with a burning, pulsating, overwhelming fury. It filled my chest and lungs and I found myself gasping, unable to speak. I made a sort of strangled croaking noise as I tried to splutter out the words.

Martin looked up from the letter in surprise. 'Hey, Cari—'

'Out!' My voice was high and hoarse. 'Out! *Out!* OUT!'

Before I knew what I was doing, I was on my feet lunging at him like a madwoman. I had the most incredible feeling of strength and power. Somehow I got him across the room and to the front door. 'Now! Out! GET OUT!' I was screaming now, my fingers dug into the skin of his jaw on both sides of his open mouth as he staggered back against the glass.

I yanked the door open and propelled him out and down the steps. He didn't resist. There was a half-smile on his face as if he couldn't quite believe what I was doing.

I heard him say, 'But that letter . . .' and then I slammed the door behind him, so hard the frosted glass rattled.

I stood and watched him through the kitchen window. He hesitated on the pavement, looking up at the house, then straightened his collar and walked off down the road.

I picked an empty coffee mug from the draining-board and threw it hard against the wall tiles. The sound of it shattering filled me with such satisfaction that I smashed three more.

Then I stood there, breathing deeply, and was filled with a strange elation. Once, I thought, a confrontation like that with Martin would have reduced me to a quivering, blubbering heap. Today I felt invigorated, empowered, strong. 'Fuck you, Martin,' I said out loud. And as I said it, the words gave me a sweet pleasure. Suddenly, finally, I realized a wonderful truth: I really, honestly, didn't want him any more.

It was at least half an hour later that I remembered his final words and thought to look at the letter he'd been reading.

It was the one from the solicitor I'd opened a couple of days previously and abandoned after the heading about Turpin Road. Now I read it right through and my mouth dropped open. Then I read it again. And again. Then I danced round and round the kitchen hugging myself. Thank you, God. Thank you. Thank you. *Thank you!*

Chapter Thirty-two

Nigel sat at my kitchen table, twisting his hands together, looking more miserable than I had ever seen him. 'They just turned up,' he said. 'Came in and went through everything, then said if I didn't find ten and a half grand pronto they'd make me bankrupt.'

I handed him a coffee.

'And they're threatening to do me for fraud. It wasn't my fault. I didn't know where Freddie had sold them. I put them through zero-rated in good faith.'

'I thought Gloria did the books these days.'

'She does, but I'd done them this time. It was a sort of deal on the side.'

Well, it would have been, wouldn't it?

'It was to make some money to get us out of the hole with Turpin Road. Because I felt so bad about it.' Nigel looked at me appealingly. 'Freddie said it was all sorted. We were going to make fifteen grand each.'

Freddie, it seemed, was a make-a-quick-buck-it-can't-go-wrong entrepreneur after Nigel's own heart.

The sure-fire plan had been to buy six diggers from a couple of bankrupt building firms and flog them to a Nigel/Freddie equivalent in Germany, called Fritz, who in turn was going to export them to some digger-depleted eastern-bloc outfit at a vast profit all round.

All went well until the diggers were just about to be shipped when not only had no money been forthcoming but Fritz had mysteriously stopped answering Freddie's phone calls, and Freddie decided to demonstrate his flair for never saying die by rapidly disposing of the diggers: he diverted the container to a tractor dealer with whom he had once been inside and who now lived in Glasgow. Only trouble was he omitted to inform Nigel of this change of plan and Nigel, who had already done the VAT return himself – so that Gloria wouldn't get wind of what he was up to – assumed they were still being exported and put them through with no VAT on them. VAT that the VAT office now wanted or else. And on hearing of this demand, Gloria had not been her usual supportive self but had said, 'This time you're on your own, Nigel,' and had taken the children to her mother's.

'I don't know what I'm going to do,' said Nigel, examining his mug sadly.

'Why can't you pay off the VAT people with your share of the digger money?'

'Well, there wasn't very much profit in the end, because Hamish didn't want to pay as much as Fritz and we had to get rid of them quick because we hadn't paid for them ourselves, and then Gloria got hold of the cheque and paid it into the bank and they took nearly all of it to pay off my overdraft.'

'And you used the rest for Trevor.'

Nigel stared blankly at me then put his head in his hands.

I'd been going to make him suffer for at least another half an hour but he looked so pathetic I knew I wouldn't be able to keep it up.

'Well, Graham's screaming for my blood, I've got bailiffs coming back any day and the house is a complete wreck,' I said. 'I'm going to have to sell this to pay them off and by the time I've settled Martin – who is being a complete bastard – I'll be penniless and homeless.'

Even as I said it my mouth was twitching but Nigel didn't seem to notice. 'I'm so sorry,' he said, wretchedly.

'No! It's all right. Look!' I was so excited now I could hardly speak. 'See this letter, Nigel? The supermarket needs our house. They want to buy it. They're going to pay us a fortune!'

Nigel gaped at me as I hugged him and thrust the solicitor's letter under his nose. 'Solicitors acting for Broadrange Food Stores Ltd. Look at the offer they've made us!'

Nigel went rigid and his eyes widened like a cartoon character's. Then he leapt to his feet with a whoop, grabbed hold of me and swung me round in elation.

'I knew it would make money for us in the end. Didn't I tell you?' He snatched up the letter and read it greedily. 'You wait and see. We can get a lot more out of them than this. Oh, Cari, it's going to be brilliant.'

'It's an awful lot of money already . . .' I said feebly, but Nigel had already reached for my phone and was dialling.

'Exactly!' he said over his shoulder. 'They must be desperate for it.' He blew me a kiss over the top of the receiver. 'Ben!' he said, moments later, 'what's the story on the back of Turpin Road, my old mate?' He grinned at me and nodded about thirty-six times to whatever Ben was saying, keeping up a steady stream of, 'Yeah, yeah, got it, yep, lovely, yeah, yeah, you bloody bet, you too mate, yeah, brilliant!'

Eventually he put the phone down. 'I knew it!' he said triumphantly. 'They've got to have our backyard! There was a mistake on the plans over the positioning of the car-wash. If they don't get our house, they're in the shit. Oh, Cari!' He gave a great sigh of ecstasy. 'I can't believe it. Ben was coming round to tell you himself. He'd already heard a rumour.'

I felt a moment's disappointment that I was now going to miss that visit. But Nigel was still talking. 'We need to get on to that solicitor sharpish and tell him they've got to increase the offer. Pity we haven't got any contacts up there. Don't suppose your boyfriend will be in the know?'

'Who?'

'Henry.'

'He is *not* my boyfriend. And, no, I shouldn't think so. He's only a manager. I've a friend on the board, though,' I finished casually, enjoying the expression on Nigel's face.

'Really?'

'I met him at the do Henry took me to. Very nice bloke. He gave me the number of his direct line.'

'Did you shag him, then?' Nigel was now looking at me in open admiration.

'Of course I didn't. What do you take me for?'

'Come on. Let's call him now.'

'Lovely champagne!' I giggled later, as I sprawled on the window-seat and watched Nigel feverishly doing calculations on the back of one of my envelopes. 'It's gone straight to my head. I feel fantastic!'

'I'd feel fantastic on lemonade right now,' said Nigel, refilling his glass anyway. 'I've always dreamt of something like this, Cari. It's brilliant.'

'Go and get another bottle, then. I feel like really celebrating.'

'Can't, Cari, I've got to drive home.'

'You can't drive. You're pissed.'

'I'm not. You've drunk most of it.'

'Well, you drink most of the next one.'

'There's no one to feed the dog.'

'Yes, there is. I've met him. Come on, Nigel, you owe me after all you've put me through.'

'OK, OK.'

'Right! Then get back down that off-licence.'

'I still can't believe Gloria's gone.' Nigel was sprawled with me now, his glass balanced precariously on his stomach.

'She'll come back.'

'I don't know. She was really fed up this time. I've never seen her like that.'

'Well, you can hardly blame her.'

'Cari, you know you said you loved me when I came off the phone to Bill . . .'

'Yeah, you were excellent. Especially that stuff about losing out on an investment opportunity and loss of earnings. Perfect mix of pretending to be a really nice guy and a businessman at the same time.'

'I wasn't pretending.' Nigel affected a hurt look.

'You know what I mean.'

'Well, anyway, I was wondering, now I'm on my own too and you are, and we get on so well, whether we could . . .'

'What?'

'You know, we'd be well suited.'

'Come off it.'

'I've always really fancied you, Cari, you know that.'

'You're just feeling randy because Gloria's left you. Phone her up and get her back. You know you're lost without her.'

'I suppose so.'

We sprawled in silence for a moment. Then Nigel drained his glass and wriggled a bit closer to me. 'I can't stay the night, then.'

'I'm not that drunk.'

'That's not what you said last Christmas.'

'I was tired and emotional then. Tonight I'm on top of the world.'

'You are mean. If I was anyone else, and you had a bottle and a half of champagne inside you, you'd be taking your clothes off by now.'

'That is not true. I am a reformed character. Anyway, you're my friend. It's not the same.'

'Guess I'd better get a taxi, then.'

I was going to suggest he stayed in the spare room but I was full of champagne and I feared I might not turn out to be as reformed as I thought I was, and would have to wake up with the embarrassing consequences, so I let him call a cab and gave him a chaste kiss on the cheek as he rose to leave.

He paused with his hand on the doorknob. 'I still think you and me would work well together.'

'We'd kill each other.'

Chapter Thirty-three

'Nigel, please!'

At this rate we were going to wear away the floor-boards. Nigel was pacing up and down my kitchen. Mobile clamped to one ear, the receiver from the land-line tucked under his chin and up against the other one. I was pacing in front of him, stopping periodically to felt-tip another note on to the back of an envelope and wave it under his nose.

He shook his head at the latest one. My stomach went into another spasm. We had been at it since nine a.m. Greggie would report the latest from the Broadrange solicitor, who kept saying it was their final offer, Nigel would say no, I would beg him to say yes, he would phone Bill and do a bit of negotiation on the side, and the solicitor would phone again, Greggie would say, 'I think this time . . .' and Nigel would say no again, and I would write him another note saying that if we lost this sale due to his greed I would set about him with the carving knife.

'Nigel, for God's sake!' I was beside myself now. 'They're offering four times the market value for a house that's a complete wash-out on every level. We can't risk losing this.'

Nigel brushed me away. 'They're desperate.' He

dropped his mobile, springing to attention as a voice sounded in his other ear. He grinned at me. 'Round it up to the next hundred and we'll sign.' He put down the phone, pleased. 'That'll get them all jumping up and down.'

'It's too much,' I whimpered. 'They're going to tell us to sod off.'

Nigel was Mr Cucumber Cool. 'They can't. It's obvious from what Bill said. They're in the shit and if they don't get our house they won't open on time. Do you know how many thousands those Broadrange tills ring up every hour? Any delay will cost them millions. A couple of hundred grand to us is chicken feed!'

And it seemed – just for once – that he was right.

I came out of a confused dream about the druggie and Turpin Road and Elsie-next-door telling me I must go up on the roof and clear away the rubbish, and for a moment I couldn't think what had happened the day before. Then it all came back to me and I sat up, grinning gleefully. Whoever said that money didn't buy happiness knew about as much as the one who reckoned weighing eight stone wasn't the joy to end all joys. I didn't care how much of my old age I had to spend clambering through the eye of a needle to reach the Kingdom of God. For the moment, my idea of heaven was being able to pay off my debts and send Martin packing once and for bloody all.

Hallelujah! I love you, Broadrange Food Stores.

I was humming as I gave the kitchen a bit of a clean, singing loudly as I whipped through the post and added today's demands to the write-to-tell-them-they'll-be-paid-very-soon pile.

Then I phoned the bank, left a mesage for Graham to say all was not lost, called Nigel to say that even if shagging him was not a good idea, I still adored him as a friend, he was the best negotiator the world had ever seen and I couldn't wait to hear how he got on with all the solicitors today, then got out all my plastic cards to work out which ones could still be squeezed for a little temporary credit. Because, looking out of the window, I saw that it was far too beautiful a morning to be inside my kitchen. Filled with the new bubbly energy that things going right for a change can bring, I grabbed my bag, slung it over my shoulder and left the house.

I got back at about five o'clock, having spent an enjoyable day bestowing love and flowers on my nearest and dearest – namely my mother, Juliette and Louise – all of whom were a little taken aback but not displeased to have blooms and my jubilant face thrust at them.

I skipped up my steps, elated that everything was right with my world again and relieved that finally things seemed pretty OK with theirs too.

I was mildly irritated to find a note from Martin pushed through the door. I had assumed that he would have slunk back to the brain-dead Sharon rather than hanging around Eastford like a bad smell. But even the thought of his odious face couldn't dampen my spirits.

The note said he was sorry about the other morning and would like to talk to me again. I bet you bloody would, I thought, now you've got a whiff that I'm about to be loaded. I thought of the unrivalled pleasure I would get from sending him a cheque for half of this house. I would attach a nice yellow Post-it note to it. Or perhaps a pink one. With some suitably thought-out closing words. Like: 'Now piss off.'

I laughed and began to unload my shopping.

Ding-dong.

There he was. Smirk on his face. Bottle of wine under one arm.

'What do you want?'

'Don't be like that, Cari. I said I was sorry. I thought we could have a drink and start again.'

'You are so transparent.'

Martin looked irritated, which he quickly adjusted to an expression of wounded innocence.

It didn't cut any ice with me. 'You're only back here because you read that letter and know that I made a fantastic business decision after all, and now you're hoping to get your hands on my dosh.'

'No, I'm not. I just want what I'm entitled to.'

I was about to launch into an explanation of what I thought he was entitled to, namely a bloody good kicking, when God came up trumps for me yet again. (Sorry, sorry, sorry I ever said I didn't believe you were there for me. I have seen the light.) Over Martin's shoulder I saw a huge and gorgeous figure making its way up my path.

Yes!

I shoved Martin aside, and held out my arms. 'Darling! How lovely! You're home early!' Ben looked startled but rose to the occasion as I pulled him towards me and stood on tiptoe to reach his mouth. In fact, he got thoroughly into his role, and clasped me to him, kissing me back until my knees began to buckle.

Eventually we let go of each other. I turned, rather breathlessly, towards Martin, whose face, I am pleased to report, was – as they say – a picture. 'Martin, this is Ben. Ben, this is my slimy ex-husband.'

'I felt almost sorry for him,' said Ben, when Martin had gone.

'No need to. He's a rat,' I said reassuringly. 'Sorry if I embarrassed you.'

'No, no, I enjoyed it.'

301

We lapsed into a slightly awkward silence.

'Do you want a coffee?' I asked, realizing that we hadn't yet established why he was there.

'Oh, yes, great.'

I spooned granules into mugs, feeling suddenly odd and shy. That's the trouble with fantasies. They work because they *are* fantasies. The moment the object of your desire is sitting in your kitchen, you don't have a clue what to say. Which was just as well, really, when that object was matrimonially unavailable.

'How do you have it?' I've always had finely honed conversational skills when I really put my mind to it.

'Black, no sugar.'

'Oh, really? How funny. So do I.' I could hear myself trilling in a most ridiculous fashion and cringed gently behind the fridge door as I shoved the milk – which anyway had gone cheesy – out of sight.

'I came round', said Ben, in a strangely gruff voice, 'to see how you were.'

'Oh, I'm fine now.'

'I'm sorry about—'

'No, look, I'm really sorry. I shouldn't have shouted at you,' I gabbled. 'I know you were trying to help and it did help and I'm really grateful to you for putting the windows back.' I stopped, knowing I had gone scarlet.

'I just wanted to make it up to you. That's why I paid Trevor.'

'You paid him? I thought it was Nigel.'

While I was digesting this startling news, Ben had turned to look out of the window. 'I came round a few days ago,' he said, with his back to me, 'but your boyfriend had just arrived and I didn't want to interrupt.'

'When was that? I finished with Guy ages ago.'

'I meant that bloke from the supermarket.'

'Henry? He's not—'

'Nigel said you'd been having some weekends away with him.'

'Nigel knows very well that there's nothing going on between me and Henry. We went to one do together. For his work. Just to help him out.'

'And then I saw him leaving here early one morning as I drove past so I thought—'

'No! He'd called in to see—'

'You don't have to explain.'

'Yes, I do. Bloody Nigel.'

'It's just that – you know – I didn't want to tread on anyone's toes.'

'What?' Henry's toes would look like pancakes if Ben's great foot ended up on them.

Ben was still talking. 'But when I heard about the Broadrange deal, which must be a weight off your mind, I wondered whether you'd like to go for a drink. To celebrate.' He met my eyes at last and smiled. 'How about it?'

I tried to keep my voice light and jovial, though things inside my stomach were leaping about all over the place. 'Wouldn't your wife have something to say about that?'

'I shouldn't think so. I haven't seen her for two years.'

Bloody Nigel.

I was so knocked sideways by this revelation, and the need to readjust my whole viewpoint and emotional responses from the No-I-mustn't to the maybe-I-can-after-all, that I barely heard the rest of what he was saying. I just caught the end of it.

'. . . no hard feelings, it just didn't work out. Last time I heard she was in Luton.'

'So don't you see the children?' I asked sympathetically, my mind still shrieking, 'He's single! He's available!' but thinking I'd better show a bit of decorum until at least we'd been for that drink.

303

'What children?'

The problem with always having started new relationships blind drunk is that I haven't been able to practise the eyelash-fluttering niceties of the pre-coital chit-chat. Having established that nothing stood in the way of Ben and me getting it together double-quick, I had no idea what to say next. I mumbled something about yes-a-drink-would-be-lovely then studied the swing-bin, feeling about thirteen.

Luckily, Ben was a bit better about coming forward. He looked at me then glanced out of the window, took a great big breath and said, 'I thought you were lovely the moment we met. Now I can't stop thinking about you.'

He stood up, walked over and put his arms around me. They were the biggest, strongest, warmest, most comforting arms I had ever been in. I put mine around his waist and pressed my face into his chest. I could feel his heart beating.

'I want you,' he said, quietly.

'I want you too,' I answered.

And my heart – like a dried bean dropped into water – swelled.

Early the next morning, the phone rang. I stretched out an arm to the receiver and answered it on automatic even before I'd struggled to open my eyes. 'Hello?'

Beside me Ben was huge and warm. He stirred and moved closer to me. I snuggled up against him.

'Cari, it's Neil.'

'Hi.'

'Sorry, did I wake you?'

'Doesn't matter,' I said, yawning, trying to work out why he was calling. Suppose he must finally want paying.

'I've been worried about you since the other morning. I should have done more. I came home that night and told

Linda about it and she said you must be having a terrible time all on your own. Are you all right? Are things better now?'

'Oh, yes, Neil,' I murmured sleepily. 'Thank you. Things are fine.'

Or as you would say, Neil, *my cup runneth over.*

Chapter Thirty-four

'Post's come!'

What a difference a bank balance makes. Or the prospect of the bank balance I'd have soon from getting mega-bucks for a dodgy house! These days I leapt up from the table, bounded towards the front door and swooped without fear on the pile of letters that had slapped on to the mat.

'What I used to like doing, when I was young,' I said, returning to my morning coffee and post-coital chocolate finger, settling the envelopes in a neat stack in front of me, 'was biting the ends off,' I held up a freshly bitten chocolate finger to demonstrate, 'and then trying to suck orange juice up through the middle. 'Oh, damn, it doesn't work with coffee.' There was a plop as the biscuit fell apart and sank to the bottom of my mug.

'You're mad,' said Ben, spreading a huge set of plans across the table. 'It wouldn't work with anything.'

I fished about with a teaspoon, dredged up a soggy mess of biscuit sludge and began to flick through the various missives. 'Ha!' I said, recognizing the bank's logo. 'Change of tune from old Graham now!' I read, '. . . have pleasure in enclosing early repayment figure you requested for your loan account . . . Anything further we can do to assist you . . .'

'Plenty, I'd have thought,' said Ben, turning the plans the other way and gazing at them critically. 'How many bathrooms have they got here?'

'Can't have too many,' I said absently, screwing my face up at the next sheet of paper. 'God, Martin is such a slime-ball. He's desperate to get paid.' Then my heart leapt. 'Hey, look! It's Charlie-boy at last. The publisher!' I held up an envelope for Ben to see the frank mark. 'Bless Bill! This could be it, Ben. I might be about to be famous!'

'Open it, then.'

'I might write *The Chocolate Finger Diet* next. Perhaps Cadbury's would sponsor me. There was the Mars Bar diet once. I remember it.'

'By the time you finish a book you'll be able to call it *The OAP Diet*. Just open it!'

'I can't.'

Ben took it from me, slit the envelope and began to read: '*Dear Cari Carrington, Thank you for sending me your manuscript.*' He stopped.

So did my breath. 'He says it's crap?'

'No. *I was intrigued by your ideas and highly original approach* . . .' Ben looked at me. 'He says it's a fine study of disintegration.'

Disintegration?

'There must have been a mix-up. It must be somebody else's book.'

Ben went on, '. . . *but I didn't feel the diet section worked very well* . . .'

'What does he mean diet *section*?' I grabbed the letter back and read the rest: '*Liked the device of the lists* . . .' Lists? '*Interesting diary format* . . .' Diary? '*Shows potential* . . .' What does? '. . . *the unique, evocative, urban ramblings of a diseased mind* . . .'

'Oh, my God.' Realization dawned. Henry had sent him my Day Book.

*   *   *

Action List Number 27

(1) Phone Juliette: share with her my very own new, exciting unlock-your-potential tips. Namely if she gets her fourteen volumes of loopy note-book out of the drawer she could be sitting on a fortune.

(2) Make calculations of how much money I'll have left after paying bank, Martin, Ben (for bridging loan used to pay off Building Supplies Co. and Electrical Bits Ltd before they dis-appeared with my car), credit cards, Louise (lent me money for telephone bill), my mother (ditto electricity), gas (who have to wait, only just got the red one), council tax (who can wait too – serves the council right for all the trauma they've caused), throwing lavish party (can't wait). Answer to calculation: brilliantly, marvellously, amazingly, LOTS!

(3) Spend some of above in anticipation, on incredibly sexy and slinky party dress designed to draw full attention to new not-full-any-more figure.

(4) Think up new and exciting investment plans for balance to go with whole new and exciting and solvent future.

(5) Dance around kitchen again.

I'd finished the invitations and was busily arranging lilies in a tall glass vase while singing 'It's A Wonderful Life' when Nigel flew through my front door. 'The old woman from next door's on the roof protesting about the house being pulled down.'

'Elsie?' I giggled. 'Is she really? Bless her!'

308

'It's not "bless her" and it's not funny! She could be a serious hindrance. They haven't had the planning meeting yet.'

He could hardly keep still.

I filled the kettle. 'What do we care? We've exchanged. If Broadrange can't pull it down that's their problem. Anyway, with their money and clout they'll soon get their legal bigwigs sorting out Eastford council.'

'It was a conditional contract.'

'What?'

'It was a conditional contract. Conditional on them getting planning to pull it down. If they don't . . .'

'But they've paid a deposit.'

'They'll get it back.'

'I've spent it.'

Nigel and I looked at each other, white-faced. I was too stricken even to shout at him.

'What are we going to do?' My voice sounded small and wobbly.

'We'd better get down there.'

Nigel did not draw breath once all the way. 'They've got the local evening-news lot there, the papers, the police, the Fire Brigade and half of the planning committee. This could really hold things up. The planning meeting's tomorrow night. If there's loads of adverse publicity they'll defer a decision until there's been an inquiry.'

'How the hell did she get up there?'

'Demolition lot have already put up some scaffolding.'

Even in the midst of crisis the word still did something odd to my knees. 'Well, you'll have to get her down.'

But that was easier said than done. A crowd had gathered on the pavement. One policeman stood in front of the door, another guarded the foot of the scaffolding.

In the front, I spotted purple-lipped Carla and my heart sank. I wasn't sure I could handle an audience with Guy right now. But she appeared to be talking to a long-haired bloke with a TV camera. I elbowed my way to her side. 'What are you doing here? Hardly a *Macho* story.'

She looked at me uncomprehendingly then recognition and boredom crossed her face. 'Left that lot. I'm with *South-east Tonight* now. This is gonna be our lead story.'

'She'll come down in a minute. She doesn't mean it,' I said hopefully.

'That's not what we've heard,' said Carla.

I looked up to where the tiny figure appeared to be waving some sort of cardboard placard. Beside me I could almost hear the frantic whirrings of Nigel's brain as he tried to think up a Nigel-solution. 'Don't worry,' he muttered distractedly.

Don't worry! Fortune handed to you on a plate then snatched back again. The house you thought you'd unloaded suddenly yours again in all its smashed-up bankruptcy-inducing glory.

I'd already written a yah-boo-sucks-to-you letter to Martin, telling him how I'd soon be rolling in it, and a see-we-told-you-so one to Graham, who wouldn't want to 'assist further' now but would come swooping in and take my home away from me. I wouldn't be able to pay anyone back.

I saw Mr Dandruff standing smugly with other council androids and I swallowed.

'What are we going to do, then?' I asked Nigel again.

He bit his lip.

I looked up again, wondering if my knees would hold out long enough for me to make it up there to sob all over her, inducing Elsie to give in, come down and make me another cup of tea. 'It's my house,' I said to the policeman on the doorstep. 'Can I go up?'

'Sorry, love,' he said.

'How are you going to get her down?'

'Sorry. Can't say.'

Suddenly I saw Ben appear around the side of the house and I shoved my way through to his side.

'Wondered what was going on,' he said.

'It won't really affect being able to pull it down, will it?' I beseeched him.

He shook his head slowly. 'They're a funny lot in Planning. No rhyme or reason. Depends what mood the guy gets out of bed in.'

Great.

'I'll see what I can find out.' He disappeared.

More friends in high places? Oh, God, Elsie, come down! What was wrong with her?

I screwed my hands into balls and looked around at all the open-mouthed spectators jostling for a better view in case something really gory happened.

Nigel came to stand beside me again. We gazed at the police, the fire engine, the ambulance waiting nearby. Carla's cameraman was on the front steps now. She was standing next to the policeman, holding a microphone under the nose of . . . Who was that? I looked at the scarf fluttering in the breeze, the megaphone and the enormous handbag . . .

Was this a set-up? *Candid Camera* or some cranky version of *This Is Your Life*?

'What's she doing here?' I hissed to Nigel. 'What are *you* doing here?' I screeched at her, running through the crowd and hauling her away from the camera.

My mother smiled calmly. 'You seem a bit over-tired again, darling. Molly and I are here as part of the Friend-in-Need scheme, helping to facilitate Elsie's articulation of her grievances to the appropriate authorities.'

'Never mind that,' I snarled. 'If she doesn't get down pronto and say she can't wait to see this house demolished, I'm going to be right in the shit.'

While my mother was hyperventilating, I turned towards Nigel. 'For God's sake, go and put your slimy salesman's ways to some use. Tell them you're her long-lost son and get up there.'

My mother's mouth opened.

'Don't you dare!' I snapped.

It shut again.

Whatever Nigel said to the police worked. They all went into a huddle, then the crowd went quiet as we watched him climbing higher and higher and finally lifting a leg over the last rail.

We all shuffled about, craning our necks to see him make his way across the roof and crouch next to Elsie. I could see his head wagging about, his hands waving.

'What's her problem?' I demanded of my mother.

'Not being given a choice. Having the fabric of her home undermined.'

'It's not her home, it's next-door. And they're sorting out her outside wall.'

'It's always been there. This building attached to her own affords her security and warmth. It's what she knows.'

'For God's sake! She was fine about everything the other day. And they've offered to move her out to a hotel while they're doing it.' I looked at my mother suspiciously. 'Why's she suddenly upset?'

My mother raised her eyes heavenwards and continued, in dramatic tones, 'Elsie has lived here all her life. These houses were built in the time of Wellington. She feels strongly about the character of the road being raped and ravaged, a part of the town's history being wiped away.' My mother gazed dreamily at the sky.

I stared at the ground. Then my mobile rang. 'Get on to Bill!' Nigel's voice came triumphantly into my ear. 'Free groceries and her electricity bill paid, and she's coming down!'

Chapter Thirty-five

Oh, the sweet relief and untold joy. Six weeks and six days and a whole host of nightmares about it all falling through, and with a single phone call my life is transformed. Completion has taken place, says Greggie gravely, and I almost rush straight to his office and smother him with grateful kisses. Almost but not quite. For there is someone considerably huger and infinitely more gorgeous much closer to hand and I am in love . . .

'Good heavens,' said Rowena, looking doubtfully around her at the candle-decked interior of 106 Turpin Road. 'What a terrible state the place is in. Not very clean, is it?'

You should have seen it three months ago. 'It's being demolished tomorrow. There hardly seemed much point in Hoovering.' I held up the champagne bottle, thinking it was a good job she hadn't seen what we *had* to do to it. 'Go on, just have a little bit. Broadrange own label. Only the best.'

'Oh, no, it gives me heartburn when I'm pregnant. And who knows? This time it might be twice as bad.' She went off into peals of tinkling laughter.

'Isn't it lovely news?' cooed my mother, appearing at my elbow as if by magic and holding out her glass instead. 'I thought Juliette was going to be twins. It was so exciting.'

What a dreadful thought. Bad enough the prospect of *three* little Lukey lookalikes inhabiting the planet but to think I might have had two sisters. The object of my thoughts wandered towards me holding a cold sausage. 'Are these all right?' she asked, turning it between finger and thumb and inspecting it.

'Of course they are. All the food came from Broadrange.'

'And it wasn't past its sell-by date?'

'Fresh this morning. And you'd better not let Henry hear you say that. He'll cry.'

Juliette looked alarmed.

'Only joking! Look, here he comes.'

Henry waddled up and planted a large wet kiss on my cheek. 'For you!'

'Oh, you shouldn't have!' I took the bumper tin of chocolate fingers into my arms and admired the red ribbon.

'Good idea!' said Ben behind me. 'She's got much too thin.'

God, how I love this man.

Skinny Barry came in with his arms full of ghetto-blaster. 'Where do you want this?' He waved the plug at me enquiringly.

'Oh!' I clapped a hand to my mouth. 'There's no power on!'

I looked at Ben. We'd thought of food and oodles of alcohol and six dozen candles and telling everyone to wear lots of clothes or be prepared to huddle together for warmth, and getting the water back on and he – my hero of modern times – had cleaned the toilet. But neither of us had thought about how Barry might drive the music. 'I'll go to the garage for batteries,' Ben said, and kissed me.

Louise, just arrived with Robert, smirked. 'Right little love-birds, you two.'

I grinned at her. 'I am *so* happy.'

She grinned back. 'Get us a drink, then.'

Gradually the room filled. I saw Rowena and Juliette huddled together peering into the murkier corners, but nobody else seemed to mind partying in a druggie's ex-squat – though they might have done before Ben's blokes had heaved out the festering mattress and other disgusting legacies from Gary, and given the place a good hose down.

At last it was all done. The house, on its final evening before being reduced to a pile of rubble, was the property of Broadrange Food Stores, the money for it was in the bank. All the anguish and *Angst* were behind me. I looked at the bare walls with affection. It was black outside and the candles threw out their flickering light making the place look romantic and exotic, highlighting the beauty of all the different faces – friends, building colleagues and associated acquaintances.

Sonia had just arrived, Jim was sucking his gums in the corner, Barry was now presiding proudly over his compilation tapes, waving his spaghetti arms and legs about to the strains of 'Dancing Queen'.

Henry was standing next to me, munching on a length of French stick. He nodded towards Barry. 'Know that waitress, Carol, he met? They're getting married.'

'Wow.'

I smiled indulgently at him, full of champagne, and threw tact to the wind. 'What about you, Henry? When are we going to find someone for you?'

'Oh, I haven't got time for that sort of thing,' said Henry ponderously.

'How's Rosie? You did invite her, didn't you?'

'Yes, she said she'd come,' said Henry distractedly.

Then he grabbed my arm. 'Oh, it's no good, I've got to tell someone!' His eyes shone. 'It's not official yet so we have to keep it quiet. So don't tell anyone but—'

'I won't, I won't. Who is she? Is it Rosie? Is it her?'

Henry looked perplexed. 'Who?'

'Your new woman.'

'I haven't got a woman. I'm going to be manager of the new ultra-store!'

As I was effusing, a pretty brown-haired girl came up to us. 'Hello Mr Chapman.' She smiled at me: 'Hello. Thank you so much for asking me.'

I smiled back, wondering who she was. Barry's waitress? I didn't remember her looking like that but I was hardly a reliable witness for anything relating to that particular weekend.

'That's OK,' I said carefully. 'How are you?'

'Well,' she giggled and cast her eyes down over her dress, 'a bit smaller these days.' Suddenly she grasped my hand. 'I can't thank you enough,' she said fervently. 'Typing out your book has changed my life. It's such a brilliant idea. Since I started using the Shelf Diet, I'm a whole new person!' She flashed me a huge smile.

I stared at the cheekbones and single chin. 'Rosie?' I stammered. 'My God! Henry?'

I turned to share the shock of this amazing vision with Henry, but he was busy at the buffet again. We watched him stuff the rest of the loaf into his mouth before he wandered off. 'Perhaps you should get him on it,' I said faintly.

Rosie looked longingly at his generous rear. 'I don't think he'd listen to me,' she said sadly.

'Sonia! Have you or Rowena got a camera? Quick before she puts it all back on!' Never mind Charlie-boy and publishers who don't know a good thing when they see it. I've got a real live before-and-after here.

317

Sonia turned me towards her and peered into my face. 'You look wonderful,' she said curiously. 'Visibly younger.'

'It's the candlelight. Brings out the best in everyone.'

'No, I noticed it the other day. Your cheeks are firmer. You've got this glow. Is it really that cream?'

'Ah.' I lowered my voice and told her about the oestrogen levels. Guy would have been proud of me.

'Really?' Her eyes widened and she looked hopefully around the room. 'Perhaps I should . . . Are there any unattached men here, apart from Henry?'

'Trevor . . .' I nodded towards where he was nursing a pint in the corner, glowering – nothing had changed there.

Sonia looked doubtful. 'What about him?'

I followed her gaze to where Nick, the young fella, him of the black eye, was engaged in conversation with – of all people – my mother. 'He had a wife last time I knew about it but he seems to be on his own tonight.'

'I was reading about affairs with younger men when I was waiting for my body-wrap,' said Sonia. 'Golden rule is: never get on top – has the opposite effect of a facelift.'

'Good God, I never thought of that.'

'And another good point we've never thought of. Hands! Biggest giveaway. We should put factor thirty on the backs every day. It's never occurred to me. Of course, I always wear gloves in the winter.'

We watched my mother pat Nick's arm before she strode towards us. 'What a lovely young man,' she said breathily. 'We had such a nice chat.'

'His wife knocks him about.'

'I know,' said my mother happily.

*   *   *

'For God's sake, Henry!' I hissed, wrenching him away from the pork pies. 'Get over there and talk to Rosie. She looks fantastic!'

Henry looked at me, cheeks bulging, as I jerked my head to where Rosie was standing alone in the corner.

'Why didn't you tell me she'd been on my diet?'

He shook his head, gulped and swallowed. 'I didn't know.' He gazed at Rosie quizzically. 'I thought she'd lost a bit of weight.'

'Only about six stone!'

Henry's eyes popped.

'And she fancies you!'

Henry looked shocked. 'Really?'

'I can't think where Nigel's got to,' I said to Ben, after I'd rescued him from Bernard and Rowena and dragged him off to smooch with me to the music so I could keep a surreptitious eye on Henry's chat-up techniques. So far they seemed to consist of devouring three plates of Scotch eggs.

'You know Nigel.'

'He promised he'd be here. It's his celebration too. He was bloody brilliant in the end. Got us so much money.' Oh dear, slurring slightly already. Never mind, it *is* a party.

'He's got the luck of the devil. He could have bankrupted you.'

'Oh, all's well and all that . . .' I shuffled closer to his great chest and gazed round the half-painted interior of white elephant turned golden goose. 'If we'd known we'd end up knocking it down, you could have carried on breaking it to bits when you first came in here.'

Ben laughed. 'Your face, you looked so horrified. There was I, thinking how beautiful you were, and you thought I was a thug.'

'Nonsense. Course I didn't.'

'You're a terrible liar.'

'You up the duff yet?' I asked Louise, when I was too drunk to dance and we were sitting on beer crates in the corner, eating peanuts.

She looked round to check where Robert was. 'Thing is, I'm not sure, really. You know I told you I had a new boss at work . . .'

'Oh, Lou! Not again.'

'Nothing's happened yet. Anyway, what are you being so sanctimonious about all of a sudden? You've never only had eyes for one!'

'I will have now.'

'Give it a couple of years.'

'I want a baby then.'

'I *thought* you were drunk.'

'No, really,' I said later, when we were sprawled on a couple of sacks on the floor, leaning back against the crates, and I'd found one more bottle of champagne in a bucket under the table. 'This is it. Ben is the one for me. There's none of that stomach-churning and feeling insecure like there was with Martin, I'm not being all needy and pathetic. It's not all sex and nothing else like it was with Guy . . .'

Louise brightened. 'I wish I'd met him.'

I giggled. 'Yes, I'll always be grateful to him. He phoned, actually, just to see how I was. He's got together with a sex-shop owner now. They seem to spend all their spare time test-driving the equipment. He says she has bits of her pierced I wouldn't believe. I said it sounded like a match made in heaven. Anyway, me and Ben . . .'

'I'm glad you're happy.'

320

'It's just like . . . right. He's all warm and strong and big and looks after me . . .'

'And – very handily – it turns out he's loaded.'

'You are dreadful. That's got nothing to do with it.'

'Only kidding.'

'It was sort of like when you suddenly, finally, realize what you've always been looking for. Like coming home.'

'Oh, my God, pass the sick bucket.'

'Shut up! I love you, Lou.'

'Love you too.'

'You'll get piles sitting on that cold concrete.' Rowena loomed above me, twin-packed stomach thrust forward. 'One more orange juice and I'll simply have to get to bed.'

I staggered to my feet and rooted around on the table among the cartons.

'I had a lovely long talk with your mum. You're lucky she's so understanding. She's going to find out where to get raspberry-leaf tea for me. Juliette says it speeds up labour. And your Ben's full of surprises.' I poured some juice into a plastic cup as she prodded my arm. 'You'll never guess what. He was at Leicester at the same time as Bernard.'

'You didn't tell me you went to . . .' I had three attempts at getting my tongue in the right position and got it out eventually '. . . university.'

Ben grinned. 'You don't have to sound so amazed. Thought I was too much of an oik, eh?'

Thank you, Louise.

'You deliberately pretended to be an oik in the beginning.'

'That's nothing. They'd think that's me gone posh where I come from.'

'Don't start that again! Posh? You were all cor-blimey-look-at-the-tits-on-that.'

'I have never said that!'

'Almost.'

'Ah, that's just building. Talking in the vernacular, my mate Vic calls it.'

'Whatever it's called, it still sends shivers down my spine . . .'

The music had slowed down again. I stood swaying dreamily against Ben as I looked benevolently round at my guests full of love and appreciation for them all. Ben swayed gently with me.

'Your mum's given Nick her phone number,' he remarked.

'Oh, God, poor sod. Why can't she leave people alone?'

'No, I think he was quite pleased.'

'What?'

'Very sexy lady, your mum.'

'Come off it.'

'Nick likes older women.'

I finished my tour of relighting the candles and put the matches down. 'Love you, Ben.'

'Love you too, darlin'.'

'What you do at university anyway?'

'Theology.'

Blimey.

'Come and meet Neil.'

Not to mention Neil's wife. I had expected a mousy, beige-cardiganed, no makeup, earnest-expressioned individual, but Linda turned out to be a dark, voluptuous beauty with glossy red lips and smouldering eyes.

As I'd approached with the orange juice I'd been startled to see her pour herself half a pint of red wine and hand a tankard to her husband.

'He's drinking beer!' I said to her in amazement, as Ben was shaking Neil's hand.

'Yes, I told him it was about time he pulled his socks up. I told him, "You've got a marraige here, Neil. It's me or God. Put that Bible down and come to bed". He's been much better since.'

I shut my mouth hurriedly, realizing I was gawping. 'I thought you were both, you know—'

'Oh, I am, love. Don't get me wrong. But you can be a Christian *and* have a life, you know. Neil gets a bit over-zealous with it all sometimes. It's stress, you know. But he's lovely, really.'

'Oh, I know he is.'

'I said to him, that day he came back from your place, "The poor girl doesn't need a load of quotations Neil, she needs a cuddle and a stiff drink." '

I grinned at her. 'He's lucky to have a wife like you.'

'That's what I always tell him.'

'You seem a bit inebriated, darling.'

Look who's talking. My one-glass-of-champagne-and-I-won't-let-anyone-else-get a-word-in-edgeways mother.

'I thought you said that now you're with Ben you won't have to drown your sorrows by abusing alcohol any more.'

'I'm not abusing anything. It's a party and I'm celebrating. Oh, look, Nigel at last!'

I rushed away from her and threw my arms around him. 'Where've you been?'

'I can see you've been enjoying yourself.'

'When will everyone stop telling me how pissed I am? Where's Gloria? She's never left you again!'

'No, she hasn't.'

'Well, where is she?'

'Oh, baby-sitter problems, you know.'

I looked at him as I handed him a glass of champagne. He definitely looked a bit shifty.

'Here's to Broadrange Stores, your marvellous negotiating skills and darling old Bill!' Nigel clinked glasses with me. 'I had a lovely card from him and Cynthia this morning,' I told him. 'He said sorry they couldn't make it but they hoped we'd have a great time. I meant to tell Henry.' I looked round and saw him proffering a chicken leg in Rosie's direction.

'Yes,' said Nigel vaguely, clearly not listening to a word I was saying.

'Nigel, are you all right? You still haven't told me what Gloria said about all the money,' I said, when I'd refilled our glasses.

'Well, she was pleased.'

'What did she say?'

'I don't remember exactly.'

'She does know about it, doesn't she?'

'Yes, Cari, of course she does. I sorted the VAT, paid off the overdraft, bought the kids' trainers, gave her two hundred quid for a new dress—'

'And she knows from where?'

'What is this?'

'I don't think you ever told her about this house. You did all the letters yourself.'

'What are you talking about?'

'You didn't tell her, did you?'

'I didn't want to worry her.'

'What? Like the diggers?'

'Don't keep on.'

I had another go at dancing. Nigel had a go at holding me up.

'You look very sexy when you're drunk,' he said. 'I think it's the way your dress keeps falling off.'

'Hah, hah. I still haven't forgiven you for telling me Ben was married with children.'

Nigel stopped and looked hurt. 'I've told you, I thought he was. I didn't mislead you deliberately.'

'And you said, "Don't be taken in . . ." '

'I just meant he puts on the old salt-of-the-earth working-class bit.'

'What about saying I was doing it with Henry?'

'I was joking.'

'Bollocks! You were keeping us apart.'

'All right. I was trying to protect you.'

'From what?'

'I was jealous.'

I gave him another hug.

I knew there was still something on his mind. It came out when I'd fetched the rest of the bottle. 'Actually, Cari, there's something I've been meaning to put to you ever since we completed the sale. It's a really brilliant investment opportunity – no, listen!' He put on his best, most earnest, trust-me expression. 'It wouldn't take all your money.'

'Oh, good.'

'And you could run everything.'

'Right.'

'It's down by the river.'

'Not a warehouse?'

'Well, it's a warehouse at the moment but—'

'It could be seven luxury flats, with a four-bedroomed, multi-bathroomed, roof-terraced penthouse on top? Idea is, buy it for cash, take out a mega-loan, convert it, sell off the flats, keep the penthouse, proceeds from the flats pays for the penthouse. Bingo: one half-a-million-quid home buckshee to live in or rent out for a fortune.'

For the first time ever I had the unrivalled and delicious delight of seeing Nigel utterly gobsmacked.

'How did you know that?' he asked uncertainly.

'Ben and I have just bought it.'

'Elsie!' I let go of Ben and gave her an I-adore-everybody hug. 'Are we making too much noise?'

'No, love, you said come round for a drink so here I am.'

Ben let go of me and bent down to touch her arm. 'What would you like?'

'Got any Guinness?'

As Ben went off, she turned to me. 'He your young man now, then?' She sniffed. 'Let's hope he's a bit more reliable than that other one.'

'Yes,' I said gaily, not looking at Nigel. 'Oh, he is.'

'She needs someone to look after her,' she remarked to my mother in the same wise-old-aunt-at-the-heart-of-the-family tone. They both looked at me knowingly, as if I were a wayward three-year-old.

'Never had a proper father,' mouthed my mother confidingly. 'Been searching for one ever since.'

I glared at her. 'Are you really sure you're not upset about the house being pulled down?' I asked Elsie. 'It will leave a bit of a gap next to you.'

'Oh, no, love. He was ever such a nice man who came to see me. He's already promised me a guided tour when the shop opens and free delivery. And they said they're going to "make recompense" for all my inconvenience.' She winked. 'I pointed out to him, of course, it won't only mean higher heating bills, being on the end like, having no insulation from the house next door. There's the resale value to think of. He said he'd take it up with the directors. I think I'll do all right.' She held out her hand for the glass of brown froth Ben was proffering. 'Bless you, love.'

'Newcastle Brown.'

'Don't mind if I do.'

'Have you seen him?' My mother – think terriers, think bones – was not to be put off by the fact that everyone else was in the party spirit.

'Who?'

'You know very well who. Your bloody father.'

I sighed, and gazed over to where Sonia was talking to the plumber. (My God, surely she wasn't that worried about her skin condition!)

'No, I have not seen him. I have spoken to him on the telephone and I am going to see him next time he comes down.' (Unless I've had the good sense to move to the other end of the country and not give any of you my forwarding address.)

'I thought he was moving to Nottingham.'

'He is.'

'Good! What's he coming down here again for, then?'

'To see me! And he's concerned about Juliette.'

'Hmmph!' My mother gave the assembled gathering a full rendition of her entire breathing range.

'As he would be!' I added, suddenly spotting who my sister was talking to . . . 'My God, look! He smiled!'

We all stared at Juliette and Trevor, who were standing by the remains of the fireplace. Juliette was clearly holding forth about something enthralling – probably the dangers of mineral deficiencies or the healing properties of radishes – and Trevor was all rapt attention, gazing at her as if she held the secret to the meaning of the universe. Which – if you favour the theory that it is the mad who have really got their finger on the pulse of things and the rest of us are the ones who should be locked up – she might well have.

Barry was playing 'Don't Ever Stop Dancing Yet' but I had to sit down. I settled myself on the stairs and leant against the wall.

Juliette emerged into the hall. 'Thanks for a lovely party, Cari. We're going now.'

I sat up. *We?*

'It's amazing. Trevor and I have so much in common. Did you know he had depression all through his teens and now takes Prozac?' Juliette smiled widely. 'He's so sensitive and intelligent.' She threw another dazzling smile over her shoulder and held out her hand. Trevor appeared, took it, scowled at me and led her off through the door.

As I continued to gape after this unlikely coupling, Jim and the plumber came up to say good night. 'All got sorted out in the end, dear, didn't it?' The plumber patted my hand.

'Thank you both for everything,' I said.

Jim nodded fervently. Ben appeared and shook his hand.

'*Can* he speak?' I asked Ben, when they'd gone.

Ben looked at me in surprise. 'Of course he can!'

Soon it was just the diehards. My mother had disappeared next door with Elsie for a cup of Horlicks and a chew over the limitations of man, Sonia had wafted off into the night to get her beauty sleep and go through her list of ex-boyfriends, Henry and Rosie had waved cheery goodbyes and left with Neil and Linda – Neil walking somewhat unsteadily, his body reeling with shock from the first injection of alcohol for years.

'That's why you're incoherent,' said Ben to me affectionately. 'It's your first drink for six days.'

Louise looked at me in disbelief. 'Really?'

Nigel laughed. 'Must be a record.'

All four of us were sitting on the stairs now, looking through the doorway at the flickering candle stumps and array of empties, listening to the last of Barry's tapes.

'Well, I'd better go,' yawned Louise, for the fourth time. 'I told Robert I wouldn't be long.'

'And me,' said Nigel.

Louise got up and kissed me. 'Great night.' She went to the front door.

'Brilliant!' said Nigel, getting to his feet and stumbling after her. 'Do you want to share a taxi?' he asked. 'Or shall I walk you home?'

'Don't think either would be a terribly good idea,' said Louise drily.

Nigel laughed good-naturedly. 'Why's that?'

'Gloria's outside.'

Ben threw the last beer can into a bulging plastic sack and picked up the ghetto-blaster.

'Don't turn it off,' I said, as he pulled me into an upright position. 'It's Stealers Wheel.' I staggered against the doorpost. 'It's very appropriate,' I slurred with difficulty.

'Shall I carry you home, darling?' asked Ben.

'Yes, please.'

He tucked the music under one arm and put the other round me, holding me up as I attempted to sing along to one of my favourite songs. 'Stuck in the Middle with You.'

Which was just where I wanted to be.

Chapter Thirty-six

We were sitting on the window-seat, Ben attending to his schedule of works for the conversion, I catching up on a little correspondence.

Dear Martin
  By the time you read this letter, the solicitors should have done their bit and you'll have had your money.
  I trust you and Sharon will be very happy wherever you go next. As happy as Ben and I intend to be when we move into our luxury new home, which I'm sure you'll be pleased to know is a cut above even Waldorf Close . . .

'We'll need to get hold of Trevor for a quote on the wiring.'
'I think he's still got hold of Juliette.'

As it is therefore a time of new beginnings, I am sure you will agree that a divorce now seems the most sensible option and to this end I have asked my solicitor to see to the necessary papers.

'Did I tell you Nick's left his wife?'

'Is that why I haven't heard from my mother for a fortnight?'

However, I should like you to recall the words I wrote when we parted. 'I am – and always will be – your friend.' Now seems a particularly fitting time to remember those sentiments . . .

'Well, we'll need another plumber. Waste disposal's going to need looking at.'

. . . and update them. For I must say that throughout this whole separation I think you have been a total and utter bastard.

'There!' I signed my name with a flourish, the way I had seen Jessica Jackson do when she held a signing in the Canterbury Waterstone's, and licked the envelope flap. 'That'll show him!'

I raised my wine-glass and clinked it against Ben's. We both drank.

I looked out of the window at the dark night sky and back to the letter lying on the table. I had a funny sort of pang that might have been salt-deficiency now I'd given up peanuts, or might have been remorse. 'Poor old Martin,' I said. 'He's not that bad, really.' Ben put down his list and drew me close to him. 'Apart from his funny moods, of course,' I said. I put my head on Ben's shoulder. 'And being mean about money.' Ben stroked my hair. 'And calling me stupid a lot.'

'Which you're not,' added Ben.

'And he was very insensitive about Sharon.'

Ben kissed my neck.

'And never once stuck up for me in front of his dreadful mother. A right mummy's boy.'

'I don't like that, do you?' asked Ben soothingly in my ear.

'And he wouldn't let me have a baby.'

'I will,' murmured Ben.

I put my arm around his waist and squeezed.

'And he was about to set his solicitors on to me.'

'Mmm.' Ben nodded slowly, putting his head to one side as if considering the situation. 'Sounds just a bit of a bastard to me.' He picked up his list again.

I stretched up and kissed his cheek. Snuggled closer to his massive, solid warmth. And took a moment to reflect. During which I silently thanked God, Broadrange Food Stores, Henry, Bill, my mother – for having the good sense to bring me into this life after all – and Nigel. Don't forget Nigel.

'I suppose I don't have to post it,' I said.

But Ben was ticking things off. 'Seen Jim, got the plasterer, just need to sort the stud work.'

'Yes, please!'

Ben put down his pen, grinned his best oiky grin and spoke in those tones I'd come to know and love. 'How yer doing there, darlin'?'

Very much better, thank you.

THE END

GOING DOWN
by Kate Thompson

Ella Nesbit is young, good-looking and has a wicked way with the violin. She also has a great job working in a Dublin recording studio. So why isn't life more fun? Could Julian, the trainee from hell, have something to do with it? Or is it really due to Ella's unreciprocated passion for her boss?

When Ella's granny wins a holiday for two in Jamaica, things start to look up. Intrepid Ella dons a wetsuit, discovers scuba, and learns something about life from Rastafarian Raphael. But closer to home, a dark horse is coming up on the outside . . .

In this brilliant, bubbly and sexy tale from the bestselling author of *More Mischief*, Ella eventually discovers what she really, really wants – and finds a sensational way to get it.

'Warm, witty, sexy and compulsively readable'
Cathy Kelly

A Bantam Paperback
0553 81299 8

VIRTUAL STRANGERS
by Lynne Barrett-Lee

Fed up, frustrated and fast approaching forty, Charlie Simpson hasn't had many high points in her life just lately. The only peak on the horizon is her ambition to climb Everest, if she could only get organized and save up the cash.

Unfortunately, though, she has more pressing things to deal with; her eldest son moving out, her father moving in, and her best friend moving two hundred miles away. She finds solace, however, via her newly acquired modem, when she stumbles upon a stranger who's a like-minded soul. Like-minded, perhaps, but no fantasy dream date. Though virtual, he's of the real life variety – he may be a hero, but he has a wife.

Charlie hasn't got a husband, but she certainly has principles, and they're about to be hauled up a mountain themselves. And, of course, her mum's always said she shouldn't talk to strangers. The question is, is now the time to start breaking the rules?

Julia Gets a Life:
'A fantastic book that gets you hooked from the first page' *New Woman*

A Bantam Paperback
0553 81305 6

A SELECTION OF FINE NOVELS
AVAILABLE FROM BANTAM BOOKS

THE PRICES SHOWN BELOW WERE CORRECT AT THE TIME OF GOING TO PRESS.
HOWEVER TRANSWORLD PUBLISHERS RESERVE THE RIGHT TO SHOW NEW RETAIL
PRICES ON COVERS WHICH MAY DIFFER FROM THOSE PREVIOUSLY ADVERTISED IN THE
TEXT OR ELSEWHERE.

81304	8	JULIA GETS A LIFE	*Lynne Barrett-Lee* £5.99
81305	6	VIRTUAL STRANGERS	*Lynne Barrett-Lee* £5.99
50329	4	DANGER ZONES	*Sally Beauman* £5.99
50630	7	DARK ANGEL	*Sally Beauman* £6.99
50631	5	DESTINY	*Sally Beauman* £6.99
40727	9	LOVERS AND LIARS	*Sally Beauman* £5.99
50326	X	SEXTET	*Sally Beauman* £5.99
40497	0	CHANGE OF HEART	*Charlotte Bingham* £5.99
40890	9	DEBUTANTES	*Charlotte Bingham* £5.99
40895	X	THE NIGHTINGALE SINGS	*Charlotte Bingham* £5.99
17635	8	TO HEAR A NIGHTINGALE	*Charlotte Bingham* £5.99
50500	9	GRAND AFFAIR	*Charlotte Bingham* £5.99
40296	X	IN SUNSHINE OR IN SHADOW	*Charlotte Bingham* £5.99
40496	2	NANNY	*Charlotte Bingham* £5.99
40117	8	STARDUST	*Charlotte Bingham* £5.99
50717	6	THE KISSING GARDEN	*Charlotte Bingham* £5.99
50501	7	LOVE SONG	*Charlotte Bingham* £5.99
50718	4	THE LOVE KNOT	*Charlotte Bingham* £5.99
81274	2	THE BLUE NOTE	*Charlotte Bingham* £6.99
81275	0	THE SEASON	*Charlotte Bingham* £5.99
81276	9	SUMMERTIME	*Charlotte Bingham* £5.99
40973	5	A CRACK IN FOREVER	*Jeannie Brewer* £5.99
81256	4	THE MAGDALEN	*Marita Conlon-McKenna* £5.99
81331	5	PROMISED LAND	*Marita Conlon-McKenna* £5.99
17504	1	DAZZLE	*Judith Krantz* £5.99
17242	5	I'LL TAKE MANHATTAN	*Judith Krantz* £5.99
40730	9	LOVERS	*Judith Krantz* £5.99
40731	7	SPRING COLLECTION	*Judith Krantz* £5.99
17503	3	TILL WE MEET AGAIN	*Judith Krantz* £5.99
17505	X	SCRUPLES TWO	*Judith Krantz* £5.99
40732	5	THE JEWELS OF TESSA KENT	*Judith Krantz* £5.99
81287	4	APARTMENT 3B	*Patricia Scanlan* £5.99
81290	4	FINISHING TOUCHES	*Patricia Scanlan* £5.99
81286	6	FOREIGN AFFAIRS	*Patricia Scanlan* £5.99
81288	2	PROMISES, PROMISES	*Patricia Scanlan* £5.99
40941	7	MIRROR, MIRROR	*Patricia Scanlan* £5.99
40943	3	CITY GIRL	*Patricia Scanlan* £5.99
40946	8	CITY WOMAN	*Patricia Scanlan* £5.99
81291	2	CITY LIVES	*Patricia Scanlan* £5.99
50489	4	THE NOTEBOOK	*Nicholas Sparks* £5.99
81297	1	A WALK TO REMEMBER	*Nicholas Sparks* £5.99
81205	X	MESSAGE IN A BOTTLE	*Nicholas Sparks* £5.99
81355	2	THE RESCUE	*Nicholas Sparks* £5.99
81245	9	IT MEANS MISCHIEF	*Kate Thompson* £5.99
81246	7	MORE MISCHIEF	*Kate Thompson* £5.99
81299	8	GOING DOWN	*Kate Thompson* £5.99
81372	2	RAISING THE ROOF	*Jane Wenham-Jones* £5.99

All Transworld titles are available by post from:
Bookpost, PO Box 29, Douglas, Isle of Man IM99 1BQ
Credit cards accepted. Please telephone 01624 836000,
fax 01624 837033, Internet http://www.bookpost.co.uk or
e-mail: bookshop@enterprise.net for details.
Free postage and packing in the UK.
Overseas customers allow £1 per book.